Changeli.   ss.com

Samurai /Phantom Duet

Harley Wylde

Samurai /Phantom Duet
Harley Wylde

ISBN: 978-1-60521-835-9

Publisher:
Changeling Press LLC
315 N. Centre St.
Martinsburg, WV 25404
ChangelingPress.com

Printed in the U.S.A.

Editor: Crystal Esau
Cover Artist: Bryan Keller

The individual stories in this anthology have been previously released in E-Book format.

Table of Contents

Samurai (Devil's Boneyard MC 9)
Harley Wylde

Grey -- Selling myself for a few hours once seems far better than my other option -- letting my mother's loan shark use me however he sees fit in order to recoup his money. I can't even be angry with Mom since she's no longer with us. She did what she'd thought was best at the time, but now I'm paying the price. I didn't count on a biker changing my life forever. Why do I keep getting tangled up with bad boys? It never ends well for me.

Samurai -- I'd never thought I'd pay to be with a woman, but not just anyone can handle my needs. The little goddess I purchased isn't anything like I expected. The way she gives into me so sweetly, and comes apart in my arms, makes it damn hard to forget. I need to fix things before my cousin, Phantom, decides to step in and claim her for himself. Grey is mine, and no one is taking her from me. Because once I'm in, I'm all in. I'll kill anyone who tries to take her from me. I promised Grey I wouldn't get sent to prison. I didn't promised to be good. I just won't get caught.

Prologue

Grey

I didn't know why I'd agreed to this. It was utter insanity. If it hadn't been for the bills piling up, and the collectors knocking at the door, I wouldn't have even considered doing something so... wild. I took shallow breaths as I smoothed my hands down my dress. I looked more like a girl fresh off the farm than someone who'd sold herself to the highest bidder.

"You understand what you've agreed to?" Mr. Knox asked.

"Yes, sir. I'll be his to use as he pleases, as long as he doesn't permanently scar me or..." I swallowed hard. "Or kill me."

He nodded. "Right. And should things go too far, all your debt will be canceled, and your child will be taken care of for the rest of his life."

Ryo. I had to make it through this for him. Money couldn't replace his mother, and his father... I wouldn't even think about that night. I'd do anything to keep Ryo away from that monster.

"Where and when?" I asked. "And what do I need to wear?"

He smiled. "Ms. Lumare, there's a reason I asked you to wear something you already owned. The client likes your girl-next-door sweet look. He's already in the room and waiting for you."

Oh. Oh! My hands shook as I fisted the skirt of my dress. I hadn't realized we were doing this right now. I'd told the neighbor I'd be back for Ryo within an hour or two. Would it take longer? As much as the man had paid for me, I didn't know if this would be an all-night sort of thing. I'd thought I'd have more time to prepare, get some sort of warning a day or so in advance.

"How long will I be here? Ryo is with a neighbor. I didn't realize…"

Mr. Knox waved me off. "If Mr. Samurai wishes to have you past the time your son needs to be retrieved from the sitter, we'll handle it. Leave the details with me."

I scribbled down the neighbor's name, address, and phone number. Then as an afterthought, I added a short note and signed it, giving Mr. Knox permission to pick up Ryo. I didn't have a choice but to trust him. I knew Mrs. Wilson wouldn't keep Ryo longer than the two hours. She'd been hesitant even then.

"Right this way," he said, ushering me back into the front entry. He pointed to a door. "Go in there and get yourself ready."

"Ready?"

He pinched the bridge of his nose. "It's like you're a fucking virgin, in which case I could have gotten a lot more money. Take off your undergarments. Pinch your nipples. Use the lube on the counter if you need to in order to prepare yourself for him. You're clearly not turned-on right now."

Oh, God. I was really doing this. I swallowed hard and entered the room, feeling slightly better when I realized it was a bathroom and not some strange sex room. I felt so out of my element. I removed my panties and bra, my cheeks flaming at the thought of being bare under my dress. I couldn't bring myself to pinch my nipples like he'd said, but I did eye the lube. Would the man pounce on me the second I met him? Since he'd paid for my time, I doubted he'd care if I was wet.

I slicked my fingers with the lube and eased them inside my pussy, wincing slightly at the pinch.

Since having Ryo, I hadn't exactly had anything inside me. I'd have thought giving birth to him would have stretched me permanently. It didn't seem to be the case. I washed my hands and saw a few small lockers on the wall. I placed my bra and panties into one of them and hoped no one would mess with them.

Stepping out into the entry again, I followed Mr. Knox up the stairs and down the hallway. The second floor of the building looked more like an old-fashioned brothel, or what I assumed one looked like. Heavy red wallpaper covered the walls. The dark-grained wood floor gleamed under faux gaslight sconces.

He pushed open a door and I stepped inside, freezing when I saw the back of the man who'd bought me. He wore a leather cut, like the bikers I'd seen around town. In fact... *exactly* like it. I wasn't sure I could do this.

I heard the door click shut behind me and realized it was too late.

Devil's Boneyard MC covered his back, along with a frightening image of a skull with horns. His dark hair had been buzzed short on the back and sides. The color reminded me of my son's hair. It was the reminder I needed. He was the reason I'd agreed to this. If I didn't get the bills paid, I'd lose our home, our car, and possibly my baby -- and even myself. The car was the least important of those, and I had a feeling I'd have to let it go.

"You still agree to be mine for the sum I paid?" the man asked, still not facing me. He had a slight accent I couldn't quite place, although it was familiar.

"Y-yes."

"Did you dress the way I'd asked?"

I looked down at my cotton dress. It flared slightly from my waist, stopping at my knees. The cream fabric had dainty pink flowers across it. "I didn't get a specific request. I was told to wear one of my regular dresses. I'm not sure if this is what you wanted or not."

He didn't say anything, and I clenched my hands at my sides. Had I already displeased him? If he walked out, would I lose the money? I couldn't remember if the contract said anything about the client leaving before anything happened.

"I'm sorry," I said. "They didn't even tell me you were here. I'd thought I was coming today to sign some papers or something. I... I don't know how all this works."

That got his attention. The man turned and my breath caught in my throat. I should have made some demands on my own. Like not having an Asian man claim me, especially one who was Japanese. Now I knew why I'd heard that accent before. My heart began to race, and my palms grew damp. The room spun a little.

I whimpered and staggered back a step, nearly collapsing to the floor. I heard his booted feet draw closer, but all I saw was my apartment door being kicked in and Ryo's daddy busting into the place. My lungs nearly seized as fear crawled up my throat, leaving an acid taste in my mouth.

"Don't hurt me," I whispered, holding my hands up to plead with him. "Please. I'm sorry. So sorry. I'll do whatever you want. Don't hurt me again."

His steps halted immediately "Again?"

I scrambled back farther, tripping and landing on the floor. I blinked rapidly. The room came back into focus, as did the man in front of me. I took deep, calming breaths, as heat settled in my cheeks.

"I..." I looked away. How did I explain what just

happened?

He knelt in front of me, reaching out to place his hand on my calf. The warmth of his skin against mine brought my attention back to his face. "Who hurt you?"

"It doesn't matter. It was a while ago. I'm sorry I freaked out."

He studied me, not saying anything. Slowly, he inched his hand up my leg. At my knee, he hesitated, his fingers toying with the hem of my dress. He pushed it up a little, sliding his hand up my thigh. When I didn't stop him, he kept going. It didn't take long before the material pooled at my waist, leaving me exposed to him. I fought the urge to slam my thighs closed and let him look. He stroked a finger over my pussy, making me shiver. The contract had stipulated I get waxed, and the Pleasure Emporium had staff to make sure it was done to Mr. Knox's standards.

"The man who hurt you. He looked like me? Or he was a biker?" he asked.

"Gang member." I audibly swallowed. "But… he was Japanese. Like you."

The man froze again, his fingers still covering me. With shaky fingers, I unbuttoned the top of my dress, letting the material gape open. Cool air caressed the swells of my breasts, and I paused a moment before unfastening more buttons. The material gaped, exposing me to him.

I needed this man to know I wasn't backing out. I couldn't afford to walk out of here empty-handed, and if he demanded a refund, I wasn't sure what Mr. Knox would do to me. I had to make this work. His gaze locked onto my breasts, and I felt my nipples harden. Looked like I hadn't needed to pinch them after all. I wasn't sure if it was from fear or if the heat in his eyes turned me on a little. I couldn't remember anyone ever looking at me like that.

"Last chance," he said, his voice deeper and raspier than before. "Walk away right now, or you're mine until I'm finished with you."

His words sounded ominous, but I didn't have any choice in the matter. I'd signed a contract, and I desperately needed the money.

I shook my head. "I'm not leaving."

He stroked my pussy again and I bit back a whimper. I'd never enjoyed a man's touch before. Why did I react to someone like him? I should be terrified, and on some level, I was. And yet... I couldn't deny the ache already building inside me.

"The papers you signed. It means you've consented to anything that happens in this room. Understand?" he asked.

"Y-yes. I think so." I licked my lips. "You aren't allowed to leave scars or kill me, but... there's an extra clause in case something happens. Mr. Knox said he can't guarantee my safety if you were to get out of control."

He nodded. "There's a reason for that. I typically have someone with me, to make sure I don't go too far. Since I paid for your time, I'm letting myself off the leash so to speak. I don't usually do this. In fact, never. But doing things the usual way hasn't been as satisfying. So, it's just us. If you've been hurt before..."

"I can handle it." I hoped I sounded braver than I felt.

"The contract promised you'd be clean. I saw your test results myself. I'm clean too, in case you were worried," he said. "Got tested a week ago and haven't touched anyone while I waited for today."

Right. Because he'd paid a lot of money to do

what he wanted with me. But once he left, he'd go right back to sleeping with other women. This was a transaction. By signing my name on all those papers, I'd become a whore. His whore, at least for this one day. I wasn't sure I could look myself in the eye tomorrow. I didn't have another way to dig myself out of the hole.

He reached down and unfastened his belt and jeans, shoving the material down. I refused to look at his cock. I saw the motion of him stroking himself, but I didn't look away from his face. He lowered himself over me and I felt the head of his cock push against my pussy. Slowly, he sank into me.

My nails bit into my palms and I took deep breaths. It burned and not in a fun way. He stopped, his intense gaze holding mine.

Samurai reached between us and rubbed my clit. I flinched at first, not having been touched like that… ever. It startled me and I felt my body tense. He used slow, soft strokes and I felt the warmth start to build inside me again. A whimper escaped me again and my hips lifted of their own volition.

"That's it, beautiful girl. It's only fun if you enjoy it too." He kept rubbing as he pulled his hips back and sank into me again. He thrust into me, slowly. The drag of his cock went from being uncomfortable to being something I craved. I needed more!

"I… I don't… I haven't…" I blinked and gasped as the most incredible sensation swept over me. I reached up and gripped his biceps, digging my nails into his skin. I cried out, my pussy clenching down on him as I came.

Samurai gave a soft growl. His hand came down around my throat, squeezing slightly. He drove into me harder. Faster. His fingers tightened as he yelled and flooded me with his release. The warmth of his cum registered in my addled brain and I tried not to panic. He hadn't used a condom. When he'd mentioned being clean, it hadn't occurred to me why he'd brought it up. No one said anything about...

He released me but kept our bodies joined.

"Fuck me," he muttered. "You didn't fake it, did you? You really came."

I nodded, then realized he could take that either way. "I didn't fake it."

A smile curved his lips. "That means all those other bitches did. Never felt anything like your pussy squeezing me and coating me in your cream. I'm keeping you as long as I can... until Knox comes and throws me out."

"You go without a condom often?" I asked. He'd said he was clean, but if he did this all the time... what if the tests were wrong? Or worse. What if he'd given Mr. Knox fake results? Could such a thing happen?

"No." He smoothed my hair back. "Never. It's why I told Knox to make sure the girl I bought was clean and on birth control. I wanted the full experience. Looks like I got all that and more with you."

Birth control. I didn't remember seeing anything about it in the documents I'd signed. But if it was in there... it meant I was in breach of the contract. What would happen if either Samurai or Mr. Knox found out? My stomach knotted and I tried to keep calm. I didn't need Samurai knowing something was wrong.

"I'm going to fuck you so good you won't be able to walk the next few days. Or sit." He squeezed my hip. "You ever let a man fuck your ass?"

I shook my head, too stunned to speak. I'd thought they only did things like that in porn movies. Men really enjoyed that? Did the women? I felt a flutter of both fear and curiosity. If he planned to enjoy me as long as possible, then I should do the same. After today, I'd go back to avoiding men. I'd store up a lifetime of memories and experiences in the next hour or two. Or however long he kept me up here.

He lowered his head, his lips near my ear. "I'm going to make you so needy, you'll be begging me to fuck you. You'll let me do anything I want and come so hard you soak us both."

"I want that," I said softly, running my hand up and down his arm.

"Only one rule, beautiful. No kissing. This isn't a fairy tale. It's a business transaction. I'll give you lots of orgasms, and you'll give your body to me until we're finished."

I couldn't help but smile. "I thought that was my line, about the no kissing."

His brow furrowed.

"Julia Roberts? *Pretty Woman*? Where she's a prostitute and he picks her up in a fancy car on the side of the road?"

"You're not normally a whore, though, are you? There's too much innocence in your eyes," he said.

"No. I'm not. This is... It's a one-time thing." I licked my lips. "I needed the money and didn't see another way to get it."

"For now, you're *my* little whore." He brushed his nose along my jaw. "Only mine."

I had a feeling the no kissing rule would be important if he kept saying things like that. It shouldn't turn me on or make me feel special. But the way he said I was only his? Dangerous words to say to someone who'd had no one except their son... I'd given up on fairy tales and romance, but those two words made me wish I could have more in my life.

I no longer worried he'd break me physically. Emotionally was another matter. He called this a business transaction, and I knew it was, but the way he touched me, the possessive look in his eyes, it all made me want someone to look at me like that for the rest of my life. Someone who could hold me at night and show Ryo what it meant to be a man.

One day. One day you'll find your knight in shining armor. A biker who'd paid for a whore wasn't that man. I'd have to distance myself from everything that happened in this room. And when I left, I'd never look back.

Chapter One
Grey -- Four Months Later

I didn't want to be here. I had a feeling this would end badly, but I didn't know what else to do. Ryo clutched my hand and I shifted from one foot to the other while the guy behind the gate looked me over. His gaze landed on Ryo and his eyes slightly widened as he took a step back.

"You said Samurai?" he asked. "Not Phantom?"

I didn't know who Phantom was, or why this man would think I didn't know who to ask for. Clearly I'd come here for a reason. Did women show up and get the men confused on a regular basis? I wasn't sure how to take that.

"Samurai." I took a step closer. "Please. It's important."

His gaze dropped to Ryo again. "I bet it is."

I breathed a sigh of relief when he opened the gates and let us through. At least we'd made it this far. Samurai might very well tell me get to lost and never show my face here again. At least I'd get the chance to find out.

He pointed to a building not too far off. "He's probably at the clubhouse. But um... you may not want to take the kid inside there. It's not too wild at this time of day. Doesn't mean people aren't smoking, or that he wouldn't see something he shouldn't."

Right. Because I was at a biker compound. Who knew what went on behind the gate, much less in the building he'd called a clubhouse. I doubted they were in there playing video games or watching movies.

"I can't leave Ryo outside on his own," I said.

The guy looked around and let out a shrill whistle. "Hey, Sam! Lady needs her kid watched for a minute."

The other man jogged over. I noticed both wore the leather vest like Samurai had, but neither had a name on theirs. It only said *Prospect*. I had no idea what that meant, and I wasn't sure I wanted to know.

"Sam, this is..." The guy rubbed the stubble on his jaw. "Sorry. Didn't catch your name."

"I'm Grey and this is Ryo," I said.

He nodded. "Right. Grey and Ryo. She's here to see Samurai."

Sam's eyebrows rose as he stared at Ryo a moment. "All right. I can sit outside with him, or I can go in and get Samurai. Might be better to have him come outside."

"Going inside doesn't bother me," I said. "But he said it wouldn't be a good place for Ryo."

Sam shook his head. "No, I have a feeling Samurai would kick my aa... uh, rear, if I let either of you into that building. You can sit in the shade. There's a few chairs up on the porch."

I led Ryo over to the building and claimed a chair while Sam went inside. I could hear laughter and music spill from the open doorway, as well as the sounds of women. My stomach soured when I pictured Samurai with them. It was stupid to come here. He wouldn't want this baby, or me. Wouldn't care about my problems or that my son was in danger.

I stood and lifted Ryo into my arms. "Come on, sweetheart. We shouldn't have come here. We'll go home and figure something else out."

I walked down the steps and toward the gate, but the guy who'd let me in was shaking his head and pointing back at the clubhouse. "Nope. Sorry. I'm not letting you leave until you see Samurai."

"Are you serious right now? It's obvious I made

a mistake coming here. Let me go before he comes out and…"

I heard heavy steps behind me and stopped mid-sentence. My nape prickled and I had a feeling the man in question was right behind me. Ryo's head remained tucked against my chest, and I tightened my hold on him. If I'd had anyone to watch him, or felt safe leaving him behind, I wouldn't have brought him with me.

"Before I come out and what?" Samurai asked. I'd recognize his voice anywhere.

Slowly, I turned to face him. He rocked back on his heels, his gaze going to Ryo. "Sorry to disappoint, but no fucking way that kid is mine. Your math is off by a few years."

"I never said he was yours." I backed up a step. "I needed help, but I shouldn't have come here. He won't open the gate and let me leave."

Samurai's gaze went over my shoulder and I saw him scanning the road. I knew what he'd see. Nothing. I didn't have a car or any other transportation. I had to walk everywhere and coming way out here hadn't been easy on either me or Ryo. Thankfully the weather had cooled a little, so I at least didn't have my clothes and hair plastered to me from sweat. Could have been worse.

"You walked here carrying him?" he asked.

"Yes, and if you'll tell him to let me go, then I'll walk right back home. I shouldn't have come."

"Why did you?" he asked, folding his arms over his chest.

I shifted Ryo in my arms and felt my dress pull tight over my stomach. I tried to hide the small bump before he noticed and seemed to have managed since he didn't say anything. Or maybe he didn't care. This version of Samurai was very different from the one at the Pleasure Emporium. The man who'd made me cry out his name, who'd melted my bones with multiple orgasms, wasn't the one eying me now.

"Some people in town have talked about the good things your club does. Toy drives and helping homeless women. I'd hoped you might know of a way to solve my problem, but it was wrong to even ask."

"You sure the kid isn't Phantom's?" the guy at the gate asked.

Samurai's eyes narrowed as he studied Ryo. The look he slid my way held a hint of hostility. I didn't know why they kept bringing up Phantom.

"I've never met anyone named Phantom," I said. "Why does everyone keep asking me that?"

"He's my older cousin, and your son resembles him," Samurai said.

I didn't want to do this out in the open, or where Ryo could hear, so I chose my words carefully. "Do you remember my first reaction to you, and why I said it happened?"

His chin went up and he cursed softly. "The guy who hurt you. The one you said was Japanese, like me."

I ran my hand over Ryo's hair. "He saw me last week, with Ryo. He knows, and he… he said he's coming for us. I survived him once. Even if I could live through it again, I won't let him get his hands on Ryo. My baby is a good boy. He's sweet and innocent. If Itachi gets his hands on him…"

"Itachi Suzuki?" Sam asked. "That's who you're running from?"

I nodded, worried how he knew the man's full name. Did they do business with Itachi and his crew? I'd thought maybe these were the good guys, despite the motorcycles and black leather. Had I been wrong?

"Sorry, little whore. Your problems aren't *my* problems," Samurai said before turning and walking back to the clubhouse.

My heart shattered at my feet, and I was thankful my son didn't know what that word meant. My cheeks flamed as Sam and the other guy eyed me. Tears burned my eyes and I motioned to the gate. "Can you please open that now?"

I tried not to cry in front of them, but the tears started slipping down my cheeks. I didn't want these men to see me as weak. Bad enough they now knew I'd spread my legs for money. Didn't matter it had only been the one time, or I'd been desperate.

An SUV pulled up to the gate and a woman rolled down her window. Her corkscrew curls were wild about her head, and she slid her sunglasses down her nose, looking first at me, then at the guys. "Which one of you made her cry?"

Sam lifted his hands and backed up. I noticed the other guy did the same. I almost laughed at the absurdity of the men looking scared of a woman.

"Samurai," Sam said. "We didn't touch her, Clarity. Swear to Christ!"

Her gaze narrowed. "No swearing in front of children. Let me in, and you..." She stared at me, her expression softening. "When I pull in, climb up front. You look like you could use something to drink, and a bit of a rest."

I looked at the men, but they were hurrying to obey her. Who was this woman? I backed up as her SUV pulled through and hesitated only a moment before I went around to the passenger side. I climbed in and noticed the soccer ball in the back seat, as well as a kid's discarded jacket.

"I'm Clarity," she said, holding out her hand.

"The VP is my husband."

"Grey." I shook hands with her and situated Ryo on my lap a little better. She noticed the swell of my stomach and shook her head, muttering about idiot men, before continuing down the road that cut through the compound.

"Your son, is he…"

"Samurai's?" I asked.

She nodded.

"No. But his father is why I'm here. I'd hoped Samurai could help me find a way to hide or disappear into another town or state. Itachi said he's coming for me and Ryo. I can't let that happen."

"And you know Samurai how, exactly?" Clarity asked.

My cheeks burned hot, and I looked away. "We had some business about four months ago. I don't know why I thought he'd care about my problems. I was desperate."

"That business give you that bump under your dress?" she asked wryly.

"Doesn't matter. He doesn't want anything to do with me. He made it clear when he called me…" I pressed my lips together.

Clarity parked in front of a large home and shut off the car. "Come on. Your boy can play or watch a cartoon while you and I talk."

I followed her into the house and set Ryo down. He clutched at my hand as we followed Clarity into the kitchen. She opened the back door and motioned to a fenced yard. "My boys are too big for the slide and swings. I just haven't been able to take them down. Every time I think about asking my husband to remove them, I realize I don't want to let go of their childhood yet. He'll be perfectly safe out there, and you can see him from the table."

I led Ryo outside and realized Clarity was right. If I sat at the table, I could watch him play. He toddled over to the slide and started to climb. I watched a few minutes to make sure he could handle the toys out there without assistance before I went back inside.

Clarity handed me a cold glass of tea and I took a seat.

"My youngest is nearly thirteen," she said. "Some of the kids here are only a year old. If I keep the slide and other play equipment, it gives them a place to hang out when their moms need a break. And I can pretend my kids won't be grown soon. I promise your boy will be fine out there."

"Why are you being so nice to me?" I asked.

She leaned back against the counter. "Because I think you're a bit like me when I was your age. You're what? Late teens, maybe early twenties?"

"Twenty-one," I said.

"That boy out there. You said his dad is coming for you and him. This guy is a bad man?" she asked.

Bad man? Understatement. I'd often wondered if Itachi had any other kids running around from his attacks on women. I knew I hadn't been the first, nor the last. Men like him got off on the pain and humiliation of forcing themselves on women.

"Yeah. Itachi Suzuki. He runs one of the local gangs." I looked out at Ryo. "I was seventeen when my mom died. Nearly eighteen. A week after her death, Itachi broke down my apartment door and attacked me. Ryo is the result of that night."

Clarity's brow furrowed and I could tell she was trying to organize her thoughts before speaking. "Your boy is a few years old. Why would this man try to come for you now? Why wait so long?"

I shrugged a shoulder. "I moved when I could and have kept to myself. I don't think he knew how to find me, or even wanted to. It was an accident I ran into him while I was out with Ryo. He took one look, and somehow knew Ryo was his."

Clarity looked at my stomach. "And the other one?"

"My mom had been really sick. I didn't know she'd taken out loans to cover her medical expenses. When I turned eighteen, the lenders started coming to me for their money. I thought I'd paid them off or had a good enough arrangement they'd leave me be. I didn't know about the more unsavory lenders until about five months ago. They gave me thirty days to pay them off, or they'd make me pay the loan back in other ways."

Clarity winced. "I know exactly what they wanted from you. Doesn't tell me how you got mixed up with Samurai. Or how you got pregnant."

I hated telling this woman all my secrets. I didn't know her. Wasn't entirely certain if I could trust her, but it wasn't like things could get much worse. If I didn't find a way to hide from Itachi, then pretty soon I'd be on my back in his bed, or worse, he'd have me on a street corner. And Ryo would turn into a monster exactly like him.

"I heard about a place where you could make a lot of money." I pressed my lips together, hoping she wouldn't judge me for what I'd done. "I signed a contract with Mr. Knox at the Pleasure Emporium. And Samurai paid for several hours of my time."

I stared at the table, not sure I could handle the disgust I'd see in her eyes. I took another swallow of the tea, just in case she threw me out. It was a long walk back home. I wondered if she'd let Ryo have something to drink first. He was innocent in all this.

"He didn't use protection?" she asked, her voice soft.

I looked up and tears blurred my vision when I only saw compassion in her eyes. "No. Apparently the contract I signed was supposed to have a clause in there about birth control. I don't remember seeing it. Only that I had to provide proof I didn't have any diseases, which I gave to Mr. Knox."

"You hoped he'd help keep you safe since you carry his child?" she asked.

I shook my head. "I didn't plan to tell him about the baby. It's clear he didn't want one. He... He called me a whore. Men don't want to claim babies they have with women like me. I didn't want anything from him except assistance staying away from Itachi. I'd heard the Devil's Boneyard helped the community. With no one else to turn to, I'd thought maybe Samurai would protect me or get me somewhere far from Itachi."

Clarity took a seat next to me and patted my shoulder. "You'll be safe here, Grey. You and your children. I'm going to call my husband and fill him in, and we'll go from there. If Samurai won't step up and help you, then we will."

I had no doubt the man wouldn't come anywhere near me. He'd made it clear what he thought about me. My throat still ached with the tears I'd shed. He'd hurt me, even though he shouldn't have had the power to do so. We'd had a few hours together, a contract signed for him to use my body, and nothing more. I'd blame pregnancy hormones if anyone asked why it felt like my heart was breaking.

"I'm not going to force him to do anything," I said. "That's not what I want."

Clarity stood and pulled a pad and pen from a

drawer near the sink. "Write down your address. I'll send someone to gather some of your things. I don't think it's safe for you to go back there in case Itachi is watching the place. That baby you're carrying is part of the Devil's Boneyard family, whether Samurai will claim them or not."

I let out the breath I hadn't realized I'd been holding and jotted down the address. I pulled my keys from my purse and set them on the table too. All the key ring had on it were the keys to the three locks on the front door and the two on the back door. When I'd rented the small house, the locks hadn't been sufficient. The landlord had agreed to add more since I was living there alone and was pregnant with Ryo at the time.

I didn't have much, but I'd worked hard for what I did have. The furniture had been secondhand, and the dishes were from the dollar store -- the one where everything is one dollar or less, not the *other* one where things can be as high as twenty dollars. I'd never understood calling it a "dollar store" if things cost more than that.

"Thank you for helping me," I said. "If there's anything I can do to repay you…"

She waved me off. "I won't get into a long, drawn-out story, but the short version? I was a single mom and homeless when my husband found me. I'd taken shelter with my son in the doorway of a shop. Didn't realize it had a security camera until a big biker showed up asking what I was doing at his shop. He took us in with no strings attached and ended up marrying me. So I've been in a similar situation to yours. I know how hard it is to have no one to rely on. You don't owe us anything, Grey."

I bit my lip so I wouldn't start crying or thanking her again. While she stepped away to make a phone call, taking my keys and the paper with her, I walked over to the door to watch Ryo. Even though he was playing by himself, I could tell he was having a blast. I couldn't remember seeing him smile so much. Samurai might not be the one helping us, but coming here had worked out after all. I'd take whatever help they offered and pay it forward if I got the chance. Anything to keep my children safe. I'd do whatever it took. My happiness came second to their needs.

I smiled, realizing there were still good people in the world. I'd started to have my doubts. Maybe our future wouldn't be so bad. I placed a hand over my belly and made a promise to my children. "Wherever we end up, you and your brother will always be loved, and I will do everything in my power to give you the best life I can. You'll be safe and happy, whatever it takes."

I only hoped I could keep that promise. I'd rather die than break it.

Chapter Two

Samurai

What. The. Fuck. I couldn't believe the woman had shown up here. Didn't matter I'd thought about her nearly every fucking day since I'd walked out of that room at Knox's place. And seeing the kid in her arms? If the bitch had thought to pawn off someone else's kid on me, it wasn't happening. I'd made sure Knox added the birth control clause for a reason. No fucking way I was going to have a kid. Ever. Yeah, she'd said it wasn't mine after I brought it up, but you couldn't trust a whore. I doubt the Prospects would have let her in if she hadn't given some sob story about that boy being mine.

My conscience pricked at even thinking of her with that label. She'd made it clear it wasn't normal for her to be in a place like the Pleasure Emporium. I could tell she'd been nervous and a bit scared. She'd needed money and had sold her body to get it. I could admit it made me an asshole to call her a whore to her face, and keep thinking of her that way, but it made it easier to keep my distance.

And what the hell had she meant by everyone bringing up Phantom? She'd clearly asked for me. Had those shitheads thought the boy belonged to my cousin? I guess I could see it. I'd even told her the kid looked like Phantom. Everyone knew my cousin wanted a family. He hadn't found the right woman to settle down with. I knew a certain lawyer had been chasing him pretty hard, and while he had fun with her, that's as far as it went. Having a lawyer tied to the club would be handy, but Phantom wasn't up for being the sacrificial lamb. His words, not mine.

As for kids… The world was too ugly, and my

past made me doubt my ability to be a good father. I'd probably be alone all my life, but that was fine. Pussy was pussy. Or it used to be. After feeling the way she responded, having her come so hard I damn near saw stars when she squeezed my cock, I hadn't been able to go back to the club whores and their fake orgasms. She'd even let me squeeze her throat and pin her down while I fucked her, and not once had she panicked or tried to break free. For that matter, she hadn't asked why I needed to take that kind of control. It wasn't just a kink, despite what my brothers thought.

In a perfect world, I'd have made the woman mine. I would have never let her walk out of the room at Knox's. But I knew I didn't have shit to offer her or anyone else, except a nightmarish past. And the way she'd flinched and freaked out when she saw me? Yeah, she'd been hurt, and bad. As much as I wanted to protect her, getting mixed up with me could put a bigger target on her back. What if I did claim her, and then some asshole decided to use her against me? Nope.

I sipped my beer and ignored the club whore plastered to my side. She'd been doing her best to get my attention since I'd walked back in, but it wasn't happening. Not after seeing that sweet face again, and that innocence I hadn't realized I needed. How sick did it make me to want to push that pretty girl to the edge and see how long she could hold onto all that light inside her?

The clubhouse doors opened so hard they slammed into the wall. I could see the VP from the corner of my eye as he stormed across the room, his boots thudding against the floor. He stopped next to my stool. I lifted my beer to take another swallow, and he knocked it from my hand, sending it crashing to the floor on the other side of the bar.

"Is there a problem, VP?" I asked, turning to give Scratch my full attention.

"You sorry piece of shit. It's been a long fucking time since I've been disappointed in anyone in this damn club. But you... You're lucky I'm the one standing here right now and not Clarity," Scratch said.

My brow furrowed. "Why would Clarity be mad at me? I haven't even seen her for a few days."

"The name Grey Lumare mean anything to you?" he asked.

"Is it supposed to?" I leaned my elbow on the bar top.

"Exactly how often do you fuck a woman without at least getting her first name?" Scratch asked.

"On average or any day of the week?" I smirked. "Because I don't need a name in order to get off."

I didn't even see it coming. One second I was running off at the mouth, and the next I was lying on the floor seeing stars as I stared up at the ceiling. I worked my jaw back and forth, wondering if he'd broken it. Scratch kicked the stool out of the way and knelt over me, pressing his knee into my chest and looking far more pissed than I'd ever seen him before.

"Listen close, motherfucker. You paid for a woman at the Pleasure Emporium, although why beats the fuck out of me when there's plenty of pussy right here free of charge. Her name is Grey Lumare. Ringing any bells now?" he asked.

Fuck me sideways. How the hell had Grey met the VP or his woman? I'd thought she was leaving when I came back to the clubhouse. Maybe I should have stayed to make sure her ass actually walked through the gates and down the street, except I hadn't wanted to see her suffering. I'd known my words had hurt her, but it had to be done.

"The whore who showed up earlier?" Wrong thing to say. His fist slammed into my face again and I heard static in my ears for a moment before everything came back into focus. "That boy ain't mine, Scratch. I was only with her the one time and the kid has to be a few years old. She even admitted he belongs to some thug."

Scratch leaned down closer. "That *whore* as you called her was attacked and raped by Itachi Suzuki, and she ran when she found out she was pregnant, so he'd never know about the baby. Until he found her last week and threatened her. She came to you for help, and you sneered at her and told her to leave."

Shit. My chest ached at the thought of some bastard doing that to her. I'd known she'd been hurt, and she'd alluded to the fact the little boy belonged to Itachi, but I hadn't realized he'd raped her. Or maybe I hadn't wanted to think about it too hard. I wasn't much better, I realized. I'd paid for her, but what had driven her to that point? She'd needed the money, had even admitted it. She hadn't said why, and I hadn't asked. A better man wouldn't have touched her and let her keep the cash. I never claimed to be a good guy. I was too fucked up.

"And for the record, the baby in her belly now *is* yours. So either man the fuck up and take care of her and those kids or be prepared to stand back and let someone else do it." Scratch stood, cursing about being too damn old as his knees cracked, and he left the clubhouse as quickly as he'd arrived.

I kept lying on the sticky floor. Baby? What baby? Was he trying to say I'd knocked up Grey when I'd bought her four months ago? Couldn't be. I'd told Knox to add to the contract a clause that whatever woman I paid for would be on birth control. I'd known I'd want to go bare and hadn't wanted to risk getting anyone pregnant. He had to be wrong, or she was lying about who the father was. Unless she'd signed the damn papers and lied through her fucking teeth about being protected. I needed to see the contract.

My cousin bent over me, his eyebrows arched. "Something you want to share with the class?"

"Fuck you."

"Nope, that's not it. So you knocked someone up, called her a whore, and kicked her out? That about sum it up?"

"It's not your business, Phantom. Leave it alone."

He tipped his head to the side. "Nah. Not my style. Think I'll head over to Scratch's place. Make sure that woman doesn't need anything. Might even offer her a place to crash. You don't care, right? She's just another hole for your dick. She's fair game for anyone, seeing as how she's not wearing your property patch."

Before I could say anything, he walked off, whistling a fucking tune like he hadn't a care in the world. I hauled myself up off the floor and knew first thing I needed was a Goddamn shower. Then I needed some time to think. If Grey was pregnant with my kid, why hadn't she said anything? She'd admitted the boy in her arms wasn't mine, so why not tell me right then and there the one in her belly was? Hell, I hadn't even realized she was pregnant, but at four months she couldn't be showing much if at all.

I walked out of the clubhouse, ignoring the stares of my brothers and the club whores, and got on my bike. I headed to my house, not stopping until I pulled into the driveway. For a moment, I stared at the place I'd called home the last few years. When the houses had started going up at the new compound, I hadn't needed one. Eventually, I'd decided I would like having my own space, but had insisted I didn't need anything large.

The three-bedroom two bath house was far more modest than a lot of the other homes. While I'd gone all out on the master suite, I'd minimized the other two rooms. Both were barely ninety square feet. I'd turned one into a weight room and the other remained empty. Since I'd never wanted kids, it hadn't mattered if I had extra bedrooms. Hell, I hadn't even thought I'd ever claim a woman.

And I wasn't now. Right?

I shut off the bike and went inside, stripping my clothes as I went straight to the master bedroom. Before I did anything else, I went to the dresser and pulled open the top drawer. My contract with Grey and Knox sat folded on top of my underwear. I opened it up and scanned the document. My stomach dropped when I realized there wasn't a damn word in it about birth control. The motherfucker had left it out and I hadn't read the contract close enough or I'd have caught that beforehand.

I folded it up again and set it back in the drawer. Didn't matter now. Too late to change things. I picked up my cut and carried it into the bathroom. I'd have to wipe off the back of it to get rid of the sticky residue. While I waited on the shower to warm, I got a damp rag to work on the nasty crap I'd gotten on my cut from the clubhouse floor. It wasn't like the damn thing was spotless, but I drew the line at possibly wearing the cum from my brothers. Some of them played a little too fast and loose with the club whores and went bare, pulling out at the last second. No fucking way would I ever do something so stupid.

Except you did. With Grey. Damnit.

I got into the shower and let the water beat down on my neck and shoulders. I pressed my hand to the wall and breathed in the steam building in the bathroom. At the clubhouse, I'd been able to lie to myself, at least a little. By calling Grey a whore, I'd tried not to think of her as more than a living, breathing sex doll. Didn't matter I hadn't fucked another woman since her. How could I when she'd come apart for me so sweetly? None of the women at the clubhouse would have ever responded the way she did. Hell, they'd been faking it for years. Not Grey.

I'd thought about her one too many times since the day I'd purchased her. Even when I'd signed the contract with Knox, I'd known what I was doing was wrong. My club fought alongside others to make sure women weren't mistreated. I hadn't forced myself on Grey, but it didn't make it right. She'd been there as a last resort, and I'd taken advantage of the situation.

And now I'd gotten her pregnant.

As much as I wanted to call her a liar, I couldn't. She hadn't been the one to tell me about the baby. I doubted she volunteered the information to anyone. Clarity had most likely asked and not given up until she'd gotten Grey to talk. I knew the VP's woman meant well. Everyone knew her story, even those of us who hadn't been here at the time, how she'd been a homeless single mom when Scratch found her. I had a feeling she saw herself in Grey, at least a little. Which meant Grey had a champion standing in her corner, whether she wanted one or not.

It would be easiest to let Phantom step in and help her. Fuck knew he'd be a much better dad than I would, and he'd wanted a family for a while. Except I hadn't been able to touch a woman since Grey. If I let her walk away, if I didn't fight for her and our kid, would I come to regret it later?

I wouldn't go to her tonight. Maybe not tomorrow either. I needed to get my head screwed on straight and decide not only what I wanted, but what would be best for Grey and the kids. I wouldn't be able to live with myself if I fucked up any of them. She'd only gotten a small taste of what life would be like with me. I wasn't sure she could handle me all day every day. Especially in the bedroom.

I pressed my forehead to the tiled wall and wished things were different -- that *I* was different. My past had made me into what I was today. For the most part, I enjoyed my life. But the darkness that touched me when I was younger had left a stain, one I couldn't wash off. I didn't want it to seep into Grey's life too.

"You're fucked up, Jin," I muttered to myself. "You damn well know she's better off without you."

I really did know it.

I just didn't know if I cared... Grey was under my skin, and I didn't think I could let her walk away.

Chapter Three

Grey

Disappointment hit me hard when I realized the knock at Clarity's door wasn't Samurai. I should have known better. The man had made it clear what he thought of me. He'd paid for my time, and in his eyes it made me a whore. I'd felt like one as I'd signed that contract, but then... Part of me had gotten attached to Samurai in those few hours we were together. I knew fairy tales didn't exist. Thinking he'd come save me was stupid. He'd wanted me to leave, not stay and make friends. He'd likely be pissed when he realized I hadn't gone home.

Phantom held Ryo on his lap, letting my son play with his keys. As Ryo shook them in his chubby fist, Phantom smiled at him. He'd claimed to be related to Samurai, yet no matter how hard I looked, I didn't see the resemblance. Their overall bone structure was entirely different, as was their build. Aside from both being Japanese, I didn't see anything similar between the two, and claiming they looked alike based off that would be like saying all blondes looked the same. Thankfully our small town didn't have many Japanese men running around. If I wasn't expecting to see Samurai today, I'd be freaking out right now. I still flinched whenever I saw anyone who reminded me of Itachi.

"Why are you here?" I asked.

"Because my cousin is an idiot. I'd hoped by coming here, it would make him realize what he'd be giving up if he let you go."

Great. So he did realize I hadn't left. If they'd thought he'd come running because I'd stayed, they were mistaken. They hadn't seen the look in his eyes, felt the cold coming off him as he'd stared at me. He probably hadn't thought about me even once since that day, and I'd gone to sleep every night wishing he was lying next to me. Pathetic. I was completely and utterly pathetic.

I sighed and looked down at the table. "He won't come for me. Not after what I did."

"It takes two to make a baby," he said.

"That's not what I meant." I locked my fingers together in my lap. "Men don't want a whore for a girlfriend or wife. By signing a contract at the Pleasure Emporium, I gave up my chance at finding love or even companionship. I knew what I was doing, and I'd do it all over again. That money allowed me to get my mother's loans current and kept a loan shark from using my body to pay off the debt."

Phantom set Ryo down and instructed him to go play. My son ran from the room and Phantom stood, moving around the table and kneeling beside my chair. He placed his hand over my folded ones and squeezed them gently.

"Grey, you did what you had to in order to survive. I think my cousin has realized that now, and he's probably at home, beating himself up for being a first-class asshole. He'll come around. And if he doesn't, then I'll do what I can to make your life easier. That's my family you're carrying in your belly, which means *you're* family."

"Clarity said the baby was part of the Devil's Boneyard and that meant I was too," I said.

He nodded. "She's right, but that's not what I meant. Samurai is literally my blood family. Our parents came to this country within a few years of each other. Mine moved to the US first, got settled, and then called for Samurai's parents. I'm quite a bit older than him so we didn't hang out much when we were younger. The fact we're both part of the same club means I get to keep an eye on him, without him realizing that's what I'm doing. I promised our family I would watch over him. And now I'm making that same promise to you. I will protect you, Ryo, and the baby with my life."

I sniffled, my eyes burning again. "I wish everyone would stop making me cry today. I feel like a weak, stupid woman. I've made so many mistakes, and I'd thought coming here was another one. Seems I was wrong. Clarity said they'd make room for me, but I don't want to intrude on their family."

Phantom kissed my forehead. "Then you'll come stay at my place. I have a spare room set up. You'll have to share the bed with Ryo, at least until we can get a toddler bed to add to the room. Might be a little cramped, but we can make it work."

I shook my head, not wanting to accept his offer. I didn't know what Samurai would think of me moving in with his cousin. The last thing I wanted to do was drive a wedge between the two men. I could tell Phantom loved Samurai like a brother, and whatever demons ate at Samurai, I knew he needed Phantom in his life. I couldn't come between them. I refused.

"I appreciate you wanting to help, but I don't think we should stay with you," I said.

"Look, Grey. I'm in my fifties now. My time to start a family has probably passed, and I've accepted that. The woman who's been after me to settle down isn't the type to have kids, so we've had our fun, but that's all it is."

"I'm not following. What does that have to do with me?" I asked.

He rubbed his forehead and sighed. "I'm not sure how to put this without upsetting you more than I have already. I have no idea what my cousin will do. It's my hope he'll come for you and realize what he's losing by letting you walk away. If he doesn't, you're welcome to stay with me... indefinitely."

I blinked, knowing there had to be a catch.

"As his old lady is what he means," Clarity said from the doorway. "And you could certainly do worse. He's an officer in the club and respected. I know he'd treat you and the kids right."

They were joking. They had to be. I didn't know him well enough to make that sort of decision. Then again, I didn't really know Samurai either, did I? We'd had sex for several hours, but we hadn't exactly had a talk about our lives or anything. He'd made me come so much I'd nearly passed out a few times, and he'd gotten off more than I realized men were capable of doing in such a short time span. We'd created a life, unintentionally, but it still didn't mean we should be together. And if I shouldn't be with Samurai, then I definitely shouldn't consider Phantom's offer. It was crazy!

"I'm not saying we need to be intimate," Phantom murmured. "I'm a stranger and I know we'd need to have a chance to get to know one another. You can set the pace, Grey. I want you to consider it if Samurai doesn't come around. I can promise I'd give you and the kids a good life."

"I'll think about it. That's all I can promise right now. I'm... overwhelmed and have so much to consider. Samurai clearly doesn't want me here. I won't do anything to jeopardize not only your relationship with him, but I also don't want to drive him away from this club. It's obvious he feels like he belongs, and he counts on all of you to have his back."

Phantom's eyes narrowed. "What aren't you saying?"

I bit my bottom lip and contemplated not uttering another word. In the end, I knew I needed to tell him. "Are you aware of what he likes to do with the women he sleeps with?"

He shrugged. "He holds them down. A lot of men do."

"It's more than that. He held me down by my throat and squeezed like he wanted to choke me. I think he needed that control, and maybe something more."

"More like what?" Phantom asked.

How did I tell this man I thought someone had hurt his cousin at some point? Call it intuition, or maybe I was projecting my own issues onto him. But I had a feeling Samurai had a secret he hadn't shared with anyone. He'd mentioned having someone with him so he wouldn't go too far, but did they know *why* he needed that extra layer of protection?

I shook my head. "I've said too much already. Forget it. It's not like he confided anything to me. I'm only guessing. Like you said, we're strangers. Other than knowing what gets your cousin off, I don't know him any better than I know you."

"If you don't want to stay here," Clarity said, "and you don't want to go with Phantom, there's one other option. We have some guest quarters inside the compound. Irish's woman, Janessa, is the daughter of a Dixie Reaper. When they come to visit, we make sure they have a place to stay. It's not just for them, though. Anyone can use it."

"I won't be in the way? What if someone visits and needs the space?" I asked. "Maybe I should go."

"You can't go home," Clarity said. "For one, it's not safe. The Prospect I sent to your place sent me pictures. That neighborhood is going to eat you alive. I don't know how you've remained unscathed since moving into that house."

"It was a step up from where I lived before," I admitted. "I know it's not safe, but it was mine. And I didn't mean I would go home. I can't. Itachi might come for me. If it isn't too much trouble, I thought maybe someone could give me a ride to another town? Doesn't have to be real far, just somewhere I could stay and get my bearings."

"You're going to run?" Phantom asked.

"I'm not a fighter, Phantom. I can admit I'm scared, and I don't want to stay somewhere I feel unwanted. Your gated compound lends a certain safety, but I can't remain here knowing Samurai dislikes me so much." I took a breath and squeezed my fingers together again. "He looked disgusted that I'd shown up here. My leaving is what's best for everyone."

"Not everyone," Clarity muttered. "You said you needed some time to come up with a plan, right? Stay with Phantom for a few days. It will give you time to figure out what you want to do, or where to go. Samurai can't begrudge you enough time to make sure your children will be safe, and if he does, I'll personally kick his ass."

"She's right," Phantom said. "No sense running off somewhere you'll be alone. Samurai might not be happy you're here, but even he wouldn't want you to put yourself, Ryo, or your unborn baby in danger."

It had seemed like he didn't care either way. How could they be so certain Samurai would want us to be safe? He'd told me to leave knowing I'd walked.

He hadn't cared that Itachi was after me and wanted Ryo. I felt so confused, and my head was starting to hurt. I rubbed at my temples and closed my eyes.

"Come on, pretty girl," Phantom said. "You need to rest. Ryo can play with my dog while you take a nap. You're so tired and stressed there's no way you could make a sound decision right now."

I nodded, knowing I didn't have the strength to fight him. If he wanted to let me sleep for a bit while he occupied Ryo, I couldn't say no. It was rare to have any "me" time so I'd take it when I could get it. I let Phantom help me to my feet and watched as he lifted Ryo into his arms. My son, who didn't usually trust strangers, had gone to the big man willingly since they'd first met.

When we stepped outside, I eyed the motorcycle in the driveway and knew there was no way we could ride to his house on it. Other than Clarity's SUV, I didn't see another vehicle appropriate for transporting a child. Except Phantom walked past the bike and went across the street. My eyebrows rose when I realized he lived so close to the VP. Since Clarity said Phantom was also an officer, it made sense. I wondered if the others were close by as well.

I followed him up to his front door and into his house. The dark wood floors gleamed, and I wondered how long before my son wrecked them. Phantom had painted the walls a soft aqua. I glanced into the living room and saw a brown leather sofa and matching chair. A media cabinet held movies on the adjacent wall, and a TV took up most of the opposite wall. The windows overlooking the yard had sheer curtains.

"Did you decorate this place yourself?" I asked, impressed with how nice everything looked.

He snorted. "Not hardly. The woman I

mentioned? I told her the sort of furniture I wanted, then set her loose on the place."

I hesitated mid-step. "She won't like me being here. Does she drop in often? What if she sees me and gets the wrong idea?"

He turned to face me, a half-smile on his face. "You worry too much, Grey."

He'd said what they shared was casual, but I had to wonder if the woman knew that. To her, it could be something more. The last thing I wanted was for her to show up, find me here, and either take out her anger on me and Ryo, or worse, break down crying.

Phantom sighed and pulled his phone from his pocket. "I can tell you won't rest until you know she'll be fine with this."

He tapped the screen, then placed the call on speaker. I could hear it ringing and my anxiety crept a bit higher as we waited for her to answer.

"Phantom! I'm so glad you called," the woman said by way of greeting.

"Celeste, I called for a reason."

She cleared her throat. "Sounds serious."

His gaze slid over me before going to Ryo, still clutched in his arm. "There's a woman and child moving into my house for at least a few days. Her name is Grey, and she's concerned how you'll react if you should decide to drop by and find them here. I told her what the two of us have is casual, but she's not going to rest easy until she knows it's not an issue."

"A woman and child?" Celeste asked softly. "You've always wanted children."

"I have," he agreed. "But they aren't mine to claim. At least… not yet."

My heart skipped a beat at his words. I shook my head at him, but he just winked. The man was causing problems where there shouldn't be any.

"Yet?" Celeste asked.

"Grey and her son Ryo came looking for Samurai. She's pregnant, Celeste, and my cousin is being an idiot. If he doesn't step up, I'm not going to toss them out of the gates and make them fend for themselves. You know me better than that," Phantom said.

"I do." She sighed. "All right. I get it. I still want to be your friend, Phantom, but I'm going to back off. I've known for a while we didn't want the same things, even if I kept hoping something would change. If they need anything, let me know."

"Thanks, Celeste. And of course, we can still be friends. I'll call you in a few days. Right now, I need to get them settled." He ended the call and slid the phone back into his pocket. "Now, if you'll follow me, I'll show you where you'll be staying. Then I'll introduce Ryo to Momo."

I followed him down the hall and into the guest room. It had the same dark wood flooring, but the walls were painted a soft peach. A brass bed took up the middle of the room. A small dresser sat along one wall with a few books stacked on top. The throw rug was mostly gray with peach and green in the pattern. I immediately felt myself relax in the soothing space and wondered if that had been the intention of the color scheme.

"The guest bath is across the hall. I keep it stocked, so use whatever you need. New toothbrushes are in the drawer, as well as travel-sized toothpaste and mouthwash. I'll call the Prospect who went to get your belongings and have him bring everything here. After you've rested, we'll discuss dinner options."

"Thank you, Phantom. For everything."

He nodded. "Ryo and I will go play with Momo. She'll be in heaven having a little boy to toss the ball for her. She's out back right now, so we'll probably hang out in the backyard for a bit. If she doesn't run out her energy, she tends to be destructive."

He stepped back into the hall and pulled the door partway shut, then I heard the thud of his boots heading back to the front of the house. I toed off my shoes and stretched before crawling onto the bed. I didn't even bother with the covers. The moment my cheek hit the pillow, I felt sleep tugging at me.

Chapter Four

Samurai

I'd slept like shit, and I damn well knew why. The devastation on Grey's face after I'd called her a whore would haunt me for a while. Every time I'd closed my eyes, I'd seen the stricken look she'd tried to hide, and remembered Scratch's words about what Itachi had done to her. She'd come to me for help, and I'd thrown her out. Good thing my VP's woman had a soft heart. If anything had happened to Grey or that little boy because I'd had my head up my ass, I'd have never forgiven myself.

I stared at the coffeemaker as it brewed a pot of caffeine strong enough to peel the paint from the walls. Despite me remaining awake nearly the entire night, I still didn't know what to do about Grey. The fact I'd thought about her a lot since I'd last seen her made me hesitant to spend more time with her. Something told me prolonged exposure to Grey would result in me wanting her with me all the time, and a sweet thing like her deserved so much better.

Even I could admit I was fucked up. Hell, if my brothers knew even half of it, they'd give me a wide berth. I probably should have told them at some point, or at least my cousin, but I'd been too ashamed. As a kid and teen, I'd been scrawny. It left me vulnerable and unable to defend myself. Over time, physical strength wouldn't have been enough anyway. I'd been broken mentally and emotionally. I hadn't started putting on muscle until I'd turned seventeen. By then, the damage had been done. But it had allowed me to pass for older, and I'd gotten away from my parents and sought out Phantom.

The machine beeped and I poured a cup of

coffee. I drained it quickly, then refilled the mug before I took a seat at the table. I'd need another cup or three before I started to feel more human, or as human as I ever felt. I hadn't even made it halfway through my second cup before I heard my front door open and slam shut. It shouldn't have surprised me to find Clarity sitting across from me a moment later.

"Are you here to remove my balls?" I asked.

"Nope." She smiled and folded her hands on top of the table. "I'm pretty sure you don't have any to remove."

Ouch! She wasn't holding her punches. I shifted on my seat and took another swallow of coffee. The VP had mentioned Clarity had felt a strong connection with Grey. It seemed to be true since she'd popped by and gone straight into attack mode. Normally, I found her to be sweet and charming. Didn't matter I'd heard about her kicking a club whore's ass when she'd first hooked up with Scratch. When it came to the club members and Prospects, she'd always been an angel.

"I'm sorry if I hurt Grey's feelings. I shouldn't have called her a whore," I said as I finished off cup two and poured a third. Probably should have put on a shirt, but I knew the VP's woman only had eyes for him. I could have been bare-assed and she wouldn't have cared. Her gaze would never stray that low. The Devil's Boneyard women were nothing if not loyal to their men.

It made me wonder if Grey would be the same way. If I were different, and there had been a chance for me to have a somewhat normal life, would she have looked at me the way Clarity gazed at Scratch? I'd never find out, but it didn't stop me from wanting it.

"Why did you do it, Samurai?" she asked. "I know you have a reputation with the girls at the clubhouse, but Grey isn't like them. The only reason she went to the Pleasure Emporium was out of desperation."

Looked like Grey and Clarity were getting close. I doubted they'd known each other before this, or Scratch would have done a lot worse yesterday. It surprised me Grey had opened up so much so fast. She hadn't seemed like the type. Then again, I didn't really know much about her, other than how she felt coming on my cock.

Shit. I closed my eyes, willing my suddenly erect cock to go down. It was a common occurrence when I thought about Grey. It had been happening ever since I'd spent those hours with her at Knox's place. I'd known then, before she'd even walked out, that it hadn't been enough. I'd wanted more.

"She mentioned needing the money," I admitted. "I should have walked away, and I knew it even then. I just couldn't. Knowing she'd give me exactly what I wanted? What I needed? It was too good to pass up."

Clarity nodded. "Grey seemed to understand you needed something from her that day, and she gave it willingly. But when she came to you for help, you called her a whore and tossed her out like trash. Did you know she was crying when I pulled up to the gate?"

Way to twist the knife, Clarity. I didn't have to be good friends with Grey to realize she wasn't the sort to show weakness in front of others. If she'd been crying at the gate, it meant I'd broken her with my words and thoughtless actions. My family hadn't raised me to be the sort of man who would walk away from a woman in need. Seeing her had fucked with my head. My family might not have been the touchy-feely sort, but my dad had made sure I knew to treat women a certain way. I couldn't say I'd been following that example since joining the Devil's Boneyard. At least, not all the time. I treated the club whores the same as everyone else.

"Nothing to say?" Clarity asked.

"She's better off without me in her life, Clarity."

"All right." She stood and put her hands in her pockets. "I guess it's okay Phantom took her home, then. I'll make sure he knows you don't want her. Last I saw him this morning, he and Grey's son were outside playing ball with Momo."

"She's staying?" I asked, running a hand through my hair and feeling antsy. I'd thought she'd leave, and I'd never see her again. If Phantom claimed her, then I'd run in to Grey everywhere around here. I'd never be able to forget her. Not like I'd been doing a bang-up job of that so far anyway.

"She needs help," Clarity said softly. "Itachi can't get his hands on the boy. He'll use her son to do horrible things to Grey, and in the end, he'll warp that sweet child into the same sort of monster as he is."

She wasn't telling me anything I didn't already know. I could admit -- to myself anyway -- that I was a chickenshit when it came to Grey. I felt too strongly for her already. Too much time in her presence, and I didn't think I'd have the power to walk away anymore.

"What do you want from me?" I asked.

"Nothing. I came. I saw. Now I'm leaving. You were probably right to stay away from her. You can't give her what she needs. And the baby... They'll need someone to look up to. A man too scared to do the right thing isn't right for the job of being a daddy. So stay here and do whatever it is you planned for today. I'll make sure Phantom takes good care of them."

She turned and walked out, slamming my front

door behind her. I shoved the mug out of the way and pressed my forehead to the table. Her words echoed in my mind, bouncing around my brain like a damn pinball. I'd always known I wasn't cut out for fatherhood. Didn't make it hurt less to hear Clarity say it too. Scared? Damn right. I was fucking terrified of being a father.

But she'd gotten one thing wrong. I wasn't scared of doing the right thing. They didn't understand that was why I'd tried to push Grey away. I didn't have anything to offer them except a life of pain and misery. Grey deserved sweet words and a soft touch, not the darkness I needed to unleash in the bedroom. I didn't think anything would change my need for control and dishing out a bit of pain. It would be part of me for the rest of my life. And one day I'd likely take things too far. If it were Grey in my bed when that happened, I'd lose what was left of my broken mind.

I stood and made my way to the bedroom. A beer at the clubhouse sounded pretty damn good right about now. Sure, I had a few cold ones in the fridge, but I needed to get out of the house, and more importantly out of my head. I pulled on a gray tee and my boots before slipping on my cut. I wet my hair and quickly styled it before heading out to my bike. The clubhouse wasn't far. It only took a minute or two to park out front and go inside.

Despite the early hour, music still pumped from the speakers in the corners, and a few club whores lingered, looking used up. Makeup smeared across their faces and their hair looked like it had been pulled all night. Probably had been for that matter. Especially Shonda's. Girl could suck cock as good as any porn star. And yeah, I'd sampled her so I knew for certain. I couldn't tell who the blonde was since she had her face buried in her arm as she snored her ass off. The other of the three I hadn't touched yet. Too skinny for my taste. Nothing against a slimmer woman, but I liked having a little more to hold onto.

I claimed the stool at the far end of the bar. Sam slid my favorite beer over to me, and I twisted off the top before taking a swallow. If he wondered why I'd decided to start drinking first thing in the morning, he kept it to himself. Smart guy. I heard the women giggle and the sound of them stumbling over in my direction.

"I'll vote you in right the fuck now if you keep them away from me," I muttered to Sam.

He snorted and gave me a half-smile. "Sorry, Samurai. You're on your own with those two. They already made their way through a fourth of the club last night."

I shook my head. Great. It would mean they'd think of me as a challenge, especially the one I'd never touched. Just what I fucking needed today. I kept drinking, hoping they'd take a hint and leave me alone. Should have known better.

"Hey, Samurai," Shonda said, sliding her hand along my shoulder. "Want some company?"

"Nope."

The other woman flanked my other side, placing her hand on my arm. "I've heard you're a wild ride. I want to play."

Shonda smiled at me. "You can have us both. Me and Darla. What do you say?"

Light spilled into the room as the doors opened. I didn't bother looking to see who else needed a drink this morning. Maybe the girls would move on to them, but I doubted I was that lucky.

"Already said it. Nope. Now fuck off. Both of you."

When I felt Shonda's nails bite into the leather of my cut, I reached up and gripped her fingers, giving them a squeeze. I clenched down tighter until she yelped and tried to back away. Darla seemed to take the hint and staggered back a few steps. I finally released Shonda, watching as she shook out her hand.

"You almost broke my fingers," she said, a whine to her voice.

"Don't fucking care. You fucking know not to touch me without permission."

"I take it this is a bad time?" The soft voice had my head whipping in that direction.

Grey wore a demure dress, much like the one she'd worn the day we'd met. Shit. No, *exactly* like it. Was the woman trying to kill me? Bad enough I still thought of our day together. I didn't need a visual. All I could think of was the way she'd unbuttoned the top and how sexy she'd looked with the skirt pushed up around her waist.

Shonda pushed her way between us and placed a hand on her hip. "Back off, bitch. I have a prior claim."

I stood, knowing I needed to end this. The club whores thinking they had more of a right to speak to me than Grey pissed me off. Yeah, I'd let Shonda suck me off several times, and I'd even fucked her once or twice, but it didn't mean shit. She was a place to put my dick. But Grey...

I reached out to grab Shonda, and my fingers slipped through air. She'd been there one second. I blinked and suddenly she was on the ground. What the fuck? I looked up and held Grey's gaze as she stepped over the club whore, shaking out her hand.

Why did I find it so hot she'd put the whore in her place? It almost felt like she'd been claiming me as her own, even though I knew nothing of the sort was going on. Grey might have come looking for me, but it wasn't to shout to the world I belonged to her. She had far too much sense for that.

"Should I apologize to her?" she asked.

"No. She had it coming. None of these women have a claim on me. If you hadn't given her a reminder that she wasn't anything special, I would have." I blinked down at Shonda, shocked as fuck Grey had put the whore on her ass. Sweet little Grey, it seemed, had claws. I wanted to smile but somehow managed to hold it back. I didn't think she'd appreciate me grinning like a damn Cheshire cat.

Shonda got to her feet and sneered at Grey. "Who the fuck does this bitch think she is?"

I sucked in a lungful of air and let it out. Moment of truth. If I said the words on the tip of my tongue, I couldn't take them back. It would cement things with Grey forever. It was easier to remind myself to keep away when she wasn't close enough to touch. The scent of her teased my nose and made me want to reach for her. Even though I knew I couldn't make her mine, I wanted to shout out to the entire club that Grey belonged to me. I didn't want her crying out anyone's name but mine. Didn't want anyone to feel her pussy squeezing their cock. In a less fucked-up world, I'd have claimed her.

Looking at her, and thinking about her walking away, made me realize something. I didn't want her to go. I *needed* to but didn't want to.

"She's the mother of my child. Show her some fucking respect," I said.

I heard Darla gasp and a softly uttered "fuck me" from Sam. Looked like I'd surprised more people than just myself. Grey's eyes went a little wide, and I saw a flash of hope before she seemed to get control of herself and blanked her expression.

"Clarity told you?" she asked.

"Actually, the VP did. Clarity did pay me a little visit this morning, though. I wasn't in the best of places mentally, and I didn't give her any answers she liked."

Although, if she hadn't come talk to me, I may not have come to the clubhouse. Would Grey have gone to my house to find me? She had to have been looking for me to come here. I couldn't think of another reason she'd visit the clubhouse. Having her all to myself, within a few yards of my bedroom, could have been disastrous. I'd have found a way to lure her to my bed and had a replay of our time at the Pleasure Emporium.

Grey licked her lips and looked around at the people gawking at us. "Can we go somewhere and talk?"

I nodded and stepped closer, placing my hand at the curve of her waist. The simple touch was enough to make my dick start to harden. The scent of her didn't help matters any. If I stayed close to her, it wouldn't be long before I couldn't hide my reaction to her. Hell, too much longer and I'd likely be lifting her skirt here and now, so I could do my best to make her come again.

"Let's take a walk."

I led her outside and into the grass beside the clubhouse. I didn't have a destination in mind. We walked alongside the road for a bit before cutting through the grass toward the back of the compound. I knew we'd have privacy for whatever she needed to say. But being out in the open would remind me not to cross the line with her. No matter how much I wanted her, I needed to keep my hands to myself... or at least in respectable places.

"I'm sorry for the way I reacted when you came

to the gate yesterday," I said. "Not my finest moment. I didn't mean it when I called you a whore."

She winced and looked away. "It hurt, but I couldn't exactly refute your statement. The moment I signed the papers with Mr. Knox, it's exactly what I became."

I pulled her to a stop. "No. Fuck, no! You're not a damn whore, Grey, and I never should have said it. I knew when you walked into that room and I saw the fear in your eyes that you weren't a regular there."

"It's okay, Samurai." She licked her lips and tucked her hair behind her ear. "I had a reason for coming to find you today. Your cousin let us stay at his place last night. I need time to come up with a plan, or an escape strategy, but I don't want to stick around if it's going to be a problem. This is your home and I have no right to barge in like I did."

I reached up and cupped her cheek a moment before letting my hand drop to my side. "You belong here too, Grey."

My gaze dropped to her stomach. I could see the small swell under her dress and wanted to place my hand there. I couldn't remember my parents being very affectionate with one another, or my aunts and uncles. For that matter, my dad had never been one to hug me. Now that I'd admitted the baby was mine, had laid claim to it in the clubhouse, I knew I didn't want to be anything like my father. If I had the chance to be part of my kid's life, I'd give them as many hugs and kisses as I could. I didn't want them to ever wonder if I loved them.

"My parents moved here from Japan when I was still young. My mother took care of our home and busied herself volunteering for one cause or another. Neither showed their emotions very often." I reached out and placed my palm over her belly, grateful she didn't swat me away. "It's a small part of why I never wanted children. I don't have the first clue how to be a dad. I don't want my kid to grow up in the same cold, emotionless environment I did."

She placed her hand over mine. "And the other reason?"

I shook my head. There were some things I couldn't discuss. Not now, and possibly not ever. For one, I didn't want that ugliness to touch Grey. For another, I didn't think I could ever tell anyone how weak and pathetic I'd been. I was supposed to be a tough, take-no-shit biker, and while I was now, I hadn't always been.

"Do you want us to stay?" she asked. "Because Itachi won't let me leave. Not after seeing his son with me. He wants Ryo, and what Itachi wants he typically gets."

"I'm not scared of a local thug, Grey. He's not as big and bad as he thinks." I gave her a smile. "And who's to say Ryo is his son? Did you confirm his suspicions? Introduce the boy to his father?"

She shook her head. "I was so scared I just stared at him until he'd left. Then I rushed home, only to realize it likely wasn't safe there anymore. So we walked here to find you."

"I can't promise you much. I'm not a good guy. I can't do soft and sweet." I looked away from her troubled eyes. "Phantom would be a better bet for you. He's always wanted a family, and I've seen him with kids. He's great with them."

"You're confusing me right now," she said.

I laughed. "Yeah, I'm doing the same to myself. Look, if you want Phantom to claim you, I'll step back and let him. He'd be great with Ryo and the baby."

Even if it would feel like I'd been gutted every time I saw them together. If it's what she wanted, what she needed, then I'd do the right thing. I owed it to her. It wasn't her fault the contract had been altered. She hadn't known I'd insisted on the woman I bought to be on birth control. I'd mentioned it when she'd walked in the room, and I didn't know why she hadn't spoken up then. Not sure if it would have made a difference. I'd wanted her, more than I'd wanted anyone before.

Her brow furrowed. "Samurai, I'm not staying there because I want him to claim me, whatever that means. I didn't understand it when he brought it up, and I still don't. He's letting us stay there while I figure things out. I came to ask if you'd be all right with us sticking around a few more days. I need a plan before I go running off to some strange town I've never been to before."

It felt like she'd punched me right in the chest. "You're leaving?"

Sure, I'd wanted her away from the compound. Moving out of town was entirely different.

She lifted one shoulder in a shrug. "Staying seems dangerous. Itachi wants Ryo. I already know what he'll ask of me if I go with them, but I could never let that monster have my son. If I leave, there's a chance he won't find me and will give up."

"You sure it's Ryo he wants?" I asked. "Because if I were in Itachi's place, it's not Ryo I'd be after. I'd do whatever it took to keep you by my side, or more accurately, in my bed. You sure he's not really after you and using the boy as an excuse? He couldn't have known he'd get you pregnant that day. And I have a hard time seeing a man like that wanting anything to do with your son. He likely has kids all over the fucking place if he goes around raping women."

"We… I mean…" Her face paled. Fuck me. All I'd done was remind her of the day Itachi hurt her.

I lifted a hand. "Wait. That's not what I meant. Shit. I'm horrible at this."

She folded her arms over her chest and waited quietly while I gathered my thoughts. I looked up at the sky again, trying to figure out what exactly I wanted to say to her. The truth? Maybe. Or at least some version of it.

"I've thought about you over the last several months. You got under my skin. Hell, I haven't even fucked another woman since that day. The way you responded to me, watching you come apart in my arms… nothing could compare to it. Not the whores at the clubhouse for sure."

"You thought about me?" she asked softly. The hope I'd seen earlier flashed in her eyes again.

I nodded and took a step closer to her. "Grey, I'm no prize. You should run far and fast to get away from me. I told you to pick Phantom if he's the one you want because you deserve the best. I'm far from that. I'll fuck up. A lot. But if you want to stay, if you think you might want to give things between us a chance, I'd like you to move into my house."

She blinked at me and didn't say a word. The longer she remained quiet, the antsier I became. Had I screwed up even more? Fuck if those words hadn't been hard to say. Asking her to live with me? I'd clearly lost my mind. I'd never allowed anyone to get that close, and now I wasn't only opening up to this woman, I'd offered up my safe space too. Except the more time I spent with Grey, the more I realized she needed the safety much like I did.

Chapter Five

Grey

Had he asked me to move in with him? I'd come to talk to him, see if he'd be pissed if I stayed a few days. He'd made it clear what he thought of me, and now... I shook my head, trying to understand what the hell was happening.

"Are you okay?" I asked. "I mean... You clearly couldn't stand the sight of me yesterday, and now you want us to live together?"

"Sorry for the whiplash." He squeezed my hip and tugged me closer. "I pushed you away to protect you. But the thought of you leaving... it twists me up inside. What if we let everyone think Ryo was mine?"

I stared at him, wondering if maybe Samurai had a twin, and they were playing a trick on me. Everything he'd said yesterday was the exact opposite of what I heard now. I glanced around, wondering if someone would jump out with a camera or something. It had to be a joke, right?

"You told the guys at the gate last night Ryo wasn't yours. Why would anyone believe he is now? And why would you even offer that?" I asked.

"If he's Itachi's son, then he's half-Japanese. Which means you could claim either me or Phantom as Ryo's dad and no one would be the wiser. Besides, if I say Ryo is mine, no one in this damn club is going to say otherwise. They'll back up my claim. Scratch and Clarity's oldest isn't the VP's son by blood, but he's raised him. Far as Scratch and anyone else is concerned, Caleb is Scratch's boy. No one will ever say different."

If he'd said any of this when I came to the gate last night, I may have jumped at the chance. It would have been the answer to my prayers. Still was, but I had to wonder if he really meant it. I felt so overwhelmed.

"I think I need to sit down," I muttered.

"We could go to my home," he offered. "It's not as big as Phantom's. I'd never planned to have a family, so I took the smallest house."

My head was starting to hurt. "I don't even know what to think right now. Could we go to Phantom's house? I don't want to be too far from Ryo."

He nodded and placed his hand at my back, leading me back to the road. By the time we'd reached my temporary lodgings, I had to wonder if Samurai had been abducted by aliens. Despite the demands he'd made of me during our only time together, he'd been almost sweet to me. Then he'd turned venomous at the gate. Now he wanted me to move in and couldn't seem to stop touching me? Were there two of him? A good Samurai and an evil twin?

Phantom's eyebrows lifted as we walked up to him and Ryo. My son launched himself at my legs, and I knelt to hug him. I needed to decide what would be best for Ryo. Nothing else mattered. As long as I kept him safe, I could deal with anything that came my way. I needed to keep that in sight while I talked to the two men standing by me.

"Let's head inside," I said.

Both of them followed and I sank onto the couch, watching as Ryo collapsed next to Momo, giving the dog a hug. Phantom had explained she was a Shiba Inu. I had to admit she was cute, and Ryo seemed to adore her. I'd have to get him a dog eventually. I had a feeling he'd be begging for one after this.

"The talk didn't go well?" Phantom asked.

"He's confusing me," I said. "See if you can make

sense of his thoughts because I can't. It gives me a headache even trying."

Phantom snorted. "Not surprised. All right, Samurai. Give it to me straight. From beginning to end, where have your thoughts been?"

I blinked. He'd worded that in a very specific way. It made me wonder if Samurai had some sort of learning disability or something. Had that been why his thoughts seemed chaotic and disjointed? Did he have a mental disorder of some sort?

Samurai blew out a breath. "All right. I'll try. I'm sure Grey told you we met several months ago. It was a one-time thing, except I haven't been able to stop thinking about her."

Phantom smiled a little. "I noticed you seemed to lack female attention lately. Or rather, you were pushing them away."

Samurai nodded. "Yeah. Because I knew they couldn't compare to Grey. Why be with someone who's going to fake it after experiencing the real thing? Seemed pointless. They no longer appeared attractive to me, not even a little."

Phantom glanced at me before focusing on his cousin again. At least he wasn't going to comment about the way I'd responded to Samurai. There was a lot I could handle but discussing my sex life openly wasn't even in the top ten things I wanted to tackle right now. Especially with my son in the room.

"She showed up out of the blue yesterday, and I didn't know what to think. I got excited to see her again, then panicked because I knew I wasn't any good for her. You know I'm all fucked up in my head, and she can do so much better." Samurai squeezed the back of his neck. "So I tried to run her off."

"She told you she needed help?" Phantom asked.

Samurai nodded. "I'm not a knight in shining armor. You know it as well as I do. Keeping her around would have only tempted to me to hold onto her, and then she'd have been drowning right alongside me."

Phantom reached over and tugged his cousin in for a hug. Samurai seemed shocked by the move and stood stiffly for a moment, before patting Phantom on the back. When they separated, Samurai kept staring at his cousin.

"Did I miss something?" I asked.

"Our family isn't known for showing affection of any sort," Phantom said. "Japanese men tend to be rather reserved. His father and mine weren't big on hugging. I can't even recall seeing either of them hug their wives. Being around the Devil's Boneyard has made me adapt to being more American. I guess I haven't hugged my cousin as much as I should have, though."

Samurai cleared his throat. "Anyway. I went home, slept like shit, and then had a visit from Clarity this morning. After she left, I went to the clubhouse to get drunk. As much as I hated the thought of Grey being with you, I knew you'd be better for her and Ryo than I could ever be."

"Not true," Phantom said.

"I'm all kinds of screwed up. You don't even know the half of it." Samurai closed his eyes and shook his head. "We're not having that discussion. Not ever, so don't ask."

"Keep going. Don't get off track," Phantom said.

"Right. So, Grey came to the clubhouse and found me. And I sort of told Shonda and Darla, as well as anyone else within hearing range, that she's the mother of my child. And we went off to talk."

"That's where the confusion really starts," I said. "He went from running me off last night to asking me to move in today."

Samurai looked my way. "When you came into the clubhouse and I was face-to-face with you, and I realized you planned to leave, I knew I didn't want that. Even if I'm a bad bet, I couldn't let you walk away. I keep touching you to convince myself you're here. I know you'd be better off with Phantom, but I don't like the idea of his hands on you. You're mine, Grey. Only mine."

I hadn't expected that. Not even a little. I glanced at Phantom to see what he thought of all this. He had a slight smile on his lips as he stared at his cousin, and what looked like pride shone in his eyes.

"If you want a chance with me, I need to know what makes you think you're so horrible," I said. "Not for myself, but I have to think of Ryo and the baby. There's clearly something you don't want to discuss. As much as I want to give you time, it's something I don't have much of. With Itachi looking for me, I need to come up with a plan now. If that means moving in with you, I need to be certain the kids and I will be safe."

Phantom rocked back on his heels. "Why don't I take Ryo and Momo for a walk across the street? They can play in the VP's backyard so the two of you can have some privacy. And, Samurai, whatever you're holding onto, bottling things up never ends well. You need to be honest with Grey. One hundred percent. You get me?"

He nodded, even though Samurai looked miserable thinking about it. I got up and went over to Ryo, hoping he'd be okay without me for a little longer. He seemed to enjoy Phantom's company, or more accurately, he'd go anywhere Momo did. The boy sure loved that dog. I hugged him to me and kissed his cheek.

"Ryo, Mr. Phantom is going to take you across the street to play on the slide again, okay? Momo is going to go with you. I'll be right here when you get back."

My son hugged me, then reached for Phantom's hand. After the door shut, I folded my arms and waited to see what Samurai would do or say. I couldn't remember seeing a grown man so uncomfortable before. Whatever weighed on him, it had to be bad. I didn't know if it would change how I felt about the situation or not. Part of me wanted to stay with him. If it were only me, I would have in a heartbeat. But I had children to consider.

"When my family moved here, my mother stayed home with me for a while. When I started school, she started volunteering for different charities. It wasn't often she was home before it was time to make dinner, if she came home at all. Sometimes she'd meet my father out somewhere. I had a babysitter from the time school let out until one of them came home."

He rubbed his hands up and down his thighs and moved over to the couch, taking a seat. I curled up next to him, reaching for his hand. I curled my fingers around his, needing to show him he wasn't alone right now. My stomach knotted, knowing something awful was coming.

"I was a scrawny kid. All the way up until I reached seventeen. Short. Skinny. I got picked on a lot at school. It also made it easy for people to bully me or force me to do things I didn't want to do." He squeezed my fingers. "My babysitters changed from year to year, until I turned twelve. My parents found a college girl to watch me from the time I got home from school until they arrived home. I'd told them I was old enough to be alone, but they wouldn't hear of it."

He got quiet. I could tell it was hard for him to talk about it. In my gut, I knew where this was going. Or thought I did.

"Whatever you need to say, I'll listen with an open mind," I said softly.

He nodded. "She'd been watching me for a few months before it happened the first time. I'd started getting hard when I saw partially naked, or fully naked, girls and women. It wasn't something I could discuss with my dad, and I didn't know how to handle it. Heather would sometimes take me out back to swim. One day, she left the bathroom door partially open while she changed. I caught her without a shirt or bra on and went instantly hard."

"It's a normal reaction, Samurai."

"Yeah. I didn't realize it, and she took advantage. Once she saw what had happened, she started flashing her tits and ass more often. Next time she changed, she lured me into the bathroom with her, and let me touch her. I came in my pants."

His cheeks flushed and I inched a little closer to him. I didn't like where this story was going, but I needed to hear all of it. And something told me he needed to get it out in the open. Even if he never told anyone else, it wasn't something he needed to keep locked up inside. It would fester, like it had already. I had a feeling the reason he liked to choke the women he slept with had something to do with this story.

"My parents started taking trips out of town twice a month. They'd leave Heather to watch me the entire time. First trip they made, she waited until the second night. I woke up and she'd... I was naked."

I covered my mouth with my other hand, horrified. "Oh, God. Samurai, I'm so sorry."

He'd suffered worse than I'd realized. I couldn't imagine how confused he must have been. His parents should have protected him. Not left him with his tormentor.

He squeezed my fingers even tighter, then seemed to realize he was hurting me. He slackened his grip. "She made me come, and… That was the first time I ever had sex."

"No. No, honey. That wasn't sex. It was rape." My heart broke for him. "You weren't old enough to give your consent and she knew that. She preyed on you, took advantage. What she did was wrong."

He shut his eyes again and his jaw tightened. "It happened every night after that. By the time I was fifteen, I was still small for my age. She'd stopped tying me down. Instead, she used blackmail to get what she wanted. It happened every. Damn. Night. She didn't even wait for my parents to go out of town by that point."

"Why didn't you tell anyone?" I asked. "Your mom? Dad?"

He shook his head. "I didn't think they'd care or understand. I put up with it until I was seventeen. Then I called Phantom and came here. I bulked up that year and made sure no one, especially a woman, would ever take advantage of me again. I hold the women down, and sometimes choke them until they pass out, because it's what I wanted to do to her. I wanted to wrap my hand around Heather's throat until she stopped breathing. It's the only time I feel like I have complete control when it comes to sex."

I reached up and turned his face toward mine. "What she did was horrible and wrong. I'm so sorry you went through that. And even sorrier you've kept it all to yourself all this time."

"I don't trust myself around someone as sweet as you, Grey. What if I get locked in the past one night and seriously hurt you? I'd never forgive myself."

And that was why I'd come here for help. The sweet side I'd seen at the Pleasure Emporium. He hadn't pushed me away for himself, but out of fear he'd harm me in some way. How could I leave knowing he'd been hurt same as me? It would be rather hypocritical of me. I leaned in and pressed my lips to his cheek. He didn't like kisses, but at least he hadn't flinched away from me.

"I think you have PTSD, Samurai. I don't know a lot about it, except that ever since Itachi broke into my apartment, certain things trigger me. I have a feeling the same is happening with you. Maybe, over time, we can learn to heal one another?"

His gaze skimmed my face before he slowly brought me closer and pressed his lips to mine. I gasped at the contact before letting him take what he wanted. His lips caressed mine. The kiss was slow, and perfect.

"You're the first woman I've ever kissed willingly," he said. "Are you sure you want to give me a chance? It could lead you down a path of destruction."

"I'm sure. You're the father of this baby." I took his hand and placed it over the small bump. "He or she is going to need you. *I* need you, and so does Ryo. You aren't a bad man, Samurai. You've been hurt and have been carrying a dark secret all these years. It would weigh on anyone. Would it help if I talked about what happened with Itachi?"

He gave a humorless laugh. "Only if you want

me to track him down and slit his throat. The fact he got you pregnant tells me enough. He raped you. Hurt you. I'm not sure I can handle hearing the details."

"Guess that makes us quite the pair," I said.

"Does this mean you're staying?" he asked.

"I still need to know one more thing." I licked my lips. "Everyone keeps talking about Phantom claiming me. What exactly does that mean?"

His eyes narrowed. "My cousin won't be fucking claiming you. Not now. Not ever."

I waited, still not having my question answered. It sounded rather barbaric and like a throwback to times past. If I hadn't already met Clarity, I'd have worried they planned to put a collar on me like a pet or something. I hoped it was only a turn of phrase and wasn't like selling myself into slavery, although I had a feeling it would be of the sexual variety with these men.

"You know anything about bikers or being part of a motorcycle club?" he asked.

"Not really. Only what I've seen on TV, and it's not like I think fiction is real no matter how much research someone does. Don't the writers for those shows tend to put their own spin on things?"

"I honestly don't watch them so I wouldn't know. Being part of the club is like having an extended family. I call the other members my brothers, same as they do with me. Phantom is my actual blood relation because we're cousins. You've met Clarity. She's referred to as Scratch's old lady. Doesn't mean she's physically old or anything, but she belongs to him. Did you pay attention to her cut?"

I shook my head. Had she been injured? I didn't know what he was talking about, or what it had to do with being claimed. Was he going to mark me in some way? Would it hurt?

He ran his hand over his leather vest. "This is a cut. The back of Clarity's says *Property of Scratch*."

"Property?" I asked, wanting to put a little space between us. "Like he owns her?"

"Pretty sure he'd say it was the other way around," Samurai said. "Different clubs do things in different ways. Here, at the Devil's Boneyard, when we claim a woman and give her a property cut, it's forever. Think of it like a marriage but without divorce."

"Wait. You're saying if I agree to stay here with you, and you give me one of those property things, then I can't ever leave?" I did slide a bit away from him that time. "What if you beat me? What if you end up being an alcoholic who hurts the kids? You could be a serial killer! We don't know anything about each other!"

He held up his hands. "Calm down, Grey. You're starting to panic. Would it help if you talked to some of the old ladies? You already met Clarity, but there are others. I could see if anyone is available. They may be able to explain things better than I can, since they're looking at it from the other side."

My heart rate started to slow again, and I nodded. Maybe I should speak with the women. I didn't want to leave, and I really did want to see where things went with Samurai, but forever? After only speaking to each other briefly at the Pleasure Emporium and just now? It seemed insane.

"I guess that would be okay. Will Phantom care if someone comes over?" I asked.

"Nope. He'll be cool with it." Samurai pulled out his phone and tapped at the screen. I glanced over and realized he was sending out text messages. "Darby and

Nikki offered to stop by. Darby is with Renegade. Nikki is with Ashes, but she's Renegade's sister."

None of those names meant anything to me. I sat and fidgeted, twisting my fingers in my lap. I didn't know how long it would take anyone to get here, and I suddenly had no idea how to fill the void with conversation. What the hell did I say after learning I'd be someone's property? And that I could never leave... I could feel my anxiety creeping up to a higher level again.

The front door opened a few minutes later and two women walked in. Both were wearing a property cut like Clarity had. They saw me and smiled before hurrying into the room.

"I'm Nikki," said the taller of the two. "I have to say we were shocked when Samurai mentioned he wanted to claim a woman. I'd thought he'd never settle down."

"It's not like I have one foot in the grave," Samurai muttered. "I'm only thirty-three."

"I'm Darby," said the other woman, giving me a little wave. "You have some questions?"

"She freaked out when I explained about old ladies and property cuts," Samurai said. "I'll step out of the room so Grey will feel comfortable enough asking whatever she wants. Be honest with her. About everything."

Darby's eyebrows shot up. "Everything? Like even club whores? Because I wouldn't have minded a warning about those."

"Think I met some already," I said, glancing at Samurai. He gave me a nod, letting me know that's exactly who those women had been. "I kind of put one on the floor after she got an attitude."

Darby covered her mouth with her hand, but I

saw the humor lurking in her eyes. Nikki didn't bother hiding it. She burst out laughing. I didn't know what to make of the women. Hadn't it been a bad thing I'd done? I couldn't remember a time I'd ever been violent before, but that woman had started running her mouth and something inside me had snapped.

I heard Samurai's booted steps as he walked out of the room and toward the kitchen. The women got themselves together and took a seat on either side of me on the couch. Nikki patted my back.

"You did good," Nikki said. "Those women like to think they have a claim on the men here, but they don't. You can't let them walk all over you."

"So what questions did you have?" Darby asked.

"I feel so lost. I never expected any of this. When I came here yesterday, I only wanted help getting away from Itachi. Everything has spiraled out of control since then."

Nikki shook her head. "Control is an illusion. I don't think any of us ever truly have control of a situation. We like to think we do, but nope. It's all up to fate."

"Are you saying it's fate that I got pregnant?" I asked.

Nikki and Darby both inhaled so sharply I heard it. They stared at me, eyes wide, jaws slack, and I had to wonder if I shouldn't have said anything.

"Wait." Darby lifted a hand. "You're pregnant and Samurai didn't toss you over his shoulder, go all caveman, and tell you that you're moving in with him?"

I had to wonder if he'd have done exactly that if it weren't for his past trauma. Since neither of them knew about Samurai's past, it didn't surprise me they expected him to act like the other men here. Assuming they were talking about their personal experiences with the Devil's Boneyard.

"He said if he claims me, it's forever. We're strangers. What if we end up hating each other? And I can't leave? I don't want to be trapped." I took a breath. "At the same time, if it meant Ryo and the baby were safe, then I'd give up anything. My happiness doesn't matter."

"Yes, it does!" Nikki patted my arm. "I know it's easy to try and sacrifice ourselves for our children, but if we're miserable, what sort of lesson are we teaching them? How can we expect them to be happy if we aren't?"

"Can I ask you something?" Darby turned to face me. "You've clearly been intimate with Samurai since you're carrying his baby. Did he do anything during your... encounter... that scared you? Anything at all that made you think you should fear for your life?"

I hesitated, thinking back to that day. My cheeks warmed when I remembered how turned-on I'd been, after I got over my shock. He'd made me come so hard, and often. Yeah, he'd held me down. He'd closed his fingers around my throat. Said filthy things to me. But I'd enjoyed all of it. I shook my head to answer her question. No, I hadn't been scared of Samurai, not after the initial jolt of realizing he was Japanese like Itachi.

"Do you really think he'd ever hurt you or the children?" Nikki asked. "Because I'd trust him with my life, and with my kids' lives."

"No, I don't," I said.

"Then what's really bothering you about all this?" Darby asked. "Because I didn't know Renegade for long at all before he made me his. In fact, I think every woman in the Devil's Boneyard fell for her guy within days of meeting him, if not from the moment she set eyes on him."

"But he said it's forever, that I can't leave," I said.

Nikki tipped her head to the side. "I can see where that might seem scary. Do you want to know what it's like to live here? To be claimed by one of these guys? Because it's amazing. Even before I became Ashes' old lady, the club looked out for me because my brother is a member. They watched over me, protected me. These guys will do *anything* for the women they claim, or those they consider family."

Darby patted my back. "I'm sure this is all new to you. I hadn't had a good experience with men before Renegade found me. Or rather, he found Fawn, my daughter. He saved my life."

Nikki smiled. "Ashes isn't the biological father of my oldest. I was pregnant with Oliver when Ashes realized I was about to lose my apartment. He took me to his house, gave me a place to feel safe, and it didn't take long before we ended up together. He's amazing, and I'm damn lucky to call him mine."

"So your men both saved you?" I asked.

They nodded. Nikki leaned closer, lowering her voice. "Every last one of us was rescued in one way or another. Our men would go to war to keep us safe, and Samurai will be the same with you and your children. I can't tell you what to do in this situation, but I think you should give him a chance. We have a good life here."

"From what I've seen and heard, the men here fall hard. If Samurai wants to claim you, then you don't have to worry about him straying. He'll never want another woman to touch him. He'll be faithful until the day he dies," Darby said. "Scratch and Clarity ended up together within a day or two of meeting. Jordan and Havoc were a thing first day he brought her here.

Rescued her off the side of the road. Sometimes you know when you've found your perfect match."

"I think the two of you may have read too many romance novels," I muttered. I couldn't imagine falling for someone so fast. And yet... I glanced toward the kitchen. I couldn't deny I wanted to spend more time with Samurai. I'd felt something that day, and even now. Every time he'd touched me today, I'd wanted to lean into him. Was that what they meant?

They'd given me a lot to think about. I didn't know how long I'd have before I needed to make a decision.

Chapter Six

Samurai

I shouldn't have eavesdropped on their conversation. Hearing the fear in Grey's voice nearly made me rush into the room. I wouldn't claim her if it scared her to be tied to me and the club forever. In a way, she already was because she carried my child. I knew she didn't see it that way. What little experience I had with women hadn't prepared me for the possibility of having an old lady and a family. I didn't have the right words to say or know what to do to soothe her.

For that matter, I'd never cared what a woman thought or how she felt. Until Grey. How had a simple transaction gone so wrong? Or had it gone incredibly right? Only time would tell.

The women had left, and Grey had looked shaken. I hadn't known if she drank coffee, but I found some apple cinnamon tea and brewed her a cup. I carried it to the living room and handed it to her. I noticed her fingers trembled as she accepted it from me. Not knowing what else to do, I folded my arms across my chest and tried to give her a little space.

"I don't think they put you at ease at all, did they?" I asked.

She shook her head. "Not really."

"Is it the idea of moving in with me, or the thought of being trapped at the compound that freaks you out the most?"

Her gaze met mine. "It's the part where it's forever and I can never leave."

I hunkered down in front of her, making sure I didn't reach for her. The last thing I wanted was to scare her more. But I had an idea.

"What if you and Ryo moved in with me, but I didn't officially claim you?" I asked.

She blinked and opened her mouth only to snap it shut again. The wariness in her eyes troubled me. She'd been right in saying we were strangers. I'd opened up with her more than anyone else, even my family, but it didn't mean we knew anything about one another.

"I can't promise the club will permit it. I'm not an officer so I'll have to at least get permission from the President if not take it to a vote at Church, which would mean getting the okay from all patched members. I'm hoping if I explain things to Charming, he'll give us some time to get better acquainted, and keep you and Ryo safe." I reached for her, placing my hand on her knee. "You and Ryo can have the extra bedroom. I just need to get it ready for you. Right now, it's sort of empty."

"Empty?" she asked. "You invited us to live with you and there's not even a guest room set up already?"

I felt my cheeks warm a little. "I don't exactly have company. I've never had a woman come over, except for the old ladies who stop by sporadically. Clarity's visit this morning was the first I've had in months. Phantom is the only family I speak to, and he's got his own place here."

I saw the pulse in her throat pounding. I didn't know if I'd made things even worse between the two of us. Speaking with Grey was unlike anything I'd done before. Sure, we'd shared a few words at the Pleasure Emporium, but I'd paid for her time. This was different.

"Would you like to see my house before you decide anything?" I asked. "It's too far to walk. When we get to the clubhouse, you'd need to ride on the back of my bike the rest of the way. I'm on the opposite side of the compound."

She turned her face toward the front door, and I knew she was thinking about Ryo. The boy would be safe with Phantom, which she clearly knew since she'd left them alone already. Did she worry something would happen to her while she was with me? Or did she not trust me to keep my hands to myself? Considering our rather unconventional beginning, I couldn't blame her.

"I can text Phantom and let him know where we're going," I offered. "Or if riding on the bike makes you nervous, I could borrow a club truck when we get to the clubhouse."

Her lips tipped up in a slight smile. "I've never been on a motorcycle before. I think I'd prefer the truck for now. Are you sure it's all right?"

I nodded. "Yep. Come on, beautiful. Let's go check out my house and see if it passes inspection. If you decide to stay with me, I'll call Charming while we're there so we can make plans if he gives me the greenlight. I want you to sleep there tonight if possible."

"You seem eager to get me under your roof, especially for someone who isn't sure they want a family." She reached over and placed her hand on top of mine where it still rested on her knee. "I want this baby to know his father, and if you want to be a dad to Ryo too, I don't have it in me to say no. But I'm worried you feel pushed to do something you'll later regret."

I reached up and touched my fingers to her cheek briefly. "You're such a sweetheart, worrying about me when you have Itachi breathing down your neck. I'll be fine, Grey. I wouldn't have offered to claim you if I hadn't meant it. Let's go see the house. You may decide you hate it and want to stay with Phantom."

I stood and took her hand, leading Grey out of the house. By the time we made it to the clubhouse, I noticed she'd slowed and shifted from one foot to the other. Clearly they were hurting. I glanced at her shoes and knew she'd need something better, especially as our child grew inside her. I didn't release her hand and led her inside, even though she balked. If the club whores were still around, I'd send them running if they dared confront Grey again.

I scanned the room and realized they were gone, and felt the tension drain from Grey. I didn't care if they were in the bathroom, off fucking one of my brothers, or had left the compound. The last thing I wanted was for Grey to feel uncomfortable. She'd already had one run in with them, and I hoped she wouldn't have to deal with them again anytime soon.

I led her behind the bar and selected keys to one of the larger trucks. If she agreed to be mine, I had a feeling we'd need to go shopping. For one, I didn't have a bed for Ryo. I didn't know how dire her situation had been, but the fact she'd sold herself to me was telling. I had a feeling the boy didn't have a lot, and I meant to rectify the situation as soon as possible. The thought of claiming him as my son would have sent me running scared only yesterday. Today, all I felt was a rightness. I knew it had more to do with the woman's hand held in mine right now. She hadn't looked at me with pity or revulsion when I'd told her what I'd been through. If she'd let me, I planned to hold onto her and the kids with both hands.

Sam smirked from his position farther down the bar, and I flipped him off. The fucker would be spreading the word about this for sure. It wasn't that I minded, but until Grey made her decision, I didn't want anyone to get the wrong idea. Or what I hoped was the right idea. I hoped I didn't fuck all this up.

"I thought Phantom said Japanese men weren't into showing signs of affection," Grey said.

"We aren't."

She tugged on my hand. "Then what's this?"

I paused mid-step and looked down, my eyebrows arching. I squeezed her fingers but didn't let go. Instead, I pulled her over to a blue four-door truck, popped the locks, and helped her into the passenger seat. The truck had been lifted and sounded like a beast. It was also one of the newer ones we had, and I'd wanted to impress Grey, as well as make sure she rode in comfort.

I reached across and fastened her seat belt. Unable to stop myself, I lightly touched her belly and marveled at the fact there was a baby in there, one we'd created together. Taking a step back, I shut the door and walked around to the driver's side. I got in and started up the engine, giving Grey one more look. She seemed settled and not as antsy. Pulling out onto the road, I headed for home, hoping it wouldn't only be mine for much longer.

I pulled to a stop in front of the house and tried to see it through her eyes. It was relatively small with a porch across the front. A stone path had been laid leading to the front steps. I could admit it was on the plain side, and the inside was much the same. The club had used generic beige everywhere. Carpet. Walls. Even the kitchen counters. It had been fine for a bachelor, but now I had a family to consider, and I had a feeling Grey wouldn't be that impressed.

I let her into the house and watched as she

wandered from room to room. I couldn't tell anything from the expression on her face and hoped she wasn't overly disappointed. She paused in my bedroom, eyeing the bed. I hadn't bothered to make it this morning. Or clean up. My dirty clothes were scattered around the room. I wasn't making the best impression right now.

"I know it isn't much," I said, looking around the space. "You can fix it up however you want. I'll give you money for whatever you need to make it look more like a home."

"How much time do you spend here?" she asked.

"I come here when I don't want to socialize with the club. Otherwise, I'm only here to sleep and eat a meal or two. I use the coffeepot more than anything else." Her features seemed pinched. "You hate it."

"No! I don't hate it. I'm not sure it's safe for a toddler," she said.

"Come sit down and tell me what I need to change. I meant what I said. I want this to feel like a home, whatever that requires."

We went back to the living room and sank onto the sofa. She ran her hand over the cushion, and I fought the urge to fidget. I'd never cared what anyone thought of my house. Hell, I never invited anyone here. The old ladies dropped in here and there, usually to try and feed me sweets or dinner, but this was my sanctuary.

"What's not safe?" I asked.

"Your weight room for starters. You'd need to lock the door and keep Ryo out. If he tried to lift anything in there, he could hurt himself. Or worse, somehow manage to knock the weights off the bar and onto his head."

I blanched and nodded. Shit. I hadn't even thought of the kid getting into that room. He could die! "Right. Okay. I can come up with something or move that stuff to storage until I come up with a better idea for it."

Maybe I could add a small building off to the side. I had plenty of land around my house. It wasn't like the club would add another home between mine and the others on this part of the street. I didn't see the VP or Pres saying I couldn't toss up a building for my weights, and anything else that might endanger the kids.

"I'm not asking you to get rid of anything." Grey's lips turned down, and she turned toward me a little.

I waved her off. "What else? You said the weight room was the first thing."

"We'll have to childproof the entire house. Outlet covers, make sure Ryo can't open the doors on his own, lock down the cabinets and drawers in the kitchen, and make sure he can't open the window in his room."

I'd never realized kids were so much trouble. I'd thought we'd pick up a few pieces of furniture, maybe some toys, and be done. It looked like this would take a while. Maybe even several days. I hoped she'd still decide to stay here tonight.

"All right. Not a problem."

She shifted on the couch, her hands twisting in her lap. "I didn't see a fence for the backyard."

"Haven't needed one."

"Well, we do if children will be in the house. We can't let them out back to play without making sure they can't wander off. What if they went into the road and got hit by a motorcycle or car? Or what if someone's dog was running loose and bit them?" she asked.

"I get it. Might take a day or three to get a fence up, depending on the type you want." The price of wood had gone through the roof not too long ago, but if that's what she wanted, I'd figure it out. Or maybe one of those iron fences?

"Nothing fancy. A regular chain link is fine." She shifted again, belying her nerves. It meant she wanted something else but didn't want to ask for it. Hadn't she realized yet I'd do whatever I could to make this a home for her? "Could we maybe put a slide or something out back? It doesn't have to be anything big or elaborate. Something for Ryo to do out back."

I'd had enough. I hated she seemed so hesitant to ask for anything. I lifted her onto my lap and wrapped an arm around her waist. Reaching up, I smoothed her hair back, letting my fingers brush over the shell of her ear. I felt her shiver and noticed her nipples tightened. I fought the urge to cuddle her closer, slip my hand under her dress, and remind her how good we'd been together.

"I want you and Ryo to feel at home here. I'll put in a playset for him, something sturdy to last for years. We'll set up that room to be a safe haven for him."

"Samurai, all that will cost so much."

I tightened my hold on her. "Grey, I'm not hurting for money. I'm not a millionaire or anything, but I can create a room Ryo will love, make a safe backyard for him to play in, and even get his beautiful mom some things too, and I won't even notice the money is gone."

Her brow furrowed. "That's not a small amount of money."

I shifted and pulled my phone from my pocket.

After unlocking it and opening the banking app, I let her see the balance. Her jaw dropped a little. Since she'd been having financial trouble, it was safe to assume she'd never seen that many zeros for a balance before. I hadn't lied. I wasn't rolling in it, but I did have a healthy six figures in my account.

"So here's what we're going to do," I said. "If you're still agreeable with moving in, we'll go to whatever store has kid-size furniture, toys, clothes, and anything else Ryo would want or need. We'll come back and I'll have the Prospects put the bed and dresser together, we'll decorate the room for Ryo, and we can bring him here for dinner tonight."

"If Ryo gets the spare room, where do I sleep?"

My cock hardened at the mere thought of where I wanted her -- in my bed! But would it be a deal breaker for her? I didn't want to push, and yet I had a feeling if I let her sleep in a different room, she'd keep her distance and not give us a real shot. "In my room. We don't have to do anything except sleep. I won't lie and say I'm not hoping for more. I want you, Grey. Have since the first moment I saw you, felt you coming on my cock, and looked at me with those innocent eyes."

"I'm not innocent," she said.

"Yes, you are. Itachi took something you didn't offer. How many men have you been with, Grey?"

She rolled her lips into her mouth and pressed down, clearly not wanting to tell me. Had it been that many? It didn't matter. It could have been five or fifteen. Wouldn't change the fact I wanted her in my house, in my bed, and raising the kids alongside me.

"Including Itachi?" she asked.

I nodded. "Sure, you can include him if you want, but he doesn't count in my book. You didn't ask him to touch you. It's not sleeping with someone unless you chose it. I believe *you* pointed that out to me today."

The way she'd accepted me, and vehemently denied I'd had sex with the babysitter and had been raped, it had broken down the walls I'd put up. I trusted my brothers, but I'd been worried they'd look at me different.

"If we discount him..." She shifted, something I noticed she did whenever she felt anxious. "One."

I blinked. Twice. "One. Excluding Itachi?"

"Yes," she admitted softly.

I swallowed hard, a knot forming in my throat. She couldn't be saying what I thought she was saying. Right? "I'm the only man you've willingly been with?"

"Yes." She held my gaze. "And you may have paid for me that day, but I enjoyed being with you. At the time, I'd wished you had been my first, except I wouldn't have Ryo then. No matter how he was conceived, he's my baby and I love him."

I didn't know how much longer I could hold back. Knowing I was the only man she'd been with made me feel like a caveman. I wanted to throw her over my shoulder, rush to the bedroom, and strip her naked. Then I'd take my time making her scream in pleasure for hours. Something told me she'd freak out if I tried that right now. I needed to earn her trust.

"We'll go slow if I need to?" she asked.

I gave a slight nod. Slow? If we went much slower than this right here, I'd likely combust. Already my cock tried to break free of my jeans. But if she didn't want me to touch her, I wouldn't. I refused to be like the asshole who'd been Ryo's sperm donor.

"And if we do start something and I decide to stop..."

"Then we stop," I said. "You've been hurt enough already, Grey. I won't add to your pain."

She cupped my cheek. "I don't want to add to yours either."

I turned my face into her hand and kissed her palm. I heard a soft sigh escape her and she leaned into me. I wanted this. Holding her, kissing her... Maybe having a family wasn't as scary as I'd thought. I still didn't know if I'd be a good father, but I knew I'd die to keep Grey and the kids safe. It was more than my parents had done for me. If anyone dared to touch my kids like that whore babysitter had done with me, I'd gut the bitch and watch her bleed out.

"You're safe with me, Grey. All of you are."

Chapter Seven
Grey

When Samurai said we'd go shopping for essential things, like a bed for Ryo, I hadn't realized his version differed from mine. Toys were a luxury, and yet after we'd selected a toddler bed and matching dresser, and three sets of bedding, he'd headed straight for the toy section. The cart overflowed with things that lit up and made noise, blocks Ryo could stack, a ball for the backyard, and a bear wearing a shirt with a motorcycle on it.

"You're going to spoil him," I said.

"That's sort of the point, my beautiful Grey. That boy deserves happiness, exactly like his mom. But I'll stop… for now. We still need the safety stuff and I want to get him some clothes."

As much as I wanted to get upset and demand to know what was wrong with what Ryo had already, I couldn't. If Samurai wanted to give my boy more things, I couldn't say no. My sweet baby had been missing out on so many things. It would be petty to deny him because I couldn't afford to buy the toys and clothes. Besides, if Samurai did end up claiming Ryo as his son, then he had every right to buy Ryo as much stuff as he wanted.

Samurai added enough outlet plugs to the cart for the entire house, safety knobs so Ryo couldn't open doors on his own, cabinet and drawer locks, and a baby gate.

"I need a way to make sure the front and back doors can't be opened by little hands," Samurai said. "I'm going to send Hunter to the hardware store. He can get one of those security locks like hotels use for the top of the doors, and I'll have him measure the yard and pick up the materials I'll need for a fence around the backyard."

"You're going to so much trouble," I said, feeling horrible.

He shook his head. "No, Grey. I'm not doing anything more than what you and Ryo deserve. I'm also going to ask Carlos to move my weights out of the house. I'll talk to Charming and Scratch about adding a separate building for anything dangerous. It can be a man cave of sorts."

He kept saying and doing everything right. After the reception I'd gotten when I showed up at the gates, I'd thought I'd made a mistake going to Samurai for help. Now it seemed like maybe it had been the right decision after all. We finished gathering everything Ryo would need, including cups and dishes, then checked out and loaded it all into the truck. Samurai called someone to meet us at the house before driving back to the compound.

I'd expected to help unload everything. Instead, Samurai ordered me to wait in the truck while he and another man took everything into the house. After the last bags had been carried inside, Samurai came back out and got behind the wheel again. It hadn't occurred to me we'd go anywhere else, but it seemed he was set to run full steam ahead and getting the house together.

"I can't stand the mall, but I thought we'd go to one of the twenty-four-hour stores and get whatever you want for the house, pick up some groceries, and you can browse the clothes if you want. I want to take you on a shopping trip somewhere nice a little later, but I know we're running out of time tonight," Samurai said.

"We don't have to do everything in one day," I said.

"Maybe not, but I want the place to feel as much like home as possible before we bring Ryo over. Phantom checked in and said everything is fine. Ryo has asked about you twice, but my cousin distracted him with Momo." He glanced at me. "We're going to need a dog, aren't we?"

I smiled. "Probably. He's never had a pet before, and he loves Momo so much. But he'd be thrilled with a puppy from the shelter. We don't need a purebred dog like Momo. Besides, if you're going to rescue me and Ryo, might as well rescue a puppy too."

He snorted and shook his head. "Long as we aren't overrun like Doolittle with the Devil's Fury. I think he has a zoo at his house. One puppy I think I can handle. I'm sure Phantom would give us some pointers on training it. He's had Momo since she was eight weeks old."

"We don't need one right away. Ryo will have a lot of adjusting to do already. He's smart. I'm not sure how much he can understand about all this. It's only been the two of us up until now. He took to Phantom quicker than I expected, so he may be fine."

"My cousin has always been great with kids. He's wanted a big family for as long as I can remember. He can't find the right woman." Samurai reached over and laced our fingers together. "I'm glad you didn't choose him. I wouldn't have blamed you, but I'm not sure I could have handled seeing the two of you together."

When he said sweet things like that, I wanted to sigh in pure happiness. I only hoped it lasted this time and I didn't wake up to the angrier version of him tomorrow. Now that I understood why he'd reacted the way he had, it was possible we'd be fine from this point forward. I'd been honest when I'd said maybe we could heal each other. Every soft word, every touch, every heated look... it all made me feel a little less broken. For the moment. Tomorrow would be another day, and once I saw my reflection in the mirror, it would all come rushing back, like it did every morning.

At the store, I picked up a few new outfits, a pair of black boots on the off chance I ever got to ride on his motorcycle with him, and new bath things. At his insistence, I found some items to add a bit of color to the otherwise drab house, including some framed animal pictures for Ryo's room, and an abstract painting for the living room. I found some throw pillows and a blanket in a deep burgundy for the couch.

Moving over to the food section of the store, I loaded the cart with groceries for meals I knew how to make and snacks I knew Ryo enjoyed. The total was a staggering amount, but Samurai swiped his card without batting an eye. I knew this wouldn't be something we did all the time. The spending today was special, since he wanted us to feel at home. It still made me a little queasy to think about how much he'd paid for everything.

Samurai drove us back to the house and I helped unload the truck this time. After the groceries were put away and I'd washed the cups, plates, and bowls we'd bought for Ryo, I set about making the house look a little homier. Samurai hung the pictures for me, then we went to Phantom's house to collect Ryo and our belongings.

My sweet boy ran to me, throwing his arms around me. "Missed you."

I knelt down to hug him. "Missed you too, Ryo. Do you remember meeting Mr. Samurai earlier?"

He nodded, glancing at the biker. Samurai moved closer and hunkered down beside us. He reached out and lightly ran his hand over Ryo's head. "Your mom said she hasn't mentioned your dad before."

Ryo shook his head, looking between Samurai and Phantom, clearly wondering if one was the father he'd never had. While he had my coloring, his Japanese heritage was prominent in his overall features. It didn't surprise me that he'd been curious if Phantom could be his father, or at least some sort of relation to him. Like I'd told Samurai, my boy was smart for his age. He had to realize the two men looked similar to him. I caught Samurai's gaze and gave him a slight smile, encouraging him to keep going.

"Ryo, what would you say if I told you I'm your dad?" Samurai asked.

I heard Phantom's sharp exhalation. I had no doubt we'd taken him by surprise. Even if Samurai had claimed me today, it wouldn't have necessarily meant he was willing to call Ryo his son. I chanced a quick glance at the other man and saw both the pride he felt in his cousin, and a flash of sadness. I hoped Phantom got the family he wanted one day soon.

"Daddy?" Ryo asked, looking up at me for confirmation.

I nodded. "Yes, Ryo. Samurai is your daddy. I've been with him all day making sure your room at our new home is just right. He picked out a bed and dresser for you, and lots of new toys. You have new clothes and shoes too!"

My son's eyes lit up and he smiled so wide his cheeks had to hurt. He threw himself into Samurai's arms, and my eyes pricked with tears when I saw the tough biker gently cradling my son against him.

Samurai held my gaze, and the emotions flitting through his eyes about knocked me down. Determination settled on his face, his jaw slightly tightening, as he hugged Ryo harder.

"I'm sorry I haven't been around before now," Samurai said. "I said something to your mom that made her think I didn't want her here with me. But it's all better now."

Ryo clung to Samurai. I liked that he'd made it seem more like a miscommunication than the fact Samurai hadn't wanted Ryo. Unless it became necessary, I never planned to tell my son that Samurai wasn't his biological father. The less he knew about Itachi the better. I only hoped this plan worked and kept the other man far away from us.

Phantom's phone rang and he answered, his brow furrowing. "Hang on, Pres. Let me put the call on speaker. Samurai is here with his family."

Samurai stood, holding Ryo in his arms. It surprised me Phantom was willing to let me hear the call. From what little I'd learned, the club didn't like their women knowing everything that went on. Which was fine with me.

"Samurai, I think we need to talk in a minute," the voice on the other end of the phone said.

"Yes, Pres. Grey and Ryo are here and both can hear you. Do we need to take this call elsewhere?" Samurai asked.

"Nope. I want her to understand what she's getting into, and Ryo is too little for this call to make sense to him. I received a message from Black Reign farther south. They need someone to infiltrate a fighting ring. Preferably someone in their early thirties, and a decent fighter," the man said.

Samurai winced. "Am I being sent?"

"No. I'd planned on it, until Phantom said your family was with you. I'll have to pick someone else and let Samson know about the change. The Black Reign VP is eager for some backup to head their way, and since it's about a six-hour ride, unless you break every traffic law between here and there, whoever goes needs to leave immediately."

"Who will you send?" Phantom asked.

"I'll send Rebel. Fuck knows the bastard is cocky enough to pull off being a fighter, and he's damn lethal when he wants to be." The man sighed. "All right. Take me off speaker, and, Samurai, go elsewhere for this conversation."

He winced a little, then handed Ryo to Phantom before walking into another room with the phone. Ryo held his hands out to me and Phantom passed him over. I clutched my son to me, hoping Samurai hadn't gotten into trouble by offering me a place to stay. I'd hoped Phantom would shed some light on the situation, but he seemed to be preoccupied, staring off into space. "Did I do something wrong?" I asked.

He jolted and turned to face me fully. "Wrong?"

I nodded my head in Samurai's direction. He'd not once mentioned he'd get into trouble by letting us stay with him. Sure, he hadn't officially claimed me as his old lady, but did that really matter right now? We were still getting to know one another. They couldn't really expect him to keep a woman forever when they were strangers, could they? The rules in this place were so different from my regular life.

"Samurai should have talked to Charming already. He'll be berated for not talking to the President before deciding you and Ryo were staying. Although, knowing the Pres, he wants to talk to your man and make sure he isn't making a rash decision.

Everyone knows how he's felt about having a family all these years, and now he's suddenly singing a different tune." Phantom shoved his hands into his pockets. "It will be fine, Grey. Although, Charming may demand that Samurai make things official pretty quick, especially with Itachi in the picture and whatever we'd bitten into with Black Reign."

"The club… I mean, will Samurai be asked to do illegal things? Could he be taken from us?" I asked.

"Sent to jail?" he asked.

I nodded. "I don't know anything about the Devil's Boneyard, except I've seen y'all around town from time to time. I've heard about the good things the club has done for the community, but… infiltrating a fighting ring? It sounds dangerous."

"Our way of life isn't for the faint of heart, Grey. Not only do we have to be tough, but so do our women. He can't leave to go on a job and make it home safe if he thinks you're there worrying over him. He needs to know you can handle any absences and trust that he'll do whatever it takes to get back in one piece. Half the battle is usually mental. He's not had an issue so far because he's never worried about anyone here at home. You understand?"

"I think so. I can't promise not to worry while he's gone. When you care about someone, you want them to be safe. But I'll try not to let him see how badly I'm freaking out."

Phantom smiled. "Good enough. Why don't I start loading your things into the truck? You and Ryo can wait here until Samurai is done with the call."

I went into the living room and sat on the couch. I could hear the murmur of Samurai's voice in the other room, even though I couldn't make out anything he said. By the time Phantom had finished, Samurai had ended his call and given the phone back to his cousin.

"Is it still okay for us to move in with you?" I asked Samurai.

He nodded. "Yep. Everything is cleared up with Charming. For now. He did give us a time limit before I need to make things more permanent. We can talk about it later."

I stood and Samurai immediately took Ryo from me. I followed them out to the truck and watched as Samurai buckled my son in, as if he'd been doing it all his life. He hadn't spared any expense on the car seat he'd purchased either. Then he helped me into the truck. Phantom came over to my side as Samurai started the engine. I rolled down the window so I could hear him.

"You're welcome here anytime, Grey. If Samurai has to go somewhere and you don't want to be alone, you can bring Ryo over to play with Momo. Or if I'm gone too, I know Clarity wouldn't mind the company. You aren't alone here, remember that. We're your family now. All of us."

"Thanks, Phantom. For everything."

He tapped the door and backed up. I rolled up the window as Samurai pulled onto the road and drove us home. I felt a little anxious about Ryo seeing his room. It was far grander than what he'd had at home. I knew he'd like it and love the toys. It was more a concern for what would happen if things didn't work out between me and Samurai. Now that Ryo thought of him as the father he'd never had, and would be given all these wonderful things, how would he react if we had to leave? Or worse, what if Samurai left on a job and didn't come home?

As if hearing my thoughts, the biker reached

over to take my hand, giving my fingers a squeeze. "Everything will be fine, Grey. You'll see."

"I guess worrying comes natural to me. There are so many what-ifs running through my mind. I'm not sure I can silence them easily, but I'll try."

"We're in this together now. You don't have to face Itachi alone. I'll keep you safe, and so will the club." He lifted my hand to his lips and kissed the back of it before settling our joined hands on the armrest between our seats. "We need to find our footing. I'm used to living alone, and you've become accustomed to raising Ryo on your own. We'll collide quite a bit the first week or so. Maybe longer. Give us time, all right? That's all I ask."

"I can do that. You mentioned Charming said something about a time limit? What if I can give us time but he can't?" I asked.

"He said he'll hold everyone off for a few weeks. But if things don't go well with Itachi, it means we need to make things official immediately." He rubbed his thumb across my fingers. "He's not trying to be a hard-ass about it all. I think he's trying to protect not only you and Ryo, but me as well."

"I'm glad you have someone who cares so much," I said. "And I understand. It freaks me out a little. Forever is a long time. I won't lie and say I'm ready to jump in with both feet. I still have reservations."

He nodded. "I know. I'll give you as much time as I can, Grey."

We pulled to a stop in the driveway and Samurai got Ryo out of his car seat. I followed them into the house, eager to see what Ryo thought of our new home and most of all, his bedroom. Samurai set him down after I'd closed and locked the door. Ryo explored the main rooms until Samurai led the way down the hall.

"Ready to see your bedroom?" Samurai asked him.

Ryo nodded, his eyes wide. Samurai flipped on the light and Ryo took a hesitant step inside. I stood in the hall and watched as he looked at everything. He toddled over to a small table with a train set up on a track. I didn't remember it being in the shopping cart and leaned closer to Samurai. "Where did that come from?"

He pulled out his phone and showed me a text on the screen.

Congrats on your new family! Left a present for your son.

I saw the name at the top said Cinder. "Who's Cinder?"

"He was the President of the club for the longest time. Not too long ago, he decided to step down and handed it over to Charming. Said he wanted to spend more time with his woman and kid. Can't blame him. Cinder has to be in his sixties now, if not early seventies. I'm not really sure of his exact age, but I do know he's the oldest of us all."

"It was nice of him to get the train for Ryo."

"I'll take you over to his place tomorrow if you want. You can meet his woman, Meg, and their son, Tanner. He's ten so I don't know if he'll want to play with Ryo or not, but it wouldn't hurt for you to make some more friends around here."

"I think Nikki and Darby weren't too impressed with me," I said.

"They'll get over it. Just because they agreed to be with their men right off doesn't mean it's the right choice for everyone. I understand why you panicked, Grey. Even if I weren't as fucked up as I am, we really don't know much about each other. You're right to be cautious, especially with a little boy to think about and another baby on the way."

"Yeah, but the baby isn't only mine." I looked at Ryo playing and took in all that Samurai had done for my son. "And neither is he. Even though you may not have officially claimed us today, I'm not sure your club sees it the same way. I don't think I do either."

"What's that supposed to mean?" he asked.

"Look at what you did for Ryo. And for me." I moved closer until I could feel the heat of his body. "For a guy who was scared of commitment, of having a woman move into his house or ever having kids, you did something really incredible today. I won't forget it. Ever."

"It's the right thing to do," he muttered. "I'm no one's hero, Grey. Don't make me out to be something I'm not."

I reached up and placed my hand on his cheek, forcing him to look at me. "You're my hero, Samurai."

"Jin," he said softly. "My name is Jin. Just don't use it unless we're alone."

I tipped my head to the side. "Getting to use your real name is a big deal, isn't it? I noticed everyone here uses the names on their leather vests."

His lips twitched in amusement. "It's a cut, Grey, and they're road names. But yeah, it's a big deal to use my real name."

"Then thank you for trusting me. And, Jin, I meant what I said. You may think you aren't anything special, and maybe to others you aren't. To me and Ryo? You're a hero."

He shrugged a shoulder and took a step back. "I'm also the asshole who called you a whore and told you to leave when you needed my help."

I sighed and let him put some distance between us. Clearly, I'd gone too far too fast. I had a feeling if I'd tried to get into his pants, I'd have met with little resistance, but talk about how wonderful he'd been today and suddenly it was like I had the plague. I wondered if I'd ever understand him, or men in general.

Chapter Eight

Samurai

Ryo played with his toys until he literally passed out in the middle of the floor. He had a block clutched in one hand and a stuffed bear in the other. Grey managed to pry the block from his fingers, but he held tight to the bear. She placed him in his bed, and the kid didn't wake even once while she wrestled his clothes off him, put on a pull-up, then dressed him in pajamas. She tucked him into bed before shutting out the light and putting the baby gate across the doorway.

I smoothed her hair back from her face as she stepped into the hall. "You look as tired as him."

She nodded. "It's been a long day. I woke up feeling so uncertain and scared. And I don't blame you! I shouldn't have shown up without any warning, much less dropped a baby bomb on you. When you mentioned birth control being in the contract, I should have spoken up then and there."

I tensed. I'd assumed she hadn't known about the change. What if she'd asked for it? "What do you mean?"

"I didn't see that anywhere in my copy. I swear I didn't."

I tipped up her chin and forced her to hold my gaze. "Grey, are you trying to tell me you weren't on anything that day? No IUD, pill, or shot? It was only you and me with no protection between us at all? And Knox didn't say a word about my requirements?"

Her face paled and she sank her teeth into her bottom lip. "I was scared of what would happen if I said anything. I didn't know if I'd missed it when I signed the document, and if you'd taken the money away, I'd have lost everything, possibly even my son."

My stomach churned at the implication. I grabbed her hand and led her to the bedroom. Opening my top dresser drawer, I pulled out my copy of the contract with Knox. I'd looked earlier and realized that clause had been left out. What else had I missed? I needed to know if someone at the Pleasure Emporium had fucked up and given us an older version, or if they'd done it on purpose... and I wanted to know why. If Grey had never known about the birth control stipulation, then Knox had kept it to himself from the beginning.

"Jin, are you mad at me?" Grey asked, her voice nearly a whisper. I'd released her to get the file and saw she'd wrapped her arms around herself, as if to protect her from whatever I'd say.

"No, beautiful. I'm not mad at you. Someone at the Pleasure Emporium gave us the wrong contract to sign. I didn't think to read over it carefully a second time. I should have."

"Is there anything else in there we don't know about?" she asked.

I went to the bed and sat on the edge. Grey joined me and we read over the document, word for word, making sure we both understood everything the same way. The last page had a section at the bottom. The regular-sized text seemed in line with everything else, but I noticed the print under it was so small I couldn't quite make it out. What the fuck?

"Grey, do you remember this being here?" I asked, pointing it out.

"I think I was so scared I didn't pay as close attention as I should have. What does it say?"

"We need a magnifying glass to find out."

She tapped my phone. "Download an app for it. There has to be one."

Humoring her, I did as she said. And fuck me if she wasn't right. There were multiple apps for it. I found a free one and gave it a try. It didn't work as perfectly as I'd have needed if this were a regular thing, but for reading the tiny print this one time it was fine. And what I read made my heart nearly stop.

Should the encounter result in a pregnancy, the woman will receive whatever aid she needs from the other party. If they fail to give her financial assistance, the Pleasure Emporium will step in with one caveat. The woman will work off the debt at a time and place of the Pleasure Emporium's choosing.

"Son of a bitch." I fisted my hand and stood up, needing to punch someone. If Grey had left the other day and Knox had found out, he'd have used this against her. What the hell had the asshole been thinking?

"Why would he put that in there?" she asked.

"Did he know you weren't on birth control?" I asked.

She nodded. "It was part of the questions I had to answer, and I also had a physical exam before I could sign the contract."

"So he probably knew you were fertile and would likely get knocked up. The motherfucker planned this!"

"Why? I'm no one special. Why would he want to force me to work for him there?" she asked.

I paced as I thought about the day at the Pleasure Emporium, and then I realized something. The mirrors on the wall. They had to have been two-way, for people who wanted to watch. It hadn't occurred to me to make sure we were completely alone and private. Knox could have easily watched us or let someone else. But the contract had been signed beforehand.

"I don't like how things aren't adding up," I muttered. "I'm calling Shade. He's the resident hacker. If there's something to dig up, he can find it, or he can talk to the people who can."

I put the call on speaker, not wanting to leave Grey out of this. It affected her as much as me, if not more. Since I'd moved her and Ryo into my house, I didn't think Knox could say shit about that clause in the contract. Still, I didn't like taking chances. If the fucker came for her, I wanted to be ready.

"What the fuck do you need, Samurai?" Shade said the second the call connected. "I'm balls-deep in pussy. Can't this wait?"

Grey squeaked and her face turned bright red. I'd have found it cute if I weren't so fucking worried about what Knox had planned for her.

"Cut the shit, Shade. Grey is here with me and you're on speaker, so thanks for that." I heard him cuss and the jangle of his belt, which told me he'd decided to stop fucking whatever slut he'd picked up for the night. He rarely went to the clubhouse anymore. Said those women weren't challenging enough. "Listen, Grey and I signed a contract with Knox at the Pleasure Emporium several months back. You breathe a word of that to anyone and I'll knock your fucking teeth down your throat. But there's something hinky about it. There's a clause that says if she's pregnant and I don't step up, the Pleasure Emporium would take care of her financially and she'd have to pay it off with them later."

"Shit," Shade muttered. "That's some kind of fucked up. This the pregnant woman who showed up with a kid in tow? Everyone's been buzzing about it."

"Yeah, and she's mine, so show some damn respect." My eyes slightly widened as I glanced at

Grey. I hadn't meant to call her mine. She'd made it clear she didn't know if she wanted to stay. But the look on her face, the way it had gone all soft with a dreamy look in her eyes, told me she wasn't pissed about it. If anything she seemed happy. Something we'd have to talk about later. "Find out what you can, Shade. I need to know why Knox would want control of her. Did he have a specific client who wanted time with her? Or did he have something else planned?"

"I'm on it. And sorry, Grey. About the, um… yeah." Shade coughed. "I'll call when I have something. If I can't dig up anything, then…"

"Call in Wire and Lavender, and anyone else you need to. I don't want the contents of this contract getting out, or anyone knowing I paid for Grey at that place. If anyone dares to look down on her for what she did, I'll gut the motherfuckers."

"Dude, chill. Do you really think anyone here would do that? Shit, look at what Meg went through."

"Yeah, but Meg wasn't paid for her time," I said. "They may not see it the same way."

"If she's yours, she's family. Simple as that. Although, I don't remember getting asked to vote," Shade said. "Is there anything *else* you need me to do while I'm at it? Maybe make her yours in a more official way outside the club?"

I paused. It wasn't the worst idea ever. I didn't know if Grey would go for it. Fuck me. She'd possibly hate me for this, but I needed her protected as much as possible. "Do it."

"You got it. I'll call soon as I know something."

The call ended and I set my phone aside. Grey still sat on the edge of the bed, but she'd started twisting her fingers in her lap. I knew she had questions, and I'd try to answer them. Well, most of them. I wasn't about to tell her I'd told Shade to marry us. If anyone went looking, everything would appear official. Far as the county and state would be concerned, Grey would be my legal wife. Which meant when our son was born, there'd be no question about who his father was. Hell.

I grabbed the phone again and shot off a text to Shade, hoping Grey didn't kick me in the balls for this one. *Add me as the father on Ryo's birth certificate.*

I got a thumbs-up emoji in response.

"What's going on, Jin?" she asked. "I didn't understand any of that."

"Shade is going to use his computer to poke around at the Pleasure Emporium. He'll look at their files, emails, any security footage they may have, and anything else. Including bank records."

"He can do that?"

"Yep. And he's not even the best we know. If he hits a snag, he'll call the others." I sat beside her again and reached over to pull her fingers apart so I could hold her hand. "I asked Shade to do two other things for me. One, I'm not ready to share with you just yet. I think we need more time. The other is about Ryo."

She tensed and tried to tug free. "What about him?"

"I told Shade to alter the birth records and list me as the father."

Grey stilled and I couldn't even tell if she was still breathing. Her lips parted and her eyes glassed over with unshed tears. She made a soft sound and threw herself into my arms. "That's the sweetest, nicest thing anyone's ever done for us. Thank you, Jin."

"You're mine now, Grey. You and Ryo." I pressed a kiss to the top of her head as I held her close. "I will do anything I can to keep the two of you out of

Itachi's hands, and Knox's. As soon as I know why he wanted you so bad, I'll deal with him."

"I'm sorry I turned your world upside down by coming here, but I'm so glad I'm not having to face this on my own. And if I hadn't come here, if Knox had found out about the baby, he could have forced me to honor the clause in the contract." She shivered. "I don't think I want to know what he'd do with me. It took everything I had to walk through the doors the day I met you. I can't do it again."

"Was it so very awful?" I asked.

"No. I enjoyed our time together and had wanted it to last longer. If you hadn't been clear about your expectations, I might have gotten fairy-tale ideas in my head. No one had ever made me feel the way you did. I didn't want to let go."

"Now you don't have to."

She drew back and looked up at me. "Do you mind if I shower and get ready for bed? I'm not sure I can remain upright much longer. I've had the weight of the world pressing down on me for so long. Having you beside me is the best gift ever, but I think all the struggling I've done since I got pregnant with Ryo has caught up with me."

"Do you need anything?" I released her hand and rubbed her back, not ready to let her go yet. I couldn't remember ever holding a woman when sex wasn't involved, and even then, I hadn't embraced anyone like this. Not until Grey. It was... nice. More than. I felt the tension drain from me as I breathed in her scent.

"I need my shower gel, shampoo, conditioner, lotion, and razor." She paused. "And clean panties and pajamas."

"I'll gather everything while you start the

shower. I'll take one when you're finished, and we can get some sleep. Does Ryo wake up early?"

She nodded, a blush tinging her cheeks. "Um, we could… I mean… It's not like you haven't seen me naked before. Would you want to shower with me?"

My cock went instantly hard, and I hoped like hell she didn't notice. I nearly groaned at the thought of seeing her naked body again, feeling her soft skin. "Yeah. I'd like that. And, Grey, if you don't want me to touch you, all you have to do is say so."

"Let's see what happens. I'm tired of feeling like I'm fighting everything and everyone. I tried to do the right thing, or what I thought was right, and keep away from you. I'd planned to raise the baby on my own and never tell you. I see now it would have been the wrong choice. So, I don't want to plan for something to happen or not happen."

Her words were slightly confusing, but I understood what she meant. Instead of trying to plot out our sex life, if there would ever be one, she wanted to let things happen naturally. I could respect that.

"All right." I patted her hip and she stood. While she went into the bathroom and got the shower running, I located the items she needed. I didn't know if she had a preference for what to wear to bed and ended up selecting some of the new things she'd bought today.

When I stepped into the bathroom, steam already billowed from the shower. I stuck my hand under the spray, worried it might be too hot. I remembered some of the old ladies saying something about how bad it sucked to not take hot baths while they were pregnant. The water was warm enough to feel good, but I didn't think it would hurt the baby.

Grey slowly removed her clothes, and I did the

same. I couldn't hide the fact I wanted her. My cock stood at attention. Her gaze skimmed over me, her cheeks flushing a deeper pink when she noticed my aroused state. Without a word, she got into the shower and held her hand out for me. I joined her, shutting the door behind us.

It bothered me that she'd planned to keep away. With the way I'd talked to her during our time at the Pleasure Emporium, I could understand her reasoning. She'd thought I'd want nothing to do with her or our child, and she'd been right. Sort of. I'd wanted her, more than anything, but the fear I might hurt her still lurked in the back of my mind.

Even now, I wasn't entirely sure I wouldn't snap and end up choking her to death during sex. I never should have started the habit, but it had been the only way to not spiral whenever I tried to fuck a woman. The babysitter hadn't left visible scars. She'd left emotional ones. At least Grey knew what to expect and why.

She wet her hair and reached for the shampoo, lathering the locks. It fell to the middle of her back, leaving it quite a bit shorter than the last time we'd seen one another. I'd loved her hair. Still did. She didn't seem bothered by me watching her every move. I eventually started to wash myself so I wouldn't be tempted to reach for her. When she'd finished and rinsed, I noticed her fingers were twitching slightly.

"If you're anxious and want out, I won't stop you." I tipped my head to wash the shampoo down the drain before swiping the water off my face. "But if you're wanting to touch me and aren't sure if you should, you have my permission. Explore all you like. I won't ever force you to do something you don't want, Grey. Unless it's for your safety or that of our kids."

Her lips curled up on the corners. "I like that. *Our* kids."

Little did she know she was also my wife or should be by now. It depended on how fast Shade had been able to work. I had a feeling she'd be pissed when she found out, at least at first. If luck was on my side, we'd grow closer between now and whenever I had to tell her. Or someone else did. No one around here knew how to keep their mouths shut when it came to things like that. Not my brothers and not the old ladies.

"Do you think you and Ryo could be happy here?" I asked.

She took a breath and seemed to ponder my question a moment. "I do. It's all so new, and a bit scary, but I think I need time to adjust."

"If I could go back and undo everything I said when you came to the gates, I would. I shouldn't have been such an asshole to you."

Grey came closer and placed her hands on my chest. "You were protecting yourself and me. Or you thought you were. I can't fault you for that."

"Yeah, well, the VP sure did. I can't remember the last time I saw him go after anyone around here. He still hits like a motherfucker."

Her eyes went wide. "He hit you?"

"Punched me. My jaw hurt, but thankfully it didn't bruise. He was right to try and knock some sense into me. I was being a jackass."

"I still don't like that he chose violence as a way to solve the problem," she muttered.

"Um, Grey. You do realize you're living at a biker compound, right? We're the Devil's Boneyard MC. If you thought you'd get puppies and bunnies, you're in for a big shock. Sometimes we fight to blow off steam."

"You're not going to teach Ryo to do that, are you?"

I grinned. "You bet your sweet ass I am. That boy isn't going to take shit from anyone. And if the baby in your belly is a girl, you damn sure better believe he's going to protect his little sister."

"I'm not going to win that battle, am I?"

I shook my head. "He needs to be tough to keep himself safe, as well as those around him. I don't want our boy getting into trouble when we aren't around and being unable to defend himself."

"Fine. As long as he doesn't start fights for no reason."

I pressed my forehead to hers. "You ready for bed?"

"Almost." She reached down and wrapped her hand around my cock. I hissed in a breath and tensed. "There's something I've been wondering."

"What's that?" I asked, my voice sounding a bit off even to my own ears.

"Can people really have sex in the shower? I've read books where they did, and seen it in movies, but is that a thing?"

"Grey, are you asking me to fuck you right here and now?"

She hesitated only a moment before nodding. "Only if you want to. I know you can't tie me down in here. Would it be better to go to the bedroom?"

Christ. The woman was killing me. So sweet. So giving. I couldn't hold back. I leaned down farther and brushed my lips over hers. She gasped, her lips parting enough for me to slip my tongue between them. I couldn't remember kissing a woman before Grey. Many had tried, but I'd never allowed it. I threaded my fingers through her hair, holding her still as I took what I wanted, what we both needed.

She melted against me, her arms going around my waist. Her breasts pressed tight to my body, and I felt her nipples harden. I should take my time with her. Remind her how good things were between us. Sex with Grey had been beyond amazing. I slid my hand down to the curve of her ass and squeezed. She gave a squeak and jolted. I noticed she didn't pull away. If anything, she tried to get closer to me.

I backed her to the shower wall, not daring to break the kiss, and caged her against the tiles. The sounds she made had me grinding against her. It had been four months since I'd been with a woman. The longest spell, by far, since I'd found a way to enjoy sex. Even still, all those other times had been a release and nothing more. Sex with Grey was completely different.

I drew back and looked down into her upturned face. "You're so damn beautiful. I know I don't deserve you, but I promise to do everything I can to make you happy, Grey. You and the kids."

She lifted her leg, hooking it over my hip. "Less talking, Jin. I need you. I ache."

I trailed my nose down hers. "Yeah? Where's it hurt?"

She reached for my hand and tugged it down between her legs. I brushed over her pussy. I felt soft hair covering the lips and my eyebrows arched. Last time we'd been together, she'd been bare. Of course, if I'd been her only sexual encounter, it made sense she wouldn't have kept it up. Especially after she discovered she was pregnant.

I stroked her slit before parting the lips and finding her clit. She moaned and closed her eyes as I rubbed the hard bud in small circles. "Eyes on me, Grey."

I could tell she struggled to obey, but her gaze landed on mine. I shifted my hand so I could rub her clit with my thumb and eased a finger inside her. Her eyes darkened as I teased her. Twice, I brought her to the edge, only to back off. I wanted her needy and begging for release.

"Feel good?" I asked.

She nodded and whined when I slowed my pace again. "Jin, please."

"Please what?"

"I need to come. I want you to..." Her cheeks flushed crimson.

"Fuck you?"

"Yes. I need your cock inside me. It's been too long."

Damn right it had been! I withdrew my hand from between her legs and settled both her thighs around my hips. My greedy girl reached between us and guided me inside her. I tried to hold back, every muscle straining as I fought not to lose control. I used short, slow strokes, working my cock deep inside her.

"Hold onto me, Grey. This might be a bit rougher than I'd intended."

The second I felt her squeeze my cock, I knew I'd lose control. I only hoped it didn't scare her when I did. I drove into her with long, deep strokes. My hips smacked against hers with every thrust. She tipped her head back, trusting me not to hurt her. I reached up and wrapped my fingers around her throat. Even though I gripped it tightly, I didn't squeeze hard enough to choke her.

I changed the angle as I surged into her again and again. She cried out and I felt her tighten on my cock. I growled and lost what little control I'd maintained. Everything went a bit hazy as I took what

I wanted from Grey, pounding into her until I came. I kept pumping into her, filling her with my cum. When I stopped, my chest heaved, and everything came back into focus.

Grey's head had slumped, and I released her throat. "Grey? Grey!"

I pulled free of her body and laid her on the shower floor. *No, no, no!* I checked for a pulse and found it beating strong, but it didn't diminish the horror of what I'd done. Already her skin had started to purple along her throat in the shape of my hand. I lifted her into my arms and got out, not even bothering to shut off the water. I dried her as best I could and dressed her. I needed to call Phantom. I'd fucked up and didn't know if there was a way back from this. Not only in the eyes of my club, but how could Grey ever trust me again?

Panic clawed at me, making me want to run. I couldn't. Ryo slept down the hall. My family depended on me. I'd let them down enough already.

Grey groaned and I saw her lashes flutter before her eyes opened. "Jin?"

"Don't talk." I rushed to her side again, sitting on the edge of the bed. I pushed the hair back from her face and took her hand in mine. "I'm so fucking sorry."

"For making me come so hard I passed out?" she asked.

It felt like everything stopped. Time ceased to exist for a moment. I hadn't strangled her? The marks on her throat indicated otherwise. Maybe she didn't remember it clearly?

"Grey, I bruised your throat. I squeezed too hard."

A small smile curled her lips. "It's all right, Jin. You didn't hurt me. I wasn't strangling. I could breathe fine."

"But the marks…" I reached out to lightly run my fingers over them.

"I had them last time too. Except they were everywhere. I bruise easily."

"I left marks on your entire body?" I asked. It was a good thing I hadn't known that back then. It might have sent me spiraling out of control.

"It will be fine." She ran her hand up and down my arm. "You dressed me for bed?"

"I thought I needed to call Phantom. I didn't want him, or anyone else, to see you naked."

"You don't need to call anyone." Her eyes narrowed and she glanced toward the bathroom. "But you should probably turn off the shower before you come to bed."

I got up and did as she said, stopping to make sure I was dry enough to not soak the sheets. Before I slid in next to her, I put on a pair of boxers in case Ryo managed to escape from the baby gate across his doorway. Grey had explained she didn't want him to feel locked in but wanted to keep him from wandering. At least until he got acclimated to his new home and figured out what was and wasn't allowed.

"You're sure you're all right?" I asked, gathering her in my arms after I tugged the covers over us.

"I'm perfectly fine, Jin. Stop worrying. If you hurt me, I'll tell you."

"It's when you can't tell me because you're dead that worries me," I muttered.

She snuggled closer to me. "You said it's always been sex except with me, right?"

I nodded and kissed the top of her head. I didn't know where this need came from to shower her with affection. It was as if confessing my darkest secret to her, and Grey accepting me as I am, broke down every wall I'd built up. Every excuse I'd had to keep her away evaporated. And now I wanted to keep her close, touch her, kiss her…

My brothers were going to give me shit over this for sure.

"Then maybe that's the difference. You didn't care if you hurt them. With me, it matters."

"Such a smart girl." I tightened my hold on her. "Get some sleep, beautiful. I'm not sure what tomorrow will bring. Best to be prepared for anything."

It wasn't long before I heard her deep and even breathing, and knew she'd succumbed to sleep. And soon after, I followed.

Chapter Nine

Grey

Sunlight woke me the next morning. I ached from head to toe, and yet, I smiled because I knew exactly why I hurt. I reached behind me, and my hand met cool sheets. Frowning, I sat up and looked around the room. Samurai had already woken and left the room. I didn't know what time it was but had a feeling Ryo would be up soon. I used the bathroom, splashed water on my face, and brushed my teeth, then pulled some clothes on before I went to find the man who'd made me come so hard I'd passed out.

I heard the low murmur of his voice in the kitchen. Passing Ryo's room, I noticed my boy was also missing. I didn't know what to expect when I walked into the kitchen, but I found Samurai at the stove, shirtless and looking far too sexy, and my sweet little boy sat in his new high chair eating scrambled eggs with shredded cheese sprinkled over them.

"How long have the two of you been up?" I asked.

Samurai smiled at me over his shoulder. "Long enough I've had two cups of coffee and fed our son. I was making another batch of eggs before I came to wake you. I didn't put ham in his because I wasn't sure he could have the small chunks of meat. But I added diced ham to ours."

"He can have it, but you'd have to make sure he chewed it properly and didn't choke."

"Um." He blinked at me. "I think I'll forgo the ham in his eggs for now. He already ate a biscuit. I left ours in the oven to keep them warm."

"You didn't have to cook breakfast," I said, taking a seat at the table. "You could have woken me."

He brought over two plates filled with the eggs. The one with two biscuits he placed in front of me, claiming the one with four for himself. Good thing. I wouldn't have been able to eat that much food. His gaze landed on my neck, and I reached up to cover the marks. I'd noticed them in the mirror of the sink, even though they hadn't worried me. They were no darker than the last time I'd been with Samurai.

"You needed your rest," he murmured before taking a bite of his food.

"Is there a plan for today? Or are we hanging out at home?"

"I haven't heard from Shade yet, or anyone else. As long as the club doesn't need me, and there are no new developments on our situation, then I don't see why we can't hang out here at home. I have a Prospect coming to put up the posts for the fence out back. I texted him when I got up this morning. They'll have to set since I'm putting them in concrete, so the chain link can't go up until tomorrow."

"Ryo will be excited to have a backyard to play in. He's enjoyed being at Phantom's and visiting at Clarity's the last two days."

"Shit." Samurai looked from my place setting to his. "Forgot to get drinks."

Before I could stop him, he'd bolted out of his chair and returned a moment later with two glasses of orange juice. I sipped mine, amused at the tough biker. I'd seen the nasty side of him, the sweet side, and the vulnerable side. Samurai was a complex guy, but I was finding I liked him quite a bit.

By the time we'd finished breakfast and I'd helped Ryo brush his teeth, I started hearing noises outside. Since I knew there were other houses around us, I didn't think much of it. Until it sounded like there were voices outside the bedroom window. I peeked through the blinds and stared in awe at the men. Two were putting in fence posts. Three were putting together a large wooden playset, and another had started to dig a hole in the yard with a machine. The last one had me a bit concerned.

"Samurai," I yelled out as I went to the front of the house to find him. Thankfully, I'd put on a pair of jeans and a tank top since it appeared we had company inside too. "Did you know they're digging a hole out back?"

"That would be my doing," one of the men said. "My name's Charming. I'm the President of the Devil's Boneyard."

He held out his hand and I quickly shook it, then released him. I moved closer to Samurai, who curled his arm around my waist. "I'm confused about the hole."

Charming grinned. "Your oldest is three, from what I hear."

"Yes," I said, drawing the word out.

"Charming is having a small inground pool put in," Samurai said. "It will be large enough for us to go swimming but will be four feet all the way around. As hot as it gets in the summer, Charming thought we'd like our own spot to cool off and not worry about the older kids being too rambunctious."

"Is there another pool here?" I asked.

"We've recently added one for everyone to enjoy. The deep end is eight feet, and there's not a lifeguard on duty. We also put in some picnic tables, a few grills, and made a nice little family area. It's great for club get-togethers that include the women and kids."

"But the older boys tend to get rough in the water," Samurai said. "They wouldn't mean to hurt

Ryo, but they could accidentally. Charming thought it would be better to give Ryo his own pool than take the chance. Might take a few days, and we can't put up the fence until the pool is ready to add water."

"I thought the fence would be finished tomorrow?" I asked.

Samurai shook his head. "That was my plan, but Charming had other ideas. I like his better. A pool would be nice, even if it's only waist-deep on me and up to your shoulders."

I narrowed my eyes at him. "Did you just call me short?"

"You're pint-size, and cute." He smirked.

"Anyone home?" a voice yelled out.

"Kitchen, Phantom." Samurai winked at me. I had no idea what he had planned. When his cousin walked in, he immediately came over to hug me. Samurai gave a playful growl and tugged me from his arms. "Get your own."

"Trying," Phantom said with a sigh. "I'm here to get Ryo. Thought he'd like to play fetch with Momo over at my place for a little bit."

"Thanks," Samurai said. "He's in his room."

"I'll grab him and be on my way. Call when you're ready for him to come home. Otherwise, I'll plan on feeding him lunch and possibly dinner. I'm sure, even after Momo gets tired, we can find something to do." Phantom gave a wave as he vanished down the hallway. As much as I wanted to be upset no one had asked me if Ryo could go, I couldn't. I'd agreed to let Samurai claim him as his son, which meant I wasn't the only person in charge of him anymore.

"Scratch bought a sandbox and some toys for your son," Charming said. "It's being delivered today."

"Ryo won't know what to make of all this," I said. "A playset, sandbox, and a pool. He's going to be so spoiled."

"We have some catching up to do," Charming said. "I know single moms sometimes have a hard time accepting help. You, Ryo, and the unborn baby are family. This is us making sure you feel welcome, ensuring you and the kids have everything they could need or want, and keeping the lot of you happy. If you're happy, this guy will be happy."

He pointed at Samurai, who was still staring at me with an odd expression on his face. My cheeks warmed when I remembered last night. My eyes went wide as I reached up to lightly touch my throat. A glance at Charming said he'd noticed. For whatever reason, he hadn't brought attention to it, until I had.

"You seem content, Grey. If you'd been in distress, I'd have removed you from Samurai's home. I know he can get rough in the bedroom. Everyone knows it. As long as you're okay with the way things are between you, I'll try not to step in, unless I think it's the best thing for either you or the club. But if he ever crosses a line, you give me a call," Charming said.

"He didn't. He saw the marks and freaked out a little, thinking he'd hurt me. I honestly can't even feel it. I bruise so easily. If I brush against a doorway when I enter a room, it leaves a bruise. He didn't grip me as hard as he thinks he did."

Charming nodded. "All right. I'll take your word for it. Now. We need to discuss Itachi. You can either let Samurai and the club handle everything, or you can sit with us while I fill him in. Shade is on his way over."

"Then I should make some coffee," I said. I went up on tiptoe to kiss Samurai's cheek before hurrying over to the coffeemaker. While I busied myself brewing a pot, the two men sat at the table. "Do I need to be worried? Should I keep Ryo inside?"

"You and Ryo are safe for now," Charming said. "Itachi should be easily handled. We have proof that Ryo isn't his son. In fact, a friend of Shade's even faked a paternity test dated one week after the boy was born."

"And you think Itachi will believe you? Or care?" I asked.

"Only time will tell."

"Where the hell is everyone?" a voice yelled out from the front of the house.

"Kitchen," Charming shouted back.

A man walked in with a laptop in his hands. I figured he must be the one they called Shade. He gave me a wink as he settled at the table. He removed a file folder from inside his laptop, having stashed it between the lid and keyboard.

"Coffee?" I asked.

"Yes!" Shade opened his computer and brought up the screen. "I think we may all need a cup. Or three."

"You're making me wonder if the three of you need alcohol instead of coffee," I said. "Or maybe alcohol *with* your coffee."

Shade snickered. "She fits in already. I like her, Samurai."

"Mine." My scary biker growled at the other man, then reached over to tug me down onto his lap. Thankfully, I hadn't started pouring coffee yet or we may have both been wearing it.

"Is all this about Itachi?" I asked, pointing at the papers and computer.

"No. This is also about Knox and the Pleasure

Emporium." Shade winced and glanced at Samurai. "Sorry, brother. Charming knows, and so do the other officers. There's a chance the entire club does."

"I didn't hide that I'd been there," I said. "While it's not my proudest moment, I did what I felt was necessary in order to ensure my son had a roof over his head and I didn't wind up being the whore of a loan shark."

Samurai narrowed his eyes and I realized I may not have confessed that last part to him, or he hadn't been listening. Clearly, he didn't like the idea of me spreading my legs for anyone but him.

"I want his name," Samurai said.

I wasn't sure I wanted to be responsible for whatever would befall the man if I sold him out to Samurai. Then again, my biker didn't look like he would be backing down anytime soon. I had a feeling I'd give up the name whether I wanted to or not.

"Later," I said. "We don't want to keep Shade here longer than he needs to be, right? Same for your President."

Shade laughed. "Nicely played, but he'll be dragging the information from you at some point."

"Fine." I folded my arms. "His name was Willis."

The humor fled from Shade's face. "Chad Willis?"

I shrugged a shoulder. "I have no idea. He only called himself Willis. Said if I didn't pay back what my mom owed, he'd find other ways for me to pay off the debt. He made it clear what that would entail."

"Who the fuck is Chad Willis?" Samurai asked.

"He's part of why I'm here," Shade said. "When I did some digging, it looked like Knox had an agreement with someone. The funny part I couldn't figure out was why they'd wanted Grey before she'd even signed the contract at the Pleasure Emporium. It wasn't like she'd been on their roster of women."

"Are you saying that clause we found was placed there specifically because of Willis?" I asked.

Shade nodded. "That's how it appears. I found communication between him and Knox about a woman who'd gotten away. Willis said he'd have her one way or another, and Knox agreed to help."

"What made you go there?" Samurai asked. "I knew the moment you walked through the door you were more innocent than the women who usually frequent that place. How did you even know about it? It's not like it's advertised around town."

"Someone told me it would be a good way to make quick cash." I worried at my lip, unable to recall the woman's name. I'd run into her before I'd even heard of Willis. "It was one of the rare times I broke down in public. My mother had recently died and left unpaid debts. A woman nearby told me to try the Pleasure Emporium."

"So Willis and Knox are in this together?" Charming asked, pulling some of the papers toward him. "You think he had someone watching Grey and went to Knox before the contract was drawn up?"

"It's the only thing I can figure," Shade said. "Far as I can tell, they haven't had any other dealings with one another."

"So I have two men after me?" I asked. "Itachi and Willis?"

"As much as I know you want to hide Grey away, I think it's time to take the next step," Charming said. "Put her out in public on the back of your bike."

"She's pregnant," Samurai said. "I'm not putting the mother of my kid on a motorcycle, which is dangerous enough with the way idiots around here drive. Not happening."

Charming raised an eyebrow and I realized Samurai had talked back to his President in defense of me. It made me feel all warm and fuzzy, and a little worried about him. What would Charming do in retaliation?

"I'll let that slide because I know you're worried about her," Charming said. "But don't forget who the fuck you're talking to."

Samurai gave a jerky nod.

"If this is going to be a problem, maybe we can set Grey up somewhere else," Charming said. "It's not like you asked permission to move her into your house before you'd already put things into motion. We have a way of doing things around here, Samurai. She's not your old lady, and honestly, I don't know which way that vote would go at the moment."

I felt the blood drain from my face. "You're throwing me out?"

"Not exactly. We can set you up someplace. Just not here," Charming said. "We don't need the extra trouble."

"She's carrying my kid," Samurai reminded him.

Charming sighed. "Look, I get it. The kid will be family, assuming they're born. She can't be far along. Might not even go to term."

My jaw dropped. "Are you kidding me right now? Did you just wish my baby wouldn't be born? What kind of monster are you?"

Samurai pulled me down onto his lap, curling his arm around me. "She's staying, Pres. I'm sorry, but I won't let her leave. Especially while two psychos are after her and one of them wants Ryo."

"You won't have a choice if I make it an order," Charming said.

Shade pushed his chair back and started gathering his things. "I'm not sure why the two of you are getting in a pissing contest, and I don't need to know. But I will say this... Charming, you may be the President, but if you do this, toss Grey and Ryo outside the gates, every last person in this club will turn against you. It's not the way we've ever run things here, and if you want to start now, then..."

"Why won't the two of you say it?" Charming asked. "I've pushed and pushed, and you're both dancing around the truth. Why?"

Samurai tensed and I had to wonder if he'd been hiding something from me, or maybe whatever he needed to say had nothing to do with me. I still didn't know him nearly as well as I'd like. Perhaps in time.

Shade eyed me. "What do you think of Samurai?"

"I'm not sure I understand the question," I said.

"Pretend he can't hear anything. You're in a bubble. If you could stay here with him, indefinitely, would you?"

"I... I guess so." What if he didn't want me here forever?

"Do you want to be his old lady, Grey? Do you want to be with Samurai, no matter what comes your way, until the day you stop breathing or he does?"

Samurai tightened his hold on me. "Don't put her on the spot."

"Yes," I whispered. "I do. But if he doesn't want that, then I'll be all right. I've made it this long on my own."

Shade pulled out a piece of paper from the file he'd gathered and dropped it in the middle of the table. "Then congratulations. You aren't going anywhere, and Charming can't fucking make you unless he wants to lose Samurai too."

I stared at the document not quite certain what I was seeing. "Is that… a…"

Charming lifted it and skimmed the page. "Marriage certificate. It seems Shade has been talking to Wire a bit too much and married you and Samurai. If anyone looks, it will appear legal. Which makes you and Ryo property of the Devil's Boneyard. So much for a vote. You know, if everyone keeps doing shit this way, we may as well toss out the rule about voting in old ladies. Makes it fucking pointless."

"I think I need a minute with Grey," Samurai said.

"That's fine. I need to call Samson anyway. Rebel should be at the Black Reign compound, and possibly have already infiltrated the fighting ring. I want to make sure our brother will make it home still breathing." Charming rapped his knuckles on the table. "Welcome to the family, Grey. I may not like how these two assholes went about it, but I'd have never denied Samurai the right to claim you, as long as it's what you wanted. Sorry if I sounded like a prick today. It's been a rough twenty-four hours."

I didn't know what to make of the President. He left, with Shade on his heels, and soon it was only me and Samurai remaining. I should be angry he'd asked the man to marry us without my knowledge. It should infuriate me he hadn't bothered to ask my feelings on the matter. So why didn't it? All I felt was a warmth because he'd wanted to keep me badly enough, he'd gone behind my back, and Charming's, in order to have the hacker create papers showing we were married.

"Is he always like that?" I asked.

"No. I have a feeling there's something brewing

that I know nothing about. Between this mess with you and whatever's going on with Black Reign, he has a lot on his plate, but something still seems off."

I hoped nothing else bad was heading our way. I was already maxed out on what I could handle.

"How pissed are you?" he asked.

In answer, I threw my arms around his neck and kissed him. I felt him smile against my lips before holding me closer. Samurai kissed me back, leaving me breathless, and wishing we were alone. I wasn't about to drag him down the hall to the bedroom with so many people in the backyard. I didn't want them to hear us and know what we were doing.

"I'll buy you a ring," he murmured before kissing me again.

"I don't need one."

He drew back and cupped my cheek. "We'll have to agree to disagree. I don't want any doubt you're mine. I'm sure Charming is ordering you a property cut as we speak, but I want more. I want a ring on your finger to warn off any asshole who even thinks you're fair game."

"Then I'll gladly wear a ring. But not anything fancy. A plain band is more than enough."

He smirked. "We'll see."

Before I knew what he was doing, he'd started backing me down the hall. We entered the bedroom and I tensed.

"I'm *not* having sex with you while everyone is right outside those windows!"

He cocked his head to the side and then tossed me over his shoulder. I shrieked and grabbed onto his beltloops to steady myself. He carried me into the bathroom, kicked the door shut, then turned on the shower, tub faucet, and the sink.

I didn't know what he planned, but I hoped he knew all the running water was a guaranteed way to make a pregnant woman have to pee. I doubted that was his end goal.

Chapter Ten

Samurai

"Now no one can hear us," I said.

"Um." She looked at all the water and back at me. "You realize I've had one baby already and I'm growing another inside me, right?"

My brow furrowed. "What does that have to do with the water?"

"It's going to make me pee," she said, her cheeks flushing.

I dropped my head and bit my lip so I wouldn't laugh. She sounded horrified, but I found her fucking adorable. I shut off all three taps and caged her in, my hands braced on either side of her hips, pinning her to the counter. "Now you won't."

"They'll hear us, Jin. I don't want everyone knowing we're in here having sex."

I leaned in closer. "Grey, they already know we've slept together. You didn't get knocked up on your own. You think any of them cares? They don't. I might get shit about it later, but they'd never dare say anything to you."

"Don't make me scream too loud."

"That's the best part." I brushed my lips across hers. "I love hearing you yell out my name. Lets me know I'm doing something right."

"Like you ever had any doubt," she said.

I tipped my head to the side, watching her. "Actually, before I met you, no, I didn't. Then you showed me what it felt like when a woman came for real and didn't fake it. Now I have to question whether or not all my previous encounters were lacking. Then again, I never gave a shit if they enjoyed it. They were an easy release and nothing more."

"If I hadn't met some of those women, I might feel bad for them, but... they were mean. They acted like they owned you because you'd slept with them."

I cupped her cheek. "And I won't be fucking any of them ever again. You're it for me, Grey. It's part of why I asked Shade to marry us. I knew I didn't want to be with anyone else."

"You might make me cry. Pregnant women tend to be emotional."

I kissed her again, soft and slow. "You can cry anytime you want, as long as you let me wipe the tears away."

She wound her arms around my neck. "You know, since deciding to go all in and not run from me, you've turned into quite the romantic. The day we met, I saw a sweeter side to you at times. The way you watched me. Touched me. You made me feel special, even if your words didn't."

"I saw the softer look in your eyes and knew I had to push you away. I didn't want you sucked into my life, Grey. I thought... I *still* think you'd be better off without me." I backed up a step. "Can we try something different?"

"Like what?"

"Since Ryo isn't home, and no one outside will bother us anytime soon, would you let me tie you to the bed? I didn't lose control as much at the Pleasure Emporium when you were cuffed."

"And you just happen to have something handy?" she asked.

"Yes, and before you ask, no I haven't used it on another woman. I always had a brother hold them down."

"I trust you," she said softly. "If you want to tie me down, I'll let you."

"Undress. I'll get everything ready."

I stepped out of the bathroom and went to my closet. I took down the duffle bag on the top shelf and removed a length of rope. There were a few toys I'd purchased and never used, and while I wanted to explore a bit more with Grey, I knew now wasn't the time. Soon.

She entered the bedroom, completely bare, except for the blush staining her cheeks. I pointed to the bed, and she crawled to the center, then turned onto her back. The swell of her belly seemed larger, and I worried I might hurt her. I toed off my boots and straddled her body, securing the rope around her wrists before anchoring them to the headboard. She gave it a tug, but the rope didn't give.

"Are you going to get undressed?" she asked.

"No. Not right now." I licked my lips and eyed her body. She looked like a goddess, and I wanted to worship every inch of her. "I'm going to make you feel good. I do anything you don't like, or if something hurts, let me know. Unless it's the kind of pain you like, in which case, I'll keep going."

"But you'll stop if I say to?" she asked.

"Yes. This isn't like before, Grey. I haven't bought you or signed a contract. You may be giving yourself to me, but only because you want to."

She nodded and I saw her muscles relax. I placed my hands on either side of her torso and lowered my head, flicking my tongue across her nipple. She gasped and her back arched, as she silently begged for more. I circled the hardening tip before sucking it into my mouth, giving it a hard pull. Grey made the softest, sweetest sounds as I lavished her with attention.

I moved to the other side, giving it the same attention, before kissing my way down her body.

Parting her thighs, I held them open with my hands, taking a moment to admire the view. The lips of her pussy spread, allowing her clit to peek out. Already my wife was wet and ready. God. My *wife*. Never thought I'd have one of those.

I traced the lips with my thumbs before opening her wider. "Hard to believe this is all mine. That *you're* all mine."

"Jin, please. I hurt. I need you."

"Not yet, Grey. I'm only getting started." I licked her slit, letting her taste explode on my tongue. I'd never voluntarily gone down on a woman, and while a part of me fought against my past, I kept reminding myself this was my woman and no one else's. I circled her clit twice before lightly biting down.

She jolted and cried out. The gush of her release coated my chin. I needed her mindless with pleasure, begging for me to fuck her. I eased a finger inside her, then curled it slightly before pulling back. I stroked my finger in and out while I sucked on her clit. Her orgasm had barely ebbed before another started.

By the time her cries had turned hoarse, and the sheets were soaked, I was more than ready to be inside her. I rose to my knees, wiping my face off on my arm before unfastening my belt and jeans. I worked them down my hips enough to pull my cock out. I didn't know if this would work, but I hoped like hell it kept me from feeling the need to choke her.

I lowered myself over her body, lining my cock up with her soaking wet pussy. I worked my way into her, slow and easy. As much as I wanted to ride her hard and fast, I held myself back. My gaze locked on her face, a constant reminder of who I was with. I paused and awkwardly removed my cut and shirt before I started thrusting again.

"Jin, please!" She opened her eyes, the irises darker than before. Sweat dotted her brow and soaked her hair. "I can't take much more."

"You'll take whatever I have to give you. Isn't that right, wife?"

Her breath hitched and tears filled her eyes as she eagerly nodded. I would have panicked if I hadn't realized they were the happy kind. I took my time, making love to her. Hell, it was the first time I'd ever attempted such a thing. She came, squeezing my dick, and I knew I was lost. I groaned and briefly closed my eyes, fighting for control.

When I opened them again, it was to watch Grey come apart one more time. As her body went slack, I took what I needed, not stopping until I'd come inside her. My chest heaved and my arms shook. Hell, my entire body trembled. I pulled free and rolled to my side a moment.

"You all right?" I asked.

"Mmm. I don't think I can move."

My lips twitched as I struggled not to smile. "Probably because you're tied down."

"Smart-ass," she mumbled.

I stripped off the rest of my clothes and turned Grey so her back pressed to my chest. I positioned her leg over my thigh, opening her up. She moaned softly as I entered her again.

"One more time, beautiful. I need to prove to myself I can do this. Besides, I like hearing you beg and watching you come. It's quickly becoming my favorite thing."

I cupped her breast in my hand, rolling her nipple between my fingers, as I fucked her with a slow, steady rhythm. It didn't take long to have her crying out my name. I quickened my pace, thrusting deeper with every stroke, until I came again. Exhaustion pulled at her as I released her wrists. She didn't even move.

As much as I enjoyed being inside her, I knew she had to be uncomfortable. I rearranged us so she lay with her head on my shoulder and my arm around her. While she slept, I analyzed why I'd been able to control myself better when she'd been tied down or handcuffed. Both at the Pleasure Emporium and here at home. Granted, at the Pleasure Emporium, I'd still wrapped my fingers around her throat, but I hadn't gone too far. Not like I would have before. The others I'd been with prior to Grey had been held down and it hadn't mattered.

Neither of the times I'd fucked her just now had I reached out to wrap my hand around her throat. Did it mean Grey had somehow healed me? Or would I ever get over what I'd been through with the babysitter? I didn't think it was necessarily me tying her down. It wasn't the first time a woman had been held immobile, and I'd used cuffs on Grey at the Pleasure Emporium. Yes, even back then it had tempered the monster inside me, but it hadn't been caged entirely. Not until now. Something was shifting... either the dark part of me, or maybe it was only a reaction to Grey herself. She brought out a side of me no one else ever had -- the need to protect.

I remembered Grey's reaction to me that first time. She'd flinched away from me in terror at first. I didn't know if either of us would ever be completely over what we'd been through, but at least together, we had a chance at building something great. She understood me and my quirks, and I knew the horrors she'd faced.

My phone started ringing in my jeans pocket and

I extracted myself from Grey and our bed before answering. I saw the number for the Pleasure Emporium on the screen and snarled.

"What the hell do you want, asshole?" I demanded.

"Good to speak with you again too, Samurai."

"Far as I'm concerned, we have no reason to talk to one another ever again. So I'll ask you one more time. What the fuck do you want?"

"Fine." Knox cleared his throat. "The woman you purchased has gone missing. She hasn't used her bank card anywhere or been seen in the last two or three days."

"If she's one of your whores, shouldn't you have kept up with her better?"

"Yes, well. As I mentioned at the time, I didn't know if any of my regular girls would accept your offer. Ms. Lumare isn't part of my staff. However, there's an interested party who'd like to make her an offer."

"I'm sure they would," I muttered. "Well, you're shit out of luck, Knox. I read your contract, including the part you thought you'd slip in. It seemed odd to me that after I'd specified I wanted someone on birth control that the woman I'd fucked would show up at my gates pregnant. So I decided to go back and read it."

"I see." I heard papers shuffling. "And where is Ms. Lumare now?"

I smiled as I watched Grey sleeping. "Where she belongs. You go anywhere near Grey, even think of trying to contact her, and I'll rip out your fucking spine. Do we understand one another?"

"Yes, of course. However, my client, the one who wishes to purchase Ms. Lumare, may not be so understanding."

"Then send him my way. I'll make sure to clear things up." I ended the call and glared at the phone. "Cocksucking motherfucker."

"Come back to bed," Grey murmured, still mostly asleep. "I'm cold without you."

I tossed the phone back down onto my jeans and slid back into bed. I gathered her close and let her sleep for a while. If Knox, or anyone else, even dared to try and take Grey from me, I'd tear them to pieces. Dance in their entrails. Bathe in their blood. And I'd make sure no one ever found their fucking bodies, whatever was left of them.

I hadn't had anything important that was mine in so Goddamn long. Yeah, my cut was mine, but it was exactly like the ones all my brothers wore, which was the point. But Grey had filled a space inside me I hadn't realized was empty. Letting her in, giving her a chance, might have been the best decision I ever made. Now that I'd taken that initial leap, I was more than all in. It had only been a day and already she was my entire world. Her, Ryo, and the baby.

I'd laughed when my brothers had talked about falling fast and hard, about knowing the second they saw their women that they would be keeping them. Hell, Rooster had claimed Alora a few years back, and he'd known the second she answered the door that he'd make her his. Maybe that's what I'd felt with Grey that day, but I'd been too stupid, stubborn, and blind to bother seeing it.

"You're thinking too hard," she mumbled. "You're keeping me awake."

"Honey, you were snoring a minute ago. I didn't keep you awake even a little. Although, we should probably get cleaned up. I bet your thighs are stuck together."

She tried to pry them apart and groaned. "Great. Your cum is like superglue when it dries. Carry me to the bathroom, please. Maybe after the shower has had a chance to warm up. I don't like cold water."

I kissed her cheek. "I think it's the least I can do. I'll be back in a minute."

I went into the bathroom and started the water, waiting until it had warmed considerably before I brought Grey back with me. I stepped into the stall and pulled the door closed before easing her down. She stood and swayed a moment. Keeping my hands at her waist, I held her steady until I knew she wouldn't fall.

I took my time washing her before cleaning myself up too. When we got out, I dried her off and helped her get dressed. She seemed nearly boneless even after her nap. After I pulled my clothes back on, I lifted her into my arms and carried her to the living room. "Pick something to watch. I'm going to get us a snack and some drinks. I think you need to refuel." I kissed her forehead and handed her the remote.

At the store, she'd mentioned liking cheese and crackers. I put a handful of each on a plate for her, then grabbed a bottle of water. I took both to her before returning to the kitchen for a bag of chips and beer for myself. I sat down next to her, tugging her against my side.

"Please tell me we aren't watching a chick flick," I said.

"Nope. We're going to watch *Tombstone*."

"Really?" I glanced at her in surprise. "You don't seem like the western type."

"I'm not."

I waited but she didn't say more. I ate my chips, drank my beer, and kept thinking she'd tell me why she'd picked this one. Had she thought I'd like it? "All right. It's killing me. Why did you pick it if you aren't into westerns?"

She smiled at me. "Because Sam Elliott is a silver fox. We can watch *The Christmas Chronicles* next. Kurt Russell makes a super sexy Santa."

"You didn't just say that to me." I stared at her, but she didn't take any of it back. "Fine, but we aren't watching a Christmas movie. It's not even Halloween yet."

"Christmas can be enjoyed all year long. Especially when sexy Santas are involved."

I gave her the side-eye. "You're working your way up to a spanking. And don't think I'll bother doing it behind a locked bedroom door. I'll bend you over my lap right here and now, yank your pants and panties down, and make your ass bright red."

She gaped. "You wouldn't!"

"Oh, hell yes, I would. No ogling men other than your husband."

"You're enjoying playing the husband card a little too much," she griped, but I saw the humor glinting in her eyes.

The rest of our afternoon was relaxed and enjoyable. I couldn't remember ever sitting like this with a woman. I hadn't bothered dating. The club whores never came to my place, even before I'd had this house. Not once had I taken them to my room. Up against the wall, in the bathroom at the clubhouse, or outside had been good enough. Didn't matter where it was, as long as someone else was there to keep me on a leash, which meant helping pin the woman. Living with a woman was turning out to be better than I'd ever realized. Or maybe it was because that woman happened to be Grey.

"Were you on the phone earlier?" she asked. "Or did I dream that?"

"It rang. I answered and dealt with the vermin who dared to dial my number."

She sighed. "It was Knox, wasn't it?"

"Yep. Don't worry. I set him straight. I doubt he'll come anywhere near you. He mentioned his client wouldn't be happy, but if the fucker comes looking for you, I'll take care of him."

"Promise you won't do anything that sends you to prison. I don't want to raise Ryo and the baby on my own. Not after finally finding someone willing to step into the role of daddy."

I leaned in to kiss her. "Honey, even if I did get arrested, you wouldn't be alone. You'd still live in our house, and the club would help you until I was able to come home again. We take care of each other around here."

"I repeat. Don't go to prison."

I chuckled. "All right, beautiful. I won't go to prison. But I make no promises about being good. I just won't get caught."

She didn't seem reassured, but it was the best I could give her. I knew damn well I'd kill anyone who tried to hurt my family. And that family now extended to Grey and Ryo. Anyone came for either of them, and I'd send the fucker straight to hell.

No one was going to fuck with my family.

Not as long as I drew breath.

Chapter Eleven

Grey

The next few days passed in a bit of a blur. Ryo and I settled into life with the Devil's Boneyard, and with Samurai. My nights were filled with the man making me scream in pleasure, and my days were busy getting acquainted with everyone. I'd even made friends with Nikki and Darby. I'd thought they'd give me a wide berth after the first impression I'd made with them. Thankfully, they hadn't held it against me.

Samurai had taken Ryo somewhere, stating it was a surprise and I wasn't allowed to go, so I found myself knocking on Clarity's door. She opened it with a smile and motioned me inside.

"Hi, Grey! You having a good day?"

"Yeah. I'm out killing time. Samurai was super secretive, saying he and Ryo had a surprise planned. I wasn't allowed to go with them."

"I'm baking a few things to take over to the clubhouse for the single guys. We try to treat them to desserts or dinners here and there. Keeps them from eating junk all the time. Want to help?"

"Sure. I'm not the best baker in the world, but I'm great at following instructions."

I let Clarity lead the way to the kitchen. She hadn't been joking about taking a bunch of stuff to the clubhouse. There already were two plates of cookies and a tin stuffed with brownies sitting on the table. I saw two pie tins on the counter, as well as a cake pan.

"Holy crap! It looks like you're feeding an army of toddlers."

She snorted and burst out laughing. "You're about right. Sometimes those men can be rather childish, and they do love their sweets. I think Janessa was planning to offset some of the sugar by bringing them a lasagna. The treats will last them a day or two, though. The dinner will be gone within the hour."

"It's nice that y'all chip in to feed them. I'm sure they like getting a home-cooked meal."

She nodded. "They do. It's my way of trying to take care of them, without smothering them too much. Plus, I'm hopeful they'll be a little less like rabid animals and find a woman of their own. That's the ultimate goal at any rate. Some of them, I think, may be bachelors for life."

"Phantom seems to want a family in the worst way," I said.

"He does. It's so sad, though. The only women I've seen him with either don't want children, or they're not in it for the long haul. The last one would have spent her life with him, but she's closer to his age and didn't want a family. Nothing wrong with that, as long as both parties are in agreement, and Phantom certainly isn't. He's great with the kids around here."

"Has anyone tried to set him up? Like on a blind date or something?" I asked.

"It would be a good idea, except for one problem. I'm noticing these guys like rescuing damsels in distress. I'm not saying any of us are weak. Far from it. But these men want to feel needed. They'd never admit it, but I think they have a hero complex. Phantom needs someone he can save, someone who will lean on him, let him shelter them, protect them from the big bad world. And if she happens to already have a kid or two, then bonus!"

"I guess I can see that. Too bad. Setting him up with a blind date would have been easier."

She smiled and handed me a bowl and a whisk. "Mix that, please, then pour it into the cake pan."

I got to work and kept my mind off Samurai and Ryo, and whatever their strange errand might be. Thankfully, I'd left a note on the kitchen table, otherwise if they'd have come back and found me missing, Samurai would have likely freaked the hell out. He seemed to like keeping me within sight as much as possible. I had a feeling it had to do with both Itachi and Willis. I didn't know what the club had planned, if anything, to handle the situation, but I was tired of being locked behind the gates.

"Hey, Clarity, is it always like this?" I asked.

"What? You'll have to be more specific."

"Me on lockdown because the big scary men want to get me. Will I be locked up in this place every time there's danger nearby?"

"He's protecting you." She smiled. "It's actually nice to see him so into someone and taking on the responsibility of not only his child but Ryo too. I didn't think Samurai had it in him for the longest time, but when you showed up, I'd hoped something would change. I've watched him keep his distance. Oh, he parties with everyone, jokes around, and has gotten to know everyone here. But at the same time, he's held them at a bit of a distance. Like he didn't want to trust them fully."

"I don't think that's it." I pressed my lips together. "It's his story to tell, but he was hurt really bad when he was younger. It hardened him, I think, as a way to survive what he went through. I can't fault him for it. After we talked, things changed. I accepted him, flaws and all, same as he's done for me. I told him maybe we could heal one another, in time."

"That's sweet." Clarity patted my back. "You can add that to the pan now. The oven is already preheated. Just pop it in there and set the timer for thirty-five minutes please."

I did as she said, then moved on to helping make the lattice tops for the pies she'd already filled. My mother hadn't been well enough to spend much time in the kitchen. When I was younger, she'd worked and wasn't home much. By the time I was a teenager, she'd already started feeling sick. So I'd missed getting to do things like this with another woman. Not that Clarity was old enough to be my mom by any means, maybe more like a sister. Either way, I had more fun with her in the kitchen than I had in a while.

"If you want to do this again sometime, let me know," Clarity said. "I'll gladly take the help!"

"Count me in."

She hugged me and sent me on my way. Although, I had a feeling it had more to do with her man pulling into the driveway. He had that same glint in his eyes I saw with Samurai right before he pounced on me.

I'd walked from the house, since I still didn't have a vehicle. Samurai said we'd pick one out together, but I knew he didn't want me leaving the compound right now. Not with Willis and Itachi still after me. I hadn't heard any updates the last few days and wondered where we stood with all that. I doubted it was permitted for me to track down Charming and ask him. If he wanted me to know, most likely he'd have told me or ordered Samurai to do it.

I hadn't realized how lost in thought I was until I bumped into someone. Strong hands gripped my upper arms to hold me steady. "You all right?"

I blinked and looked up at the rather tall man with the Russian accent. "Fine. I think. Sorry for running into you."

"It's no problem, little one. You're Samurai's

wife, aren't you?" he asked.

"Yes. I don't have one of those property things, though. I didn't think about that when I left the house. Am I allowed to roam around out here without one?" I couldn't remember ever seeing the other old ladies leave their homes without theirs.

"Usually you'd need to make sure you had it on. Especially when there are still people here you haven't met. Like me." He smiled. "They call me Stripes. Like a Siberian tiger, no?"

"Is that where you're from? Siberia?"

He shook his head. "No, my home was in another part of Russia. Were you going back home? I can walk with you."

"I didn't really have a direction in mind. Samurai and Ryo left, and I didn't like being in the house by myself. I went to see Clarity, but Scratch came home. I'd thought of asking Charming what's going on with Itachi and Willis, then decided if he wanted me to know, he'd have told me already. It's been days since I met him and we discussed it. I'm tired of being locked up."

Stripes patted my shoulder. "I understand. Even with all this space, the gates and fence make it feel like a cage. Don't worry. You'll be able to fly free soon enough."

"You know something."

He nodded. "I do. It's not my place to say, but your man has something planned for the two of you tonight. It will flush out one of your problems, and hopefully put an end to it. As for the other, that one will require more work."

"That's not cryptic or anything," I muttered.

"Do you trust Samurai?" Stripes asked.

"Yes. I may not have given that answer a few

days ago, but I do trust him now."

"Then let him do what he feels is right," Stripes said. "Now, let's get you home, little one. Don't want your man returning and going into a panic when he can't find you."

I smiled and allowed him to walk me home. It still blew my mind Samurai would even care if I were to vanish. The way he'd reacted the first day had nearly destroyed me. I'd been terrified and felt incredibly alone. Now I had him and an entire club I could call family. And Ryo would have all these people to help him grow into a man I would be proud of. Unlike if Itachi had gotten his hands on him.

I'd learned the Devil's Boneyard might not follow the law all the time, but they had good hearts. The bad things they did were for the right reasons. Maybe to some that didn't justify their actions. To me it made a world of difference. The law would throw a rapist into prison for a year or three, then release him on parole for good behavior. He'd be right back to harming women until he got caught again. But these people? They didn't take that sort of thing lightly. The fact Samurai had wanted to bury Itachi told me enough. If anyone hurt me or Ryo, they would likely pay with their lives.

Did it make me bloodthirsty for condoning such behavior? Possibly. Did I care? Nope. I felt safe for the first time since Itachi broke into my apartment and wrecked my life. I'd gotten my sweet little boy out of the deal, and I'd never wish Ryo away for anything, but I knew without a doubt the bastard had hurt other women the same way. As long as he roamed free, he'd be a threat to those weaker than him. I hated it. Couldn't do anything about it myself, but now that he was on the radar of the Devil's Boneyard, I knew they'd take care of him if he crossed that line again.

"Stripes, can I ask you something?"

"Of course! How else will people learn if they do not ask questions?"

I liked him. I didn't know if he had a woman, but if he didn't, it was their loss. Unless he didn't *want* a woman. Or a man. I didn't know if there were any gay men in the club. Was it even allowed? Or did you have to be straight to be part of the Devil's Boneyard? I wasn't sure I should even ask. At least, not one of the men. Maybe I'd ask one of the old ladies sometime.

"I'm sure everyone knows Itachi raped me. I doubt I was the only woman he's attacked. What happens if he's left roaming free and he does it again?"

"Then he pays the ultimate price," Stripes answered. "We've been watching him since you brought him to our attention and will continue to do so until we are certain he's no threat to women and children."

"Hearing that makes me feel better. Thank you."

"We've arrived at your home, little one. Will you be all right until Samurai returns?"

"I will. I'm not used to being alone. Ryo has been with me at home on the days I didn't work. With both him and Samurai out of the house, I guess it was too quiet."

"You're making friends here, yes?"

I nodded. "I am. The old ladies have been great, and I'm slowly getting to know all the... brothers? Is that correct?"

"Yes. You will meet us all in time. I'm sure the Pres and VP will be hosting a party in your honor before long. Perhaps after your safety has been guaranteed. Do you have a phone?"

I pulled it from my pocket. "Here."

"Program my number into your contacts. If you need anything and Samurai is not available, you're welcome to call anytime. You're not alone here, little one. You have a big family now."

He rattled off his number and I saved it in my phone. After I went inside the house, I locked the door. No matter how many times people insisted it was safe here, I couldn't seem to shake the feeling I *needed* those locks. What if Itachi or Willis found a way inside? What if they saw me walk into this house? No, I wouldn't take unnecessary chances. Samurai had keys if he needed to unlock the door. Better to be cautious than let the bad men walk right in.

My phone chimed and I checked my messages, smiling when I saw Samurai's name.

Shower and put on something pretty. We have plans.

Pretty left a lot of wiggle room. *Pretty as in a dress?*

He responded almost immediately. *Yes! Not the one you were wearing when we met, or we'll never leave the house.*

My cheeks warmed at his meaning. I wouldn't be opposed to a night in, but it seemed he wanted to do something special. I got into the shower and made sure to condition my hair so it would be extra soft and took my time shaving everywhere important. In another few months, I'd have a hard time reaching my legs. I'd either have to wear pants every day or ask Samurai to shave them for me. Which would likely lead to fun times in the shower. I didn't really see a downside to the scenario.

I scrubbed my skin, washed my face, then got out and dried off. Wrapping my hair in a towel, I thought of everything I still needed to do. Was this a date? We hadn't had one of those. Nothing in our life together had been what most considered normal. We'd been married by a hacker. I'd gotten pregnant the day we'd met. Oh, and he'd bought and paid for me. Probably should leave that part out of the story we told our kids and grandkids.

I smoothed lotion over my body and moisturized my face before deciding on what to wear. I didn't own much of anything I'd consider sexy. Most of my dresses were like the one he'd already seen me wear twice. The one he'd said *not* to put on today. I flipped through my meager belongings and selected a gray dress with three-quarter sleeves and small lilac flowers spread over the material. It zipped up the back instead of buttoning down the front and had a slight flare with the hem landing just above my knees.

Since comfort was more important than fashion these days, I pulled on the lilac-colored Converse Phantom had brought me yesterday. He'd mentioned one of the old ladies favoring them during her pregnancy. I'd found it to be a sweet gesture. They didn't look terrible with the dress, and I wondered if I could talk Samurai into another pair or two in neutral colors.

By the time I'd dried my hair, curled it, and done the bare minimum with makeup -- mascara and a tinted lip balm -- I was ready and waiting. I heard a truck pull into the driveway and peeked out the front window. Samurai got out and helped Ryo out of his car seat before reaching into the back and taking out a paper shopping bag. I didn't see a store logo and had no idea where they'd been all day.

Ryo burst through the door first, shooting past me and going straight to the bathroom. I eyed Samurai with a bit of amusement. "Did you deny him bathroom privileges while you were gone?"

"He drank a gallon of juice while we were out. We hadn't been in the truck more than two minutes before he started saying he had to go." He leaned in and kissed me on the cheek. "You look stunning. And the shoes are cute. I'll have to tell Phantom he was right about them."

"I was hoping we might get more."

He handed me the shopping bag and I nearly dropped it from the unexpected weight. I pulled out a leather vest. No, a cut. My eyes went wide when I realized what he'd given me.

"My property cut?" I asked.

"Yep. It was finished yesterday, but I didn't get a chance to pick it up until now. You won't be able to button it while you're pregnant. Want to try it on?"

I slipped it over my shoulders and ran my hands down the leather. "I love it."

"Turn around," he said, his voice sounding deeper than it had a moment ago. I did a slow spin and gasped when his hands landed on my hips, holding me still with my back to him. He moved in closer, his scent washing over me, and I felt his hard cock against my ass. "When we get back, I'm bending you over the bed, lifting the hem of this sexy-as-fuck dress, and I'm going to make you scream my name."

I shivered in anticipation. "Get back? Where are we going?"

"To dinner. I've heard Itachi will be at the hibachi place in town later tonight. It's one of his weekly haunts. We're going to be there too, and make sure he sees us together."

"Is that wise? What if he demands I give him Ryo?"

"Grey, I'm Japanese just like him. I'm hoping he'll see the two of us together and start to doubt whether or not Ryo is his. And if he starts shit, I'm more than capable of ending it... and him."

"Be careful, Jin. I don't want to lose you."

He kissed my neck. "You won't. Phantom will be here any minute to get Ryo. They're going to order pizza and play with Momo while we're gone."

"He really does need a dog." I looked over my shoulder. "Ryo. Not Phantom. Your cousin needs a woman."

"You're not wrong on either count. We'll work on the dog soon. As for Phantom, I hope like hell he finds someone before too long. If anyone deserves a family, it's him." He kissed my neck again. "I'm going to rinse off and put on something else before we leave. Be back in a few minutes."

I watched him walk down the hall, unashamedly checking out his ass. How I went from single mom about to lose it all, to getting to call that sexy man my own, I had no idea. But I was so very grateful.

Chapter Twelve
Samurai

I took a three-minute shower, using the body wash I'd noticed Grey seemed to appreciate, then got out and wrapped the towel around my waist. I shaved and added a splash of cologne -- something I seldom did. Tonight was special. I'd given her the property cut, but I had something else for her. Other than my cock, even if I hoped I got to give her that later too.

I pulled out a pair of my darker jeans and a white button-down shirt. I slipped on a pair of boxer briefs before I tugged on the jeans. Deodorant was next on my list, then my shirt. Once I had my shirt tucked in, my belt buckled, and had slipped my cut back over my shoulders, I put on a fresh pair of socks and a newer pair of boots I saved for special occasions.

It hadn't escaped my attention this would be our first date. Hell, even if it had, the women around here wouldn't have let me forget it. I'd already had a call from Clarity and one from Meg, both making sure I knew to dress nice. They assured me Grey would appreciate the effort. I heard my cousin at the front of the house and Ryo squealing.

Making sure I didn't forget the most important part of tonight, I reached into my discarded jeans and pulled a small box from the pocket. I shoved it into the front pocket of my new jeans and hoped like hell Grey didn't notice. Shit. She probably would. I yanked it out, removed the ring inside, and pushed the jewelry down deep so it wouldn't accidentally fall out.

Shaking my head, I made my way to the front door. Ryo already had a spot on Phantom's shoulders, and they were stepping out onto the porch. It seemed I'd been pushed aside by Phantom, or more likely,

Momo. The boy did have a one-track mind. He'd brought up the dog no less than once every ten minutes while we'd been gone. Since the fence had been finished yesterday, I didn't see a reason we couldn't get a dog. It might be a little overwhelming at the moment, but I liked seeing my son smile.

And yeah, I'd called him mine all fucking day, and he'd grinned so big each and every time. Ryo was sweet, full of energy, and I could tell he was a good kid. Grey had done a phenomenal job with him. She waved to Ryo as Phantom placed him in the back seat of an SUV I hadn't seen before.

"Did Phantom buy a car?" I asked.

"Yes. He said something about wanting to take his nephew places without having to borrow one of the club vehicles."

"That's on my list, but I want to get some of our problems out of the way first. Mainly Itachi and Willis. I don't like the idea of you leaving the compound on your own until I know it's safe."

She reached over and took my hand. "I understand. I may not like being locked up, but I get it."

"Come on, my stunningly gorgeous wife. Time for us to have our first date."

Her cheeks flushed a light pink and I saw the pleasure dancing in her eyes. Looked like the women had been onto something. I might not *have* to romance Grey, but she needed it. Hell, I probably needed it too.

I helped her into the truck and drove to the front gates. I waved to Carlos as we pulled through, and I went straight to the hibachi place. The parking lot wasn't very full yet. I scanned our surroundings and saw Itachi's vehicle a few rows over. It was hard to miss the flashy Acura NSX. Considering the part of town he called home, I had no doubts as to how he'd made enough to afford the car.

"You ready?" I asked.

She blew out a breath and gave me a nod. I got out of the truck and walked around to her side, opening the door and helping her down. I kept my hand at her waist, under her cut, so she could feel the heat of my palm against her. It wasn't just for her sake, though. I needed the reassurance she was standing next to me. If this went badly, I'd rain down hell on this fucking town until I had Grey back by my side, where she belonged.

We stepped inside and the smell made my mouth water. I heard Grey's stomach growl and I smiled down at her. "Baby hungry or momma?"

She pressed a hand to her belly. "Maybe both."

"Table for two?" the hostess asked.

"Yes. Maybe somewhere in sight of the bathroom? My wife is pregnant."

Grey elbowed me in the ribs, but the hostess smiled, grabbed two menus, and led us to a table. It happened to be within line of sight of Itachi. I knew the second he spotted Grey. I pulled her chair out for her and then sat on the opposite side.

The hostess set the menus down in front of us. "Do you know what you'd like to drink?"

"Water," Grey said.

"Sweet tea for me."

The woman hurried off while Grey and I looked over the menu. By the time she returned, we knew what we wanted and placed our order. I only hoped the sushi I'd ordered didn't make Grey turn a bit green. Some people couldn't handle it, and with her being pregnant, I knew there was a chance seeing the raw fish would make her sick. If that was the case, I'd have them box it up for later and I'd get something else.

I reached across the table and laced our fingers together. She gave me a hesitant smile. "I have something for you."

"You've given me more than enough already."

I reached into my pocket and slid the ring onto her finger. She gasped and stared at the sparkly band. I'd asked Clarity what she thought Grey might like. She'd recommended something that wouldn't scratch the kids or get caught on things. The platinum band was smooth and the diamonds were embedded all around it. I'd run my fingers over it multiple times to ensure it wouldn't scratch the kids, or Grey.

"Do you like it?" I asked.

"It's so beautiful," she said, her eyes getting glassy with unshed tears.

I stood and walked around to her side, kneeling next to her. I reached up and cupped her cheek. "It's just a ring, Grey. But I wanted something you could wear all the time. The property cut is fine when we're leaving the house, but this way, you have a reminder of how much you mean to me."

A shadow fell across the table and my gaze lifted to meet Itachi's. He sneered at me. "Isn't this touching? Where's my brat, whore?"

I stood and pulled Grey closer to me. "She's not a whore, and I'm not sure who the fuck you think is yours."

"The kid. The boy." Itachi looked around the restaurant. "Where is he?"

"Ryo?" I asked.

Itachi shrugged. "Don't know, don't care. He's mine and I'm taking him."

"Like fuck you are! Ryo is my son, as is the baby

Grey carries now. You keep the hell away from my wife."

Itachi's eyebrows lifted, and he backed up a step. "Wife? What the fuck?"

"You scared her the day she ran into you. I know all about what you did to her. Held her while she cried. But let me make one thing perfectly clear. Ryo is not now, nor has he ever been yours. If you don't believe me, I can show you the papers to prove it. Because you attacked her, after Ryo was born, we had a paternity test done. He's mine."

Itachi's brow furrowed. "Impossible. The fucking slut was a virgin. Bled all over my dick when I took her."

I ground my teeth together. I wanted to pound the fucker into the ground. "We'd been waiting, and then you ruined it all."

Itachi threw back his head and laughed. "That's rich. A biker waiting to pop someone's cherry? You don't expect me to believe that, do you?"

"Believe this..." I moved around Grey, putting myself between her and the asshole. "You come near my wife or son, and I'll make sure you disappear. You put your dick in another woman without her consent, same thing. Your reign of terror is at an end. You fucked up and hurt the wrong woman."

He spat on the floor. "Am I supposed to be scared of you?"

"Oh, it's not just me you need to worry about. It's not even the Devil's Boneyard. No, you need to be concerned with me, my club, and every club we consider an ally. Because if anything happens to Grey or another innocent, we're all coming for you, and we won't stop there. We'll wipe out your entire organization."

"Keep the whore and the brat." Itachi backed up another step. Then another. "I don't need them. Plenty of women will spread their legs for me."

"Remember what I said. We're watching you, Itachi. One wrong move and you're finished."

He tried not to show fear, but I caught it. A glimmer of hesitance in his eyes, the way his jaw tightened, the shift of his hips to bolt for the door. Yeah, the fucker was scared, and he damn well better be. I hadn't been lying. We knew his every move. I wouldn't say anything to Grey, or do anything to tip her off, but Itachi's days were numbered. Hell, his hours were. He'd stepped out of line too many times.

I reclaimed my seat and reached for Grey's hand again. I felt her shaking and wished there had been another way to handle this. I'd needed to see if he'd back down. Part of me had known he wouldn't, but after the changes Grey had brought about in my life, I'd wanted to give the man a chance. Clearly, he'd chosen the wrong path. Now my woman was terrified, worried about our kid, and I'd have to deal with that fucker's dumb ass sooner rather than later. Had I run into Itachi alone, I'd have dealt with him now.

This wasn't the way I'd wanted this night to go. Not even a little. I'd have to tell my brothers, make sure Itachi got rounded up and brought to the compound. We couldn't leave him to roam free. Not in our town.

Fury pumped through my veins. I should have paid better attention to our surroundings. Instead, I let someone sneak up on us. A business card dropped onto the table. I eyed it a moment. *Chad Willis*. I looked up, taking in the man's suit and overall polished appearance. None of it hid the coldness in his eyes.

"You're next on my list," I said.

The man smiled. "Am I now? How interesting."

"Guess warning you away from my woman won't do any good," I said.

"I think we can come to a different arrangement. As enticing as she is, money talks even louder, and I think we're about to go into business with one another."

I leaned back in my seat. "Really? What makes you think that?"

The man gave a chin nudge where Itachi had just vanished. "That parasite is trying to take over my territory. His drugs weren't an issue. Plenty of people came to me for loans to buy more, or to pay off debts to him. Even his whores weren't a problem. No, what I care about is his decision to go into the loan business too. Now *that* I can't have."

"What do you want?" Grey asked. She looked pale, even though I saw the determination in her eyes. She wanted all this over as much as I did.

"Itachi and his crew. I want them gone. I don't care how. You have until the end of the week to make it happen. You take them out, and I'll forget I ever knew your delectable little wife."

I narrowed my eyes. It couldn't be that simple. I'd planned to handle Itachi anyway. So why would he offer to walk away once Itachi was gone? Something felt off, and I never ignored my gut, not when it came to things like this.

"I've kept tabs on your club," Willis said. "For every bit of bad you do, there's much more good. Sell a little pot here, donate to a women's shelter over there. It evens things out. You aren't an issue for me."

"You've been watching us?" I asked.

"Oh, more than that. Who do you think made sure your little woman there went to the Pleasure

Emporium? I waited to call in her debts until I'd already planted the seed. Had one of my girls talk to her. Waited a few weeks and called in the loan." He shoved his hands into his pockets. "And I spoke with Knox before she'd even signed the contract. I heard you found the little hidden gem."

"Then why did you add it? If you didn't want Grey to begin with…"

"I knew your club would swoop in to save her. It's what you do, after all. Especially when we made sure you were the one to buy her. The timing was rather delicate, and I wasn't sure it would go off quite the way I'd planned. If someone else had purchased her, we'd have found a way to make the Devil's Boneyard aware of her situation. You're all horrible about taking in strays."

"You never planned to use me?" Grey asked.

"Not in the way you thought. Oh, you're still going to help me tremendously. Or rather, your husband's club will. We have a common enemy. I want them gone, and so does his club."

"Who the hell are you?" I asked.

The veneer dropped for a moment, and I saw what lay beneath the mask. A chill skated down my spine. He leaned in closer, lowering his voice so only I could hear him. "Did you think it was only Casper VanHorne and Specter meddling in things behind the scenes? You can call me Styx. I'll be paying your club a visit soon. Tell Charming to be expecting me."

He drew back and walked off, whistling a Glenn Miller tune. My heart pounded in my chest, and I wondered what the hell we'd just gotten mixed up in. First Rebel was sent to help Black Reign, now some assassin was playing at being a loan shark for what objective? I couldn't think of another reason for him to compare himself to those two men. Not unless he was just like them.

"Things got complicated, didn't they?" Grey asked.

"More than you'll ever know, beautiful. Let's try to enjoy our dinner and have a good night at home. I have no idea what tomorrow will bring."

I quickly shot off a text to Charming about Willis being Styx and hoped it would suffice for now. I didn't want any interruptions the rest of the night if it wasn't necessary. We ate our dinner and got in the truck to head back home. As I drove, I placed a quick call to Phantom to ensure Ryo would stay the night. I hadn't been certain how the night would end, but I knew I needed Grey, and I felt like she needed me too. Which meant no children in the house.

I promised to send some things over for him. When we got home, I'd pack a small bag before having a Prospect pick it up and deliver it. Then I would have Grey all to myself. Assuming I could keep my hands off her long enough to even make it home.

I had a lot of memories to make in one night. I'd promised to bend her over and fuck her while she kept her dress and property cut on, and I planned to make good on it. By morning, she'd be sore -- in a good way -- and I'd have something pleasant to think about while I talked to Charming. I didn't like the way we kept getting broadsided with shit. First Grey's pregnancy, then Knox adding that line to the contract, Willis not being who he claimed. And why the fuck hadn't Shade figured out who this guy was?

I didn't like it. Not any of it.

I gathered up my woman, carrying her out to the truck, not caring if people whispered or stared. She smiled softly as I buckled her in and walked around to the driver's side. I felt on edge, and a bit twitchy. I needed to take the edge off so I wouldn't lose control at home.

After I'd pulled out onto the road, I reached over and tugged the hem of her dress up. Not enough to expose her, but far enough it rested at the top of her thighs. She didn't protest. The heated glance she slid my way told me she wanted me every bit as much as I wanted her.

I flipped up the armrest so I could reach her easier. Sliding my hand under the hem of her dress, I pushed her panties aside and stroked my fingers over her wet pussy. The second I touched her clit, she let out a cry that had my cock going rock hard. I rubbed the hard little bud until she came on my fingers, her hips thrusting against my hand. I made her come a second time before I unfastened her seat belt and pulled onto the shoulder of the road. We were close enough to the clubhouse I didn't worry about anyone stopping to check on us, except maybe one of my brothers.

I made quick work of my belt and the zipper on my jeans. "Need you, Grey. I can't wait."

She crawled closer and she tugged my dick free, closing her lips over the head. I sucked in a breath as she swallowed me down, taking every inch. I gripped the steering wheel, trying not to grab hold of her. It didn't take long for me to lose the battle. I fisted her hair and held her still as I fucked her mouth, forcing my cock as far as I could without choking her. Her nails bit into my thighs and the way she squirmed told me she needed another release.

I pulled her off me, my cock twitching with the need to come. "Lift your dress. Show me how wet you are."

She pulled the material up and shimmied out of

her panties. Her thighs spread and the lips of her pussy parted. I groaned at how fucking beautiful she was, and how damn badly I wanted her.

"Please! I don't want to wait until we're home. Your fingers weren't enough," she said.

I patted my thighs. "Come on. Ride me, beautiful. Take what you need."

She settled over me, her pussy taking me in. I gripped her hips as she rose and fell, making the truck rock in a way that would tell anyone passing by exactly what we were up to. I didn't give a fuck. Let them know. She rode me, making the sweetest sounds, until she came screaming my name.

I held onto her as I thrust up, driving into her until I'd filled her with my cum. My chest heaved and my cock had only partially softened. I needed more, but at least I could make it to the house before ravishing her again. I hoped Grey didn't need much sleep tonight. I planned to fuck her until she was too sore to move.

I fisted her hair and kissed her hard. My tongue dominated her mouth, bending her to my will. I could feel the darkness at the edges, wanting to take over, but I held it back. Mostly.

"You're mine. My woman. My wife." I bit her lip. "My little whore. Only mine."

"Yes, Jin. Yours. Only yours."

Chapter Thirteen

Grey

Waking up not only alone in bed, but discovering the house was empty, didn't put me in the greatest of moods. The way Samurai had touched me, kissed me... he'd made love to me for hours before letting loose his darker side. I should have known it was his way of distracting me. I hadn't bothered asking more questions last night, and now I was left wondering where he was and if he would come home in one piece.

There hadn't been a note or anything. From what I could tell, he hadn't even bothered to drink a cup of coffee or eat breakfast before he'd left the house. I had yet to see the man get up without downing several cups of coffee. Had he left in a hurry? Unease settled inside me, making my stomach churn. I reached for my phone. Ryo hadn't been brought home, so I wondered if he was still with Phantom.

I dialed his number and waited impatiently for the call to connect. When it did, I heard screaming in the background that made me want to run out of the house and find my baby. Except it wasn't Ryo. No, it sounded like a grown man.

"Shit," Phantom said.

"Do you always answer like that?" I asked.

"No. It's um, a bad time." More screams. "Ryo is with Clarity. The Pres called us all in this morning. Didn't want to wake you, and Clarity was already up. He's safe. Fed. And I left Momo with him."

I couldn't get another word in before the call dropped. Or more accurately, he'd hung up. I stared at the device in my hand a moment before deciding I didn't want to be kept in the dark. Not only did the

VP's woman have my kid, but she'd likely have some answers too. I put on my shoes and stepped outside, pausing when I saw the truck still parked in the driveway. I hurried back to the kitchen and found the keys hanging on the hook just inside the door, with the extra house key and Samurai's spare motorcycle keys.

I hopped in the truck and drove to Clarity's, noticing how quiet the compound was this time of morning. The fact Phantom had said everyone had been called in and I didn't see a single bike at the clubhouse increased the feeling of dread. I pulled into Clarity's driveway and ran up to her door, knocking harder than I'd intended.

She opened it with a sigh. "Had a feeling you'd be by. Come on in."

"Where's Ryo?"

"The boys are showing him how to build stuff with Legos. They have a huge tub of them, so he'll be occupied for a while. I told them to make sure he doesn't put any in his mouth, up his nose, or in his ears. All things my boys have done at one time or another. Momo is keeping watch."

She led me into the kitchen and I sat. "I'm trying really hard not to freak the hell out."

"I can tell. You even left the house without your property cut."

I winced. "I'm not used to having one. I just got it last night."

"You going to panic every time you wake up and he's not home?" she asked.

"No. Maybe. I'm not sure." She handed me a cup of hot tea and I sipped it. "I'd have possibly been okay if he'd at least left a note. He didn't drink his morning coffee. Didn't eat anything. It scared me."

"Samurai isn't used to having a family. Not the

kind who live with him at any rate. It will take some time for both of you to adjust. Talk to him when he comes home. Let him know it scared you when he didn't leave a note. But, Grey, you're going to have to toughen up, or at least appear to be. Otherwise, the club whores are going to eat you alive and think your man is fair game."

"I already put one on her ass," I said.

"Not good enough. Great start! But no. You're going to have to do better."

"Like what?" I asked.

She tilted her head and studied me. "I'm going to tell you what I know, and then you decide for yourself what you'll do. Ryo can stay here as long as you need him to."

"Sounds rather ominous."

She shrugged. "It is what it is. Look, Charming had a meeting this morning with someone. I also know at some point either late last night or early this morning, the club dragged Itachi and his two head goons into the compound. Your man, as well as mine and the others, are out back taking care of business."

"By that you meant... killing them."

She nodded. "Does it bother you?"

"No. Those men are evil and will keep hurting people."

"Take the road through the compound. When the trees get thicker, you're close. The men are going to try and stop you. They'll claim it's not your business. It's up to you if you listen, or if you push through and go to Samurai."

"Thanks, Clarity," I said, finishing my tea and standing. "How much trouble am I about to get into?"

She grinned. "Your ass is going to hurt for a week when he's finished with you, but he's going to be proud as hell at the same time. Trust me. These men are… different. They want to protect us, but they like it when we show we can handle the darker side of their lives."

I followed her instructions and slowed when I saw the men. They blocked the road, hands up, and one of them approached my window. I rolled it down, eyeing his cut. I hadn't met this one yet. *Gator.*

"Need to turn around," he said.

"I'm not leaving. I need to see Samurai."

"You deaf? I said to turn the fuck around."

"Let her through," Stripes said, as he pushed his way through the men. "She wants to see Samurai, then I'll take her to him."

I opened my door and got out, leaving the truck running just in case. Stripes took my arm and led me toward the trees. I could hear the screams even louder now that I was out of the truck. When we stepped into the shadows, I nearly threw up. One of Itachi's men already lay dead, and in multiple pieces. The other was being dismembered while he was still breathing. And Itachi…

"Samurai," I called softly.

He turned to face me, his expression going slack as he came closer. "Grey. Is everything all right?"

"I don't know. I woke up and didn't know where you were or what had happened." I glanced at Itachi. I noticed he was no longer so smug. In fact, he knew death was only seconds away. "Are you doing this for me? For Ryo?"

He nodded. "For my family, yes. I won't let him hurt you again, or anyone else. He's outlived his usefulness on this earth, assuming he was ever good for anything other than causing people pain."

Scratch blocked my view of Itachi. "Samurai,

take your woman home. You've done enough for today. We'll handle it from here. She doesn't need to see or hear this next part."

"I need to know," I said, lifting my chin.

Scratch folded his arms. "Fucker likes to rape women, so he'll get a taste of his own medicine. Not by us, per se."

I blanched and looked around at those gathered. I saw what had to be the largest dildo ever in the hands of one of the men. But it was a woman who caught my eye. She had a split lip, black eye, and limped as she drew closer to Itachi and the man holding the toy.

"Did he rape her?" I asked.

"Yeah, he did," Samurai said softly. "We didn't bring him in fast enough and he hurt her pretty bad. He'd picked her up early yesterday, before he went to the sushi place. Had enough time to do some damage. We've roughed him up, but she's going to get her revenge before he's finished off."

I felt empty. The thought of what they'd done, what they still planned, should have sickened me. Instead, all I could think was how I wished he could experience every bit of pain he'd ever inflicted on his victims. Me. That woman. There had to be countless others. Instead, justice would be served all at once, and probably rather fast.

"Grey?" Samurai placed his hand on my cheek, drawing my attention back to him. "You all right?"

"It's not fair."

"You prefer we let him go?" Scratch asked, his voice hard and laced with disappointment.

"No. You misunderstood. You've made him bleed. She'll make him beg for mercy. And then it will all be over. How many lives has he destroyed? How many women did he violate? He's getting off too easy."

Charming folded his arms and stared at me from behind Scratch. "What did you have in mind?"

"Is there such a thing as a brothel that uses men instead of women as their whores?" I asked, thinking of something I'd read or watched in the last several months. Or tried to at any rate. Even the thought of a man being drugged and abused like that had turned my stomach and I'd had to get up and find something else.

"Yes." Charming grinned. "You want us to send him there?"

"I do, but only after she's had her chance at revenge. She deserves it. Can you guarantee he won't escape or ever come back here?" I asked.

"Consider it done," Scratch said. "Now, go home with your man. Let him get cleaned up and have him tell you about the man you know as Willis. You no longer need to be afraid, Grey. You're safe, and so is your son."

I nodded and went with Samurai away from the sounds of Itachi screaming and begging. I got into the truck and waited on him to mount his motorcycle. He took the lead and I followed him as far as Clarity's. I stopped to pick up Ryo while he continued on, and I hoped he'd have time to clean up before we arrived. I didn't want Ryo to ask why his daddy had blood spatter all over his clothes.

When we got to the house, Ryo and Momo ran to the backyard. Since Phantom hadn't come with us, I hadn't wanted to leave the dog with Clarity, and neither had Ryo. I watched as they played ball out back and waited for Samurai to join me in the kitchen. I brewed a pot of coffee for him and decided we could all use something sweet like French toast.

I'd plated eight slices when I felt his hands slide around my waist and cup my baby bump. "I'm proud of you. Pissed you came out there, but you handled yourself well."

"Clarity said if I went out there you'd likely spank me until I couldn't sit for a week."

"Hmm. Tempting. Maybe after Ryo goes to bed." He reached over and snagged a piece of toast and started eating it.

"Heathen! You didn't even put powdered sugar or syrup on that!"

He grinned and kept eating the piece he'd swiped. He poured himself some coffee and sat at the table. I made a few more slices before taking the platter to the table. I set out the syrup and got some juice for me and Ryo. Except when I called him in, he begged to play a little longer. I set aside two pieces in the oven for him to have later.

"So what did they mean about Willis not being who I think he is?" I asked.

The story he spun, about an assassin working behind the scenes, made me feel like I'd been dropped onto a movie set. It seemed Styx, as he was known, had come to town looking for someone. Instead, he'd found a place being overrun with men like Itachi and had decided to stick around. The woman he'd come to find had been raped, beaten, and left for dead on the side of the road. After he'd discovered Itachi was the culprit, he'd set things in motion.

"It all seems too elaborate," I said. "And confusing."

Samurai sipped his coffee. "I asked why he didn't just handle it himself. He's going to let the town know Itachi's crew is gone for good, except he's not taking any credit. He's spreading rumors about the club forcing Itachi to leave town."

"And they'll believe it?" I asked.

"Maybe. Maybe not. But... I did make sure we had the keys to his car, forced him to sign over the title to me, and I plan to sell it. The money will be used to set up a rape crisis center in town. It won't keep the place running, but it's a start."

Tears blurred my vision. "Really?"

He reached for my hand. "I'm calling it Grey's Place. Anyone who's been raped or threatened with rape will be welcome. Men and women both. In time, maybe it will offer other services. Once it's off the ground, and set up as a non-profit, I'll find someone to run it."

"You're amazing. You know that?" I asked.

"No, I'm just a biker who lucked out on finding an incredible woman. I was lost, Grey. So fucking lost. The darkness took me over more and more every year that passed. It wasn't until you asked me to tell you what I'd been through that I started to heal. We both went through something horrific. You came out the other side stronger than me. I let it fester and spread like a disease as it ate at who I used to be."

"I didn't get that luxury," I said. "I had a baby to think about."

"And that's another thing I'd like to offer. If someone finds themselves pregnant after being raped, and they don't want to terminate the pregnancy but know they don't want the child, we'll make sure it's adopted into a loving home. Hell, maybe Phantom can take the first one."

I leaned forward and kissed him. "Now that's a fabulous idea if ever I heard one."

"It's over, Grey. For now. I can't promise more won't head our way, or that Styx won't demand something else. Tomorrow is never promised."

"I love you, Jin," I said softly.

He audibly swallowed and his gaze held mine. "I love you too, Grey. So fucking much. You're the light to my darkness. You gave me hope when I'd had none. And I will spend the rest of my life showing you how grateful I am, and how much I adore you."

He kissed me until I was breathless, then promised all sorts of naughty things -- after Ryo went to sleep. Sadly, our boy didn't seem to be slowing down even a little. Having Momo at the house had him supercharged.

"Puppy, Jin. We need a puppy." I hoped if he had a dog of his own, one to run with every day, the two would tire each other out.

He nodded. "I'll find him one. In fact, I'll go make some calls now."

While Samurai called someone named Doolittle, I watched Ryo and Momo run around the backyard. Placing a hand over my belly, I marveled at how much my life had changed. Not just mine, but Ryo's too. We were no longer alone. No longer scared. Samurai had given us a home and shown me what love was.

I smoothed my hand over my baby bump. "You're going to be the luckiest baby ever. You'll have a big brother, a dad who loves you, an uncle who will spoil you, and a mom will who do anything to make sure you have a happy life."

Now that I'd found my happily-ever-after, I wanted everyone else to have a reason to smile too.

Epilogue
Samurai -- Two Months Later

It felt like I'd run a marathon and I couldn't stop smiling. I looked at the image on the fridge, excited and terrified over the fact we were having a little girl. I'd put up the ultrasound picture in a spot where we could all see it every day. Ryo didn't seem to care much. He'd huffed and walked off, apparently preferring to have a brother. Grey had asked me to paint the other room a lilac for our daughter, and I'd already done it. I'd also ordered the baby furniture she'd mentioned, even though she didn't know it yet.

Grey insisted I choose our daughter's name. She said it was only fair since she'd gotten to name Ryo, and she'd insisted it be a Japanese name. I'd chosen Emiko and had already painted her name on the nursery door. And since we loved our home and didn't want to make the kids double up in their rooms, we'd decided Emiko would be the final addition to the family. I'd gotten snipped three weeks ago so we wouldn't have any accidents.

What had me the most excited right now was the visitor I expected at any moment. I heard a vehicle pull up outside and waited by the front door. I cracked it open and peeked outside. The man coming up the walkway held a squirming bundle of fur in his arms.

"Ryo, I think there's someone here to see you," I yelled out.

I heard my son racing toward me. I grinned and stepped back, opening the door as I did. He gasped and shrieked before running out onto the porch.

"What on earth?" Grey came to stand beside me, wiping her hands on a kitchen towel. "Is he here already?"

"Yep. Just pulled up."

Doolittle knelt on the porch and introduced himself to Ryo, then he introduced the puppy in his arms. The pup had been abused and left for dead when Doolittle found him. He'd lost a leg and half of one ear had been cut off. It wasn't the cutest thing in the world, but he was a survivor, just like the people in my family. And I had a feeling the pup need Ryo as much as my son needed a dog.

"His name is Nozomu," I said. "Doolittle thinks he's a mix of Great Pyrenees, Husky, and few other things. He had a test run to find out what breeds might be in Nozomu's genetics. He'll likely be huge, and a bit fluffy."

"He's perfect," Grey said, kissing my cheek.

"You're not going to start filling this place with strays, are you?" I asked.

"No. I think one dog and two kids is plenty," she said.

"Good." I curled my arm around her waist as Doolittle came in. Ryo carried Nozomu, struggling with every step. I watched as my boy took the puppy to the backyard, chattering in excitement to the dog in his arms.

"You have no idea how glad I am you took him," Doolittle said. "I know he'll have a good home here, and your son is clearly excited."

"He's been wanting a dog for months," Grey said. "Thanks for driving all this way."

Doolittle waved her off. "No worries. I actually came for another reason too. I brought something."

He took a folded piece of paper from his pocket and handed it to me. The check had five zeroes and I stared at it in surprise. "What the hell?"

"For Grey's Place," Doolittle said. "The club

heard about it and wanted to help."

"It's appreciated," I said, tucking the check into my pocket. "You staying for a little bit? Want anything to eat or drink?"

"I'm here overnight. Charming already found a spot for me to crash. But I won't say no to some coffee."

"I'm on it," Grey said. "You two head to the living room. I'll get the coffee and I'll bring the cookies I made earlier in case you decide you want something sweet."

Doolittle sprawled on the couch and groaned. "It feels good to sit on a nice soft cushion."

"Yeah well, don't get too used it. The place you're staying tonight has the basics, but that couch is nowhere near as comfy as this one."

He laughed. "It's all right. One of the old ladies will be taking care of the menagerie at home, but I'd like to get back as soon as I can. It's a lot for one person, and I have a momma cat ready to deliver any day now. I like being there, even though I'm not really needed for something like that."

"You made my son very happy today. If there's ever anything you need, let me know."

"Thanks." Doolittle ran a hand over his face. "Send me pics of the pup from time to time and we'll call it even. I like keeping up with my rescues once they've been adopted out."

"I'll do you one better. I'll have Ryo send them to you."

"You're not giving our son a phone," Grey yelled out from the kitchen.

Oh, she should have known better. Didn't matter the boy was nearly four. Now she'd issued a challenge I couldn't ignore, and the look in Doolittle's eyes said he knew it too. By end of the week, Ryo would have a phone, and I'd give him Doolittle's number. He'd be sending pictures every day.

"Watch that sass," I called back. "You know what happens when you smart off."

Grey appeared in the doorway, her eyes wide and her cheeks pink. "I can't believe you just said that in front of company."

"You think he's bad, you should be around Demon and Farrah." Doolittle took a cup of coffee from her and sipped at it. I wasn't about to toss the fucker out, but the way Grey was eyeing me made me wish we were alone.

Soon, I mouthed to her, making her cheeks burn even brighter.

I was the luckiest bastard on the planet, and I damn well knew it. Good woman. Great kid. And a little angel on the way.

I'd been all kinds of fucked up until Grey had saved me.

Two battered souls had come together and something incredible had happened.

Whatever it took, I'd make sure she never regretted giving me a chance. I loved her more than my next breath, and hoped she knew it. I told her often enough, but sometimes she needed more than words... and I'd be happy to *show* her how much I loved her as soon as we were alone.

Phantom (Devil's Boneyard MC 10)
Harley Wylde

Charisma -- My mother died when I was a teen. My dad had never been in the picture, and I ended up in the system. When the high school quarterback took advantage, no one believed me. Then I landed in true hell… my foster mom was a monster who preyed on the children in her home. When I aged out of the system, I stayed in the hopes I could save the boys who were assigned to live with her. She let me, as long as I paid in blood. The never-ending cycle of abuse sickened me and wore me down. I felt powerless. Until *he* showed up. Phantom…

Phantom -- My mission was simple. Find the woman preying on young boys and end her. I didn't count on the bewitching young woman, little girl, and two boys living with the monster. Now they're mine. My family. When their demons come searching for them, I'll do whatever it takes to keep them safe. Even call in reinforcements from other clubs. Someone should have warned me I needed to protect myself as well. I never counted on Charisma's dad showing up, nor could I have ever guessed who he was. Things just got complicated.

Prologue
Charisma -- Ten Years Ago

I rubbed a hand over my swollen belly as my babies twisted and kicked at me. They were always the most active at night. Which meant I was always awake when the whimpers started. At first, I'd thought my foster brothers suffered from nightmares. Until the night I'd gotten up to use the bathroom. I peered into Jeff's room and my jaw had dropped.

He wasn't *having* a nightmare. He was living one. The woman who'd offered us a home, who was supposed to be like a mother to us, was doing far more than inappropriately touching the thirteen-year-old. I wondered why he didn't leave when he clearly didn't want her anywhere near him, until I saw she'd tied him to the bed.

A hand went over my mouth as someone tugged me from the door. I struggled until I heard my other foster brother's voice whispering in my ear. "Stop it, Charisma. You can't save him. You can't save either of us."

I turned to look up at him. Chris was taller than me, but so skinny he looked like a walking skeleton. Poor guy had no muscle mass, which meant he wouldn't be able to fight off someone like our foster mom.

"She does that to you too?"

Shame burned in his eyes and his cheeks flushed as he looked away, giving me a brisk nod. "Among other things."

"We need to stop her."

He glowered at me. "You think we haven't tried? There's nothing we can do. She's a pillar in the community. The social worker loves her. There's no one coming to save us, Charisma. We're unwanted, just like you and those babies in your belly. Focus on you and getting the hell out of here while you can."

"What's that supposed to mean?"

He eyed my stomach. "You're having twins. One is a boy. She's not going to let you keep him, Charisma. She wants that baby."

Bile rose in my throat, and I put a protective hand over my belly. Like hell would I let her or anyone else hurt my children. And I wouldn't stand here and let her hurt Jeff and Chris either. There had to be something I could do, no matter what he said. I'd stay until I figured it out, unless I aged out of the system first.

Whatever it took, I'd make Heather like me. Trust me. I'd get her to let me stay even after I turned eighteen, without her touching my babies. I had a little time to figure things out. Until then, I didn't know how I'd listen to these two suffer night after night. I knew no one wanted us, that we'd been forgotten. We were nothing. Nobodies.

I looked up at Chris. "I care. You said no one wants you. Well, I care what happens to you and to Jeff. We'll find a way to stop her."

Chris shook his head. "I'm leaving soon. She pushed an adoption through. Some guy will be picking me up next week."

"Isn't an adoption a good thing?" I asked.

"No." His jaw tensed. "Not this time. I already met with him, and he's made it clear what he expects from me. Things are going to get much worse, and when Jeff gets older, she'll do the same to him. You can't save us. Don't even try."

My heart broke for the both of them. Maybe he was right. I didn't know how to make things better, but

I had to make an attempt. What harm ever came from doing the right thing?

If only I'd realized just how wrong I was...

Chapter One

Phantom

It had been a few months since I'd learned a hard truth. Something I should have suspected, if I'd paid closer attention. Instead, I'd been too caught up with my own life to dig deep into why my cousin seemed to be wired a little different from the rest of the family. Listening to him talk about the abuse he'd suffered, and right under our family's nose, pissed me off to no end. How the hell had the babysitter gotten away with that shit without any of us knowing? Had my aunt and uncle really been that damn clueless?

It explained why Samurai had wanted to come stay here and prospect for my club. He'd been running, and no one had realized it until a tiny woman had noticed he was hurting. She'd seen something in him, a wounded creature she'd recognized every time she looked in the mirror and had been able to do something no one else had. She'd saved him.

I'd given myself a little time, let the news settle. Or more like roll around inside my brain and make my stomach burn every time I pictured that young woman hurting my cousin. Just because he'd gotten off didn't make it right. She'd given him no choice in the matter. No wonder he'd always wanted to hold women down to fuck them. It had been the only control he'd ever had when it came to females.

Samurai had settled into his new life as a dad and husband. While he'd managed to put the past behind him, Heather still needed to pay for her crimes. I'd sleep better at night knowing she wasn't out there somewhere, possibly still hurting boys. And I had a feeling it would lift a weight from Samurai's shoulders as well.

I eyed the paper in my hand before looking up at Shade. "This everything?"

"More or less."

"What's the less?" I asked.

"Heather Grant, on paper, looks like a model citizen. She's a foster parent, thanks mostly to her late husband's money, but she has some questionable cashflow. I haven't been able to trace it yet. Wire and Lavender offered to help if I can't break through soon."

"What else?"

He ran a hand over his freshly shaved jaw. "She only takes in boys, as a general rule. Until a decade ago. She took in a seventeen-year-old girl. After the girl aged out, she remained in Heather's home. But there's more. She was pregnant when she got there. Twins. One baby, a boy, was stillborn. Cord wrapped around his neck according to hospital records. I looked into the mom. Charisma Marsh. All her medical records indicate it was a healthy pregnancy, despite how she got that way. Girl claimed she was raped by the quarterback at her school. No one listened, and they brushed her aside."

"You look into it?" I asked.

"I did. From what I can tell, the school and the boy's parents did their best to make the problem go away. Official word in the files claims Charisma agreed to sex and felt guilty after so decided to yell rape. I call bullshit. The guy looks like a fucking douchebag. He went on to college, played ball there, and now he owns a car lot in town."

"Seems like my trip may need to be extended a bit. The girl's other baby was all right?"

Shade nodded. "Healthy little girl. Named her Nova Marsh. Kid is nine and seems healthy. I'm keeping tabs to make sure they make it away from

Heather Grant in one piece. I've got a friend out that way. He owes me a favor. One call and he'll get the two of them the hell out of there. I have a feeling the woman has some sort of hold over them."

"Heather have any other kids in her home?" I dreaded his answer, especially when I saw the flash of pain in his eyes. It told me plenty.

"Two boys. One is twelve and the other is his fifteen-year-old big brother. Phantom, we need to get those kids out. Now. I'm not sure how much longer they can hold on, or if the oldest will make it out at all."

"Explain." I tossed the papers aside.

"Looks like Heather keeps the boys until they're sixteen or seventeen. Once they start getting too big for her to handle, they magically get adopted. A few were placed into homes sooner. If they're too young when she gets them, she doesn't keep them more than a few months. Do I really need to tell you what happens to them afterward?"

"No. I get the picture. Can't save the previous kids, but we can do something for those boys. Get the girl and her daughter out. Call your friend now. I'm leaving immediately to handle Heather Grant. While I'm there, send me the info on the damn football player too. Fucker needs to know he has to pay for his crimes. Mommy and Daddy might have saved him, but he's a grown-ass man now. Time to own up to what he did."

"On it," Shade said, reaching for his phone. "I'll ask him to move them out of the area completely. He can help her disappear. I'll do whatever it takes to make sure she and her daughter have a fresh start. I don't think Heather has any interest in the little girl, but like I said, something isn't right with that situation."

Unless Charisma was in on it. Could be that Heather groomed her to follow in her sick footsteps. I'd find out when I checked into things in person. Until then, I'd assume she needed to be rescued. Her and the little girl.

"I'll text Charming on my way out. But not until I'm gone. I don't want him trying to talk me out of this. My shit is already packed and ready to go."

"Taking your bike or that flashy new Jeep you bought last week?"

I ignored his tone. Yeah, I'd splurged on a new Rubicon. I'd always wanted a family. Thought I might have one when Samurai didn't man up and claim Grey right off. Wouldn't have worked between us anyway. Girl had eyes only for my cousin from the beginning. I'd have to find my own woman. Too bad all the ones I seemed to like didn't want kids or came with too much fucking baggage.

"Probably the Jeep. If I need to move those boys, I'll do it. Can't carry much on the bike. Besides, I have some special tools set aside for this poisonous bitch. Watch Momo for me?"

Shade stood nodded before he pressed his screen, connecting his call to whoever was pulling the girl out. I went home, grabbed my bag, and hit the road before anyone could stop me. Only time I pulled over was to send two messages. One to Charming, and one to Samurai.

Pres, I have some personal business to handle. I'll be gone a few days and explain when I get back.

After I hit send, I pulled up Samurai's name in my phone.

I failed you when you were a kid. The entire family did. I'm making amends now. I'll be home when it's done.

I shut off my phone, not wanting any of them

calling, texting, or trying to track me. Although, Shade more than likely had chipped my damn Jeep already. I knew all our bikes had trackers on them. Too much shit not only in our past but with other clubs as well had taught us we could never be too cautious.

I sped down the highway, heading back to the town I'd called home for a while. Hard to believe that woman had never left the area. Not far anyway. She'd moved to an affluent suburb and her mailing address had a different town listed, but it was just a down the road from where Samurai had grown up.

By the time I hit the town limits, the sky had started to turn pink with the first rays of morning light. My eyes burned and I felt like roadkill. Pulling off, I found a motel where no one would ask questions. I didn't need anyone remembering who I was, or what I'd been driving. People here would mind their own damn business, just as I intended to do.

I turned on my phone, ignoring the missed calls and texts from Charming and Samurai, and sending a text to Shade.

Find me a location where no one will hear her scream, or they won't care.

I didn't know how long he'd take so I checked into a room, stretched out on top of the bed, my 9mm clutched in my hand in case any assholes decided to fuck with me, and I closed my eyes. Even though I didn't sleep hard, or for very long, I felt better after I woke up.

Shade had sent an address and I decided to check it out before tracking down Heather. Best to get the place set up ahead of time. I found the old barn easily enough. It set back off the road quite a ways, on a lot boasting a for sale sign and stating the property contained over one hundred acres. The last house I'd passed had been far enough down the road I didn't worry about anyone getting nosy. I parked the Jeep a bit farther down, pulling down a lane flanked by trees.

It wasn't a difficult walk to the barn, and I knew I wouldn't have an issue even carrying the bitch. The door creaked when I pulled it open, and I scanned the interior. Some bats rustled in the rafters, and I heard mice or rats scurrying in the abandoned stalls. Discarded furniture took up one corner. I dug through it until I found a wooden chair. It seemed solid enough, if a bit grimy. Dirt didn't matter. It would be soaked in blood by the time I'd finished.

My phone showed no reception, which probably explained why the place hadn't been snapped up by a developer. According to the records Shade found, the place had been vacant for three years. Somewhere, down another road, was a farmhouse that went with all the acreage. The amount of land would have given some construction company a lot of room for a new subdivision, or a shopping center. Unless they added a cell tower to the area, I didn't see anyone wanting the land unless they'd decided to take up farming. I went back to my Jeep and retrieved a few items, wanting to set up the area as best I could. I even stashed my tools in one of the stalls under a pile of straw. I'd need to clean the bag later, but I didn't want to try hauling it to the barn when I brought Heather here.

I drove back into the heart of town, stopping for a bite to eat, before I decided to stake out Heather's place. The park within view of her house gave me the perfect spot to watch and wait. Eating my food, I didn't look completely out of place. Just someone taking a lunch break and enjoying the atmosphere.

A Lexus pulled into her driveway and I saw the bitch get out of the car. Two boys slid out, then a slim form with subtle curves. Charisma. She lifted her face to the sun and my heart stuttered in my chest. Christ! I swallowed my food and nearly choked on the large bite. Shade had mentioned she'd been with Heather for a decade, which made her around twenty-seven now. Roughly half my age, but fuck if she wasn't stunning. She reached into the car and helped out a little girl I knew had to be her daughter, Nova.

And that's the moment I knew I'd do whatever it took to keep those four safe. Charisma, Nova, and the two boys would never be hurt again. The way she cradled her daughter against her side, the protective stance she took between Heather and those boys, told me one thing -- the girl wasn't hurting anyone. Unless it was Heather. She had murder in her eyes when she stared at the woman. Crazy bitch only smirked back at her.

I texted Shade.

Change of plans. I'm bringing them all home with me.

Those boys reminded me of Samurai when he'd been a teen. Small and wiry. And they were both at least half-Asian. It seemed Heather had a type.

I watched them go into the house with the She-Devil and shut the door. After I finished my food, I pulled out of the parking lot and moved over to her home, stopping my Jeep right behind her fancy car. Reaching into the back seat, I picked up my cut, as well as the brass knuckles I'd hidden underneath it. I slid the weapon into my pocket and got out of the vehicle. Pulling on my cut, I shut the door, locked the car, and went up to ring the bell.

Charisma opened the door, her eyes going wide when she saw me. She skimmed over my cut, her gaze locking on the patches denoting my club, name, and rank. She finished her perusal before lifting her gaze to mine again. I caught movement in my peripheral. Judging the size and shape, it was her daughter.

I pulled my keys from my pocket and tipped my head toward the driveway. "Take your daughter and get in the Jeep. Lock the doors and wait for me."

Her eyebrows went up. She stared, not moving and not speaking. She reached up to tuck her hair behind her ear and I growled at what I saw. Someone had damaged her with what looked like acid. I moved slowly, not wanting to startle her, and checked the other side. *Son of a bitch.* Whoever had hurt her, had harmed both ears. Which meant... I mouthed the words slowly. "Can you hear me?"

Her eyes widened and she shook her head.

"What else did that bitch do to you?" I asked, mouthing the words slowly again.

Her cheeks flushed and she dropped her gaze. Shame. Whatever had been done to her, she was ashamed to tell me. I had a feeling I understood why she was still here with Heather. The woman used the boys against her, and probably used her against them. If she'd touched Nova, I'd make her suffer longer.

I tipped her chin up. "Take my keys. Get your daughter and wait in the Jeep. Lock the doors. Do you understand?"

She nodded and reached behind her. I saw Nova's small fingers wrap around hers and Charisma took my keys. She hesitated, her gaze searching mine.

"I'll get the boys out too."

Her posture relaxed and she hurried to the Jeep with Nova in tow. Nothing in the reports Shade had found from social services mentioned Charisma being unable to hear. It had to have happened either right before she aged out, or after. For whatever reason, he couldn't find any updates from the social workers the months leading up to her turning eighteen. Her exit had been little more than a few notes including how wonderful Heather had been to let her stay. I didn't like being blindsided, but at least she would be safe now. All of them would be.

I felt a hand on my shoulder and jolted, having been lost to my thoughts for a moment. A man stepped up next to me, a smirk on his lips.

"Shade sent me. Looks like he was right. You need help if you're spacing out before going into the lion's den. Name's Axel."

"Phantom," I said, shaking his hand. "I need to get the two boys out, and I have a location for Heather Grant to pay for her crimes. Hadn't intended to take everyone with me, though."

"Shade sent me the coordinates for where you're taking Heather. I'll get her there. You can follow with your new family. I'll watch over them while you take care of the evil cunt. But just saying, feel free to tag me in anytime."

I gave a nod. "Let's go."

I entered the house and listened for any sounds that might tell me where the boys and Heather were located. I crept inside, with Axel shutting the door behind us. We made our way through the main areas. As I entered the hall, I saw the older boy huddled on the floor, leaned back against the wall. The devastation on his face nearly ripped me apart.

I knelt, moving slow, and gained his attention. He tensed, but I lifted a finger to my lips and whispered to him. "Charisma and Nova are outside. Go wait with them."

He shook his head frantically and glanced at the closed bedroom door. The sounds inside left little to the imagination as to what was going on. I knew he didn't want to abandon his little brother.

"I'll get him out," I whispered. "And then Heather Grant will pay for what she's done."

A spark of hope lit his eyes and he glanced at Axel over my shoulder. He stood and strode down the hall, pausing only a moment to gaze at the bedroom door again, before hurrying to the front of the house. I straightened and approached the door with Axel nearly on top of me. I felt the tension rolling off him and knew he wanted in that room as badly as I did.

"She could have a weapon in here," he said, his voice low and rough.

"I think her only weapon is herself. Ready? We do this quick and quiet."

He gave a nod and opened the door silently. The sight before me nearly made me throw up. Axel rushed the bed, yanking Heather off the boy tied down. He clocked her in the temple, knocking her out cold with one blow. I untied the boy, helped him dress, and got him the fuck out of the house.

As much as I wanted them to have extra clothes, or anything they may have kept from their life before, I didn't want to linger longer than necessary. Doing this in broad daylight had risks.

Axel had disappeared with Heather. Charisma sat in the front passenger seat of my Jeep with Nova and the other boy in back. I heard the unlocks disengage and helped the smaller boy into the back before climbing behind the wheel. I started up the Jeep and backed out of the driveway. Making sure I went the speed limit and obeyed every traffic law, I did my best to not draw undue attention to us.

"My name is Phantom," I told the kids in back. "The four of you are safe now. Heather Grant will never hurt you again, and neither will her friends."

"You can't promise that," the older boy said.

"I can, and I just did. I'm part of a motorcycle club called the Devil's Boneyard. We're based in the Florida panhandle, and I'm taking you back there with me. We can figure things out from there."

"You said she wouldn't hurt us again, but the social worker gave us to her," the older boy said. "They'll just send us back."

"They won't. I have a friend who is going to give you new identities. Charisma and Nova are safe without the extra precautions. She's an adult and has custody of her daughter." I glanced at the boys in the rearview mirror. "Any idea what you want your names to be?"

"Your name is really Phantom?" the youngest asked.

I smiled. "No. My road name is Phantom. It's what I go by now, and the only name anyone ever uses. My birth name is Kenji. Just don't say it around anyone else. It's considered disrespectful to address me by any name other than the one I earned."

"Kenji," the youngest repeated softly. "Our mother was Chinese, but our father was white. She let him name us and he chose American names. If we get to pick, I want a Chinese name."

"You can name yourselves whatever you want." I paused. "But if I could make a few suggestions for you to consider? The two of you are strong. You're brave. Survivors. Li means powerful. Hu is tiger. Heng means persevering. Jian is strong. But there are countless names you could choose. And before you ask why a Japanese man knows so much about Chinese names, two of my best friends when I was a kid were Chinese. We taught each other a lot about our names and cultures."

"We don't feel brave or strong," the older boy said. "We couldn't stop her."

I glanced at Charisma. "She used you against each other, didn't she? You, your brother, Charisma, and Nova."

The boys nodded.

"Charisma's ears…"

"Heather did that when Charisma tried to protect us. We refused to let her hurt us anymore, and she proved us wrong. Every time Charisma tried to intervene, she was punished. She should have taken Nova and left. She refused to leave us behind. Heather would let the men pay to hurt Charisma. It bought us a night off from her attentions, or anyone else's."

I pulled down the rural road behind Axel and put the Jeep in park. Turning to face them, I knew I couldn't hide the truth from any of them. They needed to know I would do whatever it took to keep them safe.

"You're going to wait in the Jeep. All four of you."

"Where are you going?" the oldest boy asked.

"I'm going to take care of Heather. She'll never hurt anyone ever again. Do you understand?"

The older boy's eyes went hard, and he nodded. "She's going to die."

"Yes." I scanned their faces. They weren't disgusted or fearful. If anything, they seemed relieved. "When I get back, we'll go home. I want to put some distance between us and this town. If you want to stop along the way and get a motel room overnight, that's fine. Or we can push through."

"Home," the youngest said. "We haven't had one since our parents died."

"It's not really home," the older one said. "It's just a stopping place."

I turned to face him. "It can be your home if you want it to be. There's only one thing I ever wanted. Something I still don't have."

"What's that?" the youngest asked.

"A family." I looked at each of them, then Nova. "I'll talk to Charisma after I handle Heather. But whether she decides to stay or not, I would be honored to call the two of you my sons."

I faced Charisma and touched her hand, drawing her attention. "Stay here. I'll be back soon. You're safe."

She blinked and didn't respond. I hoped the two boys would make sure she understood, and I got out. Axel had already carted Heather into the barn and when I entered, he'd tied her to the chair. I retrieved my bag from the stall where I'd stashed it earlier and got to work.

Chapter Two

Charisma

I didn't know what to make of the man who'd gotten us away from Heather. I'd noticed his cut. While I'd never been around bikers on a regular basis, I knew about them. There were two clubs near my hometown and the bikers often frequented the burger place that had the best milkshakes. They weren't all bad guys, but not all were good either.

Much like the man who'd been my birth father. I'd never met him. When he'd found out my mother was pregnant, he'd bolted. She'd left him off my birth certificate and listed my father as unknown. I'd only been told his road name. *Drifter*. I didn't know what club he'd been part of, or where he was now. No one had tried to find him when my mother had died, and I'd gone into the system. I'd likely never meet him.

It hadn't stopped me from trying, though. I'd been about five when I'd seen a few bikers at the burger place. I'd walked up to one of them, tugged on his leather vest, and asked if he was my daddy. The man had looked amused and lifted me onto the seat next to him.

"Why do you think I'm your daddy?" he'd asked.

"Because Mommy said he's a biker. His name is Drifter. Is that your name?"

He'd taken the time to explain what a cut was, what the different patches meant, and had talked to me until my mother had found us. She'd apologized to the man profusely before making me leave my new friend.

But this biker… When I looked into his eyes, I'd known Phantom wasn't evil. He didn't seem like the type who would abandon a woman he'd gotten pregnant. He'd handed over his keys, not knowing if

I'd steal his Jeep, and gotten me and Nova to safety. Then he'd gone inside after the boys. I'd missed everything he'd said during the drive and after we'd parked, which meant I needed to get caught up.

My foster brothers and I had learned how to sign so we could communicate, after Heather had made sure I'd never hear again. I quickly signed to them. *What did he say? Where are we going? Why are we here?*

The older of the two, Joey, smiled and signed back. I saw his lips moving and knew he spoke aloud too. "He said we can stay with him. All of us, but he wanted to talk to you about it. As to where we are... he's taking care of Heather. Permanently."

My brow furrowed. *I don't understand*, I signed.

"He's going to kill her, Charisma. Make sure she never touches anyone ever again. Then we're leaving town. He's offered to help us with new identities so no one will come after us."

I looked off in the direction Phantom had gone. Getting out of the car, I followed after him. A barn came into view, and I opened the door. Peering inside, I saw Heather tied to a chair and Phantom standing off to the side. Blood dripped onto the floor from the tip of the blade in his hand. I eyed Heather again and saw he'd cut her multiple times. Inching inside, I moved closer. Phantom saw me and froze.

I didn't know how to talk to him. If he'd known sign language, he'd have used it earlier. My fingers twisted together as I tried to figure out what to do. I glanced at Heather again. Gone was her smirk and knowing gaze. She'd accepted her fate, and any fight had been drained from her. I looked up at Phantom as he stopped within inches of me.

"You should be in the Jeep," he said, mouthing the words slow enough I could follow. I shook my head, making him scowl. "Charisma, let me handle this. I'm keeping you, Nova, and those boys safe. You don't need to be here to see it done."

I tipped my head to the side and placed my hand over his heart, patting his firm chest. My cheeks flushed. He covered my hand with his and I couldn't stop myself from getting even closer to him. It felt like a magnetic force tugged us together.

"Wait in the car, honey. I'll be done here shortly, and we'll go home. I don't want you to see this side of me."

I leaned into him, trying to tell him without words I accepted this part of his life. He wanted to protect us. I didn't care how he did it. If that meant Heather died, it was no less than she deserved. She'd ruined countless lives, and no one had ever tried to stop her. Except those of us she'd tortured. And none of us had been strong enough to take her down. But Phantom could.

The other man who'd gone into the house with Phantom came over. I tried to read his lips and only caught a few words. *Kids. Home. Let me. Should go.*

Phantom watched me and gave the man a nod. He stepped away from me, wiping off his blade on some straw before he put his things away and lifted the bag off the ground. He came toward me, holding out his hand. I placed mine in his and let him lead me from the barn.

When we reached the Jeep, Phantom put his bag into the back. I got into the vehicle and buckled my seat belt. He backed down the rural road and pulled onto the highway. He fiddled with the radio, and I felt the vibration of the music against my leg. Looking down I saw a speaker in the door. Hours passed before he stopped for gas. Everyone used the bathroom and he got back on the road, stopping again when he saw a diner.

Nova and the boys took a seat across from us in the large booth, and I slid in with Phantom taking the outside seat. A woman came over and left menus on the table, along with rolls of silverware. She said something to Phantom but spoke too fast for me to follow. He turned to me and mouthed the words, *what do you want to drink*?

I looked at the menu and pointed to the type of soda I wanted. He placed my order and his, then the kids ordered their drinks. The woman left and I perused the menu to figure out what I wanted to eat. I did the same thing when I had to order. Pointed at what I wanted and let Phantom handle it.

He pulled his phone from his pocket and unlocked it, setting it on the table. He tapped it and pointed it at me. I picked it up and noticed he'd opened a Notes app. Smiling, I typed a message to him.

Thank you. For everything.

"You're welcome." He smiled and lightly touched my cheek.

I typed on the app again. *How did you know we needed help?*

Pain entered his eyes. "My cousin. He was one of Heather's victims over a decade ago. I just found out."

And you tracked her down to exact revenge?

He nodded. "Yes, but I had a friend see if she still had a tendency to hurt kids. He told me about you, your babies, and those boys."

I pressed a hand to my belly, feeling a pang at the son I'd lost. I didn't know what had happened to him. I'd been told about his death, and Heather had said she'd handle it. If he'd been buried, I'd never been to his grave. Had he been cremated? Maybe she'd told them to throw him out with the trash. I would probably never know, and it hurt.

Phantom touched my cheek, drawing my attention to him. The understanding in his eyes made tears well in my eyes. He knew. He'd said babies, not baby. He'd known about my son, that he'd died. He curled his arm around me, and I snuggled into him, letting him comfort me. I couldn't remember the last time someone had touched me like this. Probably the last time I'd been with my mom. No one had cared since then.

I felt the rumble of his voice and knew he was speaking to Nova and the boys. I needed to be strong. To stand up for myself and the kids. I wouldn't let them go back into the system. It had failed them multiple times already, just as it had done with me.

He squeezed me and I lifted my gaze to his. He nodded to the phone, and I realized he'd written a message for me while he'd been talking to the kids. Picking it up, I read it, and my heart rate quickened.

I know about the boy who got you pregnant. Who raped you. He'll be dealt with. I'd wanted to do it myself, but getting you and the kids to safety is more important. Axel has offered to take care of it. Your monsters will be slain, and you'll have a fresh start. A new beginning.

I smiled and leaned up to kiss his cheek. My feelings were overwhelming. I'd gone from fighting the evil in our lives all by myself to having a knight swoop in to save me. As much as I didn't want to be a damsel in distress, I had to admit I couldn't have gotten away on my own, not and taken the boys with me. He'd done the impossible, and I would owe him forever. We all would. The boys had mentioned living with Phantom. Would he let me and Nova stay too?

Oh. Oh! What if he had a wife or girlfriend? I drew away from him a little. The woman in his life probably wouldn't want a twenty-seven-year-old woman and her daughter moving in. My chest ached at the thought of having to leave the boys behind. I didn't know how Nova would handle it either. She considered them her brothers. Which would make me their mom and not their sister. I'd protected them as best I could, and I'd gladly take them with us whenever Nova and I found a place to settle down and start our lives. But it seemed they wanted to stay with Phantom.

I couldn't blame them. I did too.

Nova and the boys talked non-stop. I struggled to keep up with them and gave up after a moment. With all of them talking, I didn't know where to look first. Joey seemed to understand and started to sign as he spoke. It helped a little, but it was still too much for me. I waved him off and tucked into my food when it arrived.

By the time we were ready to leave, my stomach was in knots. I didn't know what the future held for us. We'd be safe from Heather, but I didn't know the first thing about surviving on my own. No one in town had wanted to hire the deaf girl. I'd never had a job. Didn't know how to pay bills, or even find a place to live. I'd done the shopping for the house, with Heather's money. I couldn't leave. If I had, no one would have tried to protect the boys. I hadn't done a good job of it, but there were times I'd managed to distract Heather.

I reached up and touched one of my ears. I didn't regret my decision that night. It might not have saved them for long, but any reprieve had been better than none. Yes, it had cost me dearly, but I'd gained a lot too. That was the night the boys and I had become family. Unfortunately, Heather had realized I would go to any lengths to protect them, and she'd used it against me. Thankfully none of her friends had enjoyed girls, so I'd been spared that fate. It hadn't stopped them from doing other things.

Maybe my disfigured ears were a blessing. I didn't know any man who'd want an ugly wife. If my ears scared him away, then I didn't have to worry about him seeing the rest of me. The Jeep ate up the miles as Phantom put more distance between us and the town I'd called home for so long. When he stopped again, it was to pull into the parking lot of a hotel.

He shut off the engine and turned to the boys, saying something, before facing me. He made sure he had my attention before he spoke. "Follow my lead when we go inside. Don't freak out by anything I say."

I tipped my head wanting to ask what he meant, but Phantom was already getting out of the vehicle. The boys and Nova got out too, so I followed them. We went into the lobby, and I looked around, noticing the nice furniture and how clean everything appeared. He hadn't stopped at just any hotel. He'd picked one that would be comfortable for all of us.

Phantom spoke to the woman at the front desk, and I glanced at Joey, noticing he'd started to sign. *He asked for a room for his wife and kids.*

My heart nearly stopped. Was someone meeting us here? Panic started to flood my system and I wanted to bolt. Joey reached over and grabbed my hand, giving it a shake to get my attention again. *He means all of us. He called you his wife.*

Everything went still. Wife? Phantom had told them we were married? And these were our children? Longing filled me, for a life I knew I'd never have. My throat grew tight, and I fought to stay in control of my emotions. The woman gave Phantom two keycards, and he led the way to the elevators. We went upstairs and stopped in front of a room.

Phantom opened the door and motioned for all of us to step inside.

If we were all going into this room, why was there a second keycard?

* * *

Phantom

I faced the little group, making sure Charisma would be able to watch my lips and not miss anything I had to say. Claiming this was my family had been a gamble. Thankfully, none of the kids had said anything, and they'd not looked surprised. If anything, little Nova and the youngest boy had seemed excited.

"I checked us in as a family." I watched Charisma. "I told them you're my wife and kids."

"You don't seem old enough to have three kids," the oldest boy said.

I smiled. "I'm older than you think. I could be Charisma's dad and your grandpa. Guess I could have gone that route instead."

Little Nova's eyes went wide, and she looked at her mom before coming closer. She wrapped her arms around my waist, and I hugged her to me.

"I like you being my dad better," she said. "Then Mom wouldn't be alone. And then I'd have brothers for real."

"We are your brothers," the oldest boy said. "We've also decided we do want new names. We want you to pick them. Dad."

I hugged Nova even tighter as my emotions got the better of me. The only thing I'd ever wanted and been unable to have was a family. Until now. The boys clearly wanted to stay with me. I just hoped I could convince Charisma and Nova to stick around too. I didn't like the idea of the two of them leaving.

"Do you still want Chinese names?" I asked the boys. They both nodded. I pointed to the oldest first. "Your name is Li. Since you'll be my son, your full name is Li Nakamura."

The youngest stood a little straighter. "And me?"

"Jian Nakamura."

I saw tears shimmering in Charisma's eyes and I stepped a little closer to her, taking Nova with me. I reached up and cupped Charisma's cheek. Her lips trembled and she pressed them together, clearly trying to put on a brave face. I could tell the boys meant the world to her. Did she really think I'd ever try to separate her from them?

"My friend is a hacker. The one who found out about you and the boys. He can do all sorts of things, including making those two officially mine. But he can do more than that. He can make you and Nova mine too." I leaned in even more. "My wife and my daughter."

Her breath caught and a distressed sound escaped her as she stumbled back from me. I backed off, having clearly misread everything. I tugged Nova loose and sent her to her mother. It seemed I'd get half my wish. I'd get two sons, but the woman and daughter would never be mine. They'd leave, and I'd have to let them.

I rubbed my hands up and down my thighs. "Right. Well, all of you need some essentials. Li, write down everyone's sizes for me. I'll run to pick up some things at a nearby store and when I come back, we can figure out dinner. I'm sure you'd all like a shower and something clean to wear."

Li found a pad and pen next to the phone. He wrote down the information for the two of them, then asked Nova about things for her and Charisma. When I had the list, I paused at the door, looking back at the four of them. Everything I wanted was in this room. It just wasn't the right time for me to have it. Maybe I never would.

I left them and went down to the Jeep. Using my phone, I found the nearest big box store and drove straight there. I picked out four outfits for each of them as well as pajamas and grabbed a pair of pajama pants for myself since I hadn't packed any. I picked up undergarments for the four of them, trying not to think too hard about the bras I selected for Charisma. It was damn hard not to imagine her wearing them, and me getting to take them off her.

Heading to the bath and beauty section, I got combs for the boys, and brushes for Charisma and Nova. I tossed in a package of hair ties in case they wanted to pull their hair back, then found deodorant for each of them. Did nine-year-olds wear it? I wasn't sure, but I found some in the women's section that was all natural. I figured it wouldn't hurt Nova to have it. Toothbrushes and toothpaste were added to the cart. Then I realized I'd forgotten socks for all of them.

The shoes they had on would do until we got home. I'd take them shopping for more things once I knew we were safe. I perused a few other sections, grabbing puzzle books and pencils for the kids. I didn't know if Charisma liked to read, but I decided to take a chance. I grabbed two romances and a mystery. It would give them something to do until we reached the house. I could have kept driving. If it had just been me, I would have. Didn't matter I hadn't slept much since I'd first started this trip. Charisma and the kids were what was important.

My phone buzzed in my pocket, and I smiled when I saw Shade's text. *Your dog is insane!* He'd included a picture of Momo, who had somehow gotten the paper towels off the counter and proceeded to not only spread them all over the house, but also shred them. Better those than the furniture. I knew she was pissed I'd left without her.

I sent a quick response. *She's mad I left. Give her an extra treat. The good ones are in the cabinet over the fridge.*

He sent back a thumbs-up emoji and I checked out, then loaded the car. The sooner I gave all this to the kids and Charisma the better. I could only imagine how hard it had been to leave without more than the clothes on their backs. I doubted they had much, since Heather didn't seem to the type to give them toys, game systems, or even decent clothes. Although she might have just for the sake of keeping up appearances. No matter. They'd have what they needed, and what they wanted. I'd make sure of it.

I got back to the hotel and went straight up to the room. I hadn't had a chance to show them the connecting door or let them know I'd gotten us both rooms for the night. I'd hoped Charisma and I could share one and let the kids have the other. Didn't seem like that would happen. I could bunk with the boys. The honorable thing would be to let Nova and Charisma have the room with the queen bed. Except I really wanted to hold her while she slept. She'd had such a hard life, and I wanted to shelter her. Protect her. I knew I couldn't guarantee she'd never experience anything bad ever again, but I wanted to make that promise. She felt like… mine.

Knocking on the door, I waited and smiled when Li cautiously opened it. "I'm back with some things for the four of you."

I stepped into the room and set the bags down. It didn't take but a few minutes to divide everything. I left the bras and panties for Charisma in the bag, not pulling them out in front of the boys. I didn't know how she'd feel about them seeing the garments. I opened the connecting door and showed them the other room.

"You rented both sides?" Li asked.

I nodded. "I did. We can figure out who sleeps where later, but I guess it would be best for the three of us to take one side and let Nova and Charisma take the other."

The three kids shared a look before turning to face Charisma. She blinked at them and lifted her gaze to mine, her cheeks flushing. What the hell had gone on while I'd been out shopping?

"We're going to take Nova with us to the other room," Jian said. "We'll watch some TV while you and…"

"The two of you should talk," Li said.

Nova came back over to me, taking my hand. I knelt down to her level and gave her a smile. "What is it, beautiful?"

"You need to tell Mom why you wanted to make her your wife and me your daughter." She moved in closer and ducked her head, most likely so her mother couldn't read her lips. "She thinks she's ugly and no one will ever want her. You need to tell her she's pretty."

My lips twitched. Pretty? I kissed Nova on the forehead and sent her from the room. Charisma was far from just pretty. She'd damn near stolen the breath from my lungs when I'd first seen her. I'd wanted her to be mine without having even spoken to her. Sure, it had been a physical reaction, until I'd realized she'd gotten hurt protecting those boys. She was brave. Selfless. An incredible woman I knew I didn't deserve. She should have someone who could give her the world. Not a dirty biker with blood on his hands.

The kids shut the door, leaving me alone with Charisma. I walked over to the table and pulled out one of the chairs, motioning for her to have a seat, before I took the other. Facing her, I knew I'd need to speak slow enough for her to follow, and I also set my phone on the table with the Notes app open so she could talk to me.

"Earlier, it upset you when I mentioned having Shade work a bit of magic to make you my wife and Nova my daughter." She pressed her lips together and looked away. I reached out and gently turned her back to me. "If you don't want to be my wife, it's all right. I'm a lot older than you. Not to mention we're strangers."

She stared and didn't even attempt to reach for the phone. I'd hoped she'd give me something. A confirmation she just didn't want to be mine, or an agreement we needed to know one another better. Something. Anything.

"I saw you get out of Heather's car, when you pulled into the driveaway. It felt like my heart stopped a moment. I'd never seen anyone so... mesmerizing. I watched as you got Nova out of the back seat, then put yourself between the boys and Heather. The fierce way you protected them spoke to me. It also made me wonder who protected *you*."

She blinked and her lips parted before she sank her teeth into the bottom one. Slowly, she reached for the phone. *You protect me. No one has ever cared before.*

I read her message and pressed my forehead to

hers before drawing back again. "I've wanted a family for as long as I can remember. A woman to call my own, sons and daughters. My parents weren't the loving sort. They *loved* me, but they never showed affection. I vowed I'd never be like that. Japanese men in general tend to be a bit more stoic. They hold their emotions close. I never want my family to doubt how I feel about them. I'll tell them, and show them, every day."

She fidgeted with the phone a moment before she typed another message. *Are we convenient? Would any woman and children do?*

I should have anticipated her question. I couldn't blame her for asking. It wasn't like we'd had much quality time together. I couldn't talk to her in the car, since she couldn't hear me. This was my chance to have a real conversation with her. And I didn't want to waste it. I had a feeling whatever I said now would help her decide what happened between us.

"You have every right to ask me that. If our roles were reversed, I'd wonder the same thing." I sighed. "You're not a convenience, Charisma. None of you are. You're a gift. The beautiful, courageous woman who sacrificed her hearing to give two boys a night of peace. The young girl who's survived in hell and is still sweet and wants her mom to be happy. Li and Jian are damaged but not broken. They're strong and with time and love, they'll get through the nightmares and become considerate, protective men. I can already see it inside them."

No one has ever wanted me. Not since my mother died. I've never even met my father. He found out she was pregnant and left. He didn't want me. I looked down at her message and my heart ached for her. To have her dad walk off and never look back? I couldn't imagine the pain she must have felt, growing up feeling as if she weren't good enough because the man who should have protected her couldn't be bothered.

"Do you know his name?" I asked.

He was a biker, like you. I only know his road name. He's not on my birth certificate.

His road name. That wouldn't really narrow things down. I knew I wasn't the only Phantom riding the roads, just like there was more than one Scratch, more than one Dingo, and so on. Unless...

"Do you know what club he rides with?" I asked.

She shook her head. *My mom never said, if she even knew.*

"I don't know if there's a way for Shade to track him down or not. Would you want him to try?"

She hesitated a moment then shook her head. *He didn't want me then. He won't want me now. I'm damaged.*

"Hey." I curled my hand around the back of her neck. "You are *not* damaged. You're a survivor! Your scars are badges of courage. They show you fought back. You didn't just lie down and take it. Anyone who doesn't see that, who can't see *you*, isn't worth your time."

She reached up to cup my cheek, her eyes going soft. She parted her lips like she wanted to speak only to realize she couldn't. Using the phone again, she told me exactly what she was feeling, and it about tore out my soul.

I'm scared, Phantom. Terrified I won't be able to care for my daughter. That I'll fail those boys. But the worst fear of all is that I'll agree to be yours and one day you'll realize you could do better. You'll wake up, wonder why you ever agreed to keep me and Nova, and you'll regret being with us. Because you're our hero, Phantom. I don't think it would take much for us to fall in love with you. I'm not sure I could handle a broken heart, or watching my daughter be destroyed by a man she'd come to think of as her father.

I took the phone and set it down before pulling her into my arms. I ran my hand down her back as I held her close. How could anyone not love Charisma? I didn't understand how she hadn't been adopted, or how her foster families could have ever hurt her. Even if they hadn't laid a hand on her, when she'd been raped by that little punk, they hadn't stood by her side. They'd taken his. The emotional damage would have been just as bad, if not worse, than if they'd hit her. If there'd been physical abuse, it had gone undocumented. Then again, everyone thought Heather was a saint. I may have only met her earlier in the day, but some part of me felt as if I'd known her all my life.

I leaned back so she could see my lips when I spoke. "You can take all the time you need. Come home with me. You and Nova. You can stay in my house. Have your own room if that's what you want. Get to know me. Give us a chance. But I already know I want you, Nova, and the boys to be mine."

Charisma picked up the phone again. *You'll let us stay with you? Even if I'm not your wife?*

She showed me the screen and I smiled. "Yes, you can come stay with me even if you don't want to be my wife. No strings attached, Charisma. I won't expect anything of you."

She started typing again. *Then we'll go with you.*

"Are you hungry? We could either order room service or go out for something. Whatever you and the kids want to do."

Can we stay in? she asked.

"Of course. I'll check for a menu, and we can place an order. I bought pajamas for all of us. We can let the kids bathe first and get comfortable while we wait."

I wasn't sure what I'd expected when I'd said those words. The kids had eaten in the other room, and Charisma had sat at the table with me. We hadn't spoken, just ate our food and watched a movie on TV. When we finished, she got her new things and went into the bathroom. I heard the shower start a moment later.

I got up and checked on the kids. They'd all eaten and were sprawled across the beds watching a kid's movie. None of them had changed yet. I folded my arms and leaned against the wall, watching them a moment. Little Nova noticed me first. She smiled and hurried over, giving me another hug. Girl already had my heart. So did the boys, whether they realized it or not.

"The three of you need to figure out who's bathing first, but it's time to wash the day's dirt off and get dressed for bed. You don't have to go to sleep right now." I glanced at the bedside clock. "But you should at least get under the covers in the next hour. We'll be checking out before breakfast so we can get home."

"Nova can have the other bed. Jian and I will share this one," Li said.

"I don't know if Charisma wants to share a room with me. Why don't we let her decide?" I pushed off from the wall and gave Nova a nudge toward her bag of clothes. "All of you have been through a lot. I don't want Charisma to feel cornered. She's agreed to come home with us. Not as my wife."

Nova made a sound of distress. I gave her a smile. She blinked back tears and rushed into the bathroom. I knew it wasn't what she'd wanted to hear. I wished I could reassure her. No matter how much I wanted her as my daughter, and her mother as my wife, I wouldn't force Charisma to make a decision. She'd been pushed around like a pawn on a chessboard ever since her mother died. That's what happened when kids went into the system. They were shifted from one home to another, leaving them feeling as if they were unwanted and unloved. I wouldn't be another person shoving her where I wanted her to go.

I sighed and ran a hand through my hair. The boys were watching me. Their expressions were closed off, and I had no idea what they were thinking. I knew what they wanted. It's what I wanted too. But it wasn't my decision to make. Sure, I could tell Charisma she was mine. Make Shade hack into the county records and create a marriage that would bind her to me. Make Nova my adopted daughter, or hell, alter her birth certificate and school records she'd be mine in all ways... at least as far as the paper trail would show.

I could do those things. Knew brothers and men in other clubs who had done that very thing. If Charisma was anyone else, maybe I would have. Bind her to me, tell her she was mine, and never let her leave. But then I'd spend every day wondering if she'd stayed because she wanted me, or because I'd not given her a choice.

"I can't keep her if she doesn't want to be mine," I told them. "I know you don't understand. Or maybe you do. It wouldn't be right to cage her. Charisma has given up enough already. The decision to remain with us needs to be hers and hers alone."

"We know," Li said. "Even if we don't like it. Nova wants to stay. She's upset, and I don't think she gets why you won't make her your daughter. We can tell her all day, but it's something she needs to figure out on her own. We'll watch over her if she stays in here tonight."

"You're awfully smart, Li. Wiser than your years." I folded my arms. "And I'm damn sorry for how you got to this point. You didn't get a chance to be a kid. Hopefully, we can change that when we get home. We'll get the two of you registered for school within a few days. I'll have Shade get all the paperwork together. And hey! We have a dog. Her name is Momo. I think you'll love her."

"A dog?" Jian's eyes lit up. "What kind?"

"She's a Shiba Inu and is apparently a bit crazy. She shredded my paper towels after I left today. Someone sent me a picture of the mess she made. She loves playing with kids, though, so I think you'll get along just fine."

"Can Nova go to school too?" Jian asked.

"Of course. Charisma agreed to stay for a little while, so I don't see the harm in Nova going to school. We'll gather whatever she needs to get registered. But since she's younger than the two of you, she won't be at the same school. Actually, all three of you will be at separate schools. For this first year anyway."

I felt a hand on my shoulder and turned to see Charisma behind me. Her brow had pinched, and she looked concerned.

"What's wrong?" I faced her, taking her hand in mind.

She held up the phone and showed me what she'd typed. *Am I messing up things for Nova? She already told me what she wants. I didn't consider her needs when I told you I wanted time.*

That must have been one hell of a shower she'd taken to come out asking those questions. "It's okay to ask for time, Charisma. Don't feel pressured to do something you aren't ready for. Not for me. Not for Nova. You've always taken care of others. It's time to do what's right for you. Put yourself first."

She nodded, then moved a little closer. Before I realized what she'd intended, she pressed against me and snuggled close. I smiled and wrapped my arms around her. When I held her, it felt like all the pieces were coming together, like the missing parts of me had been found.

Shit. I was turning into a sappy romantic. Or maybe I'd been one for a while now. Always chasing after a dream of having a wife and kids... while my brothers partied and enjoyed their freedom, I'd wanted to be shackled to one woman. For more than a decade now, I'd dreamed of having a family. A wife and kids to make my life richer. Watching my brothers fall in love had been hard. Especially when my cousin even found his one and only.

I breathed in her scent and hoped she decided to stay. Not for me, or Nova, but because it was what she wanted and needed.

Chapter Three

Charisma

I could tell from my daughter's pleading look that she wanted to room with the boys for the night. Which meant I'd be sharing the other one with Phantom. There were two beds, and I had no doubt he'd be a gentleman. If he'd planned to force himself on me, he'd have done it already. Or he'd have paid Heather for the privilege and not bothered rescuing us and killing her.

At least the pajamas he'd bought for me were modest. He could have bought anything, and I'd have had no choice but to wear it. Or sleep in my regular clothes. Instead, he'd chosen something I'd be comfortable in, which told me he'd been thinking of my needs and not his. I'd never met anyone like him before. Which terrified me. With the men who came to Heather's, I'd always known what to expect.

Phantom came out of the bathroom, his pants slung low and no shirt on. My breath caught as I studied him. He had a few scars, and some ink across his chest. When he turned to toss the towel onto the counter, I saw more tattoos on his back. Why did I want to reach over and trace them with my fingertips? They were beautiful. Well, most were. I saw his club colors took up the center of his back, and I had to admit, the figure wasn't exactly a fluffy bunny.

He faced me and froze. My cheeks burned when I realized he'd caught me staring. I hated not being able to talk to him, except through the app on his phone. I hadn't tried to speak since I'd realized my hearing was gone. I couldn't tell how loud I spoke, and the boys had said my words sounded funny the few times I'd tried. Even though I remembered the way words sounded, it was hard to speak when you couldn't hear your own voice.

I pressed my fingers to my lips, wanting to talk to him, yet too afraid to try. He came closer, stopping near enough I could feel the heat off his body. Phantom wrapped his fingers around my wrist and tugged my hand from my mouth. He laced our fingers together and I looked up at him. I knew he had to be tall for a Japanese man. If he wasn't six feet, he had to be close to it. When the boys had told me they were half-Chinese, we'd done some research together on men from different countries in Asia. The average height for a man in Japan was five foot seven. Phantom was definitely taller than that. I might only be five feet tall, but he was roughly a foot taller.

He traced his finger down my nose, his gaze intent.

"Beautiful." I couldn't hear the word, but I read it on his lips. I didn't see how he could think I was anything other than ugly and scarred. I tried to shake my head, but he gripped my jaw and gave me a stern look. "Don't argue with me. You're beautiful."

I tugged away from him, taking a step back. Slowly, I lifted my shirt. I didn't know where I found the courage, but I needed him to see, to understand. The scars on my stomach came into view and I saw him inhale sharply. I kept going until I'd exposed myself to him. Fighting the urge to cover myself, I let him look before turning and showing him my back.

His hands curled around my biceps, and I felt his lips touch my shoulder. Tears burned my eyes as he kissed his way from one side to the other before wrapping his arms around me and holding me close. Phantom released me only to turn me so he could speak. I read his lips and I knew everything had changed.

"Did that bitch do all this?" he asked.

I shook my head.

"I will hunt them down, and I will end them. Every last fucking person who hurt you. Their time left on this earth is limited." He cupped my cheek. "There's nothing I wouldn't do for you, Charisma."

He bent down and helped me back into my pajama top. Again, he could have taken advantage and he hadn't. I swallowed hard, realizing something. The boys and Nova trusted him. They'd seen enough evil men to know when a good one came along. Not only that, but they wanted to remain with Phantom forever. As his family. And I was the only one holding Nova back from the life she'd always wanted. A dad. Siblings.

I licked my lips and tried to speak for the first time in years. "Do you still think I'm pretty?"

His eyes widened and he smiled a little. "You can speak."

I shrugged. I waited for him to answer my question. There was a sparkle to his eyes I hadn't noticed before. Had me speaking pleased him that much? I hoped I hadn't shouted my question to him. The fact the kids hadn't come running meant they hadn't heard, or were ignoring us. It could go either way.

"No. I don't think you're pretty." I tried to pull away, but he wouldn't let me. He tightened his hold. "You're stunning. The most gorgeous woman I've ever seen. Nothing you show me will change my mind."

"How?" I swallowed hard. My throat hurt. I hadn't spoken in so long, it felt like I was swallowing razor blades. "How can you see me like that?"

He brushed his thumb across my bottom lip.

"Don't talk so much if it hurts. Even though I love hearing your voice. As for how I can see you the way I do? You're strong, Charisma. A fighter. A protector. You think of others before yourself. The kind of beauty you have is more than just your looks. It's a glow you have, a light that shines bright."

A sob caught in my throat, and I couldn't hold back my tears. No one had ever spoken to me that way. I knew my mother had loved me, but she'd never told me I was special. This man who'd known me less than a day had done more for me than anyone in so long and saw me in a way no one ever had before. He could be saying everything he knew I wanted and needed to hear. Or he could be telling the truth. He'd said Heather had hurt his cousin. He'd wanted revenge, but he hadn't left us to fend for ourselves.

I cupped his cheek and stared up at him. "Hold me?"

Phantom gave a nod and led me to the bed. He stretched out on top of the covers and held his arms open. I eased down next to him and let him bring me closer. The way his scent wrapped around me made me feel secure. Safer than I'd ever been before.

Phantom tipped my chin up so I could see his lips. "The people who hurt you. What else did they do?"

I shook my head, knowing what he thought. "Not that."

Some of the tension eased from him. I knew my time there could have been worse. I could have suffered like the boys had. Instead, the men who'd wanted to "adopt" them liked hurting me.

"In the car, the boys said Heather accepted money for people to hurt you. Were they the men she'd adopt the boys out to?" he asked.

I nodded and tried not to think about all I'd been through. I'd do it again, if it meant the boys got a reprieve. It hadn't always been Li and Jian. There had been others before them. I hadn't been able to save them. I didn't know what good a night or two had been in the grand scheme of things. Now they were with men who would hurt them every day. Break them.

"Can they be saved?" I asked, my words coming slow. I didn't know how much longer I could speak tonight.

"Maybe. I won't lie to you. It won't be easy. I'll ask someone to see if they can track the others. I doubt they stayed with whoever adopted them. Assuming they're still alive, they could very well be out of the country by now. Sold time and again. Passed from one pedophile to another."

My heart broke for them. I wanted to rescue them. Give them a proper home. A chance to find happiness. How was it fair Phantom had come for me, Nova, Jian, and Li, but the others didn't get the same opportunity? I knew there were bad people everywhere. Even though he'd stopped Heather, there were others like her. He'd taken out one monster, but how many would rise up in her place?

"If I stay... If I choose you, what happens?" I asked.

"What do you know about bikers and clubs? Anything?"

I shook my head. I didn't really understand any of it. Yes, I knew what a cut was, and what some of his patches meant. Other than that, I'd been kept in the dark. Or maybe my mother just hadn't known. Even if she had, I'd been young and impressionable. There were probably things she could have never told me at that age.

"When I claim you as mine, you'll be my old lady. You'll get a cut similar to mine that will say *Property of Phantom*. But I want more than that. I want to marry you. The entire world will know you're my woman, and those are my kids. All three of them." He brushed his nose against mine and drew back a little. "And if you want more children, I'm all right with that. If not, I'm happy with the ones we have already. Or we can adopt. I will be faithful to you. Never doubt it for one second."

I pressed a hand to my stomach and felt a part of myself wither and die. He wanted more children. Of course, he would. All men wanted a son or daughter to carry on their bloodline, didn't they? Some sort of throwback gene to days gone by. He said he'd be happy with Nova and the boys. What if he changed his mind later? It wasn't like I could just decide to have more children.

He gripped my neck, drawing my attention to him again. "You can't have more children, can you?"

How could he always read me so easily? "No."

"From the damage they've done to your body?" he asked.

I shook my head and glanced toward the other room and back again. I didn't know how to tell him the birth had been difficult with Nova and my son who'd never had a chance to draw breath. "I nearly died."

"When you had Nova?" he asked.

"Yes."

"I'm so sorry, beautiful. You lost your son. Nearly lost your life. And the experience robbed you of having more children. Sometimes life isn't fair. More than that, it's downright cruel."

I snuggled against him, shutting off any other

conversation. He saw far too much, and it left me feeling raw. For so long, I'd either been unnoticed or someone's punching bag. Heather had seen me as a tool to keep the boys in line. The men she invited over got off on inflicting pain. Not once had anyone held me like this or wanted to know anything about me. Phantom didn't just see the surface things about me. It was like he could look into my soul. And it terrified me.

I could walk away. Take Nova and go. Except, I had this feeling in my gut I'd regret leaving Phantom. I didn't think men like him came along all that often. For whatever reason, he wanted me. Not just me, but Nova and the boys too. He wanted a family. Our family.

Our.

I liked that. All the times I'd thought about escaping Heather, not once had there been a man involved in our lives. I'd dreamt of running away with the boys and Nova, hitting the road and never looking back. It never occurred to me there would be a man I'd be tempted to invite along for the ride. Or in this case, one I wanted to move in with. His touch didn't repulse me. If anything, the small circles he'd been tracing on my back the last few minutes had my body coming alive.

My nipples tightened and I felt an ache building between my legs. When Nova's father had raped me, I'd not wanted more than a kiss from him. Since then, I'd not desired a man. For that matter, I'd been so young at the time, I hadn't really understood the things I'd been feeling. I hadn't been ready for sex.

Now I had to wonder what it would be like for someone like Phantom to kiss me. To touch me intimately. I didn't think I was brave enough to ask. Sure, I'd requested he hold me, which he was doing.

Kissing and other things were different. Then again, if I agreed to be his, he'd want to do those things.

I pushed back, putting a little space between us.

"Can we go slow?" I asked.

He traced his finger over the arch of my brow. "You set the pace."

"Then kiss me. Please."

He hesitated only a moment. His gaze clashed with mine before he closed the distance between us. His hand curled around the back of my neck as he pressed his lips to mine. I sucked in a breath at the spark I felt between us. I'd thought to endure his kiss, but as his lips brushed against mine, I found myself leaning into him, wanting more. His tongue flicked against my upper lip, and I opened, letting him in. His mouth devoured mine.

A whimper escaped me, and it seemed to set something free inside Phantom. I felt a vibration and wondered if he'd just growled. His hold on me tightened. The kiss deepened. Became rougher. My heart raced and I clung to him. When Phantom broke the kiss, I felt his chest heaving and saw the heated look in his eyes. More than that, he looked every bit as stunned as I felt. I reached up to touch my lips and stared at him.

"Too much?" he asked.

I shook my head. No, not nearly enough. Even now, I wanted him to kiss me again. I'd been brave enough for one day and night. Snuggling against him again, I closed my eyes and breathed in his scent. Small steps. I wasn't ready to fling myself over the cliff just yet. Kissing him had been the boldest thing I'd ever done. Or rather, asking *him* to kiss *me*. Maybe tomorrow we do it again. Or go a little further.

For now, I felt content. Happy. "I'll be yours."

He gave me a squeeze, letting me know I'd spoken loud enough he could hear me. And it seemed he was in agreement. I looked up at him once more.

"One more thing. I already told the boys. We have a dog. Her name is Momo and she's spoiled. She's also going to adore you and the kids."

"A dog?" I'd always wanted a pet and never been allowed to have one. "I can't wait to meet her."

For better or worse, Phantom was part of our family now. He'd saved us, and now it was our turn to save him. Phantom might seem to have a lot to offer, but so did we. He wanted a family? Then we'd be his family.

Perhaps one day, we'd be his everything. And Momo's too.

* * *

Phantom

There had been times I'd dated, and I'd had women fall asleep in my arms before. None of them compared to holding Charisma. It might have been because she was mine. The others had wanted me to claim them, but it hadn't felt right. My longest relationship had ended when Grey had shown up at the club with her son in tow. Even though she belonged to my cousin Samurai, I'd ended things with Celeste. A clean break had been best for both of us. She wanted forever with me, and I wanted kids -- something she hadn't been willing to budge on. I'd known for a while things weren't going anywhere. We wanted different things in life. But it had been fun and being with Celeste had kept the loneliness at bay.

The girls at the clubhouse were fine if you just wanted a quick release. They weren't exactly the sort you settled down with. Although, our VP, Scratch had gotten one pregnant a long time ago. His daughter was now fully grown and claimed by a Dixie Reaper. Hell, Scratch hadn't even realized he had a daughter until the other club had started poking around, trying to find Darian's family. I didn't think poorly about those girls. They served a purpose, but I couldn't imagine setting one of them up in my house, starting a family with her.

Then again, I had a woman of my own now. I wouldn't be using those women ever again. I hadn't touched them in a long time anyway. When I'd been with Celeste, I'd been faithful. I might not have seen forever happening for us, but it didn't mean I disrespected her. I treated her right, even when she wasn't by my side, and I'd expected the same in return. Seemed like my good behavior had paid off. I'd been given the ultimate reward -- a family.

I smoothed Charisma's hair back from her face and studied her features. She looked so peaceful while she slept. I wondered if this was how Samurai had felt when he'd met Grey the first time. I'd known something was different with him. He hadn't been the same for months, then his woman showed up, pregnant and needing help. It had made more sense, his odd behavior, but he hadn't wanted to man the fuck up and claim his family.

Thankfully, things had worked out okay for the two of them. I'd been willing to make Grey mine, even if it meant waiting a long-ass time for her to ever want my touch, just to guarantee she and the kids would be safe. Everyone kept asking if her son, Ryo, was mine. It wouldn't have been a hardship to go along with it. It just hadn't been what Grey, or Samurai, needed. She'd seen the pain in his eyes, known he was suffering, and she'd been the only one able to heal him. The rest of us had never questioned why he acted the way he did with women. Figured it was just his kink.

Now I felt like an asshole for not realizing sooner that he'd been through a trauma. I'd tried to do better. Not just with Samurai, but with everyone in the club. Who else had slipped through the cracks? Had I missed anything else? I knew Samurai better than anyone and I'd been completely blind to what he needed. Grey had been with him for one day and figured it out.

Charisma mumbled in her sleep and snuggled closer. I breathed her in, savoring the moment. She shifted again, brushing against me, and I mentally cursed as my cock started to harden. Letting her set the pace meant lots of cold showers in my future. Or giving my hand a workout. Wouldn't be the first time. I'd survive.

I eased away from her and slipped out of bed. The other room had gone quiet in the last hour, and I peeked inside, seeing all three kids were asleep. I picked up my phone and carried it into the bathroom then shut the door. I should have spoken to Charming already. Coming home with a woman and three kids wouldn't go over well if I didn't say something first.

The phone rang about three times before he picked up. Instead of a nice hello, I got a deep growl and a lot of cussing.

"Do you have any idea what time it is, you motherfucking asshole?" Charming demanded. "If you woke up…"

The Pres went silent, seeming to have said more than he'd intended. Interesting. "If I woke up who, Pres? Last I heard, you didn't have an old lady. I haven't been gone that long."

"Long enough. Next time you take off without

discussing it with me first, I'm going to kick your fucking ass. Now what the hell was so important you had to take off like that? A few lines of text and you shutting off your damn phone isn't how this works. I need details. If you're going to run off like a damn vigilante, I need to know exactly what's going on."

"I found the woman who hurt Samurai. Or rather, Shade found her for me. He also discovered she'd become a foster mom to two boys. The story is long and not something I want to say repeatedly. Can it wait until I'm back?" I asked. "I'd rather tell the entire club during Church. Well, after I let Samurai know the issue has been dealt with. I don't want to broadside him."

"Sure." Charming sighed. "So why call now? I could have just as easily cussed you out in person than over the phone. Just get home."

I cleared my throat. "I'm not coming home alone. I've never asked the club for anything. Never asked *you* for anything."

"But you are now," Charming surmised.

"Yes. The boys, Jian and Li. I'm going to have Shade work his mojo and make them my sons. They've been through hell, and I want to give them a stable home where they can learn to trust people again. I think being around the club will be good for them. A lot of the kids are close in age to the boys. Jian is twelve and Li is fifteen." I took a breath, bracing myself for the next part. This was where Charming might get a little pissed. "There's more... I'm also bringing home a woman and little girl. Charisma and Nova. They're mine. I'm not taking it to a vote. If the club doesn't like it, I'll walk."

Charming gave a humorless laugh. Yep. I'd pissed him off. I knew the guy could be a bastard when he needed to be, which was part of why Cinder had put him in charge when he'd stepped down. He'd known Charming could be compassionate, but in the end, would do whatever it took to ensure the good of the club as a whole. Which meant the guy was a total dick sometimes.

"Of course. Leaving the club would be that easy, right? Just walk out the doors?" Charming asked. "Sorry, brother. You know better. If you survived having your colors stripped, and I know damn well they're inked into your back, you'd still have to make it out there on your own. No club funds or businesses to line your pockets. No brothers to watch your six."

He wasn't wrong. Oh, I could find work and start over. I wasn't worried about that. But getting out of the club wouldn't be a cakewalk. And I wasn't sure Charisma, Nova, and the boys could handle seeing me like that. They needed me to be strong. I also knew they needed the club, even if they didn't realize it. The sense of community, of family, would go a long way to healing all four of them. It wouldn't be like Samurai. We'd know going in what they'd been through.

"Pres, they need me. They've been through more than any of us can fathom. Charisma can't hear. I don't know all the details, but it looks like that bitch poured acid on her ears. I'm guessing there's more to it than that. I don't know that damaging the outside would necessarily strip her of her hearing. They had to have hurt her inner ear too. She's got scars all the fuck over, where the woman let men hurt her. It was payment for those boys having a night off from the torment of Heather's touch, or the men she invited over."

Charming sighed. I could picture him pinching the bridge of his nose and praying for patience. I'd hit him with a lot, and it was a shit thing to do over the phone, but I didn't want Charisma and the kids walking into an unknown situation without me having paved the way a little.

"Phantom, everyone knows the one thing you've wanted most is a woman and kids. Do you really think any of us are going to say you can't keep the ones you're bringing home? As long as it's what they want, then consider it done. I'll have a property cut made. We can still take it to the table, let everyone vote, but I don't think a single brother is going to tell you no. Hell, Scratch and Clarity tried to set you up with Samurai's woman when your cousin wouldn't man the fuck up."

The tension in my shoulders eased at his words. I hadn't really thought the club would vote against me, but Charming wasn't exactly predictable these days. I now had to wonder if it had something to do with whoever I wasn't supposed to wake up. If he'd snuck a woman into his home, none of us knew about it. Why keep it a secret? I had a feeling shit was about to rain down on the club. I only hoped my family had a chance to settle in first.

"I know we have a lot of relationships in the club with a big-ass fucking age gap. Charisma is more than twenty years younger than me. I don't want anyone giving her shit about it. They might be teasing, but I'm not sure she'd see it that way. She's strong because she's had to be. Deep inside, I think she's also vulnerable and more than a little broken."

"You know better. None of us will say a word. How are the two of you communicating?" he asked. "You said she's deaf."

"Li knows sign language and talks to her. She can also read lips. At first, she used an app on my phone to type messages for me. Tonight, she actually spoke. Her voice doesn't sound like a hearing person's, and her volume is a bit all over the place, but I think it's beautiful. Like her." I smiled. "She's amazing, Charming. So fierce. You should have seen her stand up to Heather. She got between that bitch and the boys, and despite everything she's been through, she wasn't backing down. No matter the pain she's been through, she still wanted to keep the kids safe."

"What do you need? Is the house ready for them? And what about Momo?" Charming asked.

"Shade is taking care of Momo while I'm gone. As for the house... I don't know. The boys are going to need a room, and Nova will get her own. But neither bedroom is ready for kids to move into them. The boys are older, so they might be fine with something generic. They'll need two beds, though."

"Don't you have four bedrooms?" Charming asked. "Is there a reason they can't each have their own space?"

"One is set up as more of an office. Another is a guest room. And the last one is set up as a library. As much as I've wanted a family, it was looking like it would never happen. I decided to use the rooms for another purpose. Now I guess I need to figure out how to combine the two, and maybe add onto the house. No fucking clue where I'd add another room."

"Your house has an attic, right?" Charming asked.

"Yeah. Nothing up there, though, except the inside HVAC system and the hot water heater. Well, that and a shit ton of insulation. I haven't put flooring down or anything. Why?"

"It won't be an immediate solution, but I think we need to look into adding some rooms up in your attic. There should be enough space up there for two bedrooms and at least a half bath if not a full one, even if it's just a pedestal sink, standing shower, and toilet. It will give you room to grow."

I rubbed at the ache building in my chest. "Charisma can't have more kids. When she had Nova, something went wrong. She said she nearly died. Whatever happened, I think they had to give her a hysterectomy. But we'd both be open to adopting if the opportunity came along. She wants to try tracking down the other kids Heather 'placed' with adoptive fathers and probably even some mothers."

"We'll sit down with Shade after you've gotten back. Focus on your family right now and getting them home. I'll see who the hell is awake. Maybe we have some wood we can put down in the attic for temporary flooring. I'll have the Prospects start boxing up your office and the library. How long before you're home?" Charming asked.

"I thought I'd let everyone sleep in a little. I'd planned to stop for breakfast once we're on the road. Maybe four or five hours? Depends on how many bathroom breaks the kids and Charisma need."

"So you'd be here around lunch or a little after."

"Sounds about right."

"When you get close, text me. Don't bring them straight here. I'm sure there's shit they need. Take them shopping for any necessities you haven't already procured, and yes, I'm aware you've probably bought them stuff already. Get enough to last them a week or more. It should give us a little extra time to get the place ready. Any idea if they have favorite colors or anything?"

I thought about the list the boys had given me. "Nova likes pink and purple. Even though she's tough, she's girly and isn't afraid to show it. The boys are harder. Li didn't specify any colors or favorite characters or anything. I have no idea what he's into, and he may not know either. Jian likes blues and grays, and Pokémon."

"I'm sending out a text to all members, old ladies, and even Prospects to let them know what's going on. If there are any objections to you keeping the woman and kids, they can speak up now. Otherwise, we have some work to do before you get here. You've done a lot for the Devil's Boneyard over the years, Phantom. Let us do something for you now. Like you said, you've never asked for anything."

My throat got tight with emotion, and I nodded before I realized he couldn't see me. "Thanks, Pres. I appreciate it."

"We'll see you in the afternoon. Be careful. You have precious cargo now."

I smiled and ended the call. Hell yeah, I did. I stepped out of the bathroom and nearly collided with Charisma. Her eyes were wide and she'd been worrying at her lip. It was all red and puffy from her teeth digging into it.

"What's wrong?" I asked. She glanced at the phone and back at me. "I had to call my club President and let him know I was bringing you, Nova, and the boys back with me. I didn't want to surprise him by showing up with a family in tow."

Her brow smoothed and she stepped closer. "Is it okay for us to come with you?"

I nodded. "You're mine, beautiful. You agreed. Remember? I just needed to make things more official with the Devil's Boneyard. Everything's going to be fine. Promise."

She smiled and wrapped her arms around my waist, burrowing into me. I held her tight. If only I'd known about her sooner. I could have gotten her and the kids away from Heather. Ended that bitch before she'd done more damage. Maybe I'd have even found Charisma before she'd lost her hearing. Wishing wouldn't change things, though. I'd cherish my new family and show them what it meant to be loved. They'd learn to trust not only me but the men and women in the club. If Samurai could find a way to have a normal life, become a parent and find love, then so could Li and Jian. It would take time, but they had a home with me for as long as they wanted one. I didn't care if they were twenty and still living under my roof.

Well, that wasn't entirely true. At some point, I'd like to have the freedom to walk around the house in my boxer briefs if I wanted, without worrying about the kids seeing me. Then again, I wasn't exactly young anymore. By the time Nova was old enough to move out, things might be different.

I tipped Charisma's chin up so she could read my lips. "Still tired? We can sleep a while longer. It's nowhere near daylight yet."

She hesitated before speaking, and her words nearly knocked me on my ass.

"I liked your kisses. I woke up thinking I might like other stuff too."

Holy hell. "You want me to what? Kiss you again? Touch you?"

She nodded, her cheeks flushing. Before I could say or do anything else, she'd pulled her pajama top over her head and shimmied out of the pants. My heart hammered against my ribs so hard I wondered if she could see it beating. She dipped her fingers under the waistband of my pajama pants and rubbed them back and forth. When she started to tug them down, I placed my hand over hers.

"I don't have anything else on under them."

Her eyes dilated and she visibly swallowed before drawing in a breath and letting it out slow. "I want to see you."

I held my arms out to my sides a little, giving her room. She tugged the pants down and I stepped out of them. With her hungry gaze fastened on me, I turned, giving her a chance to view all of me. Instead of fear and uncertainty, when I looked at her again, all I saw was hunger and curiosity.

Fuck me sideways.

If Charisma didn't put on the brakes, I wasn't sure I'd be able to. I glanced at the connecting door, noticing for the first time, she'd shut it. It seemed she'd been waiting on me, planning this very moment. She amazed me.

"You can touch me if you want," I said. "I won't force you to do anything you aren't ready for. If you decide this is as much as you want from me right now, then that's all right."

She reached out and ran her fingers over my chest and down my abdomen. My cock hardened until it was fully erect. I heard her slight gasp. She wrapped her fingers around my shaft, and I groaned at how fucking wonderful it felt. I'd been with my fair share of women over the years. Being with her wasn't the same. She was mine. Funny how that seemed to make all the difference in the world.

I ran my fingers along her jaw, drawing her attention. "Can I touch you?"

She glanced at the shut door between our room and the kids. When she turned back to me, I could see the concern in her eyes. She didn't know how loud or quiet she was when she spoke or made noises. I knew she wouldn't want to wake them or worry them.

"We could get in the shower," I suggested. "Not as romantic as a candlelit bedroom, but we can do that when we get home."

Charisma released me, only to push at my chest. I took the hint and backed up into the bathroom. She shut the door behind us, and I turned on the water. I heard her behind me, the slide of fabric down her legs, and knew she'd removed her panties. Once the water was warm, I stepped over the side of the tub and helped her in. She slowly pulled the curtain closed and stared at me, her chest heaving, cheeks flushed. Her fingers twitched at her sides.

Reaching for the soap, I decided washing her might be the best way to ease into things. I lathered my hands and started at her neck and shoulders, rubbing the suds into her skin. I worked my way down her arm to her hand, cleaning every inch of skin, even between her fingers and all the way to her fingertips, then did the same to the other side. Placing my hands at her collarbones, I eased them down the slopes of her small breasts until I palmed them.

She made a sound, and I felt her nipples harden. Charisma subtly pushed her breasts against my hands, silently asking for more. I took my time, keeping my touch light. I explored the soft mounds, swiped my fingers over the hard peaks, and started over again. When she started panting, and I saw the feverish need in her eyes, I pinched one of the little buds giving it a slight twist.

Charisma's eyes went wide, and she cried out, her knees buckling. Her body trembled and I wondered if she'd just had her first orgasm. She clung to me as I tried to wring out every drop of pleasure, making it last as long as I could. My cock throbbed and I wanted nothing more than to be buried inside her.

Didn't mean I'd act on it. Not unless Charisma was one hundred percent certain it was what she wanted.

This wasn't about me. It was all for her.

Chapter Four

Charisma

I'd read some romances and watched movies where the couples would tumble into bed together. Not once did I ever imagine I would ask a man to touch me, much less enjoy it. No. Enjoy wasn't a strong enough word for what I'd felt. The entire world had fallen away. Even now, I wasn't certain my legs would hold me. If Phantom let go, I'd crumple to the bottom of the tub.

The water had already washed the soap from my body. Was it wrong I wanted to ask him to wash me again? I'd never realized having a man's hands on me would be so… amazing. Or maybe it wasn't just any man. Perhaps it was Phantom and only him who could make me feel like this.

"Again," I said.

A smile curved his lips and he backed me against the wall. I wasn't scared. Not of him. Having him tower over me only made me feel small and protected. He'd not used his size and strength against me so far, and I didn't think he ever would. No matter what he'd done to Heather, there was too much goodness inside him for there to be a monster lurking under his skin.

"Can I try something different?" he asked.

I nodded, eager to see what else he had in mind. He brushed his thumbs over my nipples again, making me moan. Except he let his hand trail lower, down over my belly. He didn't stop even when his fingers brushed the top of my pussy. I parted my thighs, giving him my trust and my body. He spread me open, and I felt the lightest touch against my clit.

I cried out, my fingers digging into his biceps as I tried to remain upright. He did it again and I nearly saw stars.

"Want me to keep going?" he asked.

"Yes!"

He grinned and knelt a little, lifting one of my legs over his arm. Then he stood, picking me up. My toes couldn't reach the bottom of the tub as he pinned me to the wall. My heart raced and I licked my lips, hoping I was right about him. He'd put me in a vulnerable position.

The moment his fingers slid along my pussy, I closed my eyes, my body shuddering with pleasure. A light smack between my legs had me opening my eyes and staring at him in shock. Had he just...

"Eyes on me, beautiful. I want you to know who's touching you."

Part of me softened at his words. I knew why he'd said them. He worried I'd be trapped in my head and go back to the time when Nova had been conceived. He didn't have to be concerned over that, though. His touch was nothing like my high school crush's. The asshole had pinned me down and taken what he wanted, and the louder I'd screamed, the more he'd enjoyed it. I hated that bastard with every fiber of my being.

His thumb worked my clit, and I felt him slide a finger inside me. I clenched down on it, eager for more. He worked me slowly, taking his time to draw everything out. I panted, and squirmed, wanting to make him go faster. I felt the sensation just out of reach, an orgasm cresting yet not quite getting there. When he finally gave me what I wanted, I screamed out my release. There was no way I'd been quiet, not with how much my throat ached. My cheeks burned and I waited to see if the kids would come rushing in. When nothing happened, my fears eased.

Phantom kissed me, his tongue tangling with mine and he pressed himself closer. I felt his cock, long and hard, and I realized he'd made me come twice and hadn't even tried to get me to reciprocate. He could have pushed the issue, and he hadn't. It just proved how honorable he was compared to the other men I'd met. If the experience with Nova's sperm donor hadn't been enough to turn me off men, then the guys who came to Heather's house would have finished the job. All I'd known were the rotten apples. Until now.

I reached between us, gripping his cock and giving it a stroke. His eyes darkened and his jaw tightened. I wiggled, trying to get into a better position.

"What do you want, Charisma? Ask and it's yours," he said.

"You. Inside me."

He moved so slowly I worried he'd change his mind, but he lifted my leg more, opening me farther, and then I felt the head of his cock press against my pussy. He pushed inside, stretching me. It burned a little and I bit my lip so I wouldn't make any noises. He didn't stop until I'd taken all of him. With his hand gripping my ass, he tilted my hips. Every stroke of his cock made his body brush against my clit.

His thrusts were deep yet measured. I could tell he was in complete control. I didn't know what he was waiting for until he hit just the right spot and I came again. It seemed to be the only thing holding him back. I felt the vibration of his growl as he took me harder and faster. Our hips slapped together as he took what he needed, and I was only too happy to let him.

On sensory overload, it didn't take much for me to have yet another orgasm. It seemed the slightest touch to that small bundle of nerves was enough to set me off. I came so much and so hard, I thought I might pass out. The heat of his release filled me and still he didn't stop. When he finally stayed buried inside me, his chest heaving, and his body trembling, I understood why women enjoyed sex. If their experience was anything like mine just now, I was surprised they didn't walk around begging for it all the time.

I'd never look at Phantom the same way. Every time I thought about this shower, about the orgasms he'd just given me, I had a feeling I'd want more of them. He might not have a monster inside him, but he'd just unleashed one in *me*. Whatever fear I'd ever felt when it came to sex and naked men was a thing of the past. Or at least it didn't pertain to Phantom. Let another man try to touch me, and I might lose my mind. But Phantom was different. I wanted his hands on me, his cock inside me... needed his kisses.

Holy shit! It hadn't even been a full day and already I was addicted to him.

Doomed didn't even begin to cover it.

And yet... all I wanted to do was smile and curl into him. Was this what happiness felt like? I couldn't remember experiencing it before. I knew I had. Before my mom had died, just not since then. The romances I'd read where the heroine fell madly in love with the hero within a chapter or two had always made me scoff, thinking nothing of the sort would ever happen in real life. Love at first sight was just a myth. While I wouldn't say I loved Phantom, I trusted him. To me, that was more important, and far more terrifying.

He cupped my cheek and ran his nose down the length of mine before drawing back enough for me to read his lips. "You all right?"

I nodded and kissed him. I was more than just *all right*. Putting it into words was another matter. I'd not spoken in so long, and it was rare for someone to ask about my feelings. There was so much I wanted to say, except I didn't know how to express all the emotions bubbling inside me.

"I wasn't going to push you," he said. "I told you we could wait as long as you wanted."

"I needed this," I said. My throat ached and I rubbed it. Before I could say another word, he pressed a finger to my lips.

"We'll dry off and you can use the phone to type whatever you want to say. You need to rest your voice. I promise I'll learn sign language. As much as I love hearing you speak, I don't like that it hurts you."

He quickly washed, and I did the same, before he shut off the water. We dried off and I pulled my pajamas back on, my cheeks burning at how brazen I'd been. I couldn't believe I'd undressed and told him to touch me. He picked up his phone, which I hadn't noticed he'd dropped earlier. Then he took my hand and led me over to the bed, pausing long enough to open the connecting door again. Phantom slid between the sheets, and I followed, curling up against him.

He handed the phone to me, already unlocked, and I typed in a message.

The only time I was interested in a guy he raped me. I've not wanted to be touched since then. The guys who came to Heather's only solidified my aversion to men. They may not have raped me, but they hurt me just the same. You make me feel safe. When you kissed me, it was unlike anything I'd ever experienced, and I wanted more. So I decided to be brave and take a leap.

I showed him the screen and he pressed a kiss to my forehead after reading it. The room was dark enough on this end I couldn't see his face clearly enough to read his lips. He seemed to know that and erased my message before typing out his own.

Never be afraid to ask me for what you need. I don't care if it's clothes, food, a hug, or sex. You're mine to take care of, but I'm also yours. I don't want a slave. I want a partner. A woman to stand by my side, not in my shadow.

My eyes burned and I fought the urge to cry. I'd been doing that more since meeting him than I had in forever. Well, I hadn't let the tears fall as often as I'd wanted. Just felt like I needed to. They were good tears. The kind I got from being surprised there were men in the world who weren't monsters.

He set the phone aside and held me. It didn't take long before I felt a vibration and realized he was snoring. I didn't know if he'd stayed up earlier or woken to make his call. Had he ever fallen asleep? The thought of him being tired and having to drive us to his home, our home now, didn't sit well with me. He might be taking care of us, but who had been taking care of *him*? He had to be exhausted.

With some luck, the kids wouldn't wake him anytime soon. The sun was starting to peek through the blinds. I doubted it was much past six in the morning. Maybe as late as seven. The kids often slept until eight or nine when they weren't in school. I hoped that would be the case this morning.

Breathing in Phantom's scent, and snuggling closer, I shut my eyes and let sleep pull me under.

* * *

Phantom

I'd been correct when I'd told Charming I might have to make a lot of stops with a woman and three kids in the car. The sound of the children talking and giggling had woken me around nine in the morning. Charisma still lay curled in my arms, and it was the happiest I'd ever felt. Once we'd all dressed and brushed our teeth, we'd packed up the few things we had and hit the road. First stop had been an all-day breakfast place about thirty minutes down the highway. We'd made two bathroom breaks since then, and I'd filled the car during one of those.

Not being able to talk to Charisma in the car made things a little awkward. I didn't want to speak to the kids and have her feel left out. Thankfully, she'd turned to face Li several times and he'd been able to sign for her. By the time we reached the outskirts of town, I was more than ready to get out of the car. I knew the kids had to feel the same way. Charisma had started one of the books I'd picked up for her and had nearly finished it.

"Before I show you where you'll be living from now on, we need to make another stop," I said.

The boys groaned and little Nova bounced in her seat. "Where are we going?"

"To a store. I want everyone to get at least a few more outfits, some shoes, and whatever else you need or want. Within reason. If you think something costs too much, just ask me. Pretty much any clothing you find, or shoes, will be fine. But if Nova sees a sparkly necklace and I discover it's nearly five hundred dollars, then that may have to go on the birthday or Christmas wish list."

Nova's eyes went wide as she stared at me. "Christmas. We get Christmas presents?"

My hands fisted and if Heather hadn't been dead, I'd have murdered the bitch all over again. How could she have not given the children even one Christmas gift? I had a feeling the kids were going to have a monumental list for Santa when the time came. The holiday had recently passed, and now I wished I'd kept my decorations out longer. It had always been my habit to put them away before the new year started.

"You have all year to come up with your list for Santa," I told Nova. "Same for you two. I also need to know when your birthdays are, as well as your mom's, and you'll have to give me some ideas between now and then."

The kids all shared a look, and I knew they were probably a bit overwhelmed. I couldn't imagine growing up the way they had. No one to love them. No presents. Just pain and suffering. Charisma was right. We needed to try and find the others and give them a better life. Whether that ended up being in our house or placed into homes I knew would give them loving parents, I'd make it work. Hell, maybe Havoc and Jordan would take in another one. Their oldest was graduating this year. Although, Taggart hadn't yet decided if he wanted to prospect for the club or go to college.

"There's quite a few kids at home. We live behind a gate, so it's a private community. Some of the kids are a lot younger than the three of you, and some are around your age. The oldest is Taggart. Havoc and Jordan adopted him. He'll be graduating this year, but he has two siblings. Sisters. Salem is nine and a half, I've been told that half is very important, and Lanie is nearly twelve."

Nova clapped her hands and bounced in the seat again. "Think they'll want to play with me?"

"I'm sure they will, sweetheart. There are a handful of other kids between the ages of seven and ten, a mix of boys and girls. Jian, you'll probably end up being friends with Levi and Noah. They're both thirteen. Li, you and Caleb are the same age. Allegra is a year older than the two of you and Taggart will be eighteen soon."

"So just because you're bringing us home with you, they're automatically going to like us?" Li asked, a bit of sarcasm lacing his tone.

"No. They're going to like you for who you are. Taggart and Salem were adopted by Havoc and Jordan because they'd been abused. They were going to be sold. You aren't the only ones I know who have suffered. The reason I went searching for Heather and found you... my cousin Samurai had been raped by her when he was a teenager. I know the world seems like a shit place, and you definitely were dealt a bad hand, but you aren't alone. None of you are. You not only have me and Charisma, but the entire club will stand behind you, giving you whatever support you need. You just have to let them in."

Li sighed and nodded. "All right. I'll try."

I put the car in park and opened my door, waiting on the kids and Charisma before setting the locks and alarm. I took my woman's hand and led her inside, keeping an eye on my family. Li got a shopping cart from inside the door. Since the kids' department was at the front, we let Jian and Nova do their shopping first.

I saw the jewelry counter out of the corner of my eye and motioned to Li. He paused. "I'm taking Charisma over there for a minute. Can you keep an eye on these two? We'll be within sight the entire time."

He saw where I wanted to go and smiled. "Yeah, I can do that."

I led her over to the counter and stopped in front of the wedding rings. She looked up at me, her brow furrowed. "I want to buy you a ring. It can be an engagement ring and you can plan as big a wedding as you want. Or... it can be a wedding band and I'll ask

Shade to handle the paperwork. It's your decision."

She glanced around and held out her hand. I gave her my phone, realizing she didn't want to speak in public since she couldn't hear how loud or soft she talked. When I saw her message, I wanted to kiss the hell out of her.

You really want to marry me?

"Of course, I do! You're mine, Charisma. A ring and piece of paper are just a formality as far as I'm concerned, but I want to do whatever makes you happy. If you want to wear a pretty dress and walk down an aisle, then we'll do that."

She shook her head and typed again. *I don't need a wedding. Just knowing I'm yours is enough.*

A woman came over, a smile on her face. "Can I help you?"

"I need a set of wedding bands. Preferably something indestructible for mine."

She took a moment to size the both of us before pointing out options we could buy and wear immediately, and let me know anything else could be sized, but we wouldn't get the rings for a few weeks in that case. I didn't want to wait for mine and chose a simple steel band. No matter how hard I tried, Charisma wouldn't get anything flashy. Every single diamond band I showed her got a negative headshake.

"What about this one?" I asked, pointing to a pretty white gold band with a few diamonds scattered across the time. They were embedded so the stones wouldn't catch on anything. Not to mention they were tiny as fuck. They looked more like glitter. "Come on. Just try it on."

She relented, and when it fit perfectly, I convinced her to wear it. I paid for both rings and we went back to the kids. Jian had finished picking out his clothes, as had Nova. We went to the men's department for Li before circling around to the women's section. It felt like we'd been in the store for hours by the time we checked out.

I gave the keys to Li and nudged my chin toward the door. "Take everyone out to the Jeep and start loading this stuff. I'll be there in a minute. I have one more thing I need to get."

They walked off and I pulled up the number for Charming as I walked to the back of the store. He answered right off.

"Hey, Phantom. You nearly here?" he asked.

"Just checked out at the store. The kids are loading the car. I'm going to grab a game system for Li's room and some books for Charisma. I have no fucking clue what to get Nova or Jian."

Charming chuckled. "Already taken care of, brother. We got Li the same system Taggart likes, and Jian has the one Levi and Caleb have. The women went a little crazy on Nova's room. She has dolls, stuffed animals, art shit, puzzles and all kinds of crap in there. Your dog is about to lose her damn mind trying to figure out what the hell is going on, though."

I didn't doubt for a second that Momo was either confused or excited. She'd recognize the kids' stuff as belonging to smaller humans and would likely be contemplating who was going to play with her. "So I just need some books for Charisma, then."

"The kids are covered. Just bring your family home. Everyone is anxious to meet them."

I ended the call, grabbed a few more books for my... *Shit.* I sent a quick text to Shade. *Need you to marry me and Charisma.*

When I saw his answer, I just shook my head.

Already did it. Kids are set for school too. Birth

certificates have been altered, and same for school records.

There were times my brothers not only amazed me but humbled me too. He'd somehow known, or maybe Charming had told him. Whatever the case, I owed all of them. The club had really come together for me, and for my new family. I hoped like hell I hadn't been lying when I told the kids they'd have friends right off. The kids at the compound were all good and understanding. Some had been born and raised in the Devil's Boneyard. Others had come to us later.

I hoped Li, Jian, and Nova were ready. They were about to find out what a real family was like. Same for Charisma. I had no doubt the club was going to welcome them with open arms.

I paid for the books and hurried out to the car. Someone had already started it, probably Charisma, so I slid behind the wheel and handed her the sack. When she saw what was inside, she leaned over and kissed me.

"Thank you," she said. She winced and glanced at the kids, wondering if she'd spoken too loud. It hadn't seemed to bother them, which gave her a little more confidence over using her voice.

"You're welcome, beautiful. Now, let's go home. Everyone ready?"

The kids all shouted out a *yes* as I put the car into gear and headed to the compound. I couldn't wait to see what my brothers and the old ladies had done with the three bedrooms. It sounded like the kids were more than taken care of. I only hoped they liked everything.

Hunter was at the gate when I pulled up and he let us through. I waved as I drove past him and headed for the house. Since Charming and Scratch lived nearby, they were waiting in the front yard. I saw Scratch's boys peering out the window from across the street and shook my head. I didn't think anyone would be able to hold them back for long.

Nova nearly jumped from the car in her excitement, but Li and Jian were a bit more reserved. Charisma took my hand as we walked up to the front door. I paused in front of Scratch and Charming. Facing my wife, I made sure she could read my lips.

"This is the club's President and Vice President. Charming and Scratch. They helped put together a surprise for the kids."

Scratch smiled and waited for Charisma to look at him. "Welcome to the Devil's Boneyard family. I live across the street with my wife and kids. You're welcome anytime."

Charisma frowned and glanced at me. I repeated what Scratch had said, wondering why she hadn't been able to understand. Then it hit me. His beard had grown out quite a bit and covered most of his mouth.

"VP, I think you're going to need to trim the bush on your face or learn to sign. She couldn't read your lips," I said.

He ran a hand over his beard and nodded. I had a feeling he'd go home and take care of it right away. That was just the sort of man he was. I'd have to make sure the rest of the club knew about Charisma's restrictions for reading lips if they had let their beards go a bit wild.

Charming held out his hand and Charisma hesitantly took it. The Pres pulled her in close for a quick hug, then stepped back. "We're all happy to meet you. Take some time to get settled in, then we'll plan a party so you and the kids can get to know everyone."

I curled an arm around Charisma's waist and led her into the house. Heading down the hall, we stopped at the first door. Nova's name had been painted on the door in a fancy script with butterflies and flowers around it. I pushed the door open and let my daughter inspect her space.

Her eyes were wide as she stared at all the toys. Someone had painted the walls a pale lavender and hung up girly-looking curtains. A daybed took up most of one wall with a pink, purple, and yellow quilt over the mattress. Nova ran from one thing to another, her excitement building, as did the speed with which she bounced around the space.

"Do you like it?" I asked.

"It's perfect!" She threw herself at me, wrapping her arms around my waist in a tight hug. "Thank you… Daddy."

My heart warmed at the words, and I hugged her back. We moved farther down the hall to the next room. Jian's door had a chalkboard hanging from it and someone had written his name on it. He went inside and just stared. I started to worry he hated it, until he turned to us with tears in his eyes.

I heard nails scrabbling against the floors and turned in time to see Momo race toward us. Someone must have let her in. I'd been surprised when she hadn't greeted me at the door. The fact a leash was dragging behind her told me she'd been out for a walk.

"Goddamnit, Momo!" Shade stomped into the house, his chest heaving. "Get control of your bratty-ass dog, Phantom. She yanked free and bolted."

"Probably knew I was home." I reached out and shook his hand. "Thanks for watching her."

Jian knelt and Momo immediately started licking his face. It seemed his room had been temporarily forgotten. I shook my head. Couldn't blame the kid. He'd probably never had a dog before. And Momo was

- 243 -

cute as hell, even if she could be a little bitch sometimes. Like when she shredded the paper towels.

When Jian stood again and turned back to face his room, I watched as he studied everything. "We can change whatever you want, but the club set up the room for you. Hopefully, you like it."

"It's the best room I've ever had," he said quietly.

"Check everything out while we show Li his room. Then I want to get your mom settled in." He smiled when I called Charisma his mother. I knew it wasn't something they'd done before, calling her that. Heather would have never permitted it. But maybe they'd thought it all this time. It was what she'd been to those boys, even if she hadn't had the title.

Li didn't even make it into his room. He stood frozen in the doorway. The club had left the guest room mostly the same. They'd left the wall color and hadn't added curtains. A queen bed had been put in the far corner, which would only allow him to get in and out on one side. The rest of the space now had a desk with a chair, and I noticed a new laptop waiting to be opened. A six-drawer chest had a TV on top, and a three-cube organizer set next to it with a gaming system on top and a handful of games on one of the shelves. Two controllers were on the bottom shelf, along with a charging dock.

"You can personalize the space," I said. "Posters. Framed pictures. Whatever you want. Paint the walls."

"This is really great," Li said. When he hugged me, he held on so tight I was thankful he wasn't stronger, or he might have cracked some ribs.

With the kids occupied in their own rooms, I led Charisma to our bedroom. She wandered the space while I made sure she had some empty drawers and could hang some things in the closet. Eventually, we might need another dresser, but for now we could make do.

"Welcome home," I said, when she'd faced me again. "Do whatever you want with the place. Make it your own. You don't need to ask me about changes first."

"I can't afford to buy things," she said.

"You can. I'll have you added to the bank account. We can even download the app for you so you can see how much is in there at any given time."

She started shaking her head and I cupped her cheek. "Charisma, stop. You're my wife now. I asked Shade to marry us, and the sneaky bastard had already done it. What's mine is yours. If you or the kids need anything, I want to make sure you have access to money. I don't expect you to work. You can, if you want to, but I'm not going to make you. I'd actually prefer you home in case the kids need anything, but it's your decision."

"Okay," she said. "But I don't like it."

I kissed her softly. "You're everything to me, Charisma. You and those kids. I make more than enough to take care of us."

I turned and saw the kids in the doorway, each smiling at us. I waved them in and hugged them. Momo bounded around our feet, wanting a hug too. Nova released us and started petting the dog, and Jian followed suit. It only took another moment for Li to give Momo some attention too.

I hadn't thought about stocking the kitchen. For tonight, I'd place an order and get a Prospect to pick it up. I didn't even know if Charisma cooked. If she didn't, I could cook well enough to keep us from starving. I knew a few of the old ladies liked crockpot recipes, so they could get it started and leave it going all day. Wouldn't be a bad idea to buy one and get a recipe book for it.

My house had always been comfortable, but now it felt like a home. I'd protect my family with my very life. Whatever came our way, I'd make sure they stayed safe. I'd already taken out Heather. Getting any of the other kids back would be dangerous, assuming we could even find them. But I'd told Charisma we'd try, and I would do everything I could to rescue them.

"What does everyone want to do tonight?" I asked.

"Can we play a game?" Nova asked. "A board game? And maybe throw a ball for Momo?"

I nodded. "We can do that. My nephew likes them, so I have a few in the hall closet. If you tell me which ones you like, I'll be sure to buy more. As for Momo, she has several tennis balls outside and loves to play fetch."

And that's how the rest of the night passed. Board games, dinner, throwing a ball for Momo, and a lot of laughter. Best fucking night of my life!

Chapter Five
Charisma

I stretched the next morning, then bolted upright. I glanced around the room and my heart rate slowed as I realized I was safe. For a brief moment, I'd worried I'd dreamt everything. Phantom. Heather's death. Getting a new life. But I hadn't. It was all real, which meant... I ran my hand over the opposite side of the bed. The sheets were cool even though I remembered Phantom holding me as I fell asleep. How long had he been awake?

I hurried to the bathroom to take care of my needs, brushed my teeth, and ran a brush through my hair. When I felt a little more presentable, I went to search for my husband. I looked down at the ring on my finger and warmth filled me. He'd saved me in every way possible. Not just me, but the children too. *How did I get so lucky?*

The house seemed a little too quiet. Even if I couldn't hear the kids, I usually felt their presence. Instead, there was a void. I peeked into the children's rooms and found them all still sleeping soundly. I checked the living room and finally found Phantom in the kitchen. He had his phone on the table, swiping and tapping the screen, and a cup of coffee in his hand. He hadn't heard me yet, so I tried to shuffle my feet a little as I stepped into the room. His head jerked up and a smile spread across his lips.

"Morning, beautiful. Did you sleep okay?"

I nodded and motioned to the coffee. "Can I have some?"

He got up and pulled a cup down from the cabinet by the sink, then poured coffee into it. He placed it on the table and held out a chair for me. I typically took creamer with mine, but since he hadn't been home, he probably didn't have any. I didn't want to ask. If I'd learned one thing about the man so far, it was that he took his role of caregiver and protector seriously. Which meant he'd likely be upset with himself for not anticipating my needs if I voiced my preference for creamer.

I swallowed the bitter brew and tried not to grimace. The important thing was that it was not only hot but caffeinated. "Thank you."

He lifted his phone. "I've ordered you and Li each a phone. Sent a Prospect to pick them up. I'll program in the numbers for all the club officers, as well as the schools the kids will be attending. There's going to be a few kids stopping by today. Havoc is sending over his daughter, Salem. She's about the same age as Nova. The girls can play here, or Salem can show Nova around the compound."

"And the boys?" I asked.

"Jackal and Scratch both have thirteen-year-old boys. They'll be coming for Jian. Probably try to talk him into kicking a soccer ball around. Caleb, Scratch's other boy, is Li's age. He's going to lure our oldest away to play video games across the street. I think Havoc's oldest, Taggart, might pop over there at some point. He's seventeen, but it will be good for Li to know one of the seniors at the high school when he starts."

"School?" I asked.

"Shade has the paperwork done. He's also provided school records for the kids so we can get them registered. I thought we'd go tomorrow. Give them a day or two to make a few friends at the compound before we send them off to fend for themselves."

I took another swallow of coffee. My stomach rumbled and Phantom got up again. He opened the oven and pulled out an aluminum container. Setting it in front of me, he also handed me a fork.

"It's breakfast. Had someone run by the diner. It's a casserole with eggs, cheese, ham, bell peppers, onions, and hashbrowns. I had somebody grab one for each of us. When you walked in, I was making a grocery order for pickup. Just a few things to keep us going the next few days."

I ran my finger around the rim of my cup before picking up the fork and eating. There were some things I needed to discuss with him. For one, he might have taken out Heather, but I knew she'd made appointments for me to stop by. She'd be missed, and more importantly, so would the boys. Would the social worker share pictures of the boys and ask people to watch for them? What did they call it? An Amber alert?

"What's wrong?" he asked.

"I think there are some things you didn't consider." I took another bite of food. "As much as I want to believe we're in the clear, I know we aren't."

"Explain," he said.

"The boys were under the care of a social worker. She'll come looking for them. The school will report they didn't attend classes. The men Heather let into her home will know something is wrong when we all vanish."

"You're right. I didn't consider all that when I grabbed the four of you and took off. But thankfully, Shade did. The school will see records showing a transfer. The social worker will be confused and might try to cause a stink, but the system will have an adoption in place for the boys. To a man who doesn't really exist except on paper."

"And the men?" I asked.

"That's another issue, but it's my problem, not yours. I don't want you stressing and fretting over it. My job is to keep all of you safe, and I'll do whatever is necessary to make sure that happens."

"What if someone remembers your Jeep? What if they come after us?" I asked.

Phantom leaned closer, bracing his arms on the table. "No one will hurt you or those children. They will have to go through me and every man in this club. Understand?"

I nodded even though I really didn't have a clue what he meant. How could he promise no one would hurt us? He had no control over other people, and he couldn't be with us every second of the day. The kids could be snatched on their way to school. For that matter, any time any of us left the safety of the fence, we could be targeted by anyone who tracked us here.

"Taggart and Caleb can keep an eye on Li while he's at the high school. Taggart will drive the two of them if I ask him to. He's a good kid. Nearly a man. Several kids attend the middle school and elementary school. They're used to watching each other's backs. Adding our kids to the mix won't hurt anything."

"How do the younger kids get to school?" I asked.

"The old ladies take turns carpooling. You can drive the Jeep whenever you want to. If it makes you feel better driving Jian and Nova to school, then do it. Want me to ride along, then I'll be there."

He made it all sound so easy. Phantom had an answer for everything. But I couldn't help the feeling something was going to go horribly wrong. It had all been too easy up to now. No, our lives with Heather hadn't been a picnic, but getting away from her? We hadn't had so much as one hiccup. It made me leery. After all the pain and suffering, we didn't really get to start over without having to fight for it, did we?

"I don't feel comfortable driving the Jeep. I've never driven something that big before."

"Do you want a car of your own?" he asked.

I started shaking my head before he'd even finished the sentence. Nope. I didn't want him spending enough money to buy a car. He had his motorcycle and the Jeep. It was silly I couldn't drive the vehicle. Maybe he'd let me drive it around the compound for a few days to get used to it.

Phantom leaned even closer, his nose nearly brushing mine before he backed up enough that I could see his face. "You realize if you tell me no, I'll likely just buy you one anyway? Wouldn't it be better to have some input?"

"You don't have to spend so much money on us, Phantom."

"It's just us right now," he said.

"What does that have to do with anything?"

"When we're alone, you can call me Kenji. My brothers call me Phantom. Strangers call me that. My wife can use my name, when we're at home, and my brothers or their women aren't around."

My lips turned down and I felt my brow furrow. "But I thought it was disrespectful to use your given name and not the one you earned. And I'd love to know *how* you earned the name Phantom."

"Not so sure you want to hear that story. It's not pretty."

I shrugged. "My entire life hasn't been pretty, as you put it. I'm not squeamish."

"All right." He relaxed back in his chair. "This club was different once upon a time. Before any of us had old ladies. Cinder ruled the place with an iron fist, and we didn't exactly keep our hands clean. The club ran drugs and guns, and back before my time, I think they were into even more shit. We've had wars with other clubs that resulted in casualties on both sides, and my hands have worn their fair share of blood."

I sipped my coffee and watched his lips, trying to catch every word. If he thought his speech would scare me, he was wrong. The biker I'd spoken with had given me enough information that I'd understood what some of the patches on Phantom's cut had meant. I knew what colors were, about the rockers, and noticed he didn't have a 1% patch, even though he admitted they were into some less than legal things. Which told me they were most likely outlaws.

The moment I'd learned my dad was a biker, I'd soaked up whatever knowledge I could find. The biker I'd mistaken for my dad when I was younger had been patient and informative. Since then, I'd spoken to a few others. I also knew Phantom would never harm an innocent. At least, the man he was now wouldn't do something like that. I supposed he could have been different in his youth.

"I may not always follow the law, but both I and the club do have our own moral compass. Killing Heather was an honor. I usually won't hurt women. Monsters, on the other hand, are a different matter. I don't care what gender they are."

"Seeing what you did to Heather didn't bother me. Maybe it should have, but I couldn't feel sorry for her. She'd done far worse to so many kids."

He nodded. "She had. If you hadn't come in when you did, I'd have taken more time with her."

"Does the club still do all that?" I asked.

"In a matter of speaking. We're a bit more

discerning these days. We still sell weapons, but we're selective when it comes to our clients. That's about as much as I can tell you. Club business is exactly that… which means it's not for the ears of our women and kids."

"Do you go after people like Heather often? I know she was special since she hurt your cousin."

"Me personally? Not so much. But if Charming tells me to do something, I do it. There are times that might include taking out the trash -- human trash. I don't lose sleep over it. I truly believe some people are born rotten to the core and should have never been given life to begin with."

"Are there a lot out there? Pedophiles or worse?" I asked.

"Too many," Phantom said. "For every one we take out, there are dozens more. I'm not sure the world will ever be rid of evil people."

"Vigilante justice," I said. "That's what you and the others do. Where the police fail, you step in."

Phantom smiled faintly. "More like when their hands get tied by bureaucratic red tape, we get the job done. Sometimes we take care of it before they get close enough to even try. The justice system doesn't work nearly well enough, and a lot of the prisons are overcrowded. I like to think of it as population control."

I finished my coffee and breakfast. I got up and rinsed my cup before throwing away the foil container. Stopping behind Phantom, I wrapped my arms around him, pressing my cheek to his. He spoke about taking out those people like it was nothing. Just another day at work. But I knew different. He had a kind heart. On some level, it had to affect him.

"Do you have any idea how incredible you are?

The risks you take, so other people can sleep soundly, and the way you swooped in and rescued me and the kids without hesitation. You brought us home. Made us your family. I don't know anyone else who would have done that."

He reached around and grabbed my waist, tugging me around his chair and down onto his lap. "I'm just a man, Charisma. I'm not perfect. But I'm yours."

I smiled and kissed him softly. Yes, he was mine. Maybe it was fate. Perhaps it was just luck. Whatever the case, I was going to hold onto him. If the bad guys came for me and the kids, I'd stand next to Phantom and fight any way I could. I'd finally found happiness, and I wasn't about to let it slip through my fingers. Men like him didn't come along often. At least, they didn't in my life. Or ever for that matter.

"You're mine, and I'm yours," I said. "There's no one else I'd ever want."

"Whatever comes our way, we'll face it together. You. Me. The kids. Even Momo. We're a family, Charisma. Now and always."

His lips brushed mine and I melted against him. This was as close to heaven as I'd ever get, and I was all right with that.

* * *

Phantom

It had been two days since I'd brought my family home, and that's as long as the club could last without poking their noses into our lives. I'd gotten a text to bring everyone to the clubhouse. I hoped like hell they weren't going to overwhelm Charisma. The kids were more adaptable. They'd immediately made friends within the compound and hit the ground running as far as starting over went. Charisma seemed more hesitant.

I ran my hand down her back and gave her ass a squeeze. She yelped and looked at me over her shoulder, eyes narrowed. But I saw the way her lips curved a little. She might pretend to be upset by the move, but she liked it.

Now that I had her attention... "We need to get ready and head over to the clubhouse. Kids too. It seems the old ladies put together a potluck of sorts, and our attendance is mandatory."

She winced and I knew she really didn't want to go. Clarity had stopped by yesterday and introduced herself, just so Charisma would know someone around here other than me and the few brothers she'd met so far. Didn't hurt she lived across the street. I was grateful she'd made the gesture, and in time, Charisma would be too. With the way she'd lived since losing her mom, I'd realized she wasn't used to people going out of their way to meet her or be friendly without wanting something in return. While she didn't like talking about her past much, she'd told me a bit more about where she'd been before landing at Heather's. It would take time for her to adjust, but she'd get there.

I turned her to face me and cupped her cheek. "You're beautiful. Do you have any idea how I feel every time I look at you or think about you?"

She shook her head.

"Then I'll tell you." I backed her toward the kitchen counter, caging her in. "When I wake up with you in my arms, it feels like everything I've ever wanted is finally in my grasp. A smile from you is better than any Christmas gift I've ever received. Your touch made me want to tie you to the bed and make you scream in pleasure for hours."

Her gaze softened. "Phantom…"

I pressed my finger to her lips. I hated when she called me that in our own home. For whatever reason, she insisted. Maybe she worried she'd forget when we were around other people. But the sweetest sound I'd ever heard was my real name on her lips.

"Why don't you wear your red sweater and black jeans? I have a surprise for you, so don't worry about shoes." I actually had more than one, but she'd get the other at the potluck. Cinder had already messaged to let me know he'd be bringing her property cut with him. Meg had picked it up from the lady who stitched on our patches.

"I need to shower," she said.

I waggled my eyebrows at her and grinned. "So do I. Should we conserve water?"

Her cheeks went scarlet, and her gaze darted around frantically, probably worried the kids had overheard. In the bedroom, she melted at my touch. I loved hearing her cries, listening to her beg. But when we were in the main parts of the house, it was a different matter entirely. I wanted to see that sexy, wild side of her at all times. I just wasn't sure how to bring it out yet. I knew a lot of it had to do with her comfort level. All this was new. The house. Town. Being around a bunch of bikers. And me…

"Come on. The kids are all outside. Jian and Nova went out back with Momo this morning and I haven't seen them come back through. Li was out front throwing a football with Scratch's two boys. We have the house to ourselves a little longer. The kids will be fine going as-is." I put my arms around her, tugging her closer. "Unless you don't want my hands on you? Or my lips?"

"You know that's not it."

"We'll shower and dress, then get the kids to pile into the Jeep. I was told we didn't have to bring anything other than ourselves. Everything's been handled. The club wants the chance to introduce themselves, and I think it will be good for you to see the families hanging out together."

"All right." She glanced at the kitchen doorway. "But we need to make it quick in case they come back in."

I wasn't about to remind her they slept down the hall at night when she clawed at my back and screamed my name. If I did, she might not let me undress her ever again. We might not have been together for more than a few nights, but I was already addicted to her. Ever since she'd given herself to me at the hotel, I'd craved her.

Taking her hand, I led her back to our room. I not only shut the door, but I twisted the lock too. Just to be safe. While she stripped off her clothes, I went to start the shower. I let her get in first while I undressed, then joined her under the hot spray. Her nipples had already hardened, so no matter how much she protested, I could tell she wanted me. She reached down and wrapped her fingers around my cock, giving it a stroke.

"I love when you touch me," I said.

"I like you touching me too," she admitted. "A lot."

"It makes me really damn happy to hear that."

"All those things you said you feel when you look at me? I feel that way about you too. And it scares me sometimes. I'm afraid I'll wake up and find out it was all a dream, because I never knew men like you existed."

"I'm only flesh and blood, Charisma. I'm not

perfect. Not a saint. Just a man who's completely crazy about you. The kids. You. Even Momo... You're what's important to me. Essential. I can't breathe without the lot of you. I know it's pure insanity, since we just met, but it's how I feel."

"Love at first sight?" she asked, her brow furrowing. "Isn't that a fairy tale?"

"I can't say for sure. What I do know is every man in this club who's claimed a woman did so either the same day he met her, or shortly after. When we know, we just... know." I reached down and wrapped my hand around her wrist, tugging her loose from my cock. As badly as I wanted to be inside her, I needed her to know she was more to me than a body to fuck. "You're not a convenience. I love being inside you, touching you, kissing you... but I also enjoy talking to you or holding you while you sleep. What we have is more than just sex. You understand that, right?"

She pressed herself to me, wrapping her arms around my waist. "I know. You're an honorable, kind man. I know I'm lucky to be yours."

I pulled free and shook my head. "No. No! Damnit, Charisma. Don't you see? I'm the one who's lucky. Do you think I got to be my age and single if I wanted to settle for just anyone? Because I didn't. No one tempted me to keep them by my side until you. Full disclosure, I did offer to keep Grey when my cousin wouldn't man the fuck up. It didn't have anything to do with me desiring her. I just wanted to make sure she and the kids were safe. My longest relationship was with a woman who didn't want kids. I knew there was nothing permanent there, but... being with her kept the loneliness at bay."

"I'm sorry. I didn't mean to upset you," she said. "I guess I just don't feel worthy of someone like you."

"Baby, there's no one I'd ever want by my side other than you. The things you've survived, the way you protected those boys no matter the cost to yourself, it fucking amazes me. *You* amaze me." She reached for me again, but I held up a hand to keep her back. "We should wash and get to the clubhouse. But later tonight, I plan to show you just how much I adore you. Understood?"

She nodded, a smile on her lips. As much as I loved getting to run my hands over her body, I tried to keep things on track and not get derailed by how soft her skin felt, or how much I wanted to suck her nipples. By the time we'd finished and dressed, I knew I'd catch shit at the clubhouse. An hour had gone by, and they'd assume I'd hauled her off to the bedroom before going to the potluck. Which is something I'd definitely try to do... so I deserved whatever they dished out.

Charisma kept admiring the black boots I'd given her. The way her eyes lit up told me she liked them. Hell, she'd thrown herself into my arms when she'd opened the box. At least I knew I could pick out things she'd enjoy without worrying about it so much. The guys always said how much they hated shopping for their women. With Charisma, she seemed to be thankful for anything she received.

We stepped outside and I called out to Li. "Get your brother and sister. Momo can come too."

He frowned and glanced at the other boys, clearly wanting to keep tossing the ball around. I couldn't blame him. It seemed the boys hadn't said anything to him yet. Otherwise, he'd know they were going too.

"Where are we going?" Li asked.

"Clubhouse. Everyone will be there. Bring the

football if you want. You can't throw it inside, but there's no reason y'all can't go out back to toss it around. All the kids will be there. It's a family event."

He tossed the ball to me, and I put it in the back seat before helping Charisma into the Jeep. A moment later, Jian and Nova came racing around the side of the house with Momo in pursuit. With my family crammed into the back seat, I realized we were going to need a bigger vehicle. On the way home from Heather's, I'd been more focused on getting them to safety. Long-term, the Jeep wouldn't suffice. And Li would need transportation when he turned sixteen. Maybe I'd keep the Rubicon and let him have it after he got his license. I'd start looking at larger SUVs tomorrow. Something with a third row was definitely required.

While there were a few bikes parked at the clubhouse, mostly from the single guys, the lot had filled up with trucks, SUVS, and a few cars. There were times I stood in awe as I looked at how things had changed around here. First Jackal had claimed his woman, and the little girl he hadn't known he'd fathered. Then Scratch had fallen for Clarity and her son. Havoc had literally tossed Jordan over his shoulder and walked off with her. I'd worried my time wouldn't come, but here I was, heading into the clubhouse with my wife and kids.

"Why are you smiling?" Li asked. "We aren't walking into some sort of ambush, are we? Like everyone's going to swarm us and want to know everything about us? Make us hug them and crap?"

"I'm happy, that's all. Let's get something eat and mingle for a bit."

I pushed open the doors and let the kids and Momo go in first. I heard someone cuss about the dog being in the clubhouse, but I flipped them off. It wasn't like Momo would hurt anything. Although I wouldn't put it past her to steal some food. I scanned the space, making sure she wasn't near the tables at the back wall, and realized she'd glued herself to Nova. The dog danced at her side, looking up at my daughter in adoration. Looked like I wasn't the only one who'd been wanting a family. Momo was in heaven with three kids to run after.

I led Charisma to a table and pulled out a chair for her. "Want something to eat? I can fix a plate and bring it to you?"

"Just bring me a little of all the main dishes. I'm not sure how much I can eat, but I want to try everything." Her eyes went wide, and she looked around, seeming frantic. I realized she thought she'd been yelling, which she did on occasion.

"It's fine, baby. No one here cares how loud you are. They know you can't hear, and they'd much rather get to speak to you, than have you sit here alone. No one will judge you." I leaned down to kiss her forehead then went to fix a plate for her. The kids were already in line, and I spotted Momo on her hindlegs, trying to steal a piece of chicken. "Momo! Down!"

The dog dropped to the floor and glowered at me. Until Nova broke off a bite of her chicken and handed it to her. I wasn't sure if I should scold her for giving Momo people food, or just let them have fun. The kids had never had a pet before. I didn't think it would hurt anything, for now anyway.

I glanced over where I'd left Charisma and saw Darby sitting with my wife. I liked Renegade's woman and knew she'd make Charisma feel at home. After I piled up two plates and grabbed some sodas, shoving the cans under my arm, I went back to the table and set down Charisma's things. I kissed her again, and let her know where I'd be, before heading to a spot in the corner where Scratch, Charming, and Havoc had decided to sit. I slid into the empty chair and cracked open the soda can.

"No beer?" Havoc asked.

"Don't need one right now." Light filtered into the room, and I saw Cinder and Meg come inside with their son, Tanner. He lifted a gift bag when he saw me, and I knew he'd brought Charisma's property cut. "Be right back."

I hurried over and took the sack from him. Meg followed me to where Charisma sat, still talking to Darby and Nikki had joined them. I helped Charisma to her feet, even though she looked a little worried.

"As you can see, each old lady here is wearing a cut." I tipped my head at Darby, who twisted in her seat so Charisma could get a good look. "It's called a property cut, like I mentioned before. And I have one for you."

I pulled the cut from the bag and held it up for her to see. Tears misted her eyes and one rolled down her cheek. I leaned in and kissed her, not caring who watched. When I pulled back, she eagerly took the cut from me and slid it over her shoulders, running her hands down the front with reverence.

"How do I look?" she asked, turning slowly.

"Perfect. You look like a biker's old lady, which is what you are." And I hoped like hell I could convince her to wear that cut and *only* the cut at some point, while I took her from behind. I liked the thought of fucking her while I looked down at my name plastered across her back.

She shooed me away, which made me smile. I mouthed a *thank you* to the ladies sitting with her, knowing they were why she felt so at ease right now. By the time I got back the table and my food, I growled. "Who the fuck took my corn bread?"

Havoc grinned. "Shouldn't have left it."

"You fucker! That's the best damn part of the meal." I looked around and saw Jian nearby and yelled out for him. He came over without question. "Your uncle Havoc here decided to steal my cornbread while I gave your mom her cut. Can you snatch another off the table for me?"

"On it," he said, darting off.

"We need some new rules around here. Not touching another man's bike or woman isn't enough anymore. We need to add not touching another man's food and beer to the list."

"You aren't drinking beer," Havoc pointed out.

I reached over and snatched his, draining it in one gulp before he could protest. "Now we're slightly even."

"That was a dick move," Havoc muttered, getting up to go grab another one.

Scratch chuckled. "Serves him right. He should have known better. I've seen people get stabbed for stealing a slice of that cornbread. Meg made it and sent it over earlier. She even gave the Prospects their own for helping set all this up."

"Well, now I want to kill the fucker. I didn't realize Meg made it. I don't know what she puts it in, but that shit is like crack. One piece is never enough."

"She made four huge pans of it," Charming said. "We've already put out two. If you want a second piece, I suggest you get it soon."

"How's married life?" Scratch asked. "Haven't seen the two of you out of the house much."

"I think she's overwhelmed by everything. I can't

blame her. I've tried to ease her into this new life, but..." I shrugged and dug into my food, chewing and swallowing before I continued. "She told me today she doesn't feel worthy of me. It about gutted me to hear those words come from her."

"She'll get there," Scratch said. He looked over at Clarity, who was leaning against a wall talking to Janessa. "Our women tend to think they're broken. They don't realize how wrong they are. She'll see that in time."

"At least your kids are fitting in easily enough," Charming said. "I think they've already made friends with everyone close to their age. Nova and Momo are playing a board game with Madsy, Tanner, and Salem. Should we warn them Momo will steal the pieces?"

I snorted. "No. They'll probably have fun chasing her down to get it back."

"Just saw Li head out with Taggart, Levi, Caleb, Payson, and Allegra. Any idea what that's about?" Havoc asked as he sat down again.

Jian brought my cornbread to me, and I hugged the hell out of him when he handed me three slices. Then he ran off to play some handheld video game with Noah. "I put Li's football in the back seat of the Jeep. Told him they could go out back to play if they wanted. I'm surprised the girls are going, though."

"You know they like proving they're as tough as the boys," Scratch said.

Charming took his phone out, frowning as it buzzed. He swiped the screen and read the message, paling a little. "Um. I'll be back in a bit. Need to take care of something."

He bolted before anyone could say a word. I looked over at Scratch and saw the contemplative look on his face. I remembered Charming's near slip up on the phone with me... about waking someone up. It seemed even the VP wasn't aware of what was happening with our President. And that made me even more curious.

"Anyone else find it odd our President seems to be keeping secrets?" Havoc asked. "Not to mention, he's forbidden anyone from going to his house."

Now that had my attention. "When I called, he started to say I was going to wake someone up. Then he wouldn't tell me who was at his house."

"I have a feeling everything will reveal itself soon enough," Scratch said. "Until then, we'll wait and be on guard. Because if the Pres looked that rattled over a text, and is hiding someone in his house, I have a feeling the shit will hit the fan at any moment."

"Did one of you assholes make the mistake of saying it was quiet around here?" I asked. "Because things always blow up right after that happens."

"Not that I'm aware of," Havoc said. "But if they did, I'm going to pound their asses into the ground."

There'd be a line forming behind him too. I had a feeling we'd all want a piece of whatever fuck-up did that shit.

Chapter Six

Charisma

I'd been so worried about meeting the other women, and it had been for nothing. They were so sweet, funny, and accepting. I hadn't known how they would react not only to me being deaf, but my mangled ears. Not to mention the fact I'd lived with Heather. I'd been concerned they would think I'd been in on it with her. It seemed someone had already set the record straight and let them know in advance about anything they might have found shocking.

They were also great at taking turns speaking and making sure I was facing them so I could read their lips. It warmed my heart, knowing they were taking the time to set me at ease and include me in the conversation. Phantom had been right. I was going to have a lot of friends here.

"We have to know…" Darby leaned in closer, probably lowering her voice. Wouldn't do any good because my response would likely be loud enough for the entire room to hear it. "Is Phantom as sweet at home as he is the rest of the time? He's like a big teddy bear."

Nikki nodded. "He's the favorite uncle for all the kids at the compound. And he's so amazing with them. It broke my heart every time I'd see him playing with the children, knowing he wanted a family of his own. Think he's the only one who kept having girlfriends in the hopes of finding his Mrs. Right."

I'd already heard about his dating experience, so their words didn't surprise me. "He's wonderful. The best man I've ever met. Sometimes I think I'm dreaming everything because it doesn't seem possible a guy could ever be that amazing."

Another woman came over and pulled up a chair. She waved. "I'm Josie. Jackal's woman. Mind if I join you?"

"It's nice to meet you. I guess everyone already knows who I am."

Josie laughed and nodded. "Oh yeah. The second Phantom called Charming we all knew about it. He told Charming he was bringing home a woman and kids, and that he wasn't asking permission to keep y'all, he was just telling him how it would be. That news spread like wildfire. And we were all so thrilled for him. He's the sweetest, gentlest guy here. Don't get me wrong. If I were a bad person, I wouldn't want to meet him, because I've heard he can seriously fuck someone up. But women and kids? He's a softie."

I'd already seen Phantom's handiwork. "Unless the woman is a bad person. He didn't go easy on Heather."

Darby's eyebrows rose. "You saw what he did to her?"

"I walked in while he was still... working. It didn't bother me. The woman was evil. If anything, I wish she could have suffered more. She destroyed so many lives."

"Yep, you're going to fit right in," Nikki said.

The women took turns, telling me how they'd met their men. Finding out Darby had been used and left for dead in an alley had stunned me. Nikki's story about broke my heart. But it was Josie's who fascinated me the most.

"You grew up around another club?" I asked.

"Not exactly. Tank was my half-brother. I'd been to the clubhouse for parties and some family events. The Dixie Reapers knew who I was, and mostly gave me a wide berth. I can admit I was a bit of a brat."

"That's putting it mildly from what I hear," Nikki said.

Josie elbowed her. "Shut it. Anyway, Tank tried to keep me away from the club. He worried I'd end up getting hurt. Then I found out Jackal had knocked me up, and things changed. I moved into Tank's house. He helped me raise Allegra until Jackal showed up one day. I'm surprised my brother didn't murder him."

"Meg's story is really heartbreaking," Darby said. "She'll tell you if you ask her. She's very honest about what she's been through. And Cinder was a bit of a bastard at first. Then he nearly died trying to save her. He offered up his life in exchange for hers. So fucking romantic."

"I think my brother's vocabulary is rubbing off on you," Nikki said. "You wouldn't have phrased it like that before."

"What can I say, I'm learning that a few cuss words can make you feel free. Besides, your brother says they're sentence enhancers."

Nikki rolled her eyes. "Of course, he does."

"I know you can't call because of the hearing issue, but you're welcome to text any of us anytime you want," Josie said. "Think of us as being your sisters."

"Unless one of your kids ends up falling for one of ours. Then that would be weird," Nikki said.

"Have you met the other old ladies?" Nikki asked.

"Just Clarity," I said.

"I don't see Jordan, but she's Havoc's woman. She may be running late for some reason. Meg is with Cinder. I'm sure she'll stop by at some point. Looks like she's making the rounds, checking on everyone. Cinder was the club President for a long time, so Meg got used to being the old lady in charge so to speak. Kind of like a room mom at school, but for the club." Darby looked around before facing me again. "Then again, Charming is still single, so he probably doesn't mind her doing that. One less thing on his plate."

"Your kids are also welcome to stop by whenever they want," Nikki said. "We're used to each other's kids popping up here and there without warning. I'm sure ours will be at your place too. As long as they're inside the gates, none of us really worry about them."

"So you and Phantom..." Josie leaned her elbows on the table. "How's the romance going between you two? Because we wouldn't blame you if you needed more time, but I promise if you aren't in love with him already, you will be."

"Don't ask her that! What the hell is wrong with you?" Darby asked.

Josie shrugged. "Like we didn't all fall for a biker's charms?"

"He's the only man I've ever wanted to touch me. I feel all warm inside when he holds me. And when he kisses me..." My cheeks heated. "The entire world goes away, and it's like it's nothing and no one exists but us. I've never felt like that before."

"Sounds to me like she's in love," Nikki said.

Was I? I'd thought it was too soon for something like that. Sure, I'd seen movies where they fell in love immediately, then had a bunch of fumbling dates that made it seem like they'd never get together. It was all just pretend, though. Those things didn't happen in real life, especially in *my* life.

"Looks like we gave her something to think about," Josie said. "My work here is done."

"Come on," Nikki said, standing up. "I want to

introduce you to Ashes, my old man, and my brother, Renegade. You need to get to know the men in the club too."

I stood and followed her. I met so many people I worried I wouldn't be able to keep them all straight. At least the men would have their names on their cuts, except the Prospects. Remembering which woman belongs to which man might confuse me for a while, though.

By the time I'd met everyone, Phantom had come over to kidnap me. We went back to the table where he'd been sitting with Scratch and Havoc, and a harried-looking Charming had returned after running out of the building earlier. Phantom pulled me onto his lap and held me close. I had to admit, meeting everyone hadn't been as scary as I'd feared it would be.

I liked the sense of community. Family.

Phantom had removed me from a hellish situation. It had been me and the kids, fighting to not lose ourselves in the pain inflicted by Heather and her friends. Now I had a husband, and all these wonderful, supportive people around me. I didn't think I'd be comfortable just dropping by any of their homes right now. In time, I would. For now, it just felt nice to know I had so many kind people surrounding me, and the children. Jian, Li, and Nova had kids who understood, at least to some extent. For that, I'd always be grateful.

Phantom patted my thigh and I turned to face him as much as I could while sitting in his lap. I watched his lips as he spoke.

"Ready to head home? The kids can stay and play for a while. If they notice we're gone, one of the adults will let them know where we are. Someone will drop them off later."

I had a feeling he wanted me to himself, since

our shower hadn't turned out the way he'd planned. Of course, he'd been the one to back off. Didn't mean he wouldn't want to pick back up where we left off. And I was more than all right with that. I kissed his cheek and stood. Phantom took my hand, waved bye to everyone, and led me out to the Jeep. After seeing the other families together, I didn't feel so self-conscious over his public displays of affection. It seemed to be something they all did.

When Nikki had introduced me to Ashes, he'd kissed her and hugged her to him. Renegade had lifted Darby off her feet to give her a bear hug. Jackal had bent Josie over his arm and kissed her so long and deep, I'd started to feel like I should spray them with cold water. After seeing all that today, I was more than happy to let Phantom kiss me whenever he wanted. He could have tossed me over his shoulder, and I'd have probably laughed.

"You a little less worried now?" he asked as he got into the Jeep.

"Yeah. I liked meeting everyone. They seem nice."

"They'll always have your back. You ever need anything, all you have to do is ask. You'll probably have multiple people show up to help. It's just how they are."

"Remember what you said before we left?" I asked.

"Which part? I said a lot of stuff."

"About tying me to your bed."

His eyes heated and he nodded. "I do. I've wanted that from the moment I saw you. Just didn't want to push. I know you've been through a lot, and I don't want you to try and give me too much too soon. And if you're never ready for that, I'll still want you.

You set the rules in the bedroom, Charisma."

"I want to try. I know you'd never hurt me. I trust you... Kenji."

He gripped the back of my neck and pulled me closer, then kissed the hell out of me. I nearly crawled across the console to get in his lap. My pussy ached and my clit throbbed, and all from one kiss!

He rubbed his thumb across my lip, then he drew back. "When we get home, you have thirty seconds to get to the bedroom and start taking off these clothes. Then I want you to put that cut back on."

"Why?" I asked.

"Because I want to fuck you while you're wearing it."

My heart thumped wildly in my chest, and I squeezed my thighs together. "Okay."

"Okay?" he asked. "That's all you have to say?"

"Um. Can you start driving? I'm ready to get home. I want you to tie me up, and anything else you want to do. I'm willing to try it at least once."

"Beautiful, all you have to do is tell me you don't like something, it scares you, or it hurts, and I will back the hell off. Doesn't matter if I'm balls-deep inside you at the moment or not. You understand?"

"Yes, Kenji. I understand."

He kissed me again, then put the Jeep into gear and drove us home. I hoped the kids would stay gone for a while. If they didn't, maybe I wouldn't be screaming too loud. Last thing I wanted to do was scar them for life because their mom was having sex with their dad.

* * *

Phantom

I didn't want to admit it, but Charisma had been

right. I'd been careless when I'd gone after Heather. Even worse, I'd lost my focus when I'd taken Charisma and the kids out of their hometown. I'd gotten sloppy and someone had found us. Or rather them. I didn't think the asshole cared one way or another about me.

Mason Reynolds IV had arrived in town last night, exactly two months since Charisma had voiced her concern, and immediately began poking his nose around, asking questions about the club. While the town might not love the Devil's Boneyard, they could admit we did a lot of good around town. Which meant outsiders asking questions put up red flags, and then we heard about it.

"Do we know who he's after?" I asked Charming.

"No. I can't find a single record of which boy he intended to 'adopt' which bugs the shit out of me. There should have been some paperwork, an email trail, or something. Whatever this guy has been up to, he's either a pro at hiding his nefarious deeds or he's paid someone to do it."

"So we have nothing?" I didn't like it. Not even a little. This was my family we were talking about. I'd promised they were safe.

"He's here for a reason. I know we can't tell the kids not to attend school. I guess we could say they all came down with the same virus."

"No. We don't want to draw more attention," I said.

"Dad." I looked up and saw Li standing in the door with Taggart behind him. "What's going on?"

As much as I wanted to tell him it was nothing, I wouldn't do that to the kid. He'd been through hell and come out the other side. My boy was a fighter, and he deserved the truth. Besides, I couldn't be with him every second of the day. I needed him aware of his surroundings and on his guard.

"Pres, can I call you back?" I asked.

"Yeah. Take care of your family. I'll let you decide how much to tell them. I know you want them to be aware they could be in danger."

"Thanks, Pres." I ended the call and motioned for Li to come sit at the table. He sat across from me, and Taggart hovered in the doorway. "You too, Taggart. If you're going to hang out with Li, I want the both of you to be aware of what's going on."

Taggart came up behind Li and placed a hand on his shoulder. I eyed the two of them, and noticed Li looked a little flushed and fidgeted more than usual. While I had my suspicions of what was going on, I wasn't going to say a damn word. The two of them would talk when they were ready. Although, Taggart would be eighteen soon, and Li would only be turning sixteen. The two years wouldn't be a big deal once they were both adults, but in the meantime, it could cause some problems.

Even thought there was a Romeo and Juliet law in the state of Florida, I knew a lot of the townspeople wouldn't care. The boys would have a hard road to travel, especially Taggart since he was the older of the two.

"Where the hell did you two go?" a female voice growled from the front entry. A moment later, a cute strawberry blonde stalked into the room, a scowl on her face. The attitude rolling off her made me want to smile. When she plopped down on Li's lap and Taggart put a hand on both of them, things got even more complicated.

"Boys, want to introduce me to your friend?" I asked.

"I'm Nelly," she said. "Nelly O'Gill. And you're Li's dad."

I nodded. "I am. I needed to have a quick talk with the boys. Have the three of you been hanging out a lot?"

She looked from Li to Taggart to me. "Um."

"Nelly has been my girlfriend for the past year," Taggart said. "She's sixteen."

I arched an eyebrow and eyed his hands, resting on both Li and Nelly, before staring Taggart down. The little shit smirked at me and didn't say a word. I wondered if his dad knew about this, and how Havoc felt about the situation. Something told me he'd have a few choice words to say. But I knew Li had been healing, in large part, due to Taggart. The two had spent a lot of time together over the last six or seven weeks. I'd eavesdropped on a conversation between the two and heard Li talking about one of the men who'd visited him at Heather's, and how he worried he'd been broken. The older boy had told him he wasn't broken, just a little cracked.

Nelly huffed. "Such a chickenshit sometimes. I'm dating both of them. Or rather, we're all dating each other? I'm not really sure if there's a label for what we have, but it works. Is there a problem?"

"Nope. Not with me anyway. I can't say how Havoc will react, or the rest of the club. And I damn sure don't know how the town will take it, but the three of you will figure it out. That's not what I needed to talk to them about."

"Should I go?" Nelly asked.

I held Taggart's gaze, wondering how trustworthy Nelly was. He'd been seeing her a year, and yet I'd never met her before. That alone told me he didn't typically bring her to the compound. Had Havoc and Jordan ever met her?

"I know about your club," Nelly said. "Not everything, obviously. I've seen the things you do for the town, to help people. Especially women and kids. So whatever you need to say to them, I swear I won't tell anyone. But if it involves Li and Taggart, I want to know. I care about both of them."

"Don't think I need to tell you if I hear rumblings around town, or find out you ran your mouth, it won't end well for you," I said. Li tensed and Taggart growled a little. "You two boys think you're big enough to go toe-to-toe with me? You ready to test who has the bigger balls?"

They both relented, but I saw the spark of anger in Taggart's eyes. That boy could be trouble one day if Havoc didn't keep a tight leash on him. Charming might be pissed if he found out I talked in front of Nelly, but if she wanted to help keep Li safe, I wasn't going to say no.

"Li, do you recognize the name Mason Reynolds IV?"

He paled and audibly swallowed. "Yeah. I know who he is."

"I've heard he's in town and asking questions. We think he's after you and your brother. He's been asking about the club, and any boys who suddenly came to town. He already knows you're here with the Devil's Boneyard. A few people in town gave Charming a heads-up when he started nosing around, wanting to know more about us."

"He wants Jian. Heather was going to sell him to Mason, under the guise of it being an adoption. We can't let him find my brother."

I reached across the table and put my hand over Li's. "Hey. I'm your dad and I promised to protect you.

All of you. Do you honestly think I'm going to let some asshole come in here and take any of you? Fuck no!"

"My dad will kill him if he comes near your brother," Taggart said. "The club will keep him safe."

"How?" Li asked.

"Let us worry about that. What I need from you three is simple. Keep an eye out for Mason Reynolds IV, and anyone else from your past. I'll get a picture of the guy from Shade, and you can show Taggart and Nelly. We need to let Jian know he's in danger."

"Mom and Nova too," Li said. "He'll use them to lure Jian out. He knows if he hurts Mom, we'll do whatever he wants."

My hand fisted on the table, and I felt myself start to shake. "He hurt your mom?"

Li nodded. "He's actually the one who made her deaf. Heather poured the acid on her, but the doctor said the trauma from Mason slamming her head into the wall is what actually made her hearing go. He ruptured her eardrums. The guy was a friend of Heather's, so he didn't say anything to the cops about the abuse. She had him in her pocket."

"That fucker is mine." I'd make him suffer. More than what I'd done to Heather. I'd make him cry. Scream. Beg for his life. I wanted his blood.

"If you need to ask Charming to call Church, we'll keep an eye on Mom, Nova, and Jian. Any idea where they are right now?" Li asked.

"Your mom was feeling tired so she's napping. Jian went over to Scratch's house, and Nova is at your place, Taggart. She's playing with Salem."

"Does this mean I get to meet the family?" Nelly asked.

I snorted. "Knew it. Your dad is going to freak the fuck out, and your mom might as well. Just do me a favor. If Jordan loses her shit, get my kids out of harm's way. I really don't want to go up against your dad, but I will if my kids get caught in the crossfire and end up injured."

"You said your mom was a badass, but I didn't believe you," Nelly said, her eyes widening. "I can't wait to meet her!"

"Good luck. You're going to need it."

"So are you," Li said. "You still have to tell Mom what's going on. She's going to panic."

"I'm aware. Can you get Jian and take him with you to Havoc's? I'd rather all of you be in one place. I'll send a Prospect over for some extra protection. I'm not taking any chances."

"Consider it done," Taggart said.

"All right. All of you get gone. I'm going to go wake up your mom and let her know what's up. Just... keep away from the house for a bit. Not sure how the hell I'll calm her down, but I'll figure it out. I'll drop her off with y'all before I head to Church."

"Want me to ask Dad to talk to Charming?" Taggart said. "Seems like you'll have your hands full."

I nodded. "That would be great. Thanks, Taggart. And, Nelly, I hope you're ready for the insanity because you're going to be baptized in fire. But when the shit hits the fan, there's no safer place than Havoc's house. If he's not there to kick ass and take names, his woman will step in for him. Ask her about Havoc getting captured and how she got him back. It's one hell of a story."

Taggart groaned. "Must she? I've heard that story too many times already."

"Hey, your mom earned the right to tell as many people as she wants. If it weren't for her, your dad would have been stuck in Colombia even longer. Be thankful she's as tough as she is. Pretty sure the Colombian police wanted her out of the country bad enough they'd have given her whatever she wanted."

The kids filed out of the kitchen, and I went to the bedroom to wake up Charisma. I leaned against the doorframe, just admiring her a moment. She seemed so peaceful. As much as I didn't want to confirm her worst fears were true, I couldn't keep her in the dark either. She wasn't just my old lady. She was my wife. My partner.

My everything.

I knelt on the mattress and smoothed her hair away from her face. "Charisma, I need you to wake up."

I shook my head, feeling like an idiot. She couldn't hear me so why I was talking to her? I ran my fingers over her cheeks, down her nose, across her lips. She moaned softly in her sleep but didn't open her eyes. Stretching out on the bed next to her, I pressed my lips to hers. When I drew back, her eyes fluttered open, and she gave me a sleepy smile.

"Feeling better?" I asked.

"A little."

I tried not to wince at her volume. Since she couldn't hear herself, there were times she barely whispered and others when she was loud enough, they could probably hear her outside. Not that I would ever ask her to stop talking. The fact she felt comfortable enough to speak to me felt like I'd won the damn lottery.

"We need to talk. I need to drop you off at Havoc's place. The kids will already be there."

She leaned up on an elbow. "What's wrong?"

"Mason Reynolds is here." She cried out and recoiled from me. I reached out, pulling her into my arms. I tipped her chin up so she could see my face. "It's going to be okay. We're going to call Church and come up with a plan to handle him. I'm sure a few clubs will be happy to send in reinforcements if we need them."

I felt her tremble and wiped a tear off her cheek. Li had said the bastard had been responsible for making Charisma deaf. I wondered what else he'd done to her, but I wasn't about to make her talk about such a dark time in her life. What she needed was my support and love, and that's exactly what I'd give her. I didn't need more time to know how I felt about her. But I also knew if I told her right now, she'd wonder if I'd only said it because of the threat to her and the kids.

"Once I get my hands on him, he's going to suffer. He's not leaving this town alive, and not one damn person will get in my way. We're not involving the cops. This is club business, and I will damn well handle it."

She kissed my cheek, then my lips. "Be careful. I can't lose you."

"You won't." No fucking way I'd let the bastard get the drop on me. I had something precious to defend. I'd gladly give my life to keep my family, or my club, safe. But the only one who would die this time would be Mason Reynolds IV.

Chapter Seven

Charisma

I'd met some of the old ladies over the last week, but Jordan hadn't been among them. Clutching Phantom's hand, I'd walked into their home and come to a halt. Havoc had still been home, and the huge man intimidated me. At least, he had until I saw him with his kids. The man turned to mush when it came to his girls. Phantom had hugged me once more before leaving. Now it was just me, Jordan, and a house full of kids and teens.

Jordan handed me a cup of hot cocoa, and I noticed everyone else had one too. The kids were sprawled around the living room with a cartoon playing for the younger ones. I settled in a chair near Li, Taggart, and a pretty girl who looked like she'd be sassy as hell. I hadn't had a chance to meet her yet. I lifted my eyebrows at Li, hoping he'd take the hint.

Li started signing as he spoke. "Mom, this is Nelly. She's my girlfriend."

Nelly nudged him in the ribs and Taggart leaned a little closer. "Actually, they're both mine. She's seeing both of us, and…"

Li glared at Taggart. His cheeks flushed and I saw him tremble a little. I reached over to pat him on the arm. Whatever he had to say, it wouldn't change how I felt about him. He had to know that, right? He started talking again, with both his lips and his hands. "I'm bisexual, Mom. So is Taggart. We're with Nelly, but we're also together."

I set my cup aside and hugged him tight, then hugged the other two as well. I didn't want to use my voice, knowing I would possibly be too loud, so I signed to Li and left it to him to decide if he wanted to translate.

I love you, Li, and so does your dad. All we want is for you to be happy. You have our support. I hope you know that. If anyone has a problem with who you love, I'm sure your dad will be happy to talk to them. Probably with his fists.

Li smiled. "Thanks, Mom. We weren't sure how the club would react, so we didn't say anything. Havoc was surprisingly cool about it. So was Dad."

So he'd already told Phantom. Part of me felt a little hurt that I'd found out last. At the same time, it warmed my heart to hear Li had confided something like that to his father. It meant they were building trust and bonding. Li hadn't had a male role model in so long.

Jordan came over to stand in front of me, waving her hand to get my attention. "There are some who may give the boys a hard time, even here at the club, but Havoc will straighten them out. If he doesn't, I will. I understand why they didn't want to say anything. I'm also glad they decided to come clean. I don't like the idea of them sneaking around because they didn't feel safe enough at home to be themselves."

Taggart rolled his eyes and I waited to see if he'd say something. He shook his head, looked at Nelly and Li, before talking to his mom. "Because it had nothing to do with Dad possibly scaring the shit out of Nelly. There were multiple reasons we didn't tell anyone."

Li signed and spoke. "But Jordan is right. It was mostly about the club and how they might react. I also didn't want to disappoint you and Dad."

I made a sound and placed my fingers over my throat, wanting to speak to him without having to sign. Jordan gave me a nod of encouragement.

"We could never be disappointed, Li. Well, all

right. If you bring home Fs on your report card, that would be different." I reached for his hand, giving it a squeeze. "We love you, Li. All of you. There wasn't a caveat when we adopted you. Nothing that said we'd love you only if you were a certain way."

He hugged me again and Taggart had a smile on his face. It was good to see Li happy and accepted. I knew he'd gotten to the age where he'd want to date. Or had he not been through so much trauma he would have. I hadn't known what to expect in all honesty. Until Phantom had come along, I'd not wanted anyone to touch me. The same could have happened with Li. Or maybe it had. I had to wonder if Taggart and Nelly were what he'd been waiting for. I didn't think kids met their true love, or loves, anymore, but it would be nice if he did. Li deserved all the best things in life.

"Do you think they'll be long?" I asked Jordan.

She shrugged a shoulder. "Sometimes they call Church and come back home in a half hour. Other times they're gone just about all day. It depends on how long it takes for them to find a solution."

"And we just sit and wait? Every time?"

"Yep. Sometimes the old ladies go to the clubhouse too. We commandeer the main room and talk while we wait on the guys. I'm not about to take the kids there without the place being scrubbed first, though, so we're stuck here for now."

"Am I talking too loud?" I asked.

Jordan grinned. "A bit, but it's okay. It's nice hearing you talk instead of trying to figure out what you're signing. We'll all learn. It just won't happen overnight. If it makes things easier on you, we're happy to take classes, use YouTube or whatever."

"Thank you." I signed when I spoke, thinking maybe they'd pick up a few things just from repetition.

Jordan tipped her head toward the kitchen. "Why don't you come help me figure out a snack for everyone. We can talk. Taggart, Li, and Nelly can keep an eye on everyone."

I stood and carried my mug with me. I finished off the cocoa and rinsed the mug. Jordan offered coffee but I shook my head. I hadn't been feeling very well today. Out of nowhere I'd been so tired I hadn't been able to keep my eyes open. My body felt like it weighed a ton. I wondered if all the changes were catching up to me.

"What's the deal with this Mason guy?" Jordan asked.

"He wants Jian." I glanced behind me, worried I'd spoken too loud.

Jordan seemed to understand and shut off the room with hidden sliding doors. She poured herself some coffee and took a seat across from me. Pulling out her phone, she opened the music app and started a playlist. Even though I couldn't hear it, I could feel the vibrations through the table.

"Now we can talk without worrying too much the kids will hear something they shouldn't," she said.

"What do you know about where we came from?" I asked.

Her lips thinned and anger flashed in her eyes. "The woman who hurt Samurai had control of the boys, and Havoc said you stayed to try and protect them."

I nodded. "He's right. I wasn't much good to them, but a reprieve here and there was better than nightly abuse. And I'd gladly do it all over again, even knowing I'd lose my hearing."

"What about those implants?" she asked.

"They won't work."

Her brow furrowed. "There has to be something that would make your life easier. How do you maneuver when you're out and about? What about driving? You couldn't hear a car honk, or a train whistle."

"I pay closer attention to my surroundings when I'm driving. It actually makes me a more cautious driver than a hearing person."

"I guess that makes sense. Well, if there's ever anything I can do to help in some way, please let me know. I realize I have the reputation of being the bad bitch around here, and I've earned it, but it doesn't make me heartless."

I smiled. "I know. You wouldn't have adopted Salem and Taggart if you were. You've given them a good home, loving parents, and clearly shower them with affection and whatever they might need. No one could ever say you're a bad parent."

"Did that woman ever hurt you or your daughter?" Jordan asked.

I pushed my hair back so she could see my ears. "She threw acid on me one time. Both ears got the brunt of it, and my hair. Thankfully, she didn't get it all the way to my scalp and the hair grew back."

"Is that what caused your hearing loss?" Jordan asked. "I'm sorry if that's too personal. Tell me to shut up if I ask the wrong thing."

I waved her off. "It's fine. And no, it didn't. The man who's here for Jian is why I can't hear. He slammed my head into a wall repeatedly, both sides, and it ruptured my eardrums. The damage is permanent, and nothing will help."

"What about a dog?" she asked. "Not Momo. I love her, but she's just a pet. I mean a working dog who's trained to help deaf people?"

"They're expensive. I've been fine without one so far."

"So this Mason guy... he's hurt the boys and you. Do you think he'd try to actually get inside the compound? Or will he wait and get you or the boys while you're out? I don't like being blind when our family is in danger. Drives me batshit fucking crazy. Havoc tells me more than he probably should, and by this point, the club just expects it."

"I don't think he'd try to come in. He might be tough against women and kids, but Mason will also protect himself. He wouldn't chance going up against the club to get to us. Not unless he thought they could be bought. He wouldn't hesitate to offer money in exchange for what he wants."

She tipped her head to the side. "Interesting. I bet we could use that to our advantage. Let me just text Havoc and let him know. Might be useful to them while they're plotting."

She tapped out a message and sent it to her man before focusing on me again. I hadn't talked to someone so much in forever. I spoke with Phantom quite a bit, but this was different. And really nice. I couldn't remember the last time I'd had a friend. I didn't know Jordan well enough to give her that label just yet. Didn't meant it couldn't happen quickly, though.

"I'm sure Shade will pull a picture of the guy and pass it around so everyone knows what he looks like. We'll all watch for him. Until he's caught, I'd suggest you and the kids not going anywhere alone. I know Taggart is taking Li with him to the high school. Havoc already arranged for someone to follow them and meet them when school lets out to come back home. He's not taking chances."

I could tell she was getting wound up because she was starting to talk faster. I lifted a hand. "Slower. I can't follow if you talk too fast."

"Sorry." She winced. "Anyway. Just make sure you keep someone with you. A man. As sexist as that sounds, I doubt a guy like Mason will be deterred by me or anyone else being with you."

Jordan had a good point. Mason would likely try to use another woman. He'd think he had two people to leverage for what he wanted. The last thing I wanted was anyone getting hurt because our past had come knocking at the gate. Since Samurai had been a victim of Heather, I knew we weren't the only ones with demons. He might have moved on and put his past behind him, but what if someone else had suffered a trauma? At the party, I'd learned Meg had a troublesome past, and same for Darby. What would happen if Mason got his hands on them? And what about the other children... I didn't want them in harm's way.

I wondered if Phantom had considered that. Yes, Mason was here for Jian. It didn't mean the man wouldn't hesitate to snag any other kids he could. Even if they weren't to his taste, his friends might buy them. It sickened me just thinking about any of the children here being in that situation -- or any child at all. They should be able to grow up, build happy memories, and not have the ugliness in the world touch them.

The only comfort I had with Mason so close is that I knew if anyone dared to take a child from any of the bikers here, hell would be unleashed until that kid was safe at home again. I'd seen what Phantom did to Heather. Samurai had been his cousin and was now a grown man. He'd still exacted revenge, not only for his family but for every child ever touched by that vile woman. He'd already promised to do worse to Mason.

Was it wrong I wanted to buy him more weapons so he could make the man suffer as much as possible?

"You have a ferocious look on your face," Jordan said.

Did I admit I wanted Phantom to make that man hurt and make it last? Heather had gotten off too easy, in my opinion. She'd hurt kids day after day, and yet her end had come quickly. I didn't want the same for Mason. What sort of person did that make me? I rubbed at my stomach, feeling the acid bubble.

"You want blood, don't you?" Jordan asked, tipping her head to the side like an inquisitive puppy. "It makes you feel bad because you want Mason, and all the men like him to die a bloody, horrible, nightmarish death. Am I right?"

"Yes. It's wrong to want another person to die. Except I don't just want them dead."

"I understand. Trust me. Every old lady here will get it. We've had hurdles to overcome, people we wanted our men to torture and kill. The club has come through for us each and every time. Mason Reynolds may have money, but he doesn't know what he's stepped in by coming here. You, Nova, Jian, Li... you're all family. Because you belong to Phantom, that makes you property of the Devil's Boneyard, and these men won't rest until that filth is in pieces and buried in multiple shallow graves."

"Good. I only wish we could rid the world of all of them. Every last man and woman who preys on those weaker than they are. They don't deserve to live happy lives." I leaned back and folded my arms over my chest.

Jordan smiled. "Honey, they don't deserve to live at all."

And that was the moment I knew I'd just found my best friend.

* * *

Phantom

We all eyed Havoc with varying degrees of horror.

"Did your woman seriously suggest we invite that weasel to our compound under the guise of letting him buy Jian?" Irish asked. "I'm not sure if that's diabolical, downright insane, or fucking scary as hell."

"It can't be all of the above?" Stripes asked, his Russian accent more pronounced. I'd noticed it happened when stress was high, and our women or kids were in danger.

"Can I just say I wouldn't mind a Jordan of my own some day?" Gator smiled. "That woman is a force to be reckoned with."

Ripper snorted. "Not me. I like them soft and sweet. I'm hard enough already -- pun intended."

Charming slammed his fist onto the table. "Enough! Can't the lot of you focus? One of our own is in danger and you're running off at the mouth like a bunch of teen girls. Fucking useless!"

I leaned back in my chair, surveying the room. It was my family on the chopping block. Mason Reynolds IV -- apparently the fucker really did use the full name -- was here for my son. Had they forgotten that part? I'd been as quiet as I could, but if this kept up, I'd have to leave the damn room. Charming was right. We weren't getting anywhere. We'd been here for an hour or more and other than seeing a picture of Mason, checking out his bank records, and an accounting of where he'd been the last few days, we hadn't done shit.

"I'm not putting Jian on lockdown. It's not fair to him, or to the other kids. Besides, if this man is willing to take my son, what makes you so sure he won't decide to scoop up everyone else's kids too?" I asked.

"Pedophiles tend to have a type," Magnus said.

Fucker. Like we didn't all know that? What was his point? That Mason would take my son and leave? Did that make this any less crucial? No! Which was why we were all in damn Church trying to figure this shit out.

"Yes, but do you think he doesn't know other men and women just like him? He found Jian through Heather. How many other men know my kids and might come looking for them? I can admit I fucked up. When I took out Heather, it was in the heat of the moment. I didn't cover my tracks well enough. The motel I stayed at was the type not to ask questions, but it didn't mean no one else around town saw us. Hell, Heather's neighbors could have very well been watching and reported what happened."

I heard the Pres's chair creak as he shifted. A few men around the table looked pissed, others looked concerned. I wasn't sure how to feel about the entire thing. I'd gained a wife and kids. Saved them from Heather and made sure she'd never hurt anyone again. But I'd also put them at risk by not being careful enough. If I hadn't let rage control my every step, maybe I'd have done things a little different. No way of knowing now.

"What would they have seen?" Charming asked.

I thought about the day I'd waited for Heather, watching her house from the nearby park. How Charisma had taken my breath away the moment she'd stepped out of the car. And I replayed every action I took, and every word I said. There were several things I'd have changed if I could. The end result would still have been the same... Charisma by my side, Heather dead, and three kids calling me Dad.

"The kids and Charisma getting into my Jeep. I didn't haul Heather to the old barn, though. Shade's friend took care of that part. I did head over there and take my pound of flesh. She was still breathing when I walked out, even though I left her rather bloody."

Charming's eyebrows lifted and he glanced at Shade. "Any idea what happened to Heather? Is she really dead and where did he put the body?"

"Axel isn't the type to spill all his secrets. Just know she won't be found. And yes, she's dead. He sent me an encrypted file of her last moments. I don't have it anymore." Shade closed his laptop. "I trust the guy. He could have doctored the video, but it looked legit."

I eyed Cinder and noticed he'd zoned out a bit. Or at least, he appeared to be elsewhere inside his head. He'd said he was too old for this shit, and I was starting to understand what he meant. He had roughly two decades on me, but I knew my time would come to step down and let someone else be the club Treasurer. It was more than that, though. Five years ago, I'd have never made the mistakes I did. Not even as angry as I'd been. Had I lost my edge?

"We aren't really considering letting that man into the compound, are we?" I asked. "Because I'm not sure I want him inside the gates. That's too damn close to my family."

"Too close to all our families," Cinder muttered. "I may not be President anymore, but I vote we don't let that asshole in here. If you want to set up some sort of trade to lure him in, I'd rather do it away from the compound. Cash for the kid."

I seconded that. Although, if they wanted to use Jian to get the guy's attention, they were shit out of luck. I wasn't letting my kids anywhere near that man. I didn't want them breathing the same air, and if I had my way, they wouldn't be. He'd either be six feet under, or in a prison far from here. Prison wouldn't be the ultimate goal. He'd eventually get out, want revenge, and possibly try to hurt my family again. Dead would be better. At least then I wouldn't worry about him anymore. Didn't mean someone else wouldn't come looking, but one thing at a time.

"He's not going to come if he doesn't see the kid with us," Shade said. "He's not stupid, even if he's trash. Thanks to his daddy, he's also loaded. From what I can tell, he's never had anything stick to him. A few parking violations, a drunk and disorderly, and he even got busted for a DUI. They were all thrown out and he walked away squeaky clean. Either he has a shark for a lawyer, or he's been untouchable thus far Could be paying off city officials. Wouldn't put it past him."

"No one is untouchable," I muttered. "Not even us."

I cracked my neck and stared at the table. There had to be a way to take him out. As much as I wanted to feel his blood on my hands, and watch the life drain from him, at this point I didn't care how we got rid of him. If the police wanted to lock his ass up and throw away the key, I'd deal with it. It would at least give me time to figure out a plan for when he got out. With the prisons overcrowded, as long as he followed the rules inside, he'd get an early release. The justice system was a joke sometimes.

I just didn't want him anywhere near Jian or the

rest of the family. Too much could go wrong in the blink of an eye. Besides, accidents were known to happen inside. No reason I couldn't arrange for Mason to tragically die during a fight in the yard or something. The club had some allies in a few prisons within a one-hundred-mile radius. And if he didn't end up at one of those, I'd find someone who could handle the problem.

Luring him out made sense. I just didn't agree with how they wanted to do it. There had to be something, another way... anything. A man like Mason probably did have a lawyer on retainer. If they'd gotten him off so far, they'd try to clear his name if he were accused of being a pedophile. And right now, we didn't have a damn bit of evidence against him.

Or did we...

"Shade, when you were digging up shit on Heather, how closely did you look at her bank records?"

"Which ones?" he asked. "The ones she inherited from her dead husband? Or her offshore account?"

I leaned forward and braced my elbows on the table. "The second one. What sort of deposits went in there? Were they traceable?"

He tapped at his keyboard, probably pulling up whatever he'd found on her. After looking at his screen for a few minutes, he frowned and shook his head. "I didn't dig any further. We knew it was her, and I gave you what you needed to take her out. It never occurred to me we'd need a paper trail from her to anyone else."

"How much time would you need to see if there's a connection between her and Mason, other than him looking for Jian and the fact Charisma and the kids knew who he was?" Charming asked.

"Because I don't think time is something we have a lot of. This guy has been here long enough to figure out who we are, where the kids are being kept, and he's trying to get cozy with the locals."

Shade cracked his fingers and started typing again. His eyes narrowed and his jaw tensed as his fingers flew faster over the keys. After a moment, he sat back and laced his fingers behind his neck.

"She did a decent job of hiding things, but whoever she hired wasn't the best. Give me a few hours. Maybe a little longer. If I run into any snags along the way, I'll call up Wire and Lavender. Wouldn't hurt to get them to help anyway. Maybe ask them to see what they can find on Mason. I could have missed something. While I'm good, I'm nowhere near their level." Shade reached for the laptop again. "I'll just stay here if that's all right. I have my power cord with me so I can plug in and get to work."

If I hadn't known the club hacker had installed a secure system in every damn building and house at the compound, I might have worried. He could work his mojo in here just as safely as he could at his home. Didn't make sense for him to run back and forth. But I sure the fuck hoped they didn't want all of us hanging around while he did his thing. I needed to see Charisma. Hold her. Reassure myself she and the kids were okay.

Stripes stood. "I'll have one of the girls bring you something to drink and a basket of fries."

Shade gave him a thumbs up and started getting his workspace set up for whatever the hell he did to get us the answers we needed. Computers and I didn't get along very well. Mine kept blowing up. Not literally, although I'd have preferred that to them just randomly deciding not to turn on anymore. I had the shittiest luck with the damn things.

I stood and made my way into the main part of the clubhouse. One of the club whores sat at the bar, staring into a beer like it had all the answers in the world. I knew the feeling well, and hoped she found more than I ever did. At another time, I'd have stopped to check on her. Right now, I had enough on my plate and a family to care for. Someone would either cheer her up, or figure out what the fuck was wrong, and try to fix it. Not my problem today.

I pushed through the doors and went over to my bike. After I swung my leg over, I started it up and walked it back from the line of bikes. I had to pass my house to get to Havoc's place and I stopped long enough to let Momo out. I should have sent her with Charisma. I didn't know how much protection she'd be, but at least she wouldn't have been alone. The kids might have enjoyed playing with her.

At Havoc's place, I could hear the TV playing and the kids laughing. I smiled, grateful they weren't huddling under blankets, terrified of the Boogeyman waiting to get them. Unless no one had told the younger kids yet. They'd need to know, or they might not be as cautious as they should be.

I hadn't even gotten off my bike when Charisma pulled open the door and hurried down the steps toward me. I'd barely managed to turn off the engine before she threw herself at me. I caught her and pulled her over the seat in front of me, cradling her against my chest. The way she burrowed into me made me smile. I tipped her face up so she could see my lips.

"Did you miss me?" She clung to me and nodded. If she hadn't hidden her face against my chest, I'd have told her I'd missed her too. I glanced at the house and saw Li standing in the doorway.

"Why don't you take Mom home for a little while? I've got Jian and Nova. We'll be fine here. If for some reason we go to another house, I'll let you know. And I swear we won't leave the compound or go anywhere near the fence or gate."

"You sure?" I asked, not wanting him to feel obligated to babysit his younger siblings.

"Positive. She's having a hard time keeping up with all the conversations going on, and I can tell she's getting anxious and stressed. I think some alone time with you might be what she needs right now."

"You're a smart kid, Li. And thanks for offering to stay with Jian and Nova. Call if you need us and we'll come back."

I patted Charisma's thigh and told her to get on the bike. She wrapped her hands around my waist as I backed out of Havoc's driveway and went home. I didn't know why he hadn't gone straight home, but I had a feeling he'd get an earful from Jordan when she realized I'd picked up Charisma. She'd want to know what he'd been doing that was more important than checking on her and the kids.

I pulled in next to my Jeep and waited for my wife to get off the bike before I swung my leg over the seat and took her hand. We went inside and I decided to leave Momo out for a little while. While there was a bite to the air, I could hear her racing around the backyard and knew she wasn't finished playing and stretching her legs. I led Charisma to the bedroom and shut the door behind us.

We didn't have to worry about dinner just yet, and I didn't think Shade would be calling for a few hours. Maybe longer. Which meant we had some quality time together for at least an hour or two, and I knew just how I wanted to spend it. I'd already realized I'd never get enough of Charisma. She was like a drug, and I was hooked on her. If she were to leave, I'd wither and die.

As badly as I wanted her to know how I felt, I couldn't say the words. Not yet. Instead, I'd show her and hope she understood. I shrugged off my cut and set it on the dresser before grabbing the neck of my shirt and pulling it off. I tossed it aside and Charisma's eyes flared as she licked her lips. She reached out, running her fingers over my chest and down my abs. It seemed to be her favorite thing to do. She took the same path each time, her touch light and reverent.

"I think we need a distraction for a little while. What about you?" I asked.

"Yes. Make me forget, even if it's just for now."

I kissed her, slow and deep. "We aren't going to forget, beautiful. Just put it on the back burner for an hour or so. It's been too long since I got to touch you."

"You made me scream your name so much last night I thought I'd lose my voice," she said as she took off her property cut. She placed it with mine on the dresser, and I liked the sight of the two of them together. It reminded me of how damn lucky I was. "It hasn't been all that long ago."

"That was a different day. I haven't yet held your naked body against mine today. I need you, Charisma. Want you more than my next breath. You make me feel so many things. Having you here, not just in my home or my bed, but here…" I patted my chest over my heart. "It's been the most incredible thing I've ever experienced."

"You say the sweetest things."

"Only the truth."

Her eyes went soft, and she kissed me again as she pressed herself against me. I felt her nipples harden through her shirt and knew she was telling me in her own way that she felt the same. I worked her shirt up her body, breaking the kiss long enough to divest her of the garment. My lips were back on hers as I reached behind her to unclasp her bra and let it slide down her arms to the floor.

Backing her toward the bed, I toppled her to the mattress before latching onto a nipple, sucking it hard. Her fingers wrapped around the back of my head, and she arched her back, offering herself to me. I'd take everything she wanted to give, and demand even more. I wanted to push her boundaries, watch as she blossomed and became the woman she'd always been intended to be. I'd set her free from Heather, but she hadn't yet realized I'd shackled her again. She wasn't my prisoner. If anything, I was hers. But she did belong to me. All of her. One day she'd be healed enough for all the things I wanted to do to her. With her.

I trailed kisses down her stomach and when I reached her jeans, I unfastened them and tugged them down her legs. I had to stop long enough to remove her shoes and socks, then yanked the jeans off and tossed them aside. Her panties went next, until she was bare. I kicked off my boots and finished undressing. By the time I was done, she'd scooted farther back in the bed and already waited with her thighs parted.

If she thought I was going to fall on her like a ravenous wolf… well, she'd be right. Except I wasn't going for the main prize. I'd made it a challenge of sorts, one only I knew about. She had to come at least three times before I gave us both what we wanted. Sometimes I pushed her to four or even five orgasms. She'd begged me one night, claiming she couldn't come again. I'd proven her wrong twice more.

I ran my hands up her legs and knelt next to the bed. Yanking her ass to the edge of the mattress, I smiled when she let out a squeal and flailed her arms. The glower she gave me was cute as fuck. Before she had a chance to lay into me for startling her, I bent down and blew on her pussy. She sucked in a breath and went completely still. Yeah, she knew what was coming. If she could hear me, this would be the part where I told her she was my favorite meal.

Dragging my tongue along the seam of her pussy, I pushed her thighs farther apart, giving me more room to work. Spreading her pussy open, I plunged my tongue inside her before using it to circle her clit. Her muscles tensed under my hands as she fought her desire to come. After the one and only time I'd gloated a bit for making her come on my tongue after a similar move, she'd done her damnedest to hold back. I knew I could play her body and make her beg and scream. She knew it too. For some reason, she seemed to think it was a bad thing that she reacted so strongly to everything we did in the bedroom. Making her come was my favorite thing to do.

"That's it, pretty girl. Make me work for it. Only makes it that much sweeter when you give in," I murmured to myself, knowing she couldn't hear me. I circled her clit again before flicking my tongue across the hard bud. She jerked and made a strangled sound.

I blew on her clit before sucking it into my mouth. Her thighs trembled and I noticed she'd started gripping the bedding. She didn't have to use words for me to know she was close. Releasing one of her legs, I slipped two of my fingers inside her, curling them slightly as I used shallow thrusts. I worked her clit with my tongue and within seconds she was soaking both me and the bed. She came so hard she squirted, and I lapped up all her cream.

I could hear her panting and rose over her, only to flip us. She sprawled across my chest before she sat up and straddled me. I tapped her hip and she lifted only to lower herself on my cock. "Not what I meant."

She wrinkled her nose at me as she lifted herself only to take me a little farther into her on the next downstroke. The fact I'd only made her come once made me feel like I hadn't done my job right. Taking care of her meant pleasing her too. Charisma rode me, her movements slow but steady. Until I reached between us and rubbed her clit. Her hips jerked and soon she rose and fell on my cock fast and hard. She rode me, her pussy clenching my shaft. Charisma tossed her head back, and I watched her breasts bounce as she took what she needed.

I worked her clit, feeling my own climax rising. When she came, I knew I couldn't hold back. I flipped us again, driving into her. Gripping her hip, I held her still as I thrust into her over and over. My balls drew up and my cock twitched inside her. I didn't even have enough time to draw enough breath before I was coming, filling her up with my hot cum. Not for the first time, I wished I could give her a baby. A little boy or two who was half her and half me. Didn't make me love her any less, knowing that would never happen.

I ravaged her mouth, pouring everything I felt into the kiss. My heart hammered in my chest, and it felt like I'd run a marathon when I rolled to the side and pulled her against my chest. She cuddled against me, and I breathed in her sweet scent. Running my hand up and down her back, I thought about what the future held for us. I loved Nova, Jian, and Li, but it wouldn't be long before Li was off living his own life. Jian would only be a few years behind him, then little

Nova would leave our nest. I wasn't ready for any of that. I wanted to hold onto them forever. Realistically, I knew I couldn't.

I leaned up on my elbow and traced Charisma's eyebrows, marveling at how beautiful she was. A lot of people wouldn't think so, but her scars and imperfections made her unique, and proved she was a fighter. Maybe not in the same way as Jordan. I had a hard time picturing my woman going after someone with a bat or taking them down with a well-placed punch. No, her strength was a quieter sort. More like Grey and Clarity. Although, Clarity had become a force of nature over the years.

I wondered if Charisma would be like that one day. It seemed all our old ladies became bolder, more outgoing, and overall badasses the longer they were here. Except Jordan. She'd been that way from the beginning, which was why Havoc had wanted her. They were very well matched.

"I want to enclose the attic and add two bedrooms and a bathroom upstairs." She blinked at me, and I realized I'd tossed that at her out of the blue. I needed to back up a bit since I'd clearly lost her. "The kids will be grown and gone before we know it. With Shade digging more into Heather's life and finances, I'm thinking we might get a lead on some of the kids. I want to adopt another one or two, if you're all right with that?"

"Yes! Yes, I want more children. Are you sure you don't care they aren't ours by blood?"

"Blood doesn't make someone family. All right, technically it does in a strictly biological sense, but the kids we have now aren't from my sperm. Doesn't mean I don't love them."

"You really think we'll find them?"

"Not all of them. It may honestly be too late for a lot of them. But I'm hopeful we'll find a few, or maybe stumble across some just by tracking her finances to possible pedophiles she brokered adoptions for. There's no guarantee."

"How soon can we start?" she asked.

"Tomorrow. They already added some flooring so they could store some of my stuff up there. There's enough space to section off part of the attic for storage and make rooms out of the rest. The house has more square footage than you probably realize."

"What if we find the kids before we get it done?" Her brow furrowed and I reached over to smooth out the frown lines between her eyes.

"We'll make it work. Whatever it takes."

My phone started chirping where I'd left it in my pants pocket, and I knew I had incoming texts. I rolled away from Charisma and got out of bed long enough to retrieve the damn thing so I could shut it up. Until I saw it wasn't from anyone in my club. It was from Wire. And as I read the words, my gut tightened.

Does your woman know she's the daughter of a biker? Or more specifically a Reckless King?

I looked over at Charisma and wondered if I was about to lose her. She'd thought she was alone. She wasn't. Not even fucking close. And her daddy might very well be pissed enough to try and drag her out of here.

I ran my hand up her calf and gave it a slight shake, getting her attention. I couldn't even attempt to sign. My hands were too damn shaky.

"You knew your dad was a biker. You mentioned only knowing his road name."

She nodded. "Yes. Mom said he was called Drifter."

Motherfucking fuck. "Wire found your dad."

She bolted upright in the bed. "Really?"

"Yeah." I swallowed hard. The Reckless Kings had been allies to us on more than one occasion, and we'd worked together in the past to help the Dixie Reapers. At one time, I wouldn't have thought anything of Charisma being one of their kids. Now that they'd started settling down and starting families, I couldn't help but worry Drifter wouldn't want to let her go once he came to meet her. "Do you want me to call him?"

She touched her ears and paled a little. I tossed the phone onto the bed and crawled back in next to her, wrapping her in my arms. No matter how many times I told her the scars didn't make her ugly, they still bothered her. And meeting her father for the first time? Yeah, my woman was going to be self-conscious.

"I think we need to talk to him, Charisma. He has a right to know about you. The Reckless Kings are nice guys. That's the club he belongs to, up in Tennessee."

"How did my mom meet him if he's from there?" she asked.

I brushed her nose with mine before leaning back a little. "You said his name is Drifter. I think that answers your question. I imagine he got the name because he didn't like sitting in one place for long."

"Tomorrow. I can't..." She bit her lip. "Not tonight. Please."

"All right. We'll call him tomorrow. I'll let Wire know so he doesn't run his mouth to the Reckless Kings before we're ready."

I reached for my phone and cursed before I got a chance to respond because Wire had sent another message, and this one wouldn't be good news to my wife. She was about to lose her shit.

He's on his way. Never knew about Charisma. He's pissed as fuck and not too happy with you either. Already alerted Charming.

"Worse than a fucking old woman gossiping during bingo. I swear to Christ, someone is going to end up kicking Wire's ass one of these days." I sighed and looked at Charisma who had paled again. "Sorry, beautiful. Your dad is already on his way here. Looks like you're meeting him whether you're ready or not."

"How long?" she asked.

"Maybe six hours. Have a feeling it will be less."

I held her as all the tension we'd just released built right back up. Her muscles tightened, she started shaking, and I felt her tears against my skin. Yeah. Someone was going to kick Wire's ass all right. And it was going to be me the next time I saw him.

Meddlesome fucking bastard.

Chapter Eight

Charisma

I'd thought I'd pretend to be asleep when Drifter arrived at the compound. I hadn't realized I wouldn't have to fake it. Exhaustion had pulled at me within an hour of eating dinner with my family. Phantom had been called away again for Church and had tried to send me back to Havoc's house, but I refused. I just wanted to crawl into bed and sleep for a while. Which was exactly what I did.

When I next opened my eyes, sunlight streamed through the windows. Phantom wasn't in bed with me, and it looked like he hadn't been here at all. Worry ate at me. Had something gone wrong? Or had it gone right, and he wasn't here because he'd found Mason?

I got out of bed and went to the bathroom then made my way to the kitchen. I screeched and jumped when I realized Phantom was sitting at the table with another man. Not being able to hear, with the bed being empty, I'd assumed he wasn't home. The kids had stayed the night at Jordan and Havoc's house, which meant I'd been alone. Or so I'd assumed. I placed a hand over my racing heart and tried to calm down.

Phantom held out a hand to me and I went to him, refusing to look at the other man. I'd seen the top of his cut and made out *Reckless*, which meant this was likely my father. As often as I'd wished I could meet him when I'd been growing up, I'd been through too much now to be so eager. For one, not knowing who he was before had meant I'd been dumped into a living hell. It had brought me to Phantom and given me two amazing sons and a precious daughter. For that I was grateful. It still made me angry that maybe someone would have taken up for me before I ever met Phantom if only Drifter hadn't ditched my mom before I'd been born.

Phantom cupped my cheek. "He came a long way to meet you, Charisma. Aren't you going to at least say hi?"

I stared at him, not wanting to do as he asked. So instead, I asked the other question I'd always wanted to know. I looked at the man who'd unwillingly been my sperm donor and tried not to flinch at how much we looked alike. Even if his cut hadn't had *Drifter* on it, and Phantom hadn't told me who he was, I'd have still known. I saw those eyes every morning when I looked in the mirror, and they were the same as little Nova's.

"Why didn't you want me?" I asked.

He winced and I glanced at Phantom. Was it my words or my volume? Phantom laced our fingers together and nodded at my dad. I turned to face him again and waited for his answer.

"Your husband says you can't hear."

I moved my hair back from my ears so he could see the damage. "My foster mother poured acid on me. One of her *friends* slammed my head into a wall enough times I lost my hearing permanently. If I'm shouting, I can't tell. I didn't speak until I met Phantom. It made me uncomfortable."

Drifter seemed to age before my very eyes and his shoulders slumped. When he spoke next, he signed as he talked. "I'm sorry, Charisma. So fucking sorry."

I damn near cried. I'd never anticipated my father would know sign language.

"It's not enough. I was raped. No one believed me. They *blamed me* for what happened, saying I'd asked for it, then changed my mind after the fact. My foster mother liked to prey on little boys and had been eager to get her hands on my son. Except he died before he was born. I don't know what happened to his body.

"I did whatever I could to keep the other boys in the house safe. Even if it meant letting Heather's friends torture me. I'd take a night of pain to give those boys a reprieve. It never lasted, but it was worth it. Even one night of not being groped or forced to do something they didn't want was better than never having any sort of peace at all."

The corner of Drifter's mouth lifted slightly. "Your husband is right. You're strong and a fighter. A biker's wife and daughter through and through."

I straightened my back. "What?"

"I'm proud of you." Drifter stood and came closer. I realized he towered over me and would even be several inches taller than Phantom. He engulfed me in a hug before I had a chance to back up. I tensed up, not wanting to forgive him, but... I'd longed for my dad to hug me all my life. Now that he was, it didn't take long for me to give in. I hugged him back.

Drifter released me. "I wish I could have been there for you. Your mother... I'd thought it was just a bit of fun. Assumed we were on the same page. When she started talking about babies, I made it clear I didn't want kids."

I couldn't stop myself from flinching that time. He reached out and tugged on a lock of my hair. The way he watched me, devoured me with his gaze, I realized he meant every word he'd said. He truly did regret not being there for me. Maybe he hadn't been ready to be a dad back then. He looked to be older than Phantom, but I'd always been terrible at ages. I still didn't think my husband looked like he was in his fifties. I knew my mom had been young when she had me. She'd be younger than Phantom if she were still alive.

Since he knew sign language, I spoke with not only my voice but my hands too. Phantom was learning but didn't know enough to keep up if the conversation didn't include spoken words.

"Did you know she was pregnant?" She'd made it seem like he did. Had she lied to me all these years? It would have been out of character for her, unless she'd been attempting to stop me from chasing after every man I saw in a cut. Which I'd admittedly done from the age of five until I'd turned ten. After that, I'd given up on ever meeting my dad.

"I had my suspicions. If she wasn't, I thought she wanted to be. That wasn't for me, so I left. I should have checked on her. I missed out on so much. And I'm a grandpa?" he asked.

I nodded. "My daughter, Nova, is nine. Phantom and I adopted two boys. Li is fifteen and Jian is twelve. They're in danger. Will you stay and help?"

A mask slid over my father's face, and he gave me a nod. "I'll make sure whatever fucker is trying to hurt my family pays for even contemplating such a thing. I'd liked to stay a little while. Get to know you and the kids. Would that be all right?"

"Yeah. I think I'd like that." I studied him, taking in more details. He had lines by his eyes and bracketing his mouth. His hair was turning more salt than pepper. Had my mom also fallen for an older man? "Why do you know ASL?"

He pulled his phone from his pocket and showed me a picture of a little girl. "A friend of mine with another club has a daughter who's hearing impaired. A cochlear implant works for her, but at first no one could communicate with her. Their club learned sign language to make things easier on her, and I decided to take a few classes too."

"The Devil's Boneyard are trying to learn ASL, so I don't have to always read their lips. Because of the damage to my eardrums, a cochlear implant won't work for me." I glanced at Phantom before focusing on my dad again. "One of the old ladies suggested a hearing assistance dog. I think I've done okay without one so I'm not sure it's a necessary expense."

"How long ago did you lose your hearing?" Drifter asked.

"A while. Years. At first, it was hard to adjust. Now it's just part of my life. There are things I miss, but nothing will return my hearing."

He hugged me again and kissed the top of my head. I wanted to cry at the gesture. How long had I waited for this very moment? I'd thought it would never come. Had even stopped looking for my dad after a while. Bikers riding past had still garnered my attention, but not because I hoped one of them might be called Drifter. I'd given up, and now here he was.

I felt his chest rumble and backed up so I could read his lips. I caught the last word... grandkids. Smiling I signed as I spoke. "They spent the night with their friends at the Sergeant-at-Arms' home. Do you know Havoc?"

"I've met him a few times, but we haven't really talked," Drifter said.

I worried at my bottom lip, remembering the conversation I'd had with Li yesterday. I didn't know how Drifter would handle having a grandson who was bisexual and in a relationship with both a boy and a girl. Though, after all he'd been through, I didn't think Li was having sex. I had a hard time picturing him being willing to do that after all he'd suffered. At least not this soon. Of course, I also knew Taggart was a good kid and wouldn't push Li for more than he wanted to give. I knew women could be the aggressors, like Heather, but Nelly didn't seem the type to do something like that. If anything, she seemed to follow Taggart's lead.

I cut my eyes over at Phantom. Maybe I should ask him to give them the safe sex talk. It might come better from his dad than from me. Or the doctor. But the boys needed time. Phantom had wanted to make sure they were okay physically, after all they'd been through, but neither Li nor Jian had come out of their rooms once they'd come home. It had been too much for them, emotionally and mentally.

Phantom ran a finger down the bridge of my nose, something I noticed he did a lot. I enjoyed the sign of affection. "What's wrong, beautiful? You're thinking hard."

"Li." I didn't have to say anything else. Phantom knew exactly why I'd brought him up.

"Why don't you call Jordan and have her send the kids home? I'm sure they'd like to shower and change here, then they can go back."

I folded my arms. "Really? You want me to call her?"

"Good point. Either text or FaceTime her. Just let her know the kids need to come meet their grandfather. They don't have to stay long if they don't want to. I know they've pretty much settled in now, but I don't want to overwhelm them."

I went to get the shiny new phone he'd bought me and sent a message not only to Jordan, but I sent one to Li as well. Looking down at myself, I realized I was still in my pajamas and rushed to change clothes. I couldn't believe the first time I saw my dad I hadn't even been wearing regular clothes. Or brushed my hair! At least I'd taken care of my morning breath.

Everything seemed to hit me at once and I sank onto the edge of the bed. I might have lost my mom, been through some horrific experiences, but I'd finally spoken to my dad, gotten a hug from him, and I'd found Phantom. My mom had always repeated that Alexander Graham Bell quote... When one door closes, another opens. I'd never really understood it, and I still wasn't certain I did, but it felt like I'd shut the door on my past twice now. The first time when my mom died and I went into the system, then again when Phantom found me. Although, after mom died, my life definitely hadn't improved.

I snapped out of my reverie and finished dressing. By the time I'd pulled on my clothes and made it back to the front of the house, my dad and Phantom had moved to the living room and the kids were back home. Li stood off to the side, arms folded, and attitude pouring off him. But I could see through it. He wanted Drifter to like him, to hug him like he was doing with Jian and Nova. At the same time, he probably worried he was too old to want hugs from a long-lost grandpa.

I went to Li and gave him a nudge, then signed to him. *He doesn't bite. I know you're a cool teenager, but it's all right to get a hug. Finding out you have a grandfather is a pretty huge deal.*

His lips twitched but he refused to smile. After another nudge, he went over to Drifter. My dad held out his hand and shook Li's, then before my son could figure out what was going on, my dad yanked him closer and hugged the hell out of him. It made me so damn happy, especially when Li relaxed and hugged him back.

Li spoke and signed after Drifter released him. "What does this mean for holidays? Do we go to where Grandpa lives, or does he come here?"

Drifter's eyebrows rose. When he signed as well as spoke, all three kids dropped their jaws and stared at him in wonder. "Well... you're the only family I have. Although, I do have a club I'm close to, so I don't want to spend every holiday away from them either. What if we compromise?"

The kids shared a look and nodded. I didn't know what the Devil's Boneyard did for any of the holidays. With everything else going on, I hadn't had time to talk to Phantom much about expectations and such.

"I suggest, at least for our first holidays together, you come visit me at the Reckless Kings for Thanksgiving. It will give me time to get my house set up so there will be enough beds for everyone, and a large enough table for us to sit around. Then I'll come see you here for Christmas." My dad winked at me before focusing on the kids again. "Can't have Santa confused about where you'll be."

Nova practically glowed with excitement. "Santa will come this year?"

I saw the fierce look on Phantom's face before his features smoothed out, and he hunkered down by Nova. "Santa didn't want to do anything to make Heather meaner, so he stayed away. Now that you're in a safe place, he'll come visit you every year. We can even send him a letter to make sure he knows where you are. Deal?"

Nova hugged him. "Thank you, Daddy!"

"I need to steal your grandpa for a little while. We're going to take care of that nasty man, Mason Reynolds. Be good for your mom. I'd prefer all of you go to Havoc's house again. The more people around, the safer you should be. Plus his home isn't anywhere near the fence."

"Neither is ours," Li pointed out.

Phantom nodded. "True. I'd still feel better with you at Havoc's place. When you come home, your mom and I have something to discuss with you. It involves some construction on the house, which I arranged to get started today. A Prospect will be measuring our attic and coming up with some sketches for us to look over."

"Go ahead and tell them," I said.

"You know your mom can't have more children. We love the three of you, but before we know it, you'll be off living your own lives." Phantom smiled at them. "How would you feel about us adopting one or two more siblings for you?"

"Kids who need help like we did?" Jian asked.

"Exactly. We want to give them a safe, loving home. The idea is to add two more bedrooms and a bathroom upstairs. We'll leave it to the three of you if you'd prefer to remain downstairs so all of you can be together, or if anyone wants an upstairs room, you're welcome to change bedrooms." Phantom ran his hands through Nova's hair. "Would the three of you be okay with that? With us adopting more kids?"

Li nodded and I saw the happiness shining in his eyes. Jian hugged Phantom so hard I worried he might crack something, and little Nova bounced on her toes in her excitement.

"Yes! Yes, but can I have a sister?" Nova asked.

Phantom threw his head back and laughed. "We'll see what we can do."

I couldn't have been prouder of the kids. They could have gotten upset, wanting to keep us to themselves a while longer. It wasn't like they'd had a happy homelife all this time. As excited as I was about possibly having another girl or boy come be part of our family, I made myself a promise to give the kids we already had a lot of extra attention. While they didn't seem to mind adding onto our family and taking in another child or two, I didn't want them to feel like they were being replaced either.

Drifter and Phantom hugged all of us again before heading to the front door. My husband stopped and tossed the Jeep keys to me. It looked like I'd be driving it even if I didn't feel prepared. At least we weren't going far.

* * *

Phantom

Drifter followed me to the clubhouse on his bike and we parked next to one another. The man's shoulders stooped a little, like a heavy weight had settled on top of him. I understood a little about how he felt. No, I hadn't discovered a daughter and grandkids, but hearing what Charisma and the kids had been through was enough to rip out your heart.

"You good?" I asked. "We can stay outside for a minute. Take a smoke break if that's your thing."

He shook his head. "Quit a few years ago. Heard that shit will kill you."

"Lots of things will. But at least if you die doing something you like, you might go with a smile on your face."

He grinned. "You're not wrong. Listen, before we go in there and deal with this shit, I have something I need to say. What you've done for Charisma and the kids is really fucking amazing. And I know you love her. Hell, anyone with eyes can see it. You were there

- 314 -

for them when I couldn't be, and I'll never forget it. If you hadn't gone after that poisonous bitch, I would have never known I had a daughter or grandkids."

I didn't want to risk getting punched in the face, but there was one thing I needed to know. Ever since he'd told me his side of the story, something had bothered me. "If you had even considered you might have left that woman pregnant, why didn't you ever go back and find out?"

"Because I'm a coward." His lips twisted. "I was too fucked up in the head to be a dad back then. As the years passed and I got my shit together, I guess I figured if there was a kid out there somewhere, they were better off without me. It's a kick to the gut finding out how fucking wrong I was. If I'd manned the hell up, I could have saved my daughter from all she's suffered. I'm a shit father, and I know it. There's a lot to make up for, and I know it might be an impossible task. I'm just glad she's willing to give me a chance."

"Charisma is like that. Her life could have made her hard and jaded. Instead, she's warm and loving. I already know I'm a lucky bastard to get to call her mine. I'll treasure her and the kids for the rest of my life." I clapped him on the back. "It probably doesn't seem fair you find your daughter and can't take her home with you."

"It's clear she's in good hands. All I want is for her to be happy. As much as it would have sucked, I'd have walked away if she hadn't wanted anything to do with me."

"Come on. Let's see what the club has figured out about Mason. While I'd gladly get my hands dirty taking this fucker out, if they have an easier solution, I'll take it. The most important thing is keeping my family safe. But if the club gets Mason, if I'm given the opportunity to face him, then I will have my pound of flesh."

We entered the clubhouse and the first thing I noticed was how damn quiet the place was. No club whores out front. Not even a Prospect behind the bar. We made our way to Church and when I pushed open the doors, I realized why the place looked deserted. It had been. A piece of paper lay in the center of the table.

"What's going on?" Drifter asked.

"My cousin is trying to be all noble and shit." I shook my head. "No fucking way I'm letting him do this, or the others."

Drifter read it over my shoulder.

Phantom,

We know you want Mason's blood, and you have every right. But you also have a wife and three kids who need you. You took out Heather on your own. It's our turn. You've given a lot to the club over the years, and you never ask for anything. Although, Charming just said you did ask for Charisma and the kids -- or demanded they be yours. Like we'd ever tell you no.

Cherish your family, cousin. Because of you, I have an amazing woman and two children I adore. You gave me the kick in the ass I needed. I can never thank you enough for everything you've done for me, even before I became part of this club. Handling Mason makes me feel like I'm paying you back, at least a little.

Samurai

"Did he seriously talk the club into going after this asshole without you?" Drifter asked. "And they thought you'd be okay with that?"

"I can't let them do this," I said.

"Fuck no, you can't! And neither can I. How do we find them?"

I shot off a text to Shade. *Where the hell are y'all?*

He responded immediately. *Are you trying to get me killed? They left you behind for a reason.*

"Except they didn't just leave you behind," Drifter said. "I have a lot to make up for. Protecting Charisma and the kids from this Mason guy would be a good place to start."

I typed another message to Shade. *Drifter is pissed he's not there. I'm not too happy about it either.*

The fucker sent back a string of damn emojis that made me want to gouge out my eyes. What the hell was up with him and those damn things? If he had something to say, he needed to use his words.

I finally got something that made sense from him. *We're at the barn where we took care of Grey's problem.*

I shouldn't be surprised. The club had decided to purchase that property. Even though the house remained empty, the barn had been getting some use. Although... I had an idea for the home sitting vacant. I'd just have to run it by Charming first.

"I know where they are. Let's go."

We rode through the gates, and I turned off down the two-lane road, then curved back around behind the Devil's Boneyard land. I saw the line of bikes and a few trucks outside the barn and pulled down at the end. Drifter stopped next to me, and we shut off our bikes. I could hear Mason's screams and wondered if we could soundproof the damn structure. Thankfully, there weren't other homes in the area, but if anyone wandered by, the cops could get called out here.

I pushed my way inside and a few of my brothers started cursing.

"Who the hell told you where we were?" Charming demanded.

Shade cleared his throat. "I did. As nice as our gesture was, Phantom needed to be here for this, and Drifter wants a chance to defend his daughter."

"We'll talk later," Charming said, casting a glare at Shade.

Drifter and I approached Mason Reynolds IV. The club had strung him up from the barn rafters, his toes barely brushing the ground. Someone had worked him over pretty good. Bruises were already forming along his ribs. His nose and lip were bleeding. They'd stripped him completely and the asshole had a puddle of piss under him. Looked like he could dish it out but couldn't take it.

I walked up to him and stopped far enough away he couldn't try to kick me or spit on me. Seemed like the sort of thing the pussy would do.

"Know who I am?" I asked.

"The filthy biker who took my precious boy."

Samurai stepped up next to me and I could feel the rage coming off him. Stripes strolled up beside Mason's dangling form. "Wrong answer."

"Tie his feet," I said.

One of my brothers brought some coarse rope over and bound Mason's ankles. He wiggled like a fish on a damn hook and whined like a fucking girl. No, not like a girl. I doubted my Charisma had ever made such a pathetic sound, even when this bastard hurt her. He was more like a mewling kitten.

"I need two things," I said. "Acid. If it was good enough to hurt Charisma, then he can get a sample. He might not have thrown it on her, but he probably would have if he'd thought of it."

"And the second?" Charming asked.

"I need my kit. It's in my saddlebags."

I stepped back and took off my cut, handing it to

Stripes, then yanked my shirt over my head. He took that for me as well. When Cinder handed me a glove, which I pulled on, before taking the glass container of clear liquid. I arched my eyebrow. He also had a glove on while handling the glass beaker.

"Figured you'd want the fucker to suffer this way. I made sure we were prepared." I wasn't going to ask where he'd gotten the acid. Some things were better left unsaid.

"If I do this, he won't last long. Drifter, I had them bring the kit in for you. Use whatever you want in there. I'll wait."

He got to work, yanking Mason's toenails out, slicing him open in a half dozen places, and even took off one of the man's ears. The crazed look in Drifter's eyes told me he could do this all fucking night. Except, now that I was here, face-to-face with the slimy weasel who'd hurt my son and wife, all I wanted was to get back home to them. I needed this to be over and behind us.

"You done?" I asked.

He growled and gave a slight nod. "I'll finish him off after you've done your part. That was my daughter you made deaf! My grandson that you touched. Death is too good for you, but I refuse to leave you breathing. They deserve some closure."

He took a few steps back and my brothers cleared the area around Mason. Last thing I wanted was any of this stuff getting on them. I flung the liquid at him, aiming for the bits dangling between his legs. He screamed as the acid hit his cock and balls. I eyed the empty container.

"You know, I think I like this stuff," I said.

Cinder snorted. "You would."

Charming cocked his head and watched the fight

slowly drain from Mason. "I think we can arrange to keep some of that on hand. Soon as I research how to store it properly."

"You're both fucking crazy," Cinder muttered.

"Did you forget how you earned your name, old man?" Charming asked.

Drifter rubbed his hands together before going back to the kit and selecting another weapon. The guy was like a kid at Christmas. It only took Mason another ten minutes before he breathed his last. Drifter was covered in the man's blood and would need a shower before the kids saw him. His daughter could probably handle it, as long as she knew where the blood came from.

Charming pointed to two Prospects standing near the barn doors. "You two. Clean this shit up. Drifter, use the bathroom at the clubhouse. Clean up before you see your daughter and grandkids. You look like you starred in a slasher film."

"Not the first blood my cut has worn. Doubt it will be the last."

"We sure no one else is coming here?" I asked. "No more like this fucker, or anyone searching for him when he goes missing?"

"Already arranged for it to look like Mason found what he wanted and left the country. Wire is on it. He was happy to help. As to the other thing we discussed before... we found some of the boys, and a little extra." Shade scrolled through something on his phone before showing me. I blinked, trying to figure out what the hell he meant. "One of Mason's friends seems to like both girls and boys, as long as they don't hit puberty. The little girl you see in the photo is four years old. He'd recently purchased her so he could groom her."

"I think I'm going to be sick," Drifter muttered.

"Me too." I looked at the picture again. "She needs a home."

"Exactly!" Shade grinned like a damn lunatic. "Think Nova will share her room while we work on your attic space?"

"She's mine?" I asked. "I don't understand. Did someone already rescue her?"

"She was closer to the Broken Bastards. Someone is on their way here with her. The others we rescued are pretty damaged, not just physically. Mentally. I'm not sure they'll ever live normal lives." Darkness entered Shade's eyes a moment. "The man who had them has been punished and sent straight to hell. Although the devil may not claim him either. The other kids are going to a special place where they can get the care they need."

"It's not just Shade searching now," Charming said. "Wire, Lavender, Wizard, and Outlaw are all doing their part. We'll find as many of the kids as we can. For now, that little princess needs your love and attention. I heard Nova wanted a sister. It seems the man upstairs was listening."

"How the fuck did you hear that already?" I asked.

Charming grinned. "Because your girl called her friends immediately, who told their moms, and my phone started blowing up with requests to put out a search for a sister for Nova. Like I can just go pick one up somewhere. Then this little angel fell into our laps. Seems like it's meant to be."

Drifter growled. "Isn't someone going to show me? She's my granddaughter, damnit!"

I laughed and watched his expression soften when he saw her. "Let's go back and tell the kids. I think Nova will be excited."

"Send Janessa a list of what you need," Irish said. "I'll stay with our kids."

"The daybed in Nova's room has another piece. We just didn't include it," Scratch said. "It's stored at the compound. The bed came with a trundle. One of those things that slides under the bed with another mattress? Maybe your new little one can sleep there. I'm sure Nova would like having a sleepover."

"I'll bring it by," Havoc said.

My throat was a little tight as I looked at my brothers, Drifter, and thought about all I had waiting for me at home. Family. I'd always wanted one and hadn't realized I already had one. It might not have included a wife and kids, but my brothers had always been there for me. You couldn't always choose who carried the same DNA as you, but you could damn sure pick your family... and I'd found the best one.

"I'll meet you at the house," Drifter said. "I'll bring your kit with me. Need to clean it, and myself."

"I'll hold off on telling them about the new addition to our family. You should be there."

Drifter slapped my back and went outside. I pulled my shirt and cut back on before heading back to my house. Like I'd promised, I didn't say a word about the little girl until he'd joined us. Although, I'd let him first tell Charisma that Mason Reynolds would never bother any of them again. He'd earned it. Thankfully he kept the details tame enough to not give the younger ones nightmares.

If I'd thought Nova squealed about the possibility of having a sister, it had paled compared to the eardrum shattering sound she made when she knew she had a sister arriving soon. I didn't even have to worry about her reaction to sharing her new room.

She'd immediately run off to put away everything a four-year-old shouldn't have, and then spent the rest of the night singing and dancing.

Even Momo joined in. It was complete chaos… and I was loving every second.

Epilogue
Charisma -- Three Months Later

Nova and little Ariel were out back with Momo, throwing the ball. Jian had taken off with Noah and Levi. And as usual, Li had gotten up and immediately gone over to Taggart's. I had a feeling their girlfriend was there too. I felt Phantom's arms come around my waist and I leaned back against him. Since Ariel had become part of our family, things had settled into a bit of normalcy. She was too little for school, so she stayed home with me while Nova, Jian, and Li were gone during the day. It had given us time to bond, and she'd started picking up sign language.

More kids had been found over the last few weeks. Largely thanks to me, not that I wanted a pat on the back. The information I'd given Shade had helped him track down most of the kids I'd seen come and go at Heather's place. The ones from years back were too old. Even some Heather had kept until they were nearly adults had either been murdered shortly after she "adopted" them out, or they were in the wind. Out of the ones we'd managed to find and save, some had been placed with families in various clubs. Others had families looking for them and had been reunited with aunts, uncles, and older siblings. I knew it was a never-ending cycle, but it was nice knowing we'd made a difference to at least a few children. It was better than all of them being lost forever.

Phantom turned me to face him and started signing while he spoke. "The rooms are done. Li wants to move upstairs to give Ariel the other downstairs room. I told him it was okay. I thought, since we have four kids now, we'd stop for a while. Let Li grow up and start his life. Get Jian into high school and Nova into middle school before we talk about expanding our family again. What do you think?"

I leaned up and kissed him. "I think our family is perfect as is. We don't need more kids. But if there's a child who needs *us*, then we'll welcome them with open arms."

"I love you. You know that, right?" He smoothed my hair back. "I haven't said the words because I was trying to show you how I felt."

"You have. It's in every touch. Every kiss. The way you cuddle me when you get into bed. I see it when you watch me, even if I'm just cooking dinner or folding laundry. And I love you too. So much!"

"Think the kids will be happy with our family as is?" he asked.

I nodded. "Definitely."

"Too bad the girls are home." He gripped my hips and tugged me closer. "I wouldn't mind a few hours alone with my sexy wife."

"Clarity said they could go over there any time. Think we should take her up on the offer?" I asked.

"Oh yeah. And send Momo too."

I laughed and pulled out my phone, sending a message to Clarity. *Sending the girls and dog over.*

She sent me a flame emoji and my cheeks heated. She clearly knew why we wanted the house to ourselves. Phantom called the girls in and sent them across the street, with Momo chasing after them. The only time the dog didn't need a leash was when Nova and Ariel were around. She adored them.

After he twisted the lock on the door, he scooped me up and carried me off to our bedroom. I looped my hands around his neck and tried not to squirm. I'd started to come out of my shell more when it came to the blissful hours I spent in the bedroom with

Phantom. Which meant we'd been amassing a small collection of things to try.

He set me down and I started stripping off my clothes. His hungry gaze caressed every inch of me before he undressed. The man looked like a work of art. I always loved touching him. Running my fingers along his ink had become one of my favorite things to do. I reached for him now, tracing the patterns on his chest, stopping over the last tattoo he'd gotten. A purple heart took up a decent-sized space at the top of his ribs, with a bandage over it. Across the bandage was only one thing -- my name. I'd once told him he was healing me with his kindness. He'd shaken his head and said it was the other way around. I loved the tattoo and leaned forward to press my lips there.

Phantom slid open one of his dresser drawers and pulled out the canvas bag he kept under his boxer briefs. He figured no one but me would want to rummage in there, so our goodies would be safe from the kids. Phantom removed the blindfold and padded cuffs and my breath caught. I felt my pussy get slick and I obediently turned so he could cover my eyes.

The satin cloth was cool against my skin, then he bound my wrists at the small of my back. Phantom lifted me with ease and helped me get situated on my knees on the bed, my shoulders pressed to the mattress. He spread my thighs wider and brushed his fingers over my pussy, making me shiver. We'd learned that when he took away my sight, since I couldn't hear, it made every sensation even more intense.

He slipped an egg inside me. It was one of my favorites of the things he'd bought. It had a little rubber antenna of sorts that reached up over my clit so the vibrations could be felt both inside and outside.

He'd downloaded an app on his phone and used it to control the vibrations. It barely started buzzing and I nearly came.

I felt Phantom's legs brush my arms and knew he'd knelt in front of me. He helped lift me and I blindly searched for his cock. His precum smeared across my lips before I managed to get him into my mouth. I'd never have thought I'd enjoy this part so much, but I loved the way he felt and tasted. Even if he hadn't inserted the egg, I'd have still been a needy mess by the time I'd finished sucking him.

His fingers gripped my hair, and he helped control my movements. I felt the vibrations go up a few notches and cried out around my mouthful of cock. When he changed the way it pulsed inside me, I couldn't help but suck him harder. The closer I got to coming, the wilder I got. I felt his cock get harder and jerk in my mouth, and I knew I could easily make him come. It wouldn't take much. The first time I'd done that, it had made me feel so powerful. I'd completely unraveled him only using my lips and tongue.

He changed the egg speed again and I knew I had to be screaming. My throat ached as I eagerly swallowed his cock. My body trembled as my orgasm ebbed and Phantom pulled free of my mouth.

"Kenji!" It was rare for me to use his name, but I knew he loved it when I came calling out his true name and not the one he'd earned with the club. My orgasm began cresting again as he toyed with the app on his phone. I wanted to beg him for more. He made me come three more times before removing the blindfold.

I looked up at him and the fierce look in his eyes made my pussy clench down on the egg. He tipped my head to make sure I could see his lips. It's what he did every time we'd played like this. "Does my greedy wife want to come again?"

I nodded. Yes! I definitely wanted that.

"Do you want to suck my cock some more?"

"Yes! Please, Kenji."

"I'm going to undo the restraints. I want you to brace yourself on your hands. Understand?"

"Yes." I licked my lips while he let me out of the cuffs. Once I had my hands under me and holding up my weight, he fed his cock to me. He reached over to tap the phone screen, making the egg do what he wanted, and I nearly saw stars.

He thrust into my mouth. Long, deep strokes that made me gag a little. It always seemed to turn him on more. He ran a hand down my back and up again. He slipped one hand down my side and cupped my breast, giving it a squeeze. When he pinched and twisted my nipple, I came again, harder than before. I felt my release coating my thighs and didn't know how much more I could take.

He seemed to know I was nearing my limit. Phantom pulled free of my mouth and toppled me onto my back. I spread my legs and let him remove the egg. As he settled over me, his cock pressing against my pussy, I arched into him. He drove into me, his cock slamming home again and again. I reached up to brace myself against the headboard and watched his face. If he said anything, I didn't want to miss it.

I felt the vibration of his growl as he changed his angle, sliding in deeper.

"I love this pussy. This gorgeous body. There's not a single thing about you I don't adore," he said.

"Kenji, I love you."

"It's going to be rough, beautiful. I can't hold on. You ready for a hard fucking?"

"Yes!"

It almost seemed like something possessed him as he took what he wanted, proving he owned every inch of me. When he finished, I felt the heat of his release, and my pussy clenched down on him as I came again. Sweat slicked our skin and I knew we'd need a shower. But I didn't mind the mess he left between my thighs. I felt tender as he pulled out, and yet, my clit seemed to pulse in time with my heartbeat. I still wanted more.

"My wife not satisfied?" he asked.

"I still ache," I said, shifting on the bed.

He slipped the egg back inside me. As it buzzed in my pussy, and against my clit, he sucked and teased my nipples. The beast of a man made me come many more times, but only after I begged for it.

"Do you think you could feel it inside me if you, um…"

"If I what?" he asked, looking intrigued.

"Put your cock somewhere else."

Heat flared in his eyes, and he reached for the lube. He slicked his fingers before stroking them over the little pucker between my ass cheeks. "My wife wants my cock here?"

"Can we try?"

"Not today. But soon. Doesn't mean I can't play a little."

I didn't get a chance to ask what he meant before he started working a finger inside me. He made the egg vibrations change again and between the toy and what he was doing to my ass, I was mindless with pleasure. I came twice more before he decided I'd had enough. Instead of rushing off to the shower, he cuddled me closer. I always loved this part. I snuggled against him and smiled, thinking of how perfect things had turned out.

I had a husband I loved, children who were amazing, and my dad was going to be a part of my life. I'd also made a lot of friends in the club, and one day I'd venture into town more and maybe find some new friends there too. I'd thought my life wasn't worth living. I'd pushed myself, knowing the kids needed me. Then Phantom had thrust some keys into my hand and told me to wait in the Jeep. He'd changed my entire world, and he'd forever have my heart.

Just as I knew I had his...

Harley Wylde

Harley Wylde is the International Bestselling Author of the Dixie Reapers MC, Devil's Boneyard MC, and Hades Abyss MC series. When Harley's writing, her motto is the hotter the better -- off-the-charts sex, commanding men, and the women who can't deny them. If you want men who talk dirty, are sexy as hell, and take what they want, then you've come to the right place. She doesn't shy away from the dangers and nastiness in the world, bringing those realities to the pages of her books, but always gives her characters a happily-ever-after and makes sure the bad guys get what they deserve.

The times Harley isn't writing, she's thinking up naughty things to do to her husband, drinking copious amounts of Starbucks, and reading. She loves to read and devours a book a day, sometimes more. She's also fond of TV shows and movies from the 1980s, as well as paranormal shows from the 1990s to today, even though she'd much rather be reading or writing.

Harley at Changeling: changelingpress.com/harley-wylde-a-196

Changeling Press E-Books

More Sci-Fi, Fantasy, Paranormal, and BDSM adventures available in e-book format for immediate download at ChangelingPress.com -- Werewolves, Vampires, Dragons, Shapeshifters and more -- Erotic Tales from the edge of your imagination.

What are E-Books?

E-books, or electronic books, are books designed to be read in digital format -- on your desktop or laptop computer, notebook, tablet, Smart Phone, or any electronic e-book reader.

Where can I get Changeling Press E-Books?

Changeling Press e-books are available at ChangelingPress.com, Amazon, Apple Books, Barnes & Noble, and Kobo/Walmart.

Changeling Press, LLC

ChangelingPress.com

Printed in Great Britain
by Amazon